TEARS OF ASTORIA

BOOK ONE OF THE ASTORIA SERIES

J.B. WRIGHT

NHB PUBLISHING

For anyone who has felt different.
Your differences are a strength,
learn them— use them.
You, my dears,
are the ones who
will change the world.

CONTENT WARNING

There are many themes of death, mentioned suicide, gore, massacre, reference to genocide, infant loss, infertility, betrayal, graphic sex, attempted sexual assault.

Your mental health matters. If you do not feel comfortable with these themes please do not pass this page and remember I am always available to have a discussion about it.

Be kind to yourself, always.

-J.B.

PROLOGUE

"Don't let them take me," I say. My voice shakes despite my best attempt to calm it.

Mother ignores me while watching out the large arched window of my bedroom, awaiting my transport.

Even though I know it's a useless attempt I try again to sway her. "I swear I'll be good. I'll behave. Please, Mother, I want to stay at Riverstone... with you, with my family."

She finally snaps, her first sign of any emotion. "Get a hold of yourself, Aislinn Theodora. This is why you *must* go. You're unfit for the title of a Stelleran lady. Sniveling like a toddler. You need to grow a back bone if you are to ever have a place in our society. You are fourteen and still insist on playing with the common-born and *serv* children. It is below you. You will learn how to act appropriately and lose this unruly streak of rebellion... no doubt a trait inherited by your father."

"I'll be more like Lorella. I can do it, I swear. I won't go into the village anymore. I won't scream at night. I'll do my lessons. I'll be perfect. Please don't make me leave my home."

"You will never be like your sister. You *can't* be. It isn't in your blood. You will go to the Astoria Academy until you've come of age. Then, you will marry into the Urson family and become Lady of Obsidian. Riverstone was never meant to be your home. Now, the transport has just arrived. Be a good girl, and get in without a fight."

"Never," I say under my breath before taking off down the hall. *They can't make me go if they can't find me.*

I take a turn, past the rows of arched windows overlooking part of the Vallae river, past Lorella's room, past Father's office, and finally down the serv stairwell. Mother would never come down here. I just have to wait them out.

There's a little broom closet I tuck away in. I sit on a bucket and wait. Biding my time until I am forgotten... or starve, whichever comes first.

I'm only in the closet a few minutes before I hear the clattering of footsteps, *heavy* footsteps. That of Father's security team, not of the servs'. I hold my breath and wait for them to pass.

Five, four, three, two, one.

With their fading steps I exhale, shifting on the turned over bucket. My elbow knocks into a broom and sends it clattering to the ground.

Oh Haile... here we go.

The door pops open almost immediately, and Father's guard stands before it with a disturbing smile that is only made more ominous by the blood-red of his uniform.

"Please, don't," I beg, knowing it won't do any good. My father recruits guards by their cruelty. He has no room in his guard for soft hearts.

"Found her," the guard shouts.

He grabs me by the arm and pulls me from the closet. I start screaming, kicking, and flailing, trying to get away. It's no use. A second guard grabs my other arm, and they drag me to the front of the house. When they tire of my feet kicking out behind us, making it harder for them to walk, they lift me a few inches above ground with ease. We finally walk by my parents and sister, who stand in the grand entryway with stone-cold faces.

I find each of their eyes. "Please." My voice is raspy and utterly broken. "I want to stay. Please."

My father's jaw clenches— annoyed.

My sister's gaze narrows into a thing of cruelty.

But it's my mother who truly guts me. She looks at me with disgust, and then she doesn't look at me at all. Mother walks away without so much as a backwards glance as I am dragged out of my home and thrown into the transport.

PART ONE

Obsidian Mountains

ONE

SACRIFICE

I WAS ALWAYS A disappointment to my mother.
Unfit for the position of my birth.
Attention seeking.
A burden.
Disobedient.
Clumsy child.
Stubborn.
Those were her favorite words to describe me. Perhaps the only words she had ever used to describe me. Mother couldn't wait to send me off. When I turned the appropriate age to attend the academy, a mere fourteen, she secured my rooms— not wasting a single hour. If I close my eyes, I can still feel the brutish hands of my father's guards on my body like a flesh memory. My heart still breaks as I think of how my parents watched from afar with disapproving eyes while I was thrown into the transport against my will. Begging for them to stop, promising to behave and be more like my sister... but they didn't want to hear it... they didn't want *me*.

The Astoria Academy for Young Ladies was supposed to iron out all of those traits my mother despised in me. Perhaps it did. I certainly feel tamer than I did when I came, more compliant and accepting of my role as a Stelleran lady. What Mother didn't expect was for me to make a friend like Audrina. The type of friend that feeds your flame rather than suffocating it. The kind of friend that makes you get out of bed when you're in a downward spiral and forces you to get out... despite it being past curfew.

Which is how I ended up tiptoeing down these old creaking stairs. The other girls have all gone to their beds as they're supposed to, but no one has authority over Audrina, not even the mistresses. Everyone falls prey to her charms.

We make our way through the old stone archways that lead past the rows of wooden tables and benches in the dining hall. The memories of meals spent here, laughing amongst friends, tug at my heart. I swallow down the emotion before Audrina has ammunition to tease me with.

"Wait for me in the kitchen," she says in a hushed voice.

"Why? Where are you going?"

"Just wait!" She flashes her signature mischievous smile before ducking down another hall. Whatever it is she is doing will surely cause problems later.

The kitchen smells strongly of fresh herbs and citrus soap. They must have just finished cleaning from dinner. A dinner I begrudgingly missed whilst packing my room.

My stomach rumbles angrily as I walk into the storeroom tucked in the corner of the large kitchen. I push past the jars of herbs and flour and reach into the old tea canister I know the cooks use to hide the sweets.

Cookies, freshly baked, thank the gods.

I stick one in my mouth and grab a few more as well as some crackers and cheese before exiting the storeroom.

"Perfect, bring those too," Audrina says from the archway while shaking a bottle of millberry wine at me.

"Where did you get that?" I roll my eyes and pull the cookie from my mouth.

"Oh this? Mistress Corinne wanted you to have a farewell present." She shrugs. "Well, I'm sure she would have— if she had been in her room to offer it." Her eyes sparkle as she gives another flash of that mischievous smile.

I snort. "Miss Soleil, how ever will you stay out of trouble when I leave?"

"*Out* of trouble? Oh no, Aislinn, darling, I *am* the trouble." She opens the heavy wooden door and gestures toward the open fields stretched out before the cliffs. "After you, future *lady*."

The air is thick with salt and unsaid goodbyes, and it is unusually chilly for a summer night in Astoria. Each blow of the mist-infused wind causes the skin on my arms to pimple. I lean closer into Audrina to try and steal some of her warmth as we dangle our feet over the cliffside— as we do most nights while waiting for the Tears of Astoria to fall. She takes another swig from the wine before handing me the bottle and taking some of the cheese and crackers I brought.

Below us, the Tierce Sea's waves appear almost black in the night, swallowing each glimmer of the crescent moon reflecting itself from above. It seems to beg for companionship as it drowns in darkness.

I look at my friend. There is a smile flirting its way onto her full lips. Her tightly coiled caramel hair frames her face, and her pointed chin is tilted upwards—watching the sky and allowing the moonlight to catch in her amber eyes. Even under this night sky she is the embodiment of sunshine.

"Can you believe in a few short weeks you're going to be someone's *wife*?" Audrina asks. Her gaze is still focused on the sky above, waiting for the first star to fall.

"No," I reply quietly, "I can't. I've been prepared for it all my life. I've always known it was the sole purpose of my birth, but now that it's here... I don't know. It doesn't seem real. Something inside of me says it's wrong. It's not my path, yet I know I have no choice in the matter." I fix my gaze to the reflection of the moon in the sea as I try not to dwell on things out of my control.

"Well, you could always run away and live with me on Sutton Island. You can perform the governing duties, and I'll do whatever I want since I have made it very clear to my mother that I will absolutely not be marrying some lord."

"How enticing... I feel somehow you will expect more from me than Rett will."

"I won't argue with that." Audrina laughs. "At least you actually know your future husband. Most of these girls can't say the same. Not only do you *know* him, you've grown up together— spent every summer and winter together since you were born. Your parents might be awful humans, but at least they provided you with that service."

"The *service* had nothing to do with me." I snort. "It's how our fathers grew up, spending the summers and winters together. Their fathers were so close- inseparable— almost *too* close, if you catch my meaning. They desperately wanted their children to marry, but when each side only produced males, they made our fathers promise to join our houses together with the next generation. But I *do* consider myself lucky, and if I am being entirely honest, I do *love* Rett— in a way. And how many ladies can say they *love* their husband?"

"How many indeed." Her eyes squint at the thought. Audrina has never shied away from sharing her disdain for arranged marriages. Never. She believes them to be just as barbaric as the sacrifices the people in Rousse still perform to honor gods that don't exist. "Why don't they have Lorella marry an Urson? She's older—shouldn't she marry first?"

"Mother is holding out hope for one of the younger princes. She thinks because Vallae is the center of all trade that it elevates us above the other governing houses and that a match with a prince is possible."

"She thinks *King* Carrigan will allow one of his sons— a *prince* of *Stellera*— to assume the name Delphia and govern Vallae as a consort?" Audrina can't hold back the laughter. "How absurd."

"Mother thinks *very* highly of our house."

A flicker of light soaring over the dark waters catches my attention. I look up. The stars begin to race along the edge of our realm. Faster and faster, stars shoot down from the night sky, leaving trails of lavender and silver. Diamond dust rains from sky to sea— shining brighter than any of the other stars freckling in the deep blue above us. What began as a drizzle is now a downpour. No matter how many times I see it, it still takes my breath away. Audrina's hand tightens on my own. Somehow, she knows I need the extra comfort.

My eyes burn as I fight off tears at the most beautiful sight in all of Stellera. Maybe the entire continent of Katova. Astrologers come from all over to study the Tears of Astoria. Night after night, they take notes whilst trying to find their law of reason— to find the *true* origin. None have succeeded in uncovering the secrets of the Tears. There is no consistency nor pattern to track. The only constants are they only appear over the Astorian province and they fall every night, completely mystifying all those trying to understand it.

Some lingering god-finatics, mostly from the northern nations, truly believe in the old writings. The ones of gods and magic. There are a few ruins from ancient temples where the believers will gather and worship. Not Stellerans though. Stellerans pride themselves on being scholars. *Reasonable.* We don't believe in the gods here. We believe in science—and tangible evidence. But even if the old writings *are* false, I can't help but be drawn to them. What little girl doesn't want to believe in a world of magic? In gods that can save her? The story of the Tears happens to be one of my favorites. It attributes the phenomenon to the goddess of beauty and night, Astoria—our province's namesake.

It begins with a sacrifice. One asked of her by her own father, Haile, King of Gods. He and his brother, Egon, were counterparts in every way. Where Haile was light, Egon was dark. Haile was known for kindness. Egon was known for cruelty. Haile was the god of life. Egon was the god of death. The two brothers had engaged themselves in a war. Egon believed he should be the king of the gods— for what holds more dominion over life than death?

It was only after their beloved sister, Millena, had died from standing between the two that they made a deal for peace. Egon's son, Erebus—who ruled over the Shadows—proposed he take Astoria as a wife to create a bridge between the dark and light. The two of them would serve as advisors to their fathers and boast fairness and equality.

Haile wanted his daughter to have love and happiness as he had with her mother. He worried she would wither and her light would fade if shackled to Erebus for eternity. Once a marriage vow was spoken between gods, it could not be undone. But after hearing the proposal, the good and kind Astoria agreed to it, for the betterment of the realms, both mortal and gods, and an end to the war that had already claimed so many lives.

Though she did not love her husband, Astoria treated him with respect and acted the part of dutiful wife. Soon after marrying, the two gods conceived. Astoria was overjoyed. She had always desired children. The moon never glowed quite as bright as it did during her pregnancy. Erebus, a jealous god, saw the love she held for their unborn babe. He watched as Astoria would cradle her swollen belly. She did so with such tenderness, a tenderness she never showed Erebus— and he wanted it. The moment the baby was born, he took it to our realm, the mortal realm, for it to grow up and live a life amongst us as an orphan. Erebus never even let his wife hold their child.

Not once.

Astoria wept for her lost child with tears of starlight. Starlight that burned so bright, it shredded the barriers between realms.

Over the course of a few centuries, they repeated the process. Over and over again.

Hundreds of babes were expelled from the Gods' Realm, never to know the truth of their parentage.

Each night, Astoria weeps for them— for her lost children.

Each night, her tears of starlight shred through the realms.

Each night, we see the Tears of Astoria.

It's no more than a bedtime story, created ages ago when we were incapable of finding answers for the unknown. Our ancestors made up stories about gods and magic to explain the unexplainable, and no one questioned it because there was no better explanation. But as scientists continue to find answers that explain the once thought unexplainable, the stories about the gods have become nothing but myths.

Enchanting as they may seem, no *sane* person believes in the gods anymore... aside from our neighbors in the northern nations, Dailotta and Rousse, who still honor the gods with savage sacrifice and ritual. But because no one has been able to debunk the legend of the Tears of Astoria, it has become one of the most coveted wonders of the continent.

My head rests on Audrina's shoulder as I commit this moment to memory. We continue stealing sips of wine as we watch the flashes of silver racing down the edge of the realm. Nothing compares to the night sky in Astoria, even without the Tears. It's how it came to be named for the Goddess of Beauty and Night to begin with. There is no other place where you can see all the deep colors and shimmering constellations come to life.

Not like this.

It feels like magic.

If I *believed* in magic.

Sometime in the earliest hours of morning, Audrina and I found ourselves back in the halls of the academy. We laughed and stumbled, creating entirely too much noise to go unnoticed. Not that I care. It's my last night, and I will do as I see fit. I can't even remember why I fought Audrina on going to see the Tears. Of course, she easily persuaded me. Audrina has that charm over people. In fact, I'm not sure I have ever seen her *not* get her way.

My thoughts swirl with stories of gods and falling stars as my head rests on my pillow, slowly blinking until my vision blurs into darkness.

I reach out, trying to grasp onto what light remains as panic swells in my chest. Utter darkness. The threat of it looms as the light fades. The more I extend myself, the more distance is put between the tips of my shaking fingers and the light they seek. I teeter on the edge— stretching further, further, further. Until I'm falling into the dark void.

My eyes shut as I brace for impact. When there is none, I rub my hands in the ground below me, through soil and grass.

I try to swallow my fear, but my throat is too dry

A dream. It's just another dream.

I'm surrounded by scattered daylight peeking through dense trees. My heart is still racing. I rise to my feet, realizing I am standing in an unfamiliar grove. Silver dust floats through the air, catching those precious last glimpses of sun and refracting its pink and orange rays through trees as day prepares to welcome night. An inhumanly warm hand caresses my cheek, burning deliciously. It provides my only source of comfort. Charcoal lashes try to conceal his startlingly bright eyes, the likes of which can't compare to anything of this realm. They stare at me with a softness that contrasts their very intensity.

Who are you?

I silently trace the blurred lines of his face, trying to make sense of him. I reach for the familiar stranger, begging him to come closer. Begging him to reveal his secrets. The closer I get, the more he blurs until he vanishes from sight completely and I am alone in this strange wood. Every bone aches with despair and calls for him to return. With his absence, the fear is overwhelming. A quake brings inky shadows erupting from the ground as if born of the dead buried below. They swarm like locusts.

"He's coming." They repeat the words in an otherworldly hiss while flying erratically around me.

Puffs of cloudy breath blow with each exhale, and my arms pimple with goosebumps. The warm breeze has been replaced by freezing gusts as the shadows continue to swarm.

"Who's coming?" I shout, ignoring my wild heartbeat.

With the sound of my voice, the shadows halt, becoming eerily still. At once, they all fly in my direction.

Without a hesitation, I duck low to the ground. I'm crouched on the twig and fallen leaf-covered ground. Something from below grabs me and pulls me beneath the dirt. I can't breathe. I can't scream. I can't see. Soil fills my mouth and lungs. I'm choking and surrounded by darkness.

This is how I die.

TWO

WORST YOUNG LADY

Outside my open window, the breaking of dawn serves as a reminder that my time is running out. Today, the life I've lived these last six years will cease to exist. Innocence and youth taken. I pull the pillow over my head in an attempt to block out the light. If I can't see it, it doesn't exist.

The door to my room quickly opens, ruining my plan to ignore the day, and hitting the wall beside it with enough force to rattle a hanging painting off its nail. It falls to the floor and shatters.

"Go away, Audrina," I say without removing the pillow from my head.

"You can't sleep in today. The mistresses sent me to make sure you are ready for your transport... which I can see you are not." I lift my head in time to see her kick one of my brown leather cases.

"They're going to make me pay for that, you know?" I nod in the direction of the broken frame near the door.

"They're going to make your *parents* pay for it," she says, correcting me.

"And I have to see them *today*— in a secluded mountain range," I remind her.

She grabs the broken frame and shoves it beneath my bed, sure to hide every inch of evidence.

"There, no one will know."

I roll my eyes at my friend. "You're by far the worst young *lady* to have ever attended the academy."

"Me? Look at the mess *you've* made!" She gestures to the open cases and clothing spewed throughout my room.

I sit up and throw a small decorative pillow at her.

"It's an organized mess."

"Which part is organized? The sea of clothing on this part of the floor or that part?" Her hands wave over the piles scattered across the entirety of my room.

"I've gotten everything out of the wardrobe. I just haven't put them into the cases yet."

"Okay, well, I'll start on that. *You* hop in the bath."

"Are you trying to tell me I smell?"

"I am. Now get." She pulls the blanket off me.

"No." I pull it back over my head.

Audrina crawls under the covers beside me. Her face is far more serious in this little blanket cave.

"Are you scared?" she asks quietly.

Without answering, I roll over, offering her my back.

"You're going to be great. *You're going to find happiness.* You were born for this. Don't let your parents break you," she whispers, "but first, you need a damn bath, because you really do smell."

Audrina is right. Audrina is always right. I'll be great. I'll find happiness. I was born for this. I will not let my parents break me. But first, I need a bath.

"Fine, you win. I'm up." I flip the covers off and smirk at my friend who beams back triumphantly.

The newfound confidence staggers immediately. My head betrays me, and I feel as though the room is waving like the rivers I grew up on. Audrina and I drank the entire bottle of wine last night, and I can still feel its effects.

"Maybe you overdid it last night." Audrina laughs.

My eyes dart to her in an accusation, but I don't have a retort as the room begins to spin.

Audrina's hands grab hold around my waist, helping me to the edge of the tub in my powder room. She puffs out a loud breath once she's relieved of my extra weight.

"For someone so small, you sure are dense. It's almost like there's a whole other person hanging out with you beneath your skin." She leans against the door frame of my bathroom.

"Maybe you just have no strength from being doted on your entire life," I say, snapping at her while turning the faucet.

The water pours in melodic rhythm against the copper tub.

"Are you staying to watch, or do you have something better to do?" I ask as she stares at me.

"I just want to make sure you're not going to drown yourself." Audrina studies my face to gauge just how terrible I feel.

"I'll be fine. Just go... and bring me some toast from breakfast, please. I don't want to go. It will be too awkward since everyone knows I am leaving today," I say, waving her out.

"Fine, maybe food will straighten out that attitude."

"I learned from the best."

Flipping her wild hair over a raised shoulder, Audrina glances back with her signature smile and raised brow.

Before she disappears from my room, her eyes brighten with realization. "Oh, happy birthday, Aislinn." She smiles and slips out.

I strip off the rest of my nightgown once I'm sure she's gone and I have privacy.

Happy birthday, indeed.

As I slide down into the warm water, it instantly soothes the throb in my temple. My muscles loosen as the steam rolls over my exposed skin. I pour some of my favorite lunalily oil into the water and let it overtake my senses.

Audrina was, as always, right. I desperately needed a bath.

I sink underneath the water and stare at the ceiling through the ripples of water above me. It's a blissful kind of quiet. The world outside no longer exists. I come back up and already feel better than I had.

With my head resting against the tub, I allow my eyes to close. I'm exhausted. Not that I am a stranger to exhaustion. It's kind of my permanent state of being. Since I was a child, perhaps seven or eight years old, I've been afflicted with vivid—and often terrifying—dreams... nightmares.

Wars and thousands of eyes void of life staring back at me.

People I've met and more that I haven't.

Oblivion and devastation.

Mostly Death and his shadows as they call to me.

Sometimes though—I dream of him. The boy with the blue eyes. I can never clearly see his face, but his eyes shine with a vivid intensity that cuts through the blurred edges. Those dreams are my favorite. It's almost as if he chases away the darkness, but as soon as he leaves, all that darkness floods back in. It's like the darkness is drawn to me and just waiting for me to let it in, to accept it, claim it, *become* it.

Audrina helps me braid my unruly dark brown curls so they cascade down the side of my neck and fall below my shoulder. She smears berry colored stain across my lips and cheeks as she works. I look in the mirror, admiring the way it highlights the freckles that splatter the bridge of my nose. Freckles my mother hates but I have always loved because I'm the only Delphia to possess them. My eyes are also uniquely mine. None of my living relatives have the same bright emerald green that I do.

I stare at my reflection a little longer, thinking of the girl I'd been when I'd arrived and how she is now nothing but a stranger. That girl would have done anything to escape her fate as the Lady of Obsidian. She would have run away and found adventure across Stellera, maybe even venturing to Dailotta or Rousse.

That girl dreamed up a whole life of adventure for herself.

A dream doomed to be quashed with the sense of responsibility to my name and house.

While I bathed, Audrina lazily threw all my belongings into the three brown leather cases that littered the floor. My room is now bare except the wooden furniture that has been here long before me and will remain long after. I now feel a debilitating heaviness. Sucking in my lip, I shut my eyes to try to fight off the tears.

"Hey, no, don't do that," Audrina says. She dips her head from around mine so I can see her sweet smile in the mirror. A gentle finger swipes away a tear. "I will write to you every single day. This isn't really a goodbye. "

"It's not just that. Well, of course, a large part is leaving you. I can't imagine how dull life will be when you're not a part of my every day. It's also leaving this place. It's the most I've ever felt at home in my life... it truly is goodbye to the Academy. " I let out a small sniffle and look again toward the emptiness of my room.

"My offer to run to Sutton with me remains. The island is incredible. You would love it. Or you could always refuse to marry and become a Mistress at the Academy. Then you'll never have to leave," she offers jokingly.

"Don't tempt me." A chuckle escapes my tightened lips as I imagine myself as a Mistress. A preposterous notion considering my elevated station. It would be the scandal of the decade. The look on Mother's face might almost be worth it. I smile at the thought.

Audrina pulls me into a warm hug. "I'll see you in just a few weeks for the wedding."

Her words cause a chill to crawl up my spine.

The wedding—my wedding—is in just a few weeks. I'm hit with a new wave of nausea.

Mistress Corinne clears her throat to announce her intrusion. "Miss Delphia, your transport has arrived."

With a sigh, I look back at Audrina, who in turn gives an encouraging smile.

The three of us carry my luggage down the creaky steps and through the stone halls. We pass a few familiar faces in the common rooms and stop for hugs ranging from bearish to uncomfortably awkward. We finally make it to the main entrance and leave the cases by the front door for the driver to load. The black transport is humming as it lets off small plumes of purple smoke, the sound competing with the incessant ringing in my ears.

The driver holds the door open for me, and I climb into the cushioned black leather seats in the back. My head feels too heavy for my neck, weighed down with thoughts of the future lying ahead of me and the past we are about to drive away from. I rest my head against the cool glass window as the driver closes the black drapes that act as a partition, giving me the illusion of being alone.

Again.

The gray stone building covered in vines that is the Astoria Academy grows farther and farther away until I no longer see it. We drive alongside the Tierce Sea for miles. A clear cerulean blue replaces the almost black water from last night now that the sun gleams upon it, sparkling with each rush of waves.

The road soon turns toward the center of town. We pass the public transport station and many familiar cottage-style buildings as we drive through the main road of Astoria. Navy banners embroidered with silver are hung along the wooden beams of each shop, showing off their Astorian pride. Astoria is one of the best kept provinces in all of Stellera. Even the commoners live well, and there are hardly any servs since Lady Cordelia Carro began governing. She found the treatment of servs barbaric. The first thing she did with her leadership was instill a majority voting system, so that even the smallest voices were heard. Unfortunately, her brother, Dennon, was given a small portion of the Astorian lands—to the south— and he refuses to implement his sister's system. He still uses servs and rules as though he were a king rather than a low-lord.

The familiar buildings soon turn to thickly woven together trees. They arch over the winding road we drive along create a tunnel of sorts.The trees continue as such until we come to the edge of the Egora Bog. Steam rises as toxic bubbles burst. The Egora is the largest bog on the continent and is highly acidic. Even a drop can melt flesh and bone until it resembles nothing but goo. If not for the bog we could have traveled north through Castona. It would have taken a mere four hours to make it to Obsidian. Unfortunately, the bog stretches from the Tierce Sea and curves itself around the border of Castona, forcing all to travel around it, effectively doubling the distance.

We pass by a ruin of a half finished bridge. No one knows who attempted building a bridge over such a dangerous bog, but it is said if you climb it to its end, you will find half-melted skeletons. Workers who had gotten caught in the toxic plumes and now act as guardians over the edge, making sure no one else befalls the same fate. I'm not sure if it has ever been confirmed or if it is a ghost story Astorians tell their children to keep them off the bridge, nor do I plan to ever find out.

"How much longer?" I lean forward, parting the curtains that separate me from the transport's driver.

"We are about halfway, Miss Delphia,"

I notice two gray stripes around the upper arm of his black service jacket, just below the Urson family crest. "Officer?"

"Yes, mam," he says without turning his eyes from the road ahead.

Strange for someone so young, unless he was a highborn, I suppose, but then he wouldn't be made to run an errand such as picking me up. "Why would Lord Magnus send an officer to retrieve me rather than one of his servs?"

"For your protection."

"From what?"

"Whatever dangers might be on the road, Miss."

"Is he expecting danger?"

"I can't speak on behalf of Lord Magnus' expectations other than I am expected to bring you to Obsidian safely."

"Mmm. Have you been working for the Ursons long?"

"I served with Rett on the border. He introduced me to his father and got me the position after learning I was an orphan. Raised by a general in the King's Army. I'm technically Rett's personal guard, but both Magnus Urson V and Magnus Urson VI trusted me to procure you."

My nose turns at his choice of words. "I am not a package."

"That's not what your parents seem to think." He smirks in the rearview mirror.

"Ah. So they have already arrived," I say, tapping my fingers on my seat nervously.

"They have. I hope I don't overstep when I say I much prefer your company so far. I was expecting you to be more like—"

"My sister?" I finish for him. He nods and again glances into the rearview. "Yeah, well, I've never been much compared to the great Lorella. What is your name, Officer?"

"Evander Clayne, Miss."

"Evander. It's nice to meet you. Please call me Aislinn."

"I can't, Miss."

"When no one is around, you can." Evander doesn't reply, but I see the hint of a smile in the mirror. "How is Rett? I haven't seen him in six years."

The hint of a smile fades quickly. "He is—he has been good. Preoccupied since we returned from Fort Vicanti."

"Why the hesitation?"

"I don't feel entirely comfortable discussing him. He is my employer and also my friend."

"Oh, right. Sorry." I lean back against the seat, and the transport becomes blanketed in awkward silence. At some point, Evander closes the curtain again.

We drive through open fields and farmlands. There is scarcely anything to look at to occupy my time, and I find my eyes growing heavy. I try to keep them open, but my head protests, falling forward in defiance. My breath deepens. I finally give in to the gentle sway and hum of the transport and allow myself to drift asleep.

In place of the usual dead eyes, wars, and mysterious men are doors...

I dream of many doors. I open one to find myself standing in front of another.

The large black doors marking the entrance of Obsidian Manor.

A door with black smoke pouring out from underneath.

A door with little bear carvings.

A door with a "U" engraved into the knob.

Mechanical doors.

A damaged wooden door covered in dirt.

Golden doors.

Door after door after door. I open them, and they lock as soon as I pass through, forcing me forward. After I open one leading to a small cave, I find myself surrounded by an empty abyss. It's humid yet impossibly cold. Without warning, I'm being pulled toward the stars. A shadow holds me— not tenderly, but possessively. All the doors I walked through earlier begin to spin around me.

Faster. Faster. Faster.

Until they are a blur and I'm trapped... caged... exactly how someone would contain a bird wishing to be freed.

A smoky scent awakens me from my strange and unsettling dream and tells me we are getting close. We've arrived at the town closest to the Obsidian Mountains. Ashe is unpleasant to look at. Much of the town is outdated, and the small homes are falling apart. Holes in roofs open to the sky above, providing little to no shelter from the elements. Wood is splintered and warped. The streets are nearly empty as all the town's inhabitants are either hard at work or sleeping in preparation of the work ahead. It is a hard life for the people of Ashe, yet the town's existence is essential to all of Stellera. Ashe is where all our gas refineries are kept. Their purpose is to turn the extremely poisonous oxidous gas into something sustainable that provides the fuel for transports and other types of machinery. I always wondered why the town wasn't kept better considering its importance.

The first Ursons had forbidden anyone from building in the mountains, reserving them for Urson blood only. They said it was to keep intact the natural beauty and luster of the forest that covers the mountain range. Many believe it was so they could look down on everyone else. Earlier generations of Ursons grew mad from the rising smog and toxic gasses that rose from the refineries. It wasn't enough exposure to kill them or cause symptoms of the poisoning. No one bled from their eyes or noses, but they became extremely irrational and impulsive, paranoid even. They called it the Urson Curse. After the disease claimed his father, the second Lord Magnus installed air purifying towers all the way up the mountain. They are disguised as large trees so as to not interrupt the natural landscape the Ursons are so proud of. Now the air on the mountain is some of the cleanest in all of Stellera. Whereas down here in Ashe, it is the absolute dirtiest.

The Urson's manor is nestled between the two largest peaks of a long range of dead volcanic mounds. The Obsidian Mountain range is the largest on the entire continent of Katova. They stretch across the eastern border of Stellera and Dailotta. Before the volcanoes died, their spitting lava graciously eroded tunnels deep within the mountains. The people in Ashe who don't work in the refineries or factories are usually miners, searching the tunnels for whatever precious gemstones or metals it has to offer. Especially volcorium which seems to be the most prominent metal found beneath Obsidian.

We approach the bottom of the mountain. It won't be long now. Taking out a pocket mirror, I check my reflection. As usual, my eyes are sunken from lack of sleep. I pat a small amount of powder to the thin, purple-tinged skin below my eyes in an attempt to conceal any imperfection my mother will otherwise condemn me for. I smooth my braid out and straighten my dress. I roll my shoulders as I press them back to practice the expected posture that leaves a biting feeling in my collar bones and spine.

Rett will be a good husband. I know he will. He has his own special place in my heart already. We can be happy. I haven't seen him since I was thirteen, and back then, I would have considered our bond as that of brother and sister. He was gangly; his legs were too long and skinny for the rest of his body, and his head was far too big. But he was always so kind when I needed it so desperately. I love him. It may not be in a romantic way, but I do love him, completely. This is going to be fine.

I will find happiness.

The road up the mountains is steeper than I remember. I have to hold my breath most of the way up for fear we will slide backwards off the mountain at any moment. When I was young, it felt exciting, but now, it just adds to the growing pit in my stomach.

I hold my hands together to keep from shaking, subtly picking the skin around my thumb nail. I begin counting the passing trees to curb my intrusive thoughts of falling off the mountain and other disastrous encounters. *Five... eight... twenty... sixty-three...* Of course, it is impossible to count them all, but the task provides the right amount of distraction for the remainder of the drive. As the trees begin to clear, the almost completely black manor comes into sight. It's a wonder the estate is not visible until you are upon it, considering the enormity. The massive manor stands five stories above the ground and is made of jet black brick and smokey obsidian glass.

The fortress is equally impressive as it is intimidating.

As expected, a welcome party forms up the steps to the foreboding obsidian glass doors. At the bottom of the steps are my parents and sister.

Lorella has her chestnut hair pulled into a low bun that exactly mimics our mother's. It pulls the skin on her face back in an uncomfortable tightness. She looks twenty years older than me rather than the three that she is. A sad jab of pity rises in me. Caked powder fails to conceal the prominent dark spots below her eyes, and lines of worry are creased between her brows. They show the effects of her first-born duty.

Evander opens the door for me and offers a hand to help me out. The pity I felt for Lorella quickly dissipates when she looks down at me with such fierce disgust it makes me question my entire existence. She mastered this look from our mother who stands two steps above Lorella, hands clasped tightly in front of her. She hides any form of emotion from her perfectly painted face. My mother is impossible to read unless you are skilled in the art of observing slight muscle twitches like the one her eyelid is currently practicing.

Father stands beside her, although given the way their bodies are positioned in relation to each other, they might as well be on opposite ends of Stellera. His straw colored hair is now streaked with white and is combed back behind his ears. His gray-blue eyes catch the afternoon light, making them appear ghostly. He holds a small smile on the bow of his lips, whether for the return of his daughter or joining of houses, I do not know. I hope the former but suspect the latter.

My family members coldly nod their heads as I pass in greeting. They are clearly overjoyed by the return of their second daughter. I keep my head high as I pass them, even with the stabbing pain in my chest.

The Urson children are arranged in order of birth up the grand stairs. The youngest, Orynn,was only a toddler the last time I saw him. Now, he is tall and skinny. He has gleaming brown eyes that match his hair, and his features are already symmetrical. A smile full of innocence and missing teeth is spread widely across his face, and I can't help but return it.

The twins, Lysette and Linnea, follow above him. They strongly resemble their mother with honey blonde hair flowing loose behind them in waterfall waves. I have trouble telling them apart, but they each have one brown eye like their father's and one blue like their mother's. The twins reflect each other as if they're standing in front of a mirror at all times. They nod their heads and smile pleasantly as I pass them on my climb. A curious mischief twinkles behind their mis-matched eyes as they share in unspoken communication between each other.

Rett stands just above his sisters in natural succession to the Urson line. I hold my breath as I look him over with my top lip between my teeth. He has, of course, grown in the six years since I've seen him. I expected as much. What I didn't expect was for him to fully look like a man. His body has caught up with his head, and he has filled out in both height and muscle. He has a well-trimmed beard growing along his now squared jawline. The beard is darker than the hair he no longer keeps shaggy but cropped on the sides as the men of the Kings Army often keep it. He catches my wandering eyes and gives me a goofy half grin. Even through his new beard I catch a glimpse of my childhood friend again, and a swell of hope flutters rampantly in my chest.

His mother and father stand closest to the door, waiting to welcome me. His father is by far the tallest Urson, resembling a giant and dwarfing his wife, who stands taller than any other lady I know. They are hand in hand and smile at me with an honest welcome in their eyes.

"Aislinn, welcome, we are so very pleased to have you back home with us again!" Lyrica beams as she kisses the air beside both of my cheeks.

I involuntarily cringe at the word '*home*' but am glad for the affection, especially after the greeting—or lack of greeting—from my own family.

Lyrica grabs my arm and leads me into the grand foyer. "Come, come, we have much to do, much to discuss. We've prepared a birthday dinner for you. I'm terribly sorry you had to spend the entire day traveling. Such a rotten way to celebrate."

The stairway that greets us is just as large as I remembered from my childhood. It winds on either wall and connects to a platform at the top. The stairs and platforms are covered in fresh flowers, a touch added by Lyrica who insists there must be new life daily throughout the manor. The stained glass above the entry door projects the Urson seal with refracted light from outside onto the floor in front of us. Twin mountains with a family of bears at the bottom and the initials, MEU, connect the mountains like a bridge.

"Aislinn, do tell us everything about your last six years!" Lyrica's arm is entangled with my own as she leads me down the largest hallway between the curved staircases.

"There's not much to say. I didn't leave the Academy except for the few times we went into town." I shrug.

"Astoria has always been one of my favorite places to visit. It's so quaint yet there is a feeling of..." She pauses, searching for the word before landing on "magic."

I smile in agreement. "Especially the Tears of Astoria."

"Oh, yes! I've only seen it once. How magnificent it was. Something everyone should see in their life." I nod in agreement with a genuine smile.

We enter the formal dining room. It looks the same as it did when I was a girl. One of the walls is made of floor to ceiling windows that are kept half open, allowing a small breeze from the courtyard. The rest of the walls are adorned with black molding and filigree wallpaper in shades of gray. The furthest wall is lined with tables and enough food to feed all of Ashe. The servs stand behind the tables and along each wall, waiting to dote on our every need. We move to take our assigned seats at the massive uncut obsidian banquet table that sits in the center of the room.

Already standing near the table is a man with graying dark hair and an elegant slant to his eyes, marking them distinctly Roussian. He's wearing the Obsidian uniform, and two women stand beside him. One has black hair twisted tightly behind her head and is wearing fine clothes—though the wear around her eyes and on hands tells me she is not highborn. The other is about my age and looks to be a younger version of the woman beside her. She wears her impossibly glossy-black hair down. Her dark eyes match the man's and stare at Rett with the hunger of a lover. He returns the look with a slight curve of his mouth as he fights off a smile. The interaction makes me feel as if I am intruding on something private.

As if I shouldn't be here.

THREE
EVERYTHING BURNS

"This is my head of security, Mikail, his wife, Hyacinth, and their daughter, Iris." Lord Magnus introduces the unfamiliar guests, motioning to the trio who are now making formal introductions to my parents. Now that they are on their feet, I have a full view of what the daughter, Iris, is wearing. She has on a tight form fitting hunter green dress that is striking against her complexion but much too formal for the occasion.

Rett stands behind me, and I see him squirm out of the corner of my eye. The daughter is facing away from us, greeting my parents and sister as she expertly pulls her long hair over the front of her shoulder, showing off her exposed back, with scarcely there lines of ribbons hardly holding the fabric together.

Rett clears his throat a few times while a bead of sweat forms at his hairline. Clearly, these two have been engaged in some kind of dalliance. Maybe I should feel upset as his future wife, but watching Rett squirm is more fun than I expected to come from this evening. This is Stellera, after all. Given the nature of most of the marriages, it is not uncommon for the lords or ladies to take on a consort. Or two. Or twelve, if you believe the rumors about Lord Fillistius down in Ezolle.

"A little warm in here, Rett?" I don a smug smile as I follow his gaze to the prominent dimples just barely visible on Iris' low back.

Iris turns. The apples of her cheeks have reddened, and her eyes are daggers at my side.

She musters out a bitingly formal, "Hello."

"Hello. It's lovely to meet you, Iris." I keep my voice polite despite her glare twisting my stomach.

She smirks, "is it?"

Lyrica spots the brewing tension and expertly dismantles it. She waves for the servs to start filling drinks and plates before turning her attention back to Rett. She shoots him a silent scolding that demands for corrected behavior. He sinks into himself, appearing as a small child rather than a twenty-two year old man about to be married.

To my disappointment, my assigned place card is beside Lorella, probably my least favorite person currently in the room... though Iris seems to be trying to claim that title for herself. At least Rett is beside me and not my mother. Thank gods for small mercies. Our fathers are at either end of the large table and their wives beside them. Every person at the table is strategically arranged like pieces on a chess board. I notice Lord Magnus tracking Evander, almost as if he's studying him before taking a bite, signaling for the rest of us to do the same.

My sister's body is angled away from me. Rett keeps his head low and focused on his plate of oxen and creamed root vegetable. Iris stares at him with wanting eyes. She leans slightly forward, ensuring the tops of her breasts are on full display. Rett pretends not to notice, but the red rushing to his cheeks gives him away. Iris pretends to fiddle with a strap of her obnoxiously over the top dress. Her fingers lightly trace down the length, moving lower and lower until Rett chokes on a mouthful of food.

Trying to keep from rolling my eyes at the display, I turn to my sister.

"How have you been, Lorella? What is new in Vallae?" I ask the almost stranger beside me, growing more uncomfortable by the second.

She turns to me, disgust written in the scrunch of her nose as if she can't believe I'd dare to speak to her. It appears as if she is having some internal conversation before she finally lets out a sigh and replies, "We've been doing *very* well the last *six years*. No incidents to speak of since *you've* been away. Trades fare well. The lands are prosperous. Our people are content enough."

Lorella offers the most diplomatic response she can muster, ever the dutiful first born and never *just* my sister.

"That's all good news." I smile weakly, feeling my heart crack as she turns away from me yet again, signaling the end of the conversation.

Well. It would appear we will not be doing any sisterly bonding. With a drop of my shoulders, I turn to Rett.

"And you? How have you been?"

His mouth is full of food as he lifts his head. Daring not to speak, I'm sure in fear of being chastised further by his mother. He politely nods and smiles, puffing out his cheeks with food.

This dinner is a far cry from the laughter filled dinners I spent in Astoria. My cheek grows raw as I chew the inside of it repeatedly.

You will find happiness. Audrina's voice echoes in my mind.

I will not be deterred by a few awkward moments.

Things will take time to feel normal. I haven't seen any of these people in more than six years. They are all but strangers now. It will get better. We will be happy.

This is fine.

I will find happiness.

Lyrica ordered carts of spirits and an assortment of desserts for my birthday. She said a short but sweet toast and then everyone began shifting seats. My father has joined with Lord Magnus and Mikail on one end of the table. They're engaged in a heated conversation about the happenings in the Capital. The women discuss the upcoming engagement party and guest lists, excluding Hyacinth and Iris, who are huddled deep into their own hushed conversation. I try to pay attention to the conversations at either end of the table as they fight for attention by seeing whose voice carries over the others. I become distracted by the longing glances shared between Rett and Iris, glances that I've only ever read about in romantic novels, glances we all secretly desire.

They are secretive, eyes lusting over one another's features. Iris subtly licks her top lip. In turn, Rett's eyes darken, the temptation working its way through his mind and written clearly in his features. The distraction of their interaction causes me to clumsily knock over the glass of celebratory wine, spilling the contents over my cake and lap. I jump up at the sudden cold and meet my mother's wildfire gaze that I swear causes actual burns on my exposed skin.

A serv comes immediately to clean the mess I made. He offers me a clean linen napkin to clean myself. I wipe at my lap before dipping down to help him with the floor. I finally look upon him, and my breath catches in my throat. His unnaturally bright blue eyes are almost identical to the stranger's from my dreams, the one who chases away the darkness... but the stranger's eyes from my dreams are always so full of life. This serv's eyes are cold and unfeeling, the blue appearing more like ice than the hottest burning fire. He looks about my age, but the years of a working life has aged him more than the highborns I usually keep company with.

Still, he isn't bad-looking. In fact, I'd say that if he'd been born in different circumstances, he'd be attractive... perhaps the most attractive man I've ever seen. Black hair falls in messy waves around his olive-toned face. The contrast between light and dark makes his already bright eyes shine brighter. There is something inexplicably interesting about him. I can't bring myself to look away. It's as if the air has been sucked out of the room, and a ringing in my ears blocks out all other chatter.

He, on the other hand, won't look my way at all. I suppose it would be considered inappropriate and disrespectful for a serv to peer upon their lord or lady for too long... but still, I wish he'd meet my eyes, if only for a moment.

Still using the napkin he handed me, I move to help him clean the remainder of my spill. The side of my hand briefly slides against his. That small bit of unexpected contact sends a rush of heat that ignites every nerve ending in my body and rushes to my cheeks.

He quickly removes his hand as if repulsed and steps back into position, standing straight and looking to the ceiling, ignoring me entirely.

"If you'll all excuse me, now that I've ruined my cake *and* my dress, I'll be going to get settled into my room now," I say with an embarrassed half-laugh that is met by a room of blank stares.

Lyrica blinks, no doubt remembering her role in this house. "Yes, Rett, dear and... you, DeLuca—" She snaps her fingers toward the serv who helped to clean my mess. "Please escort Aislinn to the east wing and get her settled in."

The serv I now know is called DeLuca dips his head in compliance, and Rett immediately rises from his chair, obeying his mother. In my peripherals, I see a pout form on Iris' lips, but her mother is quick to shoot her *the look,* and she straightens up, looking utterly unaffected and bored.

"It was getting stuffy in there anyway." Rett smiles as we make our way up the eastern staircase.

"Or slightly uncomfortable?" I reply with a cocked brow.

He ruffles a hand through his hair, obscuring my view of his face, which I suspect is again turning red. "I don't know what you mean."

"Iris." I elaborate with a knowing look.

Rett looks uncomfortable. There is no hiding the red in his face now as it extends its way down to his neck.

"Well... yeah...I mean... she's lived here since her father got promoted to head of security, and when I got back from my tour in the King's Army... well, things happened... but she's always known about you... and me.. and that we are... betrothed. She understands. We talked about it. I never gave her hope of anything being more than it was. Her family is without title. She knows that means nothing can come of it, but her father has been very loyal to mine for years. He's worked here long before I was born... and the mountains get lonely." Rett's words tumble over each other until they become incoherent babbling.

I keep a fake scowl until I can no longer keep up the ruse. I burst into laughter at the guilt that contorts his face. I'm *not* jealous, well, not in the way he would think. I may be a little jealous of the freedom he has had to explore and live and find himself before being bound to someone for life. The academy offered a bounty of knowledge but not experience, and I find my shadow aching for adventure.

"I'm not naive, Rett. *Of course,* you've lived a life. I don't care about the things you've done, but I don't think *she's* as understanding as you think she is based on her performance at dinner."

His shoulder's relax as he exhales. Rett's smile is wide and boyish as he wraps an arm around my shoulder, pulling me into him, and planting a kiss on the top of my head. "I'm glad that fancy academy didn't change you, Ailie-cat... and I'm glad you're back."

Being so close to him allows me to smell his familiar musky soap. It smells like the woods we played in as kids, bringing a wave of comforting memories with my childhood friend. I want to stay here and breathe it in forever. Instead, I push him off and say, "Of course, you are," doing my best impression of Audrina's confidence with a cocked brow and half-grin.

Rett smiles, shaking his head as he follows me down the eastern hall. The serv, DeLuca, is close behind, impressively carrying all three of my cases without faltering in step, but his jaw is clenched, and he has a kind of violent look in his eye. I stare at him for a second longer and watch as he shakes the emotion off of his face.

I open the farthest door down the hall, expecting to find the pastel pink and white room. The same room the Ursons have reserved for me since the day I was born, the room I have stayed in for thirteen winters. Instead, I find a room I'm unfamiliar with. The layout is the same. Canopy bed against the back wall. Writing desk in the corner. Vanity near the powder room. But everything has been completely redecorated. All the pastel pink has been replaced by navy sprinkled with silver strands, resembling the night sky in Astoria. The once blond wooden furniture has been stained so dark that it appears almost black but with a reddish hue when the light touches the right places. It's gorgeous, exactly what I would've designed for myself had I been given the opportunity. It makes me feel more at ease... more at home.

"The twins' idea, for your birthday," Rett says, noting my awestruck silence.

"I love it. Honestly, it's perfect." The effort they made is enough to almost bring me to tears. I feel my words are inadequate to describe just how much I love this room, and I make a mental note to thank the twins.

"Well," Rett says with a loud awkward clap of his hands, "I guess I'll call it a night."

"I'm sure you will." I roll my eyes. "Have fun *sleeping*."

He kisses the top of my head again. "Goodnight, Ailie. Oh, and happy birthday. " With a wink and that boyish grin, he disappears down the hall as DeLuca sets my bags down.

"Thank you for your help, DeLuca." I offer him my most gracious smile.

The serv's brows knit together. He is clearly not used to being thanked for doing his job. He bows and stands in the doorway. I keep staring at him, trying to uncover what it is about him that draws me in so fiercely. Looking over his features, his frame is most definitely masculine—tall, not as tall as Lord Magnus, but definitely taller than the average man. His stiff, boxy service uniform makes it hard to imagine what is beneath. Not that I am at all interested in what's beneath. At least, I think I'm not. His eyes though; I can't get enough of them. They're not fit for this realm. Eyes like those belong to the gods.

"Will you be needing anything else, Miss Delphia?" he asks after I fail to realize what he's been waiting for—a dismissal.

"Uhm, no, well, thank you for your help."

The corners of his mouth twitch in what appears to be amusement. "You said that, Miss."

My cheeks burn. "Right, but for earlier. The spill."

"Anytime, Miss. It's my job."

"Right..."

His smile is more evident now, and I can't stop staring at it, even if he won't bring his eyes up to mine. I swallow, forgetting how to form words.

"Miss Delphia?" he asks.

My voice comes out with a squeak. "Yes?"

"Will that be all?"

Oh... right...

"Uhm, yes, DeLuca. That will be all. Thank you... again." I inwardly cringe at myself.

For the first time, he allows himself to look upon me, curiosity forming in the lines between his brows.

"Goodnight, Miss Delphia." He dips into a bow.

"Goodnight, DeLuca." I chew at the bottom of my lip, not breaking eye contact. His face returns to an impassive expression as he politely nods.

I'm finally left alone for the first time today.
Happy birthday to me.

I'm suffocating. Purple smoke is filling my lungs. No one else in this sitting room seems to notice it. They continue their idle conversation as though nothing is amiss. I'm screaming at them.
"We have to leave! Please! We have to go!"
But they are all sitting around, drinking tea and eating little cakes, ignoring me completely. Why don't they care? This isn't right. None of this is right. I choke on the smoke. Blood splatters with each hack, spraying the cream colored sofa. I feel tears start to roll down my cheek. I swipe them with the back of my hand. Blood. It's not smoke... It's gas. I go to Rett and shake him, but he doesn't notice me. His usually soft brown eyes are a milky white. Black goo oozes out his ears. He doesn't seem to care. No one can see me.
The gas is filling the room, and I try to scream, but no noise comes out. It's sliding down my nostrils to the back of my throat. Bitter and metallic.
Everything burns.
"Miss Delphia! Miss Delphia! Wake up, Miss Delphia. Please, miss, wake up!"
I wake with a jolt, dripping in sweat and my heartbeat racing.
Gods, it's hot in here.
Nothing is on fire. There's no gas.
I exhale in relief, eyes closed as I try to convince my trembling body we are not in danger.

"Apologies, Miss Delphia. I wouldn't have disturbed you, but we could hear the screaming throughout the entire east wing. We were worried." An older woman looks over me, apologetic.

Finding my bearings and rubbing the sleep from my eyes, I process the words '*we were worried*'. We. Plural. How many people heard?

"Please don't apologize. I'm sure I've woken the entire house. I am the one who should be apologizing. What is your name?" Feeling embarrassed by my inability to control the night terrors, I pull the covers tightly to my chest as if they are some kind of shield I can hide my shame behind.

"Elinor, Miss Delphia. My name is Elinor. I've been assigned to you specifically."

I feel a pang of guilt for not having remembered this gentle woman's name considering she's been doting on me since I arrived a few days ago.

"Thank you, Elinor, and if you are to be with me specifically, please call me Aislinn. No need for the formalities," I say, taking her hand and patting it gently.

"Surely, Miss Del... Aislinn. I'll go ring for some coffee or perhaps tea, and we can start our day, shall we?"

"Coffee would be wonderful. A splash of cream, please." I yawn. She nods as she walks out of the room.

My throat still burns. The taste of blood is on my tongue. *There's no gas, no fire. There's no gas, no fire. There's no gas, no fire.* I repeat the mantra to myself over and over until I believe it, then fall back in bed, not yet ready to face the day of a proper lady.

A soft knock raps on the door. I grab the long silk robe draped across my night table and shrug it over the matching short nightdress. Expecting Elinor, I lazily open the door without looking.

"Come on in," I beckon from behind the open door.

The wheels of a service cart squeal as they roll in. The cart has a steaming pot of coffee upon it with a lone cup, a saucer of cream, and a tiny bowl containing cubes of sugar. The cart is being pushed by the serv who is now all too familiar with a mop of black curls upon his head and startling blue eyes.

DeLuca.

I try to conceal my smile. I've seen him around the manor a few times since that first night. I feel like we are playing a game of sorts. I stare at him like an idiot and see how long it takes him to look at me. He usually wins... because he doesn't look at me much. Or at all.

Okay, so maybe I'm the only one playing this game.

"Apologies, Miss Delphia. You asked me to come in. I assumed you already had Elinor dress you." DeLuca isn't quick enough for me to miss his eyes rolling up the length of my exposed legs before he can tear them away.

My fingers quickly pull my robe shut and securely tie it. "Don't worry, the fault lies entirely with me." I rest an assuring hand against his upper arm. He stares at my hand on his arm like it is some bizarre monstrous creature, and I quickly pull away.

"How do you take your coffee, Miss Delphia?" he asks, eyes steady on the ceramic pot of steaming coffee.

"Just a splash of cream. I don't like it too sweet." I fold my arms over my chest for added security over my state of undress.

"That's surprising," he murmurs.

"Why's that?"

He looks up in shock. I don't think he meant to say that last bit out loud. Which, of course, I find amusing. Especially the way his eyes widen and he pales.

"Apologies, Miss Delphia, I misspoke," he says quickly as he mixes my coffee.

My hands move to my hips, and I cock my head to the side playfully. "No, now you *must* continue. Why are you surprised that I don't take my coffee sweet?" I study the worry upon his face. "You won't get into any trouble. I'm merely curious."

"It's just"—He pauses, searching for the words—"you're very kind compared to the other lords and ladies I've served. There's a sort of calm energy around you... I would expect you to take it more sweet than bitter... because you're more sweet... gods. That sounds so incredibly lame. Apologies, Miss Delphia. I should not have said anything." He keeps his eyes low, but I can feel the warmth from his flush. It's potent and fills the room.

His answer provokes an unexpected nervous giggle, and I am suddenly all too aware of my body.

Why are my hands so sweaty?

Still not raising his eyes, he offers the cup to me.

I go to grab the coffee from him but the ceramic mug is burning hot. The shock causes me to drop it, sending it crashing to the hardwood floor of my room. It shatters and the hot liquid hisses where it splashes against the cold metal cart.

"Apologies, Miss Delphia!" DeLuca immediately begins to clean my mess, flustered and apologizing repeatedly.

"It was my fault." I examine my burning red fingertips. "How did... how did you hold that mug? It was so hot... unbearably hot."

"It didn't feel hot to me. I wouldn't have handed it to you if I had known." He pauses with a small glimmer of emotion that I do not recognize. "I wouldn't hurt *you*. It must be the calluses. They might have reduced the sensitivity in my fingers." He holds his hands out to show the rough evidence of hard work etched deeply in the creases of his fingers and palm.

"Must be," I say warily while still examining the intense burning on my fingertips.

He continues to pick up the pieces when he pulls back his hand suddenly with a hiss. A lengthy shard from the broken mug has lodged itself deeply into the fleshy part of his palm below his thumb. He goes to pull the shard free.

"Stop!" I grab hold of his opposite wrist. "Don't pull it. Hang on, follow me."

I lead him into my powder room. He looks at me in confusion, forgetting his place as serv for a moment and allowing his eyes to rise to my face.

"You can't just yank it out if it's deeply lodged. It's like a dam. Right now, the shard is holding your blood in place. If you remove the plug, it will flow out rapidly."

"Hmm." DeLuca looks so much younger with his amused expression. "How would you know that, *Miss* Delphia?"

I pull up my robe, revealing a deep silver scar on the back of my calf.

"Experience. It's what the healer told me when I fell into a river bank and got a sharp stick lodged into my leg... I was nine, so, of course, I pulled it out and lost a ton of blood." I drop the robe, concealing the scar once more.

DeLuca's eyes follow the hem of my robe as it falls.

He unsuccessfully tries to conceal his smile. "I don't think I will bleed out from a broken shard stuck in my palm."

"Maybe not, but at least you won't bleed all over my floor." I raise my eyebrows and grab a cloth from the shelf beside my tub, fingering through the row of vials on the next shelf up until I find the one I am searching for. A vial of disinfecting *limpar* serum.

Using the clean cloth, I hold his hand open with his thumb out. I then pull the shard out from his palm, acting quickly to squeeze the cloth over the wound and applying pressure. With my hand firmly closed over his, our eyes meet, and the blue in his blazes with a vibrancy unlike anything else in this realm. It starts a fire in my chest that spreads quickly throughout the rest of my body. Instinctively, I move to close the distance between us, drawn to him by an invisible rope being pulled tighter.

"Miss Delphia." He breathes low and full of warning, reminding me of our place and roles.

I shake my head to rid myself of the trance and then smile.

"Hold that tight," I order, referencing the cloth around his hand. I unscrew the vial, getting ready to drop its contents on the wound. At my command, he opens the cloth, revealing a deep gash pooling with blood. I drop the serum over the gash. It sizzles on impact and turns blue. A reaction I've never seen before. He doesn't flinch.

Deciding it would be rude to inquire further about the odd behavior of his blood, I wrap a clean cloth around his hand and tie it in a neat little bow. My fingers linger over the wrappings for seconds longer than necessary.

"I should get back to the kitchen... I'll have Elinor bring you a new cup of coffee," he says abruptly, pulling his hand away, and yet again unwilling to meet my eyes.

"Uhm, right." He goes to move and I grab hold of his uninjured hand to stop him. "Wait."

DeLuca raises his brow.

"Just hold on a second." I begin searching among my creams and vials until I find what I'm looking for—a tub of healing ointment. I grab the round little jar and hand it to him. "For quicker healing... I know you use your hands a lot while working."

DeLuca turns the jar over in his hand with the deepest furrow in his brows. "I can't accept something like this. It must cost a small fortune. Not to mention, I've seen you stumble more than a few times since arriving, and I have a feeling you'll be needing it pretty soon yourself."

There is no hiding my embarrassment as it crawls up my neck, heating my ears and face. "You have to. It's a gift. Please, I want you to have it. Besides, I'm sure we have more of it floating around somewhere. If not, Lord Magnus can get some from a healer."

"If you're sure."

"I'm sure."

He stares at me for several seconds before nodding with a small smile and taking the ointment.

When DeLuca makes his exit, I flop on my bed and stare at the silver strands woven in the canopy above.

What am I thinking? Why am I so drawn to the serv? I've never felt this way. Never. Well... I also haven't known many men other than Rett... I'm probably just lonely, and he's easy company. Company without pressures.

But gods... his arms... his eyes...

Stop. Stop it, Aislinn. He's a serv. You're his future lady. There are boundaries that must be upheld.

Boundaries I already came close to violating.

I flail myself violently in my bed, frustrated and trying to shake him from my thoughts.

He is infuriating.

My own mind is infuriating.

"Shall I come back later, Miss Aislinn?" Elinor calls from the doorway. She brings with her a fresh cup of coffee in a mug identical to the one that had been broken.

Immediately, I stop my flailing and sit up, composing myself—like the lady I am supposed to be.

"I was just having a moment."

She nods with a warm smile. "Lots of changes happening to be sure. Take all the moments you need."

I nod in agreement, thankful she doesn't further pry for the cause of my *moment*.

After handing me my warm coffee, she pulls two garments from the wardrobe. Elinor alternates between holding out a pale blue dress with cap sleeves and a sweetheart neckline and a white dress with sheer bell sleeves and a squared neckline.

"The blue or the white?" she asks.

"We'll do white today. It will pair nicely with this sunny weather we are having. Don't you think so?"

"Yes, I think so. Good choice, Miss." She sets the dress over the full length mirror and pats the chair in front of my vanity, inviting me over so she can fix my hair. She lets my dark waves fall over my shoulders, pinning half of them up in intricate twists and braids. I dab color on my lips and cheeks as she adds the final touches. I don't want to give my mother anything to scrutinize if I am to run into her.

"A vision, Miss Aislinn. A true vision." Elinor claps her hands beneath her chin and gazes at me with true adoration once I finish dressing. "Young Lord Urson won't be able to take his eyes away from you, if I may be so bold."

My nose scrunches. "He has been rather busy looking at the head of security's daughter." I try to push away thoughts of what DeLuca's reaction would be instead and wonder why I'm even having them. *He's a serv. I am a future lady. I don't even know him. This is ridiculous.*

Elinor gives me a reassuring squeeze on my shoulders.

"Men are fools, no matter the age."

FOUR
THE WALLS HAVE EARS

I've only been in the mountains a few days and already can imagine how my days will be spent, wasting away in these halls—lonely and bored. I set out in search of Rett to see if he wants to go for a walk in the woods like we used to do as kids. Instead, I run into Linnea and Lysette. They are wearing matching pastel pink floor-length dresses with their hair flowing in golden waves behind them. It is a little unnerving when they dress the same, but I have gotten pretty good at telling them apart.

I smile at the pair as they quicken their pace toward me. They shared their eighteenth birthday last fall and have a line of suitors that could stretch across all of Stellera. Beautiful and quick witted, the Urson girls are highly sought after. It is hard to picture them ever parting, and I wonder if that is the reason they haven't committed to any marriage offers yet.

"We found you!" the twins say in unison as they each grab hold of an arm.

"You found me."

"Walk with us," they say—again in unison.

"Of course. Where are we going?"

"We were just wandering. There's not much else to do here." Linnea sighs, her face contrite with boredom.

"Don't say that. You have so many rooms and passages, I'm sure it could be quite the adventure to explore them," I don't disclose my own boredom from being cooped up in the mountains.

The twins share a flicker in their gaze as they silently communicate.

"There is this *one* room that's quite interesting." Lysette's face brightens.

Linnea beams at her twin.

"Why are we still standing here then? Show me this *interesting* room."

The twins lead me to the fourth floor and through a maze of hallways. Each turn looks exactly as the one before, down to the same portraits lining the walls, a design to confuse would-be intruders. Without the help from the twins, I'd never again be able to find my way through it.

They stop before a plain wooden door. Nothing stands out about it at all. It could pass for a storage closet. Linnea opens the door. Air soured with mildew hits the three of us in a gust.

It *is* a storage closet.

"I know that seeing things like this may be rare for people of our station, but brooms and boxes aren't exactly what I would call *interesting*." I laugh, wondering how I'll ever keep my mind intact whilst living in the mountains with little more to do than explore storage closets.

"It's not what it appears." Lysette smiles mischievously. Her mismatched eyes twinkle in anticipation.

"Trust us," they say together. They lead me into a dark corner of the room and move a box to the side, revealing a small door the size of a cabinet.

Lysette pulls it open, and Linnea crawls through first. "Come on, Ailie!" Her soft voice echoes from behind the small door.

"If you are attempting to murder me, I am going to be really angry and come back from the Afterlands to haunt you." I climb through the door on my hands and knees while lifting my dress to make sure I don't drag the white through settled dust. My bare knees throb in protest against the hard concrete, but I push on, hoping whatever is at the end of this tunnel is worth it.

"If we were trying to murder you, we'd be much more creative about it. Mom has a wonderful conservatory near the eastern courtyards, full of all sorts of exotic plants, many of which are extremely poisonous." Lysette chuckles.

I hear the flip of a switch from somewhere behind me, and in procession, a dim purple light illuminates the room, just enough to see ahead of us. It smells stale as though it has sitten undisturbed for many years. A low hum from the purple light rings through my ears, effectively bringing the twinge of an impending headache behind my brow bone. The light is cast from oxidous energy, something rarely used in homes after so many accidental poisonings. Its main purpose has been fuel, but some of the older Stelleran structures still use it despite the danger it poses. Mostly ones without the funds to remodel.

Now partially illuminated, I see that the room is small. Scarcely tall enough to stand in fully. I have to crane my neck to the side or risk hitting the ceiling. There's nothing in the room but a hole in the center of the floor.

"We're not going down there, are we?" I ask. My nerves are getting the best of me, and I'm questioning my own judgment. Perhaps boredom isn't the curse I thought it to be.

Maybe they *are* leading me to my murder.

"Of course, we are," they answer together.

With a tightening in my chest, I follow the twins down the hole containing a slim ladder. The dim purple light continues to shine through the narrow tunnel. It seems never ending as we descend into the unknown until we finally drop below into a room with only one chair and a small table, a quill standing upon it—awaiting its master's return. There is nothing remarkable about the room other than the wall the chair faces being made entirely of a window, the edges of which are mirrored, leading me to believe it is a half-silvered mirror. I press my face against the cold glass, trying to get a glimpse beyond it. The other side is blanketed entirely in darkness, but with the help of the dim purple light, I can make out large shapes of furniture. A conference table is centered in the room, and the walls are lined with shelves. Edges of books come into focus as I strain my eyes on a set of shelves directly across from me.

Rectangular shapes that I take to be frames are almost visible in the low light, though their contents remain a mystery.

"How do we get in?" I touch the edges of the window, feeling for a draft.

"We haven't figured it out yet." Linnea shrugs.

"Papa forbade us from going anywhere near it once we told him we discovered the room," Lysette adds.

"Did he say why?" I'm becoming more and more eager to unlock the secrets of this hidden room.

"He said he'd 'tell us when we're older,'" they both answer.

"Well. You're older now," I muse. "It looks like an old library or archive hold."

"We thought that too." They nod.

"Interesting, indeed. Why hide it?" My hand presses flush against the glass. In the dark part of a blink, I see a flash of a room filled with people rustling through books. The image leaves as fast as it comes. I squint and strain against the glass for as long as I can before giving up on conjuring the image again. The twins declare we make it our summer's mission to find our way into the room beyond the glass.

After we've climbed out and made our way back to the main chambers of the manor, a serv informs the three of us that our presence was required by our mothers in the main gardens. Both of them.

We walk out together and find the two ladies pointing all over the gardens in ordering and frantic gestures.

"We can't simply cut down trees that have been here since the beginning of time, *Sescily*." I overhear Lyrica talking with my mother once we are within earshot.

"Oh pish, we can do anything we'd like, Lyrica. We need to make more room for the tents."

Lorella nods in agreement with my mother but keeps silent.

They pause their conversation to acknowledge our presence.

"Ah, ladies, we are glad you're here to provide some input," Lyrica wears a look that dares me to side with her rather than my own mother.

"What have I walked into?" My shoulders drop ever so slightly. Mother notices and shoots me a look that makes me instantly straighten them again.

"Well, your mother insists we will be needing twenty tents at the engagement party. I believe that will be far too many. It will cover the entirety of our magnificent garden and take away all the natural luster of the forest that surrounds us. What, then, is the point of hosting outdoors?"

Lyrica makes her point by using both hands to gesture around the full and blooming garden, which is indeed magnificent.

"Ailie loves the stars," Linnea interjects.

"We could entertain beneath the night sky," Lysette concludes.

"What if it rains? And what of the food?! We simply can not risk any outdoor *contaminations*." My mother's foul look directly implies the oxidous gas and smog from down below in Ashe. Her words are surely meant as a polite insult between ladies.

"Then we can move into the formal ballroom as we normally do," Lyrica responds, ignoring the slight with a small muscle twitch in her cheek.

"This is a union between Delphia and Urson! Riverstone and Obsidian! It has to be a spectacle. It has to be the largest event of not only the season but the decade! *Normal* has no place in this celebration." My mother's eyes are hard, focussed on a grove of trees nearby, no doubt silently plotting their downfall.

"Why don't we do three tents? Just over top of the food in the west courtyard. That way it won't obstruct the view of the gardens and then we can open the smaller ballroom up for seating. We can serve cocktails in the formal ballroom as well as entertainment and transform the gardens for socializing and evening entertainment?" I suggest, hoping to placate them both.

"And we simply must have—" Lysette starts.

"Fireworks," Linnea finishes, nodding enthusiastically in agreement with her twin.

"Ah, see, problem solved. We just needed another point of view. You will make an excellent lady, Aislinn." My cheeks redden at Lyrica's praise.

Mother looks as though she wants to say more on the subject but thankfully refrains with her lips set in a hard line, knowing her place is not lady of *this* house.

"Come dears, let's take lunch in the garden." Lyrica gives a look to an older serv with deep purple bags under her eyes. The serv nods in compliance before heading to the service door hidden behind a vine covered trellis.

The servs bring our finger sandwiches and an assortment of iced teas to a wrought iron table that sits near a large pond full of lilies. The sound of the centered fountain is composing a soothing serenade with the addition of birds happily singing in nearby trees. This is the kind of day that begs to be enjoyed.

For the first time in a long time, my mother is not eyeing me in judgment but seems rather relaxed, and there is a shadow of a smile upon her stoney face. The conversation flows easily, and I find I have been missing this kind of connection since my arrival.

But such is my luck I almost choke on a grape when the servs bring out desserts and coffee.

Rolling one of the golden carts is DeLuca. I swear he is glowing beneath the golden rays of sunlight like some kind of god.

I swallow, trying to show indifference to his presence in front of the other ladies.

Don't look at him.

Don't look at him.

Don't look at him.

I keep my eyes fixed on Lorella who is telling another self-indulgent story about visiting the Capital last fall and being a personal guest in King Carrigan's palace. She and Prince Leopold seem to have hit it off rather well, and she expects him to visit Vallae in the spring. Her story drones on and on. It takes all I have to actively listen. Even Lysette and Linnea are completely uninterested, their eyes glazing over while they examine the tea cakes placed before them.

Don't. Look. At. Him.

My cursed eyes shift to catch a glimpse of the maddeningly handsome serv. He averts his eyes quickly but isn't quick enough for me to miss that they were scanning me the moment before.

There is a strange pull of energy between us. It feels as if we are magnets being forced toward one another, and fighting it is almost physically painful.

"I need some air." I interrupt my sister who stares at me as if I'd called her the most vulgar of names imaginable.

"We are *already* outside, Aislinn." My mother gestures around us and her familiar scowl returns.

"Yes... I know... What I meant was..." I rack my brain for an excuse to leave—any excuse. The long open sleeve of my dress catches on a sharp bit of welding on the wrought iron table. When I pull it free, the force knocks a pitcher of blackberry tea over. It would be my luck that the contents would spill entirely on me. The prickle of murderous stares from my mother and sister dance uncomfortably on my skin, but I have my excuse.

Lyrica's eyes are much softer but also wide with surprise at my odd behavior.

"Ugh, Helena spare me! I roll my eyes, "I apologize, Lyrica. I've seemed to have muddled up another one of your lovely meals."

This is the third time I've spilled a beverage in the days since my arrival. My mother will have me thrown in an institution with the invalids if I keep it up.

DeLuca is, again, quick at my side, cleaning the mess I made on the table. What must he think? Always cleaning up my messes.

"We have to stop meeting like this." I awkwardly laugh.

"Miss Delphia..." His voice is low as he nods toward my dress, keeping his eyes fixed on the plates in front of him.

I follow his nod and look down. The once white linen of my dress is now soaked through completely with the deep-purple tea, turning the dress translucent, exposing all my assets and leaving nothing to the imagination. I try, unsuccessfully, to cover myself with my arms.

"For the love of Haile! DeLuca, give her your coat!" Lyrica orders.

"Lady Urson?" His face is filled with too much shock to remember his place.

"Your coat, boy, your coat. The future Lady of Obsidian cannot be walking about the grounds so exposed! Give her your coat and escort her back to her room through the service doors!" Lyrica waves her hands frantically at my exposed body.

DeLuca slides his black uniform coat off, and with hesitant hands, wraps it over my shoulders. It's warm with his lingering body heat and has a smokey musk. Thankfully, the coat is far too big on me and covers everything I need it to.

I am the one who stands practically nude, but somehow DeLuca is the one who seems exposed. The ripples of muscles are now prominent beneath his tight-fitting undershirt. He has what looks like burns running up the length from his left wrist to his shoulder. They take the shape of smoke, only made more intense by the silvery hue they've obtained with age. He catches me staring and crosses his arms, trying to cover the marks.

I've made him uncomfortable.

I *hate* that I've made him uncomfortable.

"This way, Miss Delphia." He tilts his head toward the hidden service doors.

I follow DeLuca to the passage. I'm not sure what I expected, but given the extravagance of the manor, it was more than this. There is nothing but rows of doors and exposed black brick walls. These passages are not meant to be seen by the highborns.

It is evident I am out of place from the looks we receive by all servs we pass. But this is the quickest way back to the east wing because they have their own lift that can move horizontally and vertically through its shafts hidden within the walls. It opens to each floor, allowing them to easily move carts full of refreshments or take the laundry or whatever else it is that the servs do.

DeLuca wears a stoic expression, but his breath is heavier than it should be, and there's a darkening in the blue of his eyes. The temperature seems to increase with each passing moment. This is awkward. Why do I feel so awkward?

Get a grip, Aislinn. You're an embarrassment.

"Your hand looks healed." I notice his unbandaged palm which doesn't have so much as a scar.

"I'm a fast healer, and your ointment helped." His reply is curt, and he keeps his eyes fixed ahead.

That ointment *does* work wonders... but I've never seen it completely heal a wound in less than a day.

He must be a *really* quick healer.

I'm racking my brain, trying to think of something more to say when I hear something slam behind us. DeLuca carries on, but my curiosity begs me to follow the noise. Not just curiosity... a pulling sensation. I'm *supposed* to go this way. I feel it in my bones.

DeLuca calls for me. He's telling me I'm going the wrong way, but a ringing in my ears muffles his words. An exotic herbal smell I don't recognize fills the air. It's potent and brings a fog over my thoughts. The pull leads me past a dozen doors before stopping. Black smoke flows from underneath a door at the end of this hall, then disappears as soon as I am upon it.

There are frantic husted voices behind this door.

"It will work. I need more time to figure out the correct dosage. Too much could be disastrous, lethal even," a shaky female voice says.

"We've run out of time! The secrets we keep threaten to expose themselves within the weeks to come. Our whole lives will have been a waste if we don't do something now. We might as well go back to Rousse now to avoid retribution if you can't make it work," a man's voice responds. Even when speaking low, it is strong with authority.

"She's close. I know she is. If I make it any stronger...it could... I don't know how much one person can take. It's a science I've never studied." She stammers. It is clear from the way her voice carries that she is afraid to upset the man.

"Figure it out," he commands.

Straining to hear more, I move closer, nearly pressing my ear to the door when someone covers my mouth and pulls me back by my waist. DeLuca whirls me around and puts a finger to his lips as he nods his head in the direction of the lift. I look back to the door. Something sinister is transpiring behind it, and I want to uncover its mystery. As if reading my thoughts, DeLuca shakes his head in warning. I choose to follow him, against the pull at my core telling me to stay.

We get in the lift, a room big enough to only fit a handful of bodies, maybe as much as seven if they stand shoulder to shoulder. My mouth opens to ask him whose room is behind the door, but he doesn't give me a chance. DeLuca leans close to me. His smoky scent makes me dizzy with uninvited desire that I try to choke down. He makes it impossible as he leans in even closer. His hands expertly work the levers beside me that cause the lift's gears to shift.

With his lips so close to my ear that the tiny hairs on my neck raise to greet his warm breath, DeLuca whispers, "The walls have ears." When he pulls away, there is no expression upon his face, as if he hasn't said a word. A shiver crawls up my spine in warning, and I keep the onslaught of questions to myself... for now.

The gears groan in dismay as they lift us through the manor. We go up, to the left, and then up again. The lift silences, and the doors open as we reach the third floor of the east wing. My floor. DeLuca gestures to let me walk ahead. He keeps a few steps behind me as servs are taught to do. I wish he'd walk beside me. It has always bothered me the way servs are treated as lowly creatures when, in reality, they could have been us, or we could have been them if there was even the slightest shift in fates.

When we arrive at my door, DeLuca bows his head in goodbye. "I'll send for Elinor to help you dress." He keeps his eyes low.

"But, your coat?" I ask, hoping he'll stay. I want to know more about what we'd overheard... about the *'ears'* he warned about... and though I don't want to admit it, I want to learn more about him.

"I'll get it from Elinor, to give you privacy, Miss Delphia. It would be inappropriate for me to remain in your chambers when you're so... indisposed." He briefly allows his eyes to travel to the opening of his coat that exposes the delicate dress still clinging to me with dampness. For a second, I think he might walk towards me, the way his gaze lingers. I bite my lip as he drags it back up to my face, but he just shakes his head slightly before turning to leave.

A wave of unexplainable disappointment hits me like running into a brick wall as the door shuts between us. But I don't have time to think about that or the sudden emptiness his absence brings. Strange secrets are unfolding in Obsidian Manor. I can feel it. The voices beyond the door confirm it. I will not allow plots and schemes under my roof. They've brought down dynasties, and I will not have Obsidian Manor endure such a fate. I need to talk with DeLuca. somewhere safe from whatever *ears* are listening.

I pace around the room, thinking of how I can get him alone. A letter from Audrina that arrived this morning sits opened on my bedside table. I've already read it backwards and forwards since Elinor brought it to me. There is no news of import other than when she and a few other girls witnessed some kind of protest through the streets of Astoria. Apparently, a man was rallying groups of the underprivileged from neighboring villages in Astoria. She said mostly the ones who live in Dennon's lands to the south were listening to him, the ones still trapped in the circumstance of their birth. Though, she wasn't sure what the protest was for, exactly. Just that the people were very riled up.

I tear a corner piece of the letter, dip a quill in an ink pot, and quickly scribble.

We need to talk.
Somewhere free of "ears"
-ATD

I fold the paper and stuff it into the front pocket of the service coat that is still draped around my body. I pull the collar over my nose and inhale the familiar smoky scent. Beneath the smoke, I get a hint of the man the coat belongs to. The smell is distinctly male in the best of ways and similar to a river stone back home. The mixture is addictive and further fuels my enthrall with its owner. My fingers trace the stitching in the fabric, stopping at a loose thread as someone lightly knocks on my door.

"Well, Miss, it seems the blue will be the one for the day after all." Elinor opens the door, snapping me out of whatever impossible daydream I was about to walk into.

I smile at the sweet woman. "I suppose it was fate, and who am I to argue with fate?"

"How very true that is, Miss. Wouldn't want to upset the Weavers." Elinor helps me out of my wet dress and into the blue one from earlier.

"Elinor... I don't suppose you know about the serv who helped me earlier? DeLuca?"

Elinor's smile falls. "I do, Miss."

"What can you tell me about him?"

"Oh, Miss Del–Aislinn, please don't have him fired. That poor boy has had the most rotten luck just about his whole life." She pleads with the worry of a mother.

"Fired? No, Elinor, I am only curious because he's been very kind to me. I enjoy his company."

Elinor's creased eyes widen with surprise, but her face relaxes, and she composes herself. "Apologies... I just thought... well, each time there's been an incident, he's been there... I thought maybe he was to blame."

"I take credit when it is due. I know I can be a bit jumpy at times. To no one's fault but my own." I give her a half-smile. "Elinor, what did you mean by 'he's had rotten luck?'"

She lets out a long sigh. "His story is a sad one to be sure. Found on the streets as a newborn. A family took him in that already had nine children they could hardly feed. The father died of oxidous poisoning when working in the mines... terrible conditions those mines... and the mother followed just a year later. Suicide. Nasty business. I suspect she struggled keeping the family afloat after her husband passed, and I'm sure she succumbed to the grief of it all. Poor DeLuca was only five when she went, but he still remembers. He was the one who found her. The two oldest boys joined the royal army and were sent to the border of Dailotta. They always sent home money to the younger siblings—until they didn't. All eight remaining children needed to find work after. The two little girls were able to assist tailors. The oldest sister I believe served in the tavern. The second eldest girl left for the capital and hasn't been heard from since. The rest of the boys, DeLuca and his brothers, went to work in the mines. They use children as runners. They are quick and can get supplies to and from faster than the adult workers."

Tears fill the brim of Elinor's eyes, telling me the story doesn't end there.

"Then what happened?" I prod.

"Oh, Miss, it was terrible. An explosion. Twelve years ago. Some of the oxidous gas leaked from the pipeline into the mine, and the second someone came in with a lamp, the gas ignited. The entire mine collapsed, and whatever miners survived the blast were blocked in and left to starve. All of Ashe was covered in the toxic smoke and ash. The townspeople had to wear masks for over a year. The town still hasn't recovered. There was only one survivor of the blast, little DeLuca, no more than nine years old at the time. It was a true miracle... I lost my husband in the very same blast."

She lets a tear fall but quickly swipes it away.

Remembering the smokey scars on DeLuca's arms, I feel a heaviness in my heart for the horrors endured by a single child. I pull my knees to my chest and shift in my vanity chair, squeezing Elinor's hand, which rests gently on my shoulder.

"I am so sorry you lost your husband, Elinor. I'm so sorry for what the town lost that day. It must have been horrible." My words feel too little, but I don't have any others for such an atrocity befalling an entire town.

She nods and continues. "All of his sisters have married now. I believe there may be one that stayed in Ashe, but the rest left in search of better lives. His oldest two brothers still haven't been heard from. It is presumed they are dead... as the little ones are. It's just him now. He's doing the best he can, the dear thing." Her expression is haunted.

The hardships they have endured... that Ashe has endured... I wonder what Lord Magnus has done to help them. Surely *something*.

I squeeze her hand once more as she takes a deep inhale, shaking her head as though she can shake away the sadness.

"Well, that's enough talk of tragedy for the day. I'll bring you some warm tea."

I notice the coat lying across my vanity and remember the note I stuck inside it. "Oh, hold on a moment, Elinor. Can you kindly return DeLuca his coat?"

"Of course." She smiles and nods, folding the coat over her arm.

She shuts my door quietly, leaving me alone with my thoughts of Ashe and DeLuca, wishing I could hug him.

No, Aislinn. That's horribly inappropriate.

But would it really be so wrong?

FIVE
SOMETHING ISN'T RIGHT

It's been over a week since I've last seen DeLuca. There's been no reply to my note or any indication that he's gotten it. After the third day, I asked Elinor where he'd gone, and she informed me he took a leave, that he had personal business to attend to. She was vague and uncertain of when he'd return.

My heart jumps each time I hear a serv rolling a cart, only to fall with disappointment. I have found distractions. The twins and I have been trying to find a way into the hidden room, the one behind the window, with no luck. Whoever designed the mysterious room wanted to be sure its existence remained secret.

Orynn and I played a few games of chess. He's much smarter than any other boy of nine I've ever known. It's entirely possible he will grow to be one of our nation's brightest minds. Of course, I'd never tell him so. With each win he gains, his ego inflates to an unbearable level. After every win, he makes sure to run through the manor, telling anyone who will listen that he's bested me yet again. I, of course, tell him I intended for him to win... that I am going easy on him. But honestly, he is just *really* good... or I am really bad. Strategy has never been my strong suit.

My parents and sister shall return from Vallae in a few days for my engagement party. At least I have not had to shoulder their attacks while also adjusting to a new normal. Lord Magnus travels to and from the Capital often. Each time he returns, it's like he's aged another half decade. Something is weighing heavily on his soul. He takes most of his meals in his study, with Mikail close by his side.

Rett is still here, I think. I haven't seen much of him— or any of him—except the back of his head when he spots me coming and turns the other direction. His behavior over the last week has been strange. I thought our relationship picked up where we left off six years ago based on our exchanges the night of my arrival, but apparently, that was too much to hope for.

There has been an eeriness in the air lately as well. Something dark flows through these halls, setting me completely on edge. It could be the nightmares, still of doors, shadows, death, blood, fire, purple gas, and the screams of children. Same as they always are—always have been. They're unbearable, and I wake up drenched in sweat each time.

The sun is beginning to dip behind the mountain. I'm sitting in a meadow near the treeline outside the main gardens, reading a fascinating historical-fiction book about 'the gifted' people born in the mortal realm with powers similar to those of the mythical gods. Such people existed before the Trinity War, but the dictator who'd taken power in Rousse, Edgar Dukkah, had been sure to wipe them out. He claimed all who were born different were born 'wrong' and 'cursed,' that they could only bring with them wickedness and immorality. He is recorded as the most evil mortal man in the history of any of the nations. He committed atrocities that make me shudder, uncaring as to whether his victims were grown men or innocent babes. No one was safe from his genocide aside from the full-blooded Roussians. The ones with dark hair and dark eyes.

They were a plague of darkness.

When the light grows too dim to make out the letters on the page before me, I sigh and close the book. The scent of old pages briefly escapes the bindings from the rough collision. I lay back in the dew-dotted grass with my arms behind my head, waiting for moonrise. The brightest stars appear before the sun has made its final bow beyond the treeline. Three to the west that are used to track direction. Forbis, Opari, and Viitor, the stars named after the three children born to the Goddess of Balance, Millena. It's said the stars represent the sight her children possessed and, therefore, were named after them—so that all who seek to truly see will never be lost.

I hear the growls of what sounds like large animals somewhere beyond the treeline. The growls are restless, and I have no desire to meet the creatures responsible. I pick up my book, ready to head back to the manor when a shadowy figure approaches from the distance, tall and imposing. It is hard to make out distinct features without the light from the sun, and the moon hasn't found its position in the sky just yet. Still on edge from the distant growling, I hold my breath. My nerves dance aggressively beneath my skin, urging me to run. The only place to go is into the woods, toward the growling beasts lurking beyond. The figure blocks my direct path back to the manor.

Whatever you're going to do, Aislinn, do it now.

Taking a calming breath, I search for anything that I can wield as a weapon and settle on a fallen branch. I hold it close as I rise to my feet.

"What do you plan to do with that?" A familiar voice coming from the approaching figure chuckles.

As he grows closer, I can see his mop of black curls.

"DeLuca." I breathe out a sigh of relief, and my blood returns to its steady flow through my veins. "My heart nearly jumped out of my throat. Don't scare me like that!" My hand instinctively holds my chest as I relax. The other lands on his bicep.

He looks at my hand, my fingers splayed around the curve of his upper arm. I pull it back quickly, flushing with embarrassment.

"Apologies, Miss Delphia. I wasn't trying to sneak up on you. I got your note but only just returned from my leave." He reaches into his pocket and pulls out the folded paper I'd placed inside it.

"My note? I sent you that note over a week ago! You could have had the decency to send some kind of word. Any kind of word...especially after such an ominous warning." My fists move to my hips, and a scowl tugs the corners of my lips downward.

The twinkle in his eyes, caught by the starlight above, is disarming, and I lose myself staring for a moment. I find that I am unable to be angry with him. Especially with his head cocked to the side in confusion at the edge in my voice.

"I had business in the Capital. It could not wait."

"I know. I asked Elinor where you'd gone."

"You asked for me?"

"Mhmm." I let out an exasperated sigh. "I hope all is well?"

DeLuca's eyes darken and his jaw clenches. "It will be."

I nod, not believing him, but he obviously doesn't want to discuss his business, and I don't want to push him. "Anyway, what I wanted to ask you is whose door was that the other day." I pull forth my memories of our last encounter. "The voices of the man and woman? Then you said...you said...the walls have ears? What does that even mean? Whose ears? Was it entirely necessary to be so incredibly cryptic because, honestly, I've been losing my mind trying to figure out what is happening in the manor."

"Miss Delph-"

I place a hand up for him to stop as I interrupt him. "Please, just Aislinn. I despise being called '*Miss Delphia*'."

The contortion of his face is almost comical, and I have to bite my lips together to keep from showing my amusement. It is my turn to take him by surprise it seems.

"Miss *Aislinn*, you have many questions, but the answer is the same." He looks me directly in the eye, his features far more serious than moments ago. *"Mikail,"* he finally says, practically spitting the name.

"I need you to elaborate." I'm aware my tone is sharper than usual as I grow impatient with his obscure answer.

"Sometime else," he promises, looking behind his shoulder toward the manor. "I have to go before I'm noticed." He pauses before leaving. "Be careful in the manor, Miss Aislinn. You will not find safety here." His fingers run along my arm, leaving a trail of goosebumps despite his heat.

His hand grasps mine, giving it a gentle squeeze. Then, he disappears toward the house, leaving me shivering in the dark meadow alone. My jaw is still slack, and I am staring at the empty spot on my hand where his had been. I make a tight fist, digging my nails into my palms to provide a distraction from their loneliness. The pain is better than the emptiness that seems to deepen after each interaction with DeLuca. I've known something felt off since returning to the manor, but it wasn't until he spoke those words that I truly realized there may be danger lurking in the halls of Obsidian Manor.

And I'm not safe.

Sleep evades me yet again. Shocking to none. I toss and turn, reflecting on the series of events that have taken place since my arrival. There is an aura of danger encapsulating the manor.

You will not find safety here...

But why? From Mikail? Who's charged with the security of the household? If we can't trust the head of security, who can we trust? Mikail's ears? Spies? Or something else? I suppose it would make sense for him to need to know all the happenings within the manor as he is the head of security... but then, why wouldn't *I* be safe? And why wouldn't we be able to talk freely? I have more questions than answers after DeLuca's visit, and I can't shake the feeling that something catastrophic is on the horizon.

The lamp on the table burns bright beside me. My quill sits neatly beside the stationary I purchased in Astoria. The borders are engraved with wisps of silver swirls and a sprinkling of small stars. My finger runs along the little bumps the design makes in the rigid parchment as I think of my true home—Astoria.

I knew life in the Obsidian Mountains would take some getting used to, but I never dreamed it would be *this* hard. That already my intended would be deeply in the midst of a relationship with another woman. That there would already be so many secrets. Already be lies. Never would I have guessed of my growing infatuation with a serv. It feels like *more* than infatuation though. I know it mustn't be. It can't.

How I long for the simplicity of life in Astoria. Even at the Academy. *Especially* at the Academy. I want to write to Audrina. I do. But I don't know where to start. What I can even say...without sounding pathetic? With a sigh, I set the paper down again.

The wind seems to call my name from outside my window. I feel like I am being watched. I'm well aware it is likely my tired mind playing tricks on me, but that doesnt stop the shiver from creeping along my spine. I've always hated being alone in the east wing but especially now, given the unsettling atmosphere within the walls. It feels as though I'm being watched at all times, like the walls have eyes following my every step.

Decidedly, I will not be sleeping tonight. In slippered feet and with my warmest robe tied snug around me, I hop out of bed. I have no intended destination. I never do. Letting my feet lead the way, I wander aimlessly down the corridors, twisting and turning through halls with rows of nearly identical doors. I've essentially grown up in these corridors but still only know my way to a handful of rooms without the help of a serv or Urson.

A portrait of the first Lord Magnus catches my eye. He is said to be the greatest of the Ursons...or was until he lost his mind near the end of his life—the Urson Curse. He'd become incredibly paranoid. Suspicious of all, including his own family—most of all, his wife and servs. He looks proud in the portrait. His mustache curls in happy spirals above the curve of his prominently bowed lips... the same lips the current Lord Magnus has. The twins have it too, but it skipped Orynn and Rett. He wears a military uniform, decorated fully with medals. He'd been a general in the King's Army during the Trinity War and was responsible for saving hundreds of Dailottan refugees. If I remember correctly, there is a statue in his honor in Dailotta, somewhere near the border but still beyond the Thickett Woods close to where they settled.

I touch my hand to the painting, feeling sad for this proud hero of a man to have lost himself. When my hand makes contact with the canvas, my ears begin to ring loudly. I clap my hands over them, trying to subdue the sound threatening to burst my eardrums, and I shut my eyes tightly as if I can block the sound from all my senses.

When I open them, I see a man identical to the one in the portrait, but this man is older, sadder...his eyes haunted. He is having a heated argument with a woman. She is small with dark hair and hazel eyes.

"You must stop this madness, Mags! You have servs up at all hours. They need rest. The house needs rest. I need rest. People have begun to talk... the other governing houses... they wonder how capable you are... Think of the children. What they will lose if the king decides you're unfit to govern?!"

The man from the portrait, the one she called 'Mags', grabs her by her shoulders. I can see his nails dig, and she winces at the pressure, letting out a small whimper as fear replaces her hardened features.

"You don't understand, Fiorah. I can't. I can't stop. He's coming. They're coming. Everything will end in fire and smoke, and we must have a way to escape. I'm doing this for the children. Can't you see that? Can't you see everything I do is for the future of this house? Of our family?" His words are slow and deliberate as if explaining something to a child.

Fiorah's eyes well up with tears as she searches the man's face, looking for familiarity. He, in turn, releases her shoulders from his grasp and sighs. The deep purple below his eyes is more prominent against the flicker of light dancing upon his face from a sconce nearby. Without a backwards glance, he side-steps past her and disappears down a hall.

She falls to her knees in complete defeat.

I try to reach for her, to comfort her. When I blink, I am again alone in the hall with my hand against the portrait.

What the Haile was that?!

My uncontrolled dreams are starting to bleed into my waking life.

I'm heading back the way I came when I cross paths with a familiar door. My random wanderings through corridors has somehow landed me in the west wing. This is without a doubt Rett's door. I'd recognize the bears carved into the frame anywhere. When I was around the age of eight or nine, we named them all. Haile, Agnar, and Felix for his favorite stories of gods, and he'd let me name one, Millena, after my favorite goddess. I have always admired her ability to stand her ground between right and wrong without fear. The carvings also include other animals, trees, and birds. But the bears are most prominent. This room has always belonged to the firstborn of house Urson. It was his father's growing up and his grandfather's before that. Hundreds of years of little lords in the making.

I run a gentle finger down the deep grooves of the bear I'd named Millena. A smile forms as I relive the memory she brings forth. Rett and I were sitting on the outside of the door. We'd been playing with wooden figures he had gotten for his birthday the week prior. My sister had never shared anything with me, and I felt as though I'd get in trouble. When I asked him if he was sure I could name one of the bears, he said, 'of course, what is mine will eventually be yours anyway. I want to share everything with you, forever.'

If only we could have maintained such sweet innocence.

When I hear hushed whispers beyond the door, I draw my hand back from the carvings as if a viper is waiting to strike. It's well after midnight. Everyone should be long asleep. Leaning closer to the door, I strain to listen to the voices that are so soft they could be mistaken for the wind outside. It's no use. They are too low. I can't make out words or tones.

It occurs to me that it's very likely Iris on the other side of this door. My blood sours at the thought. Gods, this has to be the most awkward moment of my life...well, in the top five at least. I slowly and carefully back away, trying not to make a sound. The very last thing I need is to be caught outside my future husband's door while he is taken with his lover. I turn the nearest corner when I hear the springs in Rett's door knob bounce and click as they twist open.

Please, no.

Flattening myself to the wall, I pray to whatever gods will hear me that I become a shadow or sprout wings. Whichever. I'll take either. The hair on my arms stands at attention as I recognize the low voices now unmuffled by a closed door.

"Was it enough?" the man asks, his voice low.

"It should be," the woman says. There is a small quiver of uncertainty in her voice.

I peer around the corner in time to see two figures vanish down another corridor. I catch just enough of a glimpse to see long black hair streaked with silver...*Hyacinth.*

My heart races wildly with adrenaline. They are the same voices I heard in the servs' corridor. The long black hair with silver... Hyacinth...Mikail...DeLuca was right—

Was what enough?

What did they give him?

My breath stops completely.

Any rational thought vanishes as the flood of realization hits me.

Rett.

Flinging the door open, I rush into his room to find him sound asleep.

My head lowers to his chest as I check his breathing. Fine.

I use the back of my hand to feel his head. Fine.

His room looks normal. It smells of his usual woodsy scent. There is nothing out of place as far as I can tell.

"Rett?" I ask gently, sitting beside him. No response. I rub a hand gently on his shoulder. "Rett, wake up." No response. The blood rushes from my body. I yell and shake him rapidly. "Rett...Rett. Rett! Come on, wake up, Rett!" I shake and shake. "Oh, gods, Rett!" I slap him across his face, ignoring the sting of my palm.

Finally, he rubs his eyes that refuse to fully open. "What are you doing here?" There isn't a trace of the warmth in his voice.

"I...they...Someone was in here." I realize how strange it must appear for me to be in his room at this hour.

"No one is here but you." He turns over, pulling his quilt higher above his shoulder. "Go back to the east wing where you belong." His voice is cold. Hollow. Utterly not his own.

"Rett...what—" The words won't form as I notice an inky black goo dripping from his ear. "Oh my gods! Rett, you have to get up. Now!" I shout, not caring who hears me.

"I'm not supposed to see you anymore," he replies sleepily.

"What? Why? That doesn't make sense."

"I don't know. I'm just not supposed to." He shrugs.

I take the light from his bedside table and hold it to his ears so I can get a better look at the goo. The light catches his eyes. There's a milky gray film over them. I jump back from the bed and stumble out of his room.

"A healer!!" I shout, running down the hall at full speed toward his parents' chamber. "A healer! Call a healer at once!"

Lord Magnus and Lyrica open their door just as I get to it. I nearly topple them to the ground, unable to command my feet to slow.

Lord Magnus frantically searchers me for signs of injury. "What is it, child? What's happened?" Lyrica strokes my hair in the soothing motions, perfected by motherhood.

"It's Rett. He's been poisoned. We need a healer now!" I sob, and thick tears soak the top of my nightgown.

They look at each other, their faces turn grim once my blurted words process. In a split second, they are running down the hall. Lyrica pushes past Lord Magnus to get through the doorway. They look to each other, then back to me, their expressions riddled with confusion. Rett's sitting up in bed, and his mother is holding his face. The light she shines against him reveals soft brown eyes, as they've always been. The milky film is gone.

That makes no sense.

"His ears! Check his ears!" I choke on the words.

She turns his head and shakes her own. The inky goo is gone.

"I...I don't understand. He had black goo coming out his ears and his eyes.. They weren't right...I saw it. I saw it." My voice quivers in confusion.

I know what I saw.

"My dear, is it possible you had *another* nightmare?" Lyrica asks.

"I know what I saw. I was awake. I couldn't sleep. I heard whispers coming from Rett's room. There were two others in here. They were talking about giving him something. I don't know what. When they left, I came to check on him. His eyes were milky, and he had black goo coming out of his ear. I know what I saw." I say the words firmly, but the bleeding daydream I had only moments before discovering Rett casts a shadow of doubt in my mind.

"She's crazy, Mother. She's always been crazy." Rett's words slur together as though he's had too many spirits. "It's why she had to go to the Astoria Academy with all the other crazy girls without a place in society. I can't be expected to marry someone crazy. Think of the future of our house." Rett's lips are moving, but the words coming out are not his own. This man is a stranger inhabiting the body of my oldest friend.

"Rett!" Lyrica's shock is undeniable.

"You will not speak in such a way about your future wife!" Lord Magnus' voice is full of authority, a voice more inline with a governing lord than a father.

"Something isn't right with him. Please believe me," I beg them both.

Rett scoffs.

"Something isn't right with *her*!" He pulls the quilt back over his shoulders, queuing us to take our leave. Lyrica refuses. She strokes his head and settles under the blankets beside him, motioning for Lord Magnus and me to go.

I catch Lord Magnus by the arm before he can go back to his room.

"Lord Magnus, please, please have a healer look at him. I know what I saw, and I know how it sounds and looks, but what if I'm right? What if someone has been sneaking in at night and poisoning him?"

"Ailie, my girl, of course, we will. He is our *son*. It was very clear that something *is* wrong with Rett from his strange behavior. He has always been so fond of you. I can't understand why he'd say those uncomely things." Lord Magnus shakes his head. His eyes fixate on my own with a softness...with concern for *me*. "I do wonder though...if maybe you'd like the healer to visit you as well... For the nightmares. You have always been like a child of our own. Hearing you scream throughout the night.. Well, if I'm being honest, it brings pain to Lyrica and myself."

Heat rises, coating my entire face and neck...possibly my entire body, down to the very core of my being. I never thought they could hear me so far away in the west wing. No one has ever mentioned it before.

"I'd appreciate a visit from a healer, thank you. I apologize for tonight...and...all the other nights."

Lord Magnus smiles limply and nods, offering a gentle kiss to my temple before heading back to his room and leaving me alone yet again. Though, the bitter cold piercing the back of my neck tells me I'm not alone...not entirely.

Someone *is* watching me.

SIX
PROVINCE WELL CARED FOR

I've been staring at a spec on the wall for hours, waiting for the sun to rise and the house to wake. What caused that little gray smudge near the powder room? It's too high up to have been me. Maybe it was caused during the redecorating? Or, perhaps, someone was in my room while I was gone? Servs are always in and out of each room. Privacy is something highborns know very little about. Maybe it is the exhaustion, but something about that spec is making me irrationally angry. It's possible I'm only angry because I feel so helpless. Like nothing I say or do matters and I won't be taken seriously. I know in my bones that danger is lurking. And Rett. Rett is in danger. Or he *is* the danger... I'm not entirely sure. My head is spinning. I haven't slept. I haven't tried. I just continue to look at the godsdamned spec on the wall.

I'm acutely attuned to my surroundings, having sat in silence for so many hours. So when a tiny piece of paper slides below my door, I jolt at the unexpected movement. It takes me a few moments before I realize what it must be. A message. Given that it was slid under the door, probably a secretive message. Quickly picking up the dirty piece of paper, I carefully unfold it:

> **Meet me at the lift.**
> **Alone.**

I flip it over multiple times, looking for more, but that's it. That's all that is written in the barely legible writing. There's no signature, but I'm sure it's from DeLuca.

I hope it is.

But why?

Why do I want to see him so godsdamn much?

I feel like a ridiculous first-year at the Academy the first time they see a local boy.

Elinor isn't due for a few hours to help me get ready for the day. While at the academy, we were made to get ourselves ready. The mistresses said it was so we were never caught off guard while not looking our best. I'm pretty sure they just did not want to fork out the higher wages Lady Carro would require the servs to be paid.

I tie my tangled waves back with a ribbon and decide on black pants with a charcoal gray cloak—clothes that are plain and easy to move around in. I don't want to draw attention to myself, whatever we may be doing. As I lace my boots, doubts flood through my mind.

What if it isn't DeLuca? It could be dangerous. What kind of lady follows the command scribbled upon dirty paper? Especially with all that has been happening. You're smarter than that, Aislinn.

Despite the warnings shouting in my mind, everything in my body tells me to go. I'm not the best at anything, but trusting my gut hasn't failed me yet. With a hand on the knob, I glance toward my writing desk, noticing the letter opener that sits on the corner. I grab it and tuck it between my boot and sock—just in case. The sharp, uncovered blade digs into the flesh beside my ankle bone, drawing a dribble of warm blood that slides below my foot. I like having the constant reminder that I'm armed. It helps steel the voices of doubt. I am not entirely useless.

The house is eerily quiet at this hour. The servs have yet to begin the morning preparations. It is still night, so no light sneaks in from the slits of the closed drapes. I make my way down the hall to the lift, going off memory from when DeLuca brought me back to my room. I step lightly so as to not alert anyone of my movements. When I approach the lift's doors, they are already open, yet the room is empty. My heart sinks with disappointment.

Perhaps there is another note waiting for me. I enter the lift with my eyes fixed on the floor, looking for any scrap of paper or sign of what to do next. A warm hand touches my shoulder, causing me to jump back with a small yelp.

"Shh!" He hushes me, holding his hand over my mouth, pulling my head against his shoulder and my back flush against him. My chest rises heavily as I feel the heat radiating around us. His breath swells against my ear. DeLuca shushes me once more. When he feels me relax, he turns me around and places his finger to his lips, telling me to be quiet. I nod and step back against the wall, holding tightly to the railing until my hands turn white. I try to focus on something other than the lingering heat of our bodies being so close together. DeLuca begins working the lift gears. We go sideways and then down.

It feels like we're never going to reach the bottom. When we finally do, DeLuca grabs my hand in silence and leads me down a dark corridor I've never seen before. The walls are a mix of compacted dirt and stone. I believe we are underground. We must be, given how long we were descending. It smells of old earth as we follow the dim purplish lit concrete path. Logically, I know I should be weary about following an almost stranger down mysterious dark corridors. Instead, I focus on how my breath hitched when his hand grabbed hold of mine. I feel safe with him. With this almost stranger. I have no idea why, but I do.

I wonder if he notices how sweaty my palms have become.

Breathe, Aislinn. It doesn't mean anything. It's dark. He's just leading you. Breathe.

DeLuca looks back at me. The look is one that tells me he is assessing me. He's making sure I'm okay, searching for insecurity. I reassure him with a tight smile that says *I'm fine. Don't worry.*

We reach the end of the corridor. A rusted metal door is set into the dirt and stone wall. It appears completely sealed off, no knob or handle in sight. DeLuca lets go of my hand—leaving it incredibly cold without his warmth—and pushes the door with both hands. It squeals as if screaming for its last breath as it slides open. The door disappears within a small opening between the stone and a rusted metal wall.

DeLuca walks in without hesitation. Now, I'm feeling those jitters that should have hit in the lift. When I don't move, he pulls me in by my elbow. The door quickly shuts behind us. After seeing the rows of seats big enough to hold maybe thirty people, I realize we are in a large pod-like transport, the likes of which I've never seen before. The seats are all worn, and the cushions are falling apart and peeling. There are windows encircling the vessel, but they're so dirty that they're rendered useless. It is obvious by the conditions that this transport hasn't been maintained.

DeLuca pulls a lever and fiddles with some small switches before the transport starts moving. It's quicker than any kind of transport I've ever been on, and the force throws me back against one of the seats. Immediately, warm hands are beneath my back and easing me up again before guiding me to a seat.

"What is this?" I ask as DeLuca takes the seat beside mine.

"It's a transportation system used for servs. Many of us live in Ashe rather than staying in serv quarters in the manor. Our trams only run through town and since most of the people in Ashe are too poor for their own transport we had no way to get back and forth. The Urson's built this transport system in some of the unused mine shafts. It takes fifteen minutes either way."

"That's brilliant. Why don't more people use it?" I remember the steep road up to Obsidian Manor with a shudder.

"Would you *want* more people to know how easy it is to gain access to the manor? With the way things are in Stellera?" he replies with a cocked brow.

"What do you mean how things are in Stellera?"

DeLuca's eyes squint like he's trying to read my face. "You really don't know?"

"Don't know what?"

His brows are drawn so tightly together I wonder if he will give himself a headache. "There's been riots in the Capital...all over, actually. They're demanding change, demanding an end to governing houses and the monarchy, just about anyone born in privilege. They want all wealth to be distributed equally like it is in Rousse. It's been getting violent lately. Almost all governing houses have been receiving threats. I'm sure that Lord Urson knows about this."

I gnaw at the inside of my cheek, thinking about how many trips Lord Magnus has taken to the Capital since I've been at Obsidian Manor. About how I've seen a change in his demeanor. He fades with each visit.

"No, I hadn't heard any of that. What people are so discontent? All the common borns I have met seem happy enough. I used to play with the common children in Vallae. It's actually part of what got me sent to the Academy...but the people in Astoria all seem happy. Is that why...why you said I'm not safe? Do you think we are under threat?"

The bright blue of his eyes almost glows in the dark of the tunnel and magnifies whatever concern lies behind them. "No, that's something else..."

"Well?" I prod.

"The servs hear things behind manor walls, things we aren't meant to. We know our place and don't insert ourselves in the business of *highborns*. Usually." He takes a pointed look at me. "Before you arrived, I overheard Mikail and his wife talking about how they'd need to get rid of you. I didn't hear how or why. When they heard my footsteps, they stopped talking. I assume it will make way for their daughter, Iris, to elevate their position. She's been trying to get to Rett for years, unsuccessfully, until he returned from the King's Army. Now, they're together each night. He wasn't even considerate enough to try to be discreet. Even in front of you, his future bride." The air around DeLuca heats, and a muscle in his jaw ticks.

"Go on."

He exhales through his nose. "Being head of security, Mikail has devices planted all over, allowing him to hear things throughout the manor. He calls them his *ears*. He's constantly listening to everything that goes on. I said you're not safe because when Mikail wants someone gone...they disappear." He bites his lip. "Mikail is not known to be gentle, and thinking of—" DeLuca groans in frustration with a clenched fist but doesn't finish his sentence. He doesn't need to. The temperature continues to increase around us, causing sweat to form at my hairline.

"Is this...is this all the information you have?" My face turns, betraying the disgust I feel. The idea of being listened to all the time is beyond violating. Far beyond the invasion of privacy that typically accompanies highborn life. My gut is twisting the longer I dwell on it. To what lengths will Mikail go?

"It's all I have to *tell* you, but, if you're willing, I'd like to show you something...well, somewhere. If that's alright, Miss Aislinn."

Not paying attention, I nod and try to wrap my head around Mikail constantly invading the privacy of every member of the house. What he must hear. I shiver at the thought. I am only half listening to DeLuca, but it doesn't feel right for the formality given our surroundings. "Outside the walls just call me Aislinn, please, or really anything else as long as it doesn't bear a title."

"Anything else?" An almost playful smile seems to hide in the twitch of his lip, "Okay Ail— Aislinn." He explores the informality as the temperature starts to cool again.

The pod screeches to a halt, and the blinking purple lights overhead steady themselves. DeLuca gets off first and holds out his hand to help me over the small step up. The blade in my boot digs slightly at the movement, and I feel reassured by its presence. We are in a small, dark cavern. If it weren't for the pod we just came off of, I would think it abandoned. DeLuca leads me to a slim set of stairs made of nothing more than hardened black clay native to the cave. I can barely make out a small opening at the top.

DeLuca stops mid step and turns to face me as if he has remembered something important. His hands graze my shoulders as he lifts the hood of my cloak. Trying not to let any sound escape, I take my bottom lip between my teeth. He tucks the loose strands of hair behind my ears. His fingers move gently as he pulls the hood lower, concealing most of my face. The close proximity of our bodies causes my heart to beat erratically.

"I don't want anyone to recognize you, for both our safety." His voice is a whisper, and his hands linger on the trim of my hood. I catch him staring at my mouth, and my lips part ever so slightly in invitation.

DeLuca releases his hands and takes a step back, creating more distance between us.

With his back to me, I exhale all the breath I was holding and roll my eyes at my own stupidity.

Get over yourself, Aislinn.

We walk through the charred remains of the forest at the foot of the Obsidian Mountains.

Everything feels dead.

Everything smells dead.

The air is suffocating.

Ash mixed with powdery sand kicks up with each step, covering my boots and pants. The almost full moon is gracious with her silver glow, even as she retires, providing us with our only form of light. We walk in an awkward sort of silence for ten minutes before we make it to a clearing and find ourselves on a worn-down cobblestone street.

"This is Ashe," DeLuca says with the faintest hint of sadness.

My brows knit. "I know this is Ashe. I've been through many times," I reply, wondering what the Haile we are doing here.

"But have you really been *through* it? Have you ever gotten out of your transport and gotten to know its bones? Its scars?" he rubs his arms reflexively.

I pull my gaze off his disgustingly beautiful face and force it to take in our surroundings. Boarded up buildings line the street we stand on. Holes in windows. Roofs caving in. A distinct smell of rot mixed with smoke flows freely through the air.

A crash of glass in the alley a few buildings down makes me inch a little closer to DeLuca. My hand twitches, thinking about grabbing the letter opener as my eyes dart in the direction of the abrasive sound. There's a dirty bearded man sleeping on the edge of the road. He is wearing nothing but holey socks and a long shirt that doesn't cover his manhood—leaving it fully on display as he lies with his legs spread.

DeLuca tracks where my eyes have landed after taking in the horror splashed across my face. He puts himself between my line of vision and the man. I've never seen a naked man before. other than the half destroyed sculptures depicting the gods near one of the temple ruins in Astoria. It is regrettable that my first time seeing one in the flesh is so unsettling.

"I...I haven't ever gotten out of the transport." I try to take in my surroundings without letting the pity show in my face.

"We don't have much time. I'll have to get you back soon so you're not missed, but I want you to see... to understand." He leads me through a series of seemingly deserted shops. Through each threshold, we step over broken glass and wood rot. There are very few people. The ones we do come across are covered in soot and look sickly, covered in lesions, with a yellowish hue to their skin. DeLuca pulls my hood down each time he hears footsteps. I wonder if he's embarrassed to be seen with me.

After walking through what can only be described as a ghost of a town, DeLuca brings me to a tavern. It appears to be the only building in workable condition. Someone has taken the time to repaint it recently, and the roof is whole and intact. The bell atop the pulley system hanging above us rings as we open the door.

"Yes, hold on, hold on. Early in the day, innit? Sun's not even awake, and you bastards already want to piss away the day," a woman's voice rasps from somewhere behind the bar.

There is a man sleeping in one of the wooden booths, but the tavern is otherwise void of patrons.

"It's just me, Valera," DeLuca calls toward the voice. He looks at me and mouths '*sister*'.

Valera appears from beyond the bar and hugs DeLuca.

Her dark hair is cropped below her ears, accentuating her sharp cheekbones. She, like the others who live in Ashe, has smudges of soot wiped across her tan face, but she contains a spark of life that they do not. Something motivates her. She hasn't given up.

"Luc! I wasn't expecting you yet! We're not due to leave for a few—" She stops mid sentence when she spots me, her smile dropping into a deeply angry scowl. Valera hisses through her teeth. "What have you done?"

"Hello, Im—" I'm cut off by the women who had only moments before shown so much warmth to DeLuca.

"I know exactly who *you* are. There's no cloak in the world that can hide a *highborn*." She speaks with so much disdain you would think I single-handedly slaughtered her entire family.

I step back, my fingers itching again for the small blade in my boot.

"Val, please, she's not the same as them." DeLuca's tone is soft as he pleads with his sister.

"How could she not be? Look at her!" Valera points at me.

"Same as what?" I look between the two, trying to figure out what is happening.

"Aislinn, excuse us for a moment. I need to talk with my sister." DeLuca looks at me apologetically, but when he turns to his sister, his features harden and his jaw clenches. He ushers her to a room behind the bar, leaving me to wander the small tavern alone.

The floors and walls are covered in a layer of black dirt. You can't even see out the windows; they have layer upon layer of thick black soot. There are very few booths and a few small round tables with mismatched chairs. I'm drawn to a cluster of posters hanging on the back wall. I move closer to examine them and let out a small gasp.

One is a propaganda poster calling for an end to *"Oppression"* by the *"Liberators"*. Another is a flier for an anti-monarchy rally in the Capital with an appearance by a man named *'Pierce Decatur'*.

The last one shocks me most of all—a formal portrait of Lord Magnus and his family, including Rett, with a bright red handprint smudged across all of them. The words 'Death to Highborns' are scribbled atop.

I feel the anger radiating from the walls.

"You smell pretty." A raspy voice slurs from near my hip.

I look down and find myself standing next to the man who'd been sleeping. I was so distracted by the alarming posters that I failed to realize I wandered near his booth.

The white of the man's eyes are completely yellowed with disease, and he smells as if he's already been dead for quite some time. I try to step away from him, but his dirty hand grabs hold of the end of my cloak.

"Let go!" I order with as much command in my voice as I can muster.

"I just want to smell you. Nothing else smells like you." He grunts as he bundles my cloak into his sweaty dirt-covered face.

"I said let go!" I pull the letter opener free from its hiding place in my boot and point it at the man. It drips crimson from the blood I've drawn from my ankle in the quick movement.

DeLuca runs out from behind the bar and places himself between us, his back to my chest as he pushes me back with his body.

Valera slowly follows behind him with her arms crossed and a scowl plastered on her face. She takes in the scene and rolls her eyes.

"Go home, Walter." She helps the man to his feet.

"Lovely, Val. You know this *is* my home." He smiles, revealing all but three of his teeth are missing, and the ones that remain are black with rot.

"I'll be sure to tell that to your *wife*." Valera nudges him through the door.

"Just like I'll be sure to tell our friends of your new extravagant guest." He taps his nose before stumbling out the door.

DeLuca turns his attention to me, searching me over for injury with rushed and frantic movements. His relief is obvious from the way his shoulders relax after not finding a scratch on me.

His head quirks to the side. "Have you had that this entire time?" He gestures toward the letter opener that still has a faint red discoloration on the edge.

I nod yes—struggling to find words.

"Where did you keep it?" His eyes search my tight fitting pants and my cloak with no pockets.

I roll my sock and boot down, revealing the shallow cuts from where the sharp blade had been hiding.

DeLuca crosses his arms and raises his brows with a half-smile "You continue to surprise me, Aislinn. I would have had no idea you were armed if you hadn't shown it." He takes the blade from my shaking hands and gently tucks it between my sock and boot, shielding my ankle from further injury, "I'm glad you thought to bring a weapon. That kind of thinking will keep you alive in the weeks to come."

"Keep me alive..." My voice shakes. "When you said....I didn't realize that it was included here,"

I'm still in disbelief over the level of distraught. Though, after walking amongst Ashe, I can't say I'm truly surprised by their anger. The only building that isn't falling into itself is this one that provides escape with an obstructed view of the outside world and loaded spirits.

How could things have gotten so bad? Why hasn't Lord Magnus done more for Ashe?.

"Of course, *you* wouldn't. How could *you*—living in a castle hidden away from anything *real*?" Velera chides.

DeLuca shoots her a harsh look of warning, met by his sister with a mere shrug.

"There was an explosion about twelve years ago. Even after the air was deemed breathable again, most of the town got very sick, many of them dying. Children were born with deformities. Most people are too sick to work now. The small handful of us that are able-bodied are either set to work in the factories, the mines, or Obsidian Manor. Some have been able to leave, but when there weren't enough workers left for the factories, Lord Magnus decreed all children over the age of six were to be sent to work too." DeLuca speaks his words carefully.

"No, no he wouldn't do that. Lord Magnus is kind, especially to children! He's one of the kindest men in this world!" I defend the man who filled my childhood with warmth and welcome.

"Look around, *Princess*. Does this look like a province well cared for? Is he not in charge of the well being of Ashe? If he were doing his job, would we be struggling so greatly? My fa-" Velera's voice breaks "family would still be here. *All* of them."

"He is but..He... Ashe is..." I have no words. There are no words. I want to defend the man I consider family, but looking around, how can I? Velera is right. Lord Magnus is in charge of the well-being of Ashe and its people.

He is failing them.

A pit forms in my stomach, and I feel sick.

A whistle blows outside.

"Shift change..." DeLuca looks toward the door. " We need to go now, Aislinn." He places a hand on his sister's shoulder. "See you soon, Val."

"Don't be stupid," she says while still glaring at me.

"Love you too." He kisses her cheek.

DeLuca's hand finds its way to the small of my back, radiating heat so powerful I can feel it through my layers of clothing. He leads me back down the cobblestone path. Workers carrying pickaxes and other tools are filing through the street. Occasionally, one notices how out of place we are, but they seem too exhausted to care. Their eyes are as hollow as their sunken cheeks and are covered head to toe in dirt. Their hair is all the same color of gray—coated in dust. They walk as one group, without any life left in them.

A group opposite of us, dressed in factory uniforms, approaches the street we are on. Instead of dirt, the majority of them are covered in an oily substance. Their steps are less dragging, but their eyes are just as hollow as the miners'. DeLuca swiftly pulls me between two of the forgotten buildings lining the road. I nearly fumble over my feet from the unexpected change of direction.

"Why are we in an alley?" I ask him with a wince as I crunch on broken glass.

"The miners are essentially brain-dead. They don't have the energy to care about you. I have less faith in the factory workers.

I don't trust them with you—how they would react, and I don't feel like fighting today."

I try to conceal the shake of my voice. "Would you? If you had to? Fight, that is."

"Are you asking if I *can* fight or if I *would* fight to protect *you?*"

"Both, I suppose." I say.

"Yes."

"Yes?"

He locks eyes with me, "yes."

When the group of workers passes the alley we stand in, DeLuca pushes me against the wall, creating a cage with his body. There is less than an inch of space standing between us.

"What are you doing?" I whisper as my breath catches.

He doesn't reply, only lowers so that his forehead rests on mine.

I taste the sweetness of his breath on each exhale, and I swallow down the urge to wrap my hands around his neck and crush my lips to his. The sound of footsteps marching along the cobblestone gets louder. I remain motionless, partly to avoid the people and partly waiting for DeLuca to give me a sign that he wants this too. Our lips brush for the briefest of moments, just before he pulls away, releasing my body from his entrapment. The group of workers have passed. I shut my eyes, not wanting to ever open them again.

"I think we can go now." He breathes out heavily, as though we'd just climbed our way back up the mountain.

"Fine." I cross my arms over my chest and follow him out of the alley, out of town, back through the skeletal woods, and finally back into the cavern. We climb back into the rusted transport pod. DeLuca works the same levers and switches as I settle into a seat.

It feels like someone is slowly pouring lead over my body, anchoring me to this spot. My lungs burn as I fight the urge to cry. The adrenaline of our morning wears off, leaving me weak.

I allow my weighted head to fall into my hands. "I didn't know how bad it is."

"I didn't think you did." DeLuca responds even though I hadn't actually been talking to him.

My head raises slightly to peer up at him through my lashes. "I'm going to fix it, DeLuca. I will. When I am Lady of Obsidian, all of it will change. We can rebuild Ashe. We can bring in more healers. Create better jobs with better hours. I can fix this. As soon as I marry Rett, I can fix this."

DeLuca's face hardens into a scowl, and I swear I almost hear a growl low in his throat. He sits a few seats away. I wonder now if I repulse him because of the station I was born to. I'd be repulsed by all highborns if I grew up in *that* place too. Maybe that's why he has a hard time looking at me. Why when I thought we were about to share a kiss he pulled away as if my lips were dripping with poison. All these desires that have been building within me are completely one-sided, and I have just been embarrassing myself.

People are suffering. Truly suffering. It doesn't matter what you feel for him. His people suffer because of mine.

"It may be too late. Things are in motion. The people...they're tired...we're tired. I just wanted you to know. So you can prepare yourself for whatever is coming. The discord. The rebellions. You're not like the rest of them. I...I don't think you should be thrown into a category just because of who you were born to." He looks at the floor near my feet, his mouth pressed in a hard line.

"Too late to fix it? Then why even show me? You say all this like you know, DeLuca." My voice hardens. A realization I don't want to believe worms through the chaos of my thoughts. A realization I force out of my mind. One that would mean death for DeLuca if I were to ever speak a word of it. So I shove it down. Deep down.

"I *do* know, Aislinn." His voice is barely above a whisper. It's quiet enough that I pretend not to hear his admission.

We ride the rest of the way unable to look at each other. Both of us are drenched in guilt and regret. We continue without speaking even after the transport comes to a stop and we walk through the tunnel. The unsaid creates more tension as our minds race. I'm sure he's debating whether or not he can trust me. I'm still reeling from the discovery that the province I am to care for is in such disarray.

As I am about to step into the lift, DeLuca puts an arm on the wall next to me, yet again using his body to box me in. His hot breath trails the back of my neck, deepening the unwanted desires I feel for him despite where his allegiances may lie. I clench my fists at my side and command them to stay.

"No matter what happens, I *will* keep you safe, Aislinn. I will protect you, whether it is from my people or yours." His voice is low and has a rough edge.

My teeth ache from how hard I am biting them together. Every bone in my body aches for DeLuca, screaming at me to turn around and kiss him, fully and deeply. To give myself over to him. Right here. Against the very wall he has me pinned against. I'm fighting a battle against myself, and I don't even know why. It's not like I know him that well. I hardly know anything about him at all.

So why am I so drawn to him?

His chest rises against my back, and I want to curve into it. Instead, I dip under his arm and ignore his declaration completely.

SEVEN
STRANGE BEHAVIOR

The healer arrives mid-afternoon, a blind woman called Sylvie. Her silver hair is so long it almost touches the floor even while braided. She enters my room burning a bundle of herbs that burn my nose and make my eyes water.

"Two drops of rutide before bed to keep the nightmares away." Sylvie tosses a small vile toward me. Surprisingly, it lands right in my outstretched hand.

"Will there be side effects?" I shake the bottle and watch with curiosity as tiny seeds swirl around the red liquid.

"You will have no nightmares." Her voice is sharp. "Strange energy around you, child. You don't belong *here*. Strange, indeed," she says, mostly to herself. Her burning bundle continues wafting smoke as she traces swirls in every corner of my room.

"I notice you have an accent. Where are you from?" I ask, trying to ignore the slight.

"Northern Rousse, in my youth. Been here since being called as a healer. No use for healers in Rousse when the *gods heal all*."

"And do they?" It still shocks me at times that an entire nation could hold such a preposterous belief system.

"They do not." She waves a hand over her white eyes.

I look at my feet, feeling the heat of embarrassment. "Oh."

"Do not pity the blind, Miss Delphia. We see more than most."

"I'm not sure what you mean."

"Yes, I suspect you do not... yet." She pauses while contemplating something. "*Young* Magnus Everett Urson...it is you who claims the poison, is it not?" Sylvie asks.

"Yes. I know it."

She smells the air around me and moves closer until our faces are inches apart. The exotic herbal smells intensify, making me nauseous. "How? How do you know it?"

I tell her about the night before, the whispers, black tarry ooze, the milky eyes, the harsh change in personality, all of it except the waking dream I had just before finding Rett. I'm not sure she would understand, and I don't want her to write this off as some delusion from a jealous girl who cannot control her own mind.

"Poison...yes." She nods, feeling the air around us, and continues. "Hmm, perhaps not poison but something else. Yes. Let's go see young Magnus Everett Urson." She rubs her index finger and thumb to her ear as if they are whispering to her.

All healers I've been met with have been strange. Sylvie may be the strangest yet.

Lord Magnus is pacing outside Rett's room. His eyes brighten when he sees us.

"Ah, did we find something to help then?"

I nod with a thankful smile. In truth, I can't wait to try the Rutide drops tonight. It has been too long since I've had a restful sleep. I honestly can't even remember the last time.

"The boy?" Sylvie asks, motioning to the door she can not see.

"I fear Aislinn may have been right. He appears himself yet not. In body, he is healthy, but his mind is not his own." Lord Magnus shakes his head and opens the door. We walk in together and are met with a pillow thrown in our direction, missing us and instead knocking over a hand painted antique vase, sending it shattering to the floor.

"I told you I can't see her!" Rett shouts. "I can't see her! I cant, I cant! Take her away. Make her leave! Make her!" He's thrashing himself violently in bed. The veins on his neck are protruding as if, at any moment, they will burst.

"Aislinn, dear, wait outside, will you? Your presence is agitating him further." Lord Magnus looks at me with apologetic eyes, then turns to Sylvie "This is not my boy. He loves Aislinn, yet the mere mention of her name sends him into a fit of rage. When she is not around, he is himself, but the mention of her..." He shakes his head.

When I walk into the hallway, I find Lyrica waiting.

"Well?" she asks.

I shake my head. "I was sent out. I was agitating him"

She looks perplexed. "Hmm. Such strange behavior indeed."

"I think I know who did this," I quietly say, unsure if I should.

She looks at me expectantly.

"Mikail and Iris." I let out on an exhale.

"Aislinn. Please do not say such things out of jealousy. I know Rett has been acting foolishly, but Mikail is my husband's most trusted man. He would never betray the family. We've been good to them. What reason do they have?"

"If Iris were to marry Rett, they'd all be titled. They'd have to be for the king to recognize it. They'd gain power and influence. It's actually not surprising when you consider a life serving others. Families like theirs don't do well taking orders."

Lyrica ponders over my words before responding. "Even if you weren't in the picture, Rett could never marry Iris. He's our first born. By law he has to marry someone from Stellera already titled. It just doesn't make any sense." She shakes her head.

"Lyrica, I *know* it's them. Please, trust me."

The drop in her shoulders is so subtle I hardly notice it. She nods while tapping her fingers along her chin. "Aislinn, I trust you. This is a complex matter and must be handled carefully. Magnus trusts Mikail more than anyone in the realm, maybe more so than us and—"

Rett's scream cuts through the air like a sword.

"No! You will not touch me. No!" he shouts as Lyrica and I run in.

Lord Magnus is restraining him while Sylvie holds a dropper of silver liquid over his eyes.

Without turning she says; "Miss Delphia, would you please assist me? Hold his eye open."

I run over and do as I am told. The second he is steady, she releases a few drops. The liquid lets off an angry hiss as it lands on his eye. Sylvie instructs us all to let go. We back away as Rett holds his head, yelling out in pain. Black tarry ooze drips from his ears, nostrils, and eyes. He keeps his lips shut, but the ooze still finds its ways out of the corners. No longer able to hold it back, he opens his mouth and spews the black ooze all over himself. It's dripping down his chin. I pinch my elbow to make sure I am still awake. The scene before me may as well have been taken directly from one of my nightmares.

"What's happening to him?!" Lyrica watches in horror as her son convulses. She runs to hold him.

"The *hopea* is working," Sylvie responds. She turns her head slightly to the side, listening to the air once more.

Lord Magnus shoots me a quick look filled with shock and realization.

I was right.

"What is it?" he asks Sylvie. The worry in his voice is undeniable.

Sylvie swipes at the goo running from Rett's ears. She rubs it in small circles between her fingers, bringing it up to her nose to whiff. She nods as though someone is whispering the answer to her.

"A concoction from Rousse called *ivlodeas*," Sylvie answers, still rubbing the goo between her thumb and index finger.

"Ivlodeas? No, that cannot be," Lyrica says in disbelief.

Lord Magnus remains silent, but a fury hardens his already fierce features.

"What is *ivlodeas?*" I ask.

Sylvie responds with a monotone voice. "A concoction made of strovia herb and the extremely rare indicus oil—a thick black oil taken from indi blossoms. They are only to be found in the Roussian village of Eurel. This concoction is known to make its victims susceptible to influence and alter their way of thinking. It was used three hundred years ago on the Roussian ruler, Dukkah. The assailant convinced him to invade Dailotta and Stellera, beginning the Trinity war. It has since been outlawed by punishment of death."

Tears warm trails down my cheeks as I shoot a pleading look at Lyrica. She looks at Rett who is now unconscious and so pale he can pass for dead. Trying to find the courage, she closes her eyes, mentally preparing for what comes next.

"Magnus. It is possible that Mikail is responsible." Her voice is quiet, her gaze fixed on her son's hair.

Lord Magnus snaps his head, looking at her with wide eyes. "That is a mistake!"

"I thought so too. When Aislinn tol—"

Lord Magnus interrupts Lyrica with a laugh. "Ah-ha! Aislinn! It would make sense for her to believe this with the way the boy has been behaving!."

"Lord Magnus, please. You must believe me. I have good reason to believe it was him and his family," I beg.

Lord Magnus rubs his chin. "Do not repeat this *theory*. To anyone." His voice is full of command. It makes me feel small. *Weak.*

"How can we be safe if it was him?" I refuse to crumble beneath him and lean on the heat of anger rising beneath my skin instead.

"Aislinn... you must understand...he knows things that can destroy this family. If it *is* him, he will be dealt with accordingly, but we must be absolutely sure beyond a shadow of a doubt," Lord Magnus says.

"He poisoned your son!" I yell. "Who knows what he was trying to influence him for? Maybe to marry his daughter? To kill me? To kill you?!"

"All will be dealt with, Aislinn." His voice is calm.

I look at Lyrica, hoping she will come to my aid, but instead, she just shakes her head and goes back to stroking Rett's hair.

Sylvie is giving Rett some kind of tonic, pretending not to hear what is going on in the room.

Pretending not to hear.

Seeing Sylvie ignore the hostile conversation provokes a memory of something DeLuca said. *Servs hear things they shouldn't.* It's obvious whatever Mikail knows is worth risking the safety of every person in the house. If Mikail knows something, I'm positive some other servs do as well, and even if they don't, maybe one of them has the indisputable proof against Mikail that I need to sway Lord Magnus to get rid of his whole wretched family.

I look between Lyrica and Lord Magnus again, giving them a final moment to change their minds before storming out of the room, a scowl plastered to my face.

When turning the corner, I find myself face to face with Iris, whose eyes are swollen and red around the rims. She looks at my feet when realizing who I am, and her long hair falls in a way that hides her face.

"Is he okay?" she asks with a small, shaking voice.

"How dare you ask me that?! How dare you?!" I use every bit of self control not to push her down the obscenely large staircase to send her plummeting down to the obsidian tiled floors below.

Her voice breaks between sobs.

"Please–They-on't-Allow-Me-In. No- One-
Will-Tell-Me-Anything."

"Good. It's your fault he's in the mess," I say.

"M-my fault?" She looks genuinely confused, snapping her out of her fit.

"Don't pretend you don't know." I use my shoulder to push past her.

"But I don't know anything!" she calls from behind me.

I ignore her, keeping my eyes forward as I march down the hall. The anger beneath my skin itches as it boils to the surface.

I order the first serv I pass—who is arranging the new daily florals in a corridor—to send for Elinor. She bows and complies immediately.

I storm to my corridor without thanking the serv.

Too many thoughts run rampant in my mind to worry about niceties.

How many times can I pace the same steps in my room? The anger building inside me is too much. I feel as though I will burst into flames. The emotional toll from everything that has happened today is fueling the fires inside me. Learning about Ashe, the discord in Stellera, Lord Magnus, Rett and the ivlodeas, Mikail and his snakey family. It's all too much. My head is pounding. My ears are ringing.

I see a flash of light so bright it burns my eyes and blinds me completely. When it disperses, I am no longer in my room.

I'm in the woods. They look similar to the woods Rett and I have always played in. It's snowing, but it's warm out. I smell smoke but cannot see a fire. Something is biting my arms. I look down and realize they are covered in tiny embers that turn to ash as they drop. It's not snowing. It's raining ash. Behind me, there is rustling through the leaves. A small figure about the size of a child skidders through brush. Before I can go to it, a group of people runs through, toward me, from the other side of the trees. Rett is leading them, followed by Iris, one of the twins, Audrina, DeLuca, Sylvie, and...myself. There is terror written across each of our faces. Bloody footprints trail behind. I try to reach out to the strange version of myself. She's covered head to toe in blood, and I'm not entirely sure it truly is me I'm looking at, but she has the same emerald green eyes. When my fingers are about to land on her shoulder, the same light that blinded me earlier flashes. When it's gone, I'm on the floor of my room.

Nauseous.

Head threatening to split in two.

Sweating and breathing heavily.

It was exactly like one of my nightmares, but I was awake.

I know I was.

I don't understand what has been happening to me. I'm losing my grip on reality. It has to be the stress. *It has to be.* I rub the itch on my arms, agitating it further. I look down to examine them and find they're speckled with tiny burns.

What is happening to me?

Elinor knocks while opening the door. "You sent for me, Miss Aislinn?"

She gasps when she sees me on the floor and hurries toward me. "Oh! What's happened, Miss?!" she asks in alarm while looking me over. "I'll send for the healer! I don't think she's left!"

"No, don't. Please. I'm okay, Elinor, I'm okay," I'm not sure if I believe my own words, but I push myself up off the floor anyway. I rub the back of my head and feel a small tender knot.

I must have fainted. The stress. It has to be the stress.

I try to reason with myself.

Another voice in my head argues. *But what about the burns?*

I rub my arm along pocked burns, trying to make sense of them, but the spinning thoughts hurt my already throbbing head.

Motioning Elinor to close the door, I turn my focus back to *this* reality. "Elinor, I have to ask you something that may seem strange. Can I trust you?"

A look of worry forms new creases in her forehead. "Yes, Miss, I believe you can."

I give a small smile and nod. I do feel as if I can trust her even though I haven't known her for long. I have to place my trust in someone. I choose that someone to be Elinor.

"Something has been happening in this manor. I fear something treacherous. I have felt uneasy about my arrival even before coming, and the longer I've been here, the stronger these feelings get. I believe we are on the precipice of something very bad. I don't know what exactly."

I pause, looking her in the eye and lowering my voice. "Have you ever heard any secrets in this house? The kind that can permanently damage the Urson family? The kind that if the wrong person knew, could perhaps, cast influence upon Lord Magnus?"

She only shows her surprise for a second before schooling her features into a cool calm. "No, I don't believe so, but I have always been assigned to the children's corridors. I was with young Orynn before your arrival. I don't have much interaction with Lord Magnus or the Lady wife, Lyrica. But I could perhaps inquire with some of the other servs?"

"Only if you are careful. Only the most trustworthy. I fear danger here and no one is safe."

She nods. I see a glimmer of hesitation.

"Elinor...just one more thing."

"Yes, Miss?"

I pick at the skin around my thumbnail and bite my lip. "Are you happy here?"

"Why, yes, Miss Aislinn. You are very kind to me, and I consider myself fortunate to be in your service," she says without hesitation.

Relief floods through me. I don't think I would be able to live with the burden of fueling the discord amongst classes. "Good. Should that ever change, please let me know."

EIGHT
USUAL CONSPIRACIES

I've taken the rutide drops nightly, and to my relief, they have worked wonderfully. Each night, after I drift off to sleep, my mind goes peacefully blank. When I awake, it feels as if no time has passed at all yet, somehow, I've traveled through the rifts of our realm and woken up in the future. A dreamless sleep. Real sleep. I feel better than I have in years.

Rett has been resting under guard in his room for days. I am told he's back to himself. I have been unable to visit, and he hasn't been permitted to leave the confines of his room. Only his parents are allowed entry until their investigation finding whoever slipped him the ivlodeas is concluded, though, we know who did it. They have to know. Otherwise, the guards in the house would have tripled.

Iris has been sulking about the house. She can mostly be found pacing in front of Rett's door or very near to his corridor. Whenever she catches me coming her way, she wisely turns the opposite direction. I rarely see her parents. Who knows what Hyacinth is up to? Probably mixing more potions like the witch she is. Mikail has remained *dutifully* by Lord Magnus' side. The few moments I have spent in their presence, I make sure they catch my glare. They need to know that I know what they've done, even if Lord Magnus won't take me seriously.

Each morning, I await Elinor's arrival in hopes that she has learned a secret of importance. So far, she has learned only that

Lord Magnus keeps a family of bears as pets in the forest; he has a special team of servs look after the beasts with as much care as one would look after a child—which may be interesting but isn't entirely helpful. Keeping such wild animals as pets might be odd, but it is not against any of our laws.

DeLuca has been working in the food service. At the Urson dinners, I find what I crave most are the forbidden glances we share. Each gaze is heavy and loaded with questions we do not dare voice within these walls. We haven't spoken at all since the lift. I'm not entirely sure what I would say if we did. He can't be trusted. I know this. He is somehow involved with the *Liberators* threatening the great houses of Stellera, but he's entangled himself in the entirety of my mind, refusing to separate from it. Part of me doesn't want him to. I find myself lying awake at night imagining what life could be like, if I didn't disgust him...if titles and houses and duty were no longer of importance...what that could mean for DeLuca and me. I quickly shake such impossibilities from my mind.

He's not on our side.

My engagement party is only days away.

I must stay focused.

Rett, it's always been Rett and will always be Rett. Magnus Everett Urson VI is my future. Not DeLuca. Definitely not a serv.

I tap my quill repeatedly on my desk, searching for the words to write Audrina. They escape me. I still haven't managed a single letter to my best friend even though she has stayed true to her word and written nearly every day. My mind remains too crowded and it scatters any intelligible thought.

I release a sigh, dropping the quill.

A soft knock raps on my open door's frame.

"Young Lord Magnus requests you join him in the west wing's sitting room." Evander, the officer who brought me here, offers a friendly smile.

I nod and smooth my skirt as I stand, noticing a small spot of ink from my hesitation with the quill. I try to rub it out with no luck. It's small, likely unnoticeable. My mother isn't here to scrutinize every aspect of my appearance anyway. Pushing the hair from my cheek, I smile back at Evander and follow his heavy booted steps.

"How is he?" I swallow back the memory of our last encounter.

"Himself," Evander replies. "I shouldn't say too much, but he feels terrible about everything that was said, his behavior. I can see how hard it has been weighing him down."

I chew the inside of my cheek. Rett and I haven't spoken since he was under the influence of the ivlodeas. His mind wasn't his own. I know this, but his words still cut into the fabric of our bond.

I take a deep inhale and force my feet forward. Evander leads me to the west wing's third floor sitting room. There are two other guards outside the large doorway, standing at attention, hands remaining on the hilt of their swords and wearing impassive expressions. Evander walks me past them before turning back and heading down the corridor.

Rett is sitting on the oversized plum chair closest to the fireplace that is tiled with pieces of broken obsidian glass. I hesitate before approaching him, but when he spots me, his wide smile is infectious, steadying the anxiousness within me. He runs and picks me up, spinning me in a tight embrace.

He holds me tightly against his barrel chest. "I owe you a realm of thanks!"

With no space between us I feel the steady drum of his heart. Mine slows to match it.

"You don't need to thank me. I didn't really do anything other than cause enough of a commotion to be heard"

"Ailie... of course, I do! If it weren't for you, no one would've known about the ivlodeas! It's nearly undetectable once it's absorbed. Ailie, you saved me. If not my life, then surely my shadow. For who knows what my puppeteer would've commanded of me." He kisses my cheek which immediately flushes beneath the touch of his lips. Rett's smile widens as if amused. "You have a smudge of something black, just here." He rubs his thumb along the side of my face.

My entire body warms, thankful for the return of my oldest friend. The way his eyes are alight. His goofy grin. His very demeanor. This is *my* Rett. I grab his hand before he can take it off my face and cup it with my own, holding it in place along my cheek.

Rett's smile fades into something more serious. His honey flecked eyes search mine as if he is seeing me for the first time. The fire crackles behind us, and a log breaks, sending a flurry of embers through the air. Rett moves both of his large hands to either side of my neck and tilts my head up to meet his as he bends down to kiss me again. This time, instead of my cheek, his kiss lands on my lips. Rett's eyes remain softly closed. Mine are open, studying him. By all means, this should be a monumental moment in our lives.

The first kiss shared between husband and wife.

Butterflies should dance in our bellies, and time should freeze.

But I feel nothing.

The clank of a cart hitting a wall outside draws our attention, prying our lips apart. We look toward the doorway, and DeLuca's intense blue eyes are staring back at us, burning. When his golden cart rammed against the wall, some of the dishes atop it had been knocked over. My chest tightens, and my breath stalls. I haven't done anything wrong...so why does it feel like I have?

"Be careful, serv! Just one of those dishes costs more than a year's worth of your earnings." Rett's voice is fit for a lord and makes me cringe.

I jump in. "I'm sure it was an accident, Rett."

"Apologies, Young Lord Magnus, bad wheel. I'll be sure to have it corrected." DeLuca speaks quickly while straightening the cart.

He glances at me for a moment that feels entirely too brief before rolling his cart toward the service lift.

"Accident or not, servs need to handle *our* property with care. All of this is supposed to be *ours*, Ailie-cat. They can't break everything, leaving us with nothing before we even inherit it," Rett says jokingly, still holding my neck.

I don't find the humor.

"A giant manor made of obsidian glass on top of a mountain is hardly *nothing*," I reply. All the building aggression I've felt the last few weeks is boiling to the surface.

His face falls, feeling the tension, and he removes his hands from my neck, running them through his close cut hair.

"Listen, Ailie, I've been meaning to, well, apologize. For kind of..."

"Ignoring me for your consort the weeks leading up to our engagement party?" I finish for him.

"Yes...for that...and my parents told me how I was speaking to you...speaking about you...I want to apologize for that as well, but in all honesty, I don't remember it so much." He winces at his words.

"Honestly, Rett, I've been preoccupied, and your behavior, while concerning, is accompanied on a long list of concerns."

"Oh? With what?" His eyebrows raise.

"The usual conspiracies that plague governing houses," I reply vaguely, unsure of how much to divulge or where to even begin. The look on his face tells me he's not going to let me off the hook that easily.

I release a sigh. "I went to Ashe...the people there...they're not well. Rett, they're angry...and rightfully so. The conditions they're forced to live in...I can't imagine subjugating *our* people to that."

"You went to Ashe? How in the world did you get to Ashe?" His reaction tells me he already knows of the conditions and the people suffering. I'm hit with a flood of disappointment.

There's no chance I'm going to tell him that DeLuca took me. Not after the way he was just acting. It's possible Rett would be totally understanding. There's also a chance that he'd have him killed for it. It's not worth the risk.

"I was exploring the grounds and came across a tunnel deep under the manor that the servs use to get to and from Ashe. There's a pod type transport. It goes really fast...faster than any kind I've been on."

Rett's proud smile spreads as he looks off to the distance. "Ah, yes, I'd forgotten the tunnels. The pods run on a magnetic track system that is much faster than the transports running on oxidous gas. The first Lord Magnus Urson had them built. Quite the visionary. We never use them, so I forget they exist. Well...father does to get to the Capital, but the rest of us don't."

I look at him in confusion.

He laughs. "They don't only go to Ashe. There are three tunnels. One for Ashe—which is the one you found. One goes to the Capital, and there's one my great-grandfather put in that runs completely through the Obsidian Mountains and comes out in the Thickitt Woods...in Dailotta. He wanted it as an escape route. After serving during the Trinity War his mind was never quite the same. He became obsessive and paranoid. Some of that can be blamed on the Urson Curse."

I get lost in my mind remembering the waking dream I had where I thought I saw the first Lord Magnus and his wife. His behavior could have been described as erratic. How would I have known that? I couldn't have seen it in a dream. The memory travels through the rest of that night. To when I found Rett. Inky goo dripping from his ears. Milky glazed eyes. My face turns down into a scowl.

"What is it?" Rett touches below my chin delicately to get a better view of my face.

"It's about the night I found you. Your parents don't believe me...or they don't want to...I'm not sure, but I'm positive that Iris and her parents are the ones who gave you the ivlodeas." I feel the bile rise in my throat as I think of the treacherous family.

"Honest to gods?" There's a glint of sadness in his eyes. "You think it was Iris?"

I nod and soften, feeling pity. "I do. I know it in my bones. I know it."

He deflates. "That can't be true."

"Rett, I'm sorry. I can't tell you how I know. I just do, and I need you to trust me."

"I trust you, Ailie. You and my family are just about the only ones I trust completely in this whole realm."

I smile at him but he doesn't return it.

He looks down at his hands. His face transforms into that of a small child who's lost their way. "I know I shouldn't talk to you about this because we are to be married, but you are my oldest friend too...I think...well, I thought, maybe I might have loved her."

The hurt in his voice is too much. I pull him to the sofa and put his head on my lap, stroking his hair. There are no words I can say to bring him comfort. What do you say to someone when they find out they're being manipulated by someone they love? I can only be here for him. How strange it is that I am consoling my fiance on the betrayal of his mistress.

Rett's breath falls into a smooth and steady rhythm. He's asleep. I can't bear to move him. I trace the lines of his face with a gentle finger. What could Mikail have over this family that would be worth putting him in harm's way? Especially because he is a first born of Stellera. What could possibly be worth that risk? My mind wanders over all the possibilities as my eyes grow heavy.

A woman is screaming. I follow the sound that rattles the windows of the manor. Passing the banisters, I notice the flowers that usually adorn them are all dead. The flowers in the vases are also dead.

The screams are coming from the very end of the corridor. From Lord Magnus and Lyrica's chambers. I can see my breath in the frigid air. The curtains haven't been closed—snow covers the treetops through the fogged over glass. Another scream echoes throughout the hall. Mikail is keeping guard outside the closed master chamber door. He looks decades younger. His full black hair is slicked back, and he wears an obsidian guard uniform that has no indication of his elevated position. He fixes his eyes forward in a bored expression, completely unphased by the screams behind the doors.

The screaming stops abruptly, and a few short moments later, the door opens. Lord Magnus comes out holding a bloodied knit blanket. He shakes his head and hands the bundle to Mikail. Lord Magus' eyes are haunted. His face is pale as he leans in to whisper something to Mikail, but I can't make out what. I am too far away. Mikail, still holding the bloody bundle, starts walking. Lord Magnus collapses against the wall. His head falls to his hands. When Mikail passes me—as if I don't exist—I follow him into the service lift. We go down, to the side, and down again. He opens the bloodied blanket just enough for me to see the blue face of a sleeping newborn baby covered in thin green vines.

No... not sleeping. Dead.

The baby is dead.

Mikail shakes his head and covers the infant's face again.

When the lift's metal doors creak open, I recognize the tunnel as the one that leads to Ashe, the one DeLuca took me to.

With the baby gently cradled in his arms, he boards the transport, pulling a hood to cover his face.

"Mikail!" I shout, trying to get his attention.

He looks toward my direction as the pod's doors close, but his eyes don't find mine. The pod's magnets release, and the transport races away.

Gasping, I sit up quickly, knocking Rett off my lap. The floor receives his weight with a loud thud. We're still on the sofa in the sitting room. The fire still roars, bringing warmth to my cheeks.

"Ow. Ailie, what are you doing?" Rett rubs at the sore spot where his elbow made impact with the floor.

"I...uh...bad dream, I guess." My brain tries to focus on the details while adjusting to the waking world.

A bad dream...I hadn't taken my red drops before falling asleep... It felt so real.

My heart is still racing, as is my head. I think I know *the* secret, and it changes everything.

I've been sitting at the vanity in silence while Elinor combs through the tangles of my hair. My quiet contemplation hasn't gone unnoticed, and Elinor frowns at me in the mirror. "You're less chatty this evening."

"Sorry, Elinor. I have a lot on my mind is all."

"I wonder if it's not something I can help with?" she asks, her eyes soft and nurturing.

"I don't think so. The thoughts plaguing me are...dangerous...the kind of danger that could probably get you killed." I chew the inside of my cheek until it's raw.

Elinor replies with a devious smile. "What fun. I haven't been involved in a scandal for ages."

I can't help but smirk. "Okay, Elinor. I actually can use your help with something. Can you find me the midwives who assisted for each of the Urson children's births?"

"I can, Miss. I can because I've been in the manor since before any of them were born. I already know the midwife who delivered them. It was Hyacinth. The head of security's wife."

My mouth goes slack, and I am unable to hide my surprise. Though it is convenient. I won't have to go on a manhunt for the midwife like I originally planned.

"Elinor...you said you've always been placed with the children. Was that also when they were newborns?"

She wears a proud smile. "Why yes, Miss Aislinn. I've been with all the children."

"And was anything strange about the babies? Or their births or pregnancies?"

Elinor's brows shoot up with curiosity. "No, not that I am aware of." She pauses as she searches the banks of her memory. "Come to think of it, the twins had unusual scaring up their legs and torsos. It looked almost as if they'd been tied together by ribbon or something similar while in the womb. The healers were able to fix them right up, not even a trace of the marks. I believe they said their umbilical cords had been the cause."

"The twins?" I croak out my surprise. I had only been thinking about Rett. He was the only winter-born child the Ursons had.

"Yes, the twins. They were also the only ones we were immediately asked to look after. With the others, we had to wait a full day at least. Two with young Orynn. Lady Lyrica had a harder time with the boys. She slept for days after they were born. With the twins, she was back to herself within hours."

"Hmm." I nod my head. This information is helpful to confirm the theory I have been working on since the dream in the sitting room. Helpful but not quite proof. If I were to accuse Lord Magnus of something so evil, it had to be irrefutable. A secret like this would be exactly what Mikail could use to destroy the family. Not only that. If it got out...it would have a ripple effect, wreaking havoc across Stellera.

"What are you thinking, Miss?" Elinor's voice is hushed, and she studies my face for a clue as to what I'm thinking.

I speak automatically as I try to sort through my theory. "I'm thinking it is entirely possible that Rett, the twins, and Orynn are not biologically the children of Lord Magnus and Lyrica." I vocalize my suspicion for the first time. "I think that Lord Magnus sent Mikail to switch the babies with ones from Ashe so that it would appear his bloodline was thriving and strong...which makes Rett...and his siblings.... Well, they wouldn't be Ursons. Actually, they wouldn't be highborn at all. They'd get nothing, no notoriety, no rights. No status whatsoever. Lord Magnus would be stripped of his as well for kidnapping...and for deceiving the realm...the king."

While the thoughts run rampant through my lips, I start to consider fully what impact this secret will have, no longer sure it's a secret I should have uncovered. It can ruin everything for a family I love so dearly, especially the children. I suddenly understand Lord Magnus' willingness to dismiss the rumors I presented and the hold Mikail has over him...and I've just told it all to a serv.

I force my eyes to her after having long spent staring at a void while the threads of realization wove mercilessly in my mind. She's white as a ghost. Realization must be striking her as well. She recognizes the shape that takes hold behind my gaze, and I see a shiver in her shoulders.

"Elinor, you must swear to secrecy. Swear it. I have no proof. It's a dirty rumor, probably untrue. Pretend you've never heard it. For this house...and for you...." I plead, taking her trembling hands into my own.

"I-I h-heard nothing, Miss Aislinn." She dips into a curtsy, leaving me alone to bear the weight of knowledge on my own.

NINE
TRUTH

"We've searched the entirety of the fourth floor, and there's no entrance or hint of one. I say we go to the fifth floor next," Lysette says. We walk out of one of the beautifully arranged guestrooms on the fourth floor. Nearly identical to the eight others down this hall. Each room has a large canopy bed with black bedding, dark stained wooden furniture, and paintings of forests—simple, elegant, unmistakably *Obsidian Manor*.

"Shouldn't we go lower, not higher? The watching room is definitely below ground." Linnea stretches as she yawns.

"Don't think about where the room is. Think about the last place you'd think to find an entrance... like a broom closet," Lysette reminds her.

"What do you think, Ailie? Up or down?" Linnea asks.

I've been lost in thought and only half-listening to the two. "Whatever you think." My reply is met by a scowl from both twins.

"You're not yourself today, Ailie. What's going on with you?" Lysette asks.

"Oh, you know, wedding jitters," I lie, unconvincingly.

"Wedding jitters?" Lysette's brow raises in skepticism.

"Fine, don't tell us, but at least get your head in the game," Linnea says with her hand on her hip.

"I say down. If it were me, I'd put the entrance somewhere my guests wouldn't venture. Maybe in the service corridors." I shrug.

"Brilliant, we can search the service corridors." Lysette's eyes sparkle at the prospect of going somewhere so *improper*.

"Okay, good. Let's do it." Linnea pushes our upper backs in the direction of the stairwells.

"Why are you in such a hurry today, Linnea?" I pick up the pace so her bony fingers can no longer dig into my shoulder blade.

"She gets like this when she hasn't been outside for a while," Lysette answers for her twin. "We both do—but Linnea more so."

"It's hard to explain. Like a craving, I guess. I need to take off my shoes and dig my toes in the soil. I need to feel the freshness of the growth and smell the trees. When I haven't been out in a while, I go through a type of withdrawal." Linnea looks distantly through the large window ahead of us.

"There are stranger addictions, I suppose." I bite down a laugh.

"Yeah, at least we don't eat the dirt like Mama did while she was pregnant." Lysette laughs.

Linnea's face floods red.

"No," Lysette and I say in unison before bursting into an uncontrolled fit of laughter.

"Stop it, you two! It's perfectly normal. My body craves the metals in the soil. That's what the healer told Mama."

"How have you kept this from me?" Lysette fights to speak between giggles, wiping tears from her eyes.

"You don't know everything, Lysette." Linnea sticks her tongue out.

We barely set foot on the second floor landing when a serv in an Obsidian guard uniform comes up to us. One I do not recognize. "Miss Delphia, Lord Magnus requests your presence in his study."

"His study?" I've never been summoned to a lord's place of business before. It's not proper.

The twins share the same shock in their expressions that I feel within.

"Yes, Miss Delphia," the guard confirms.

"When?" I look to the grandfather clock at the entrance to the landing. It's not yet the eleventh hour.

"Immediately." He gestures back up the staircase that I just climbed down.

With a sigh, I nod to the twins. "I'll see you two later, tell Orynn I'll be late for our game."

They both give the guards a foul look before they trot off down the hallway.

The guard leads me up the stairs to the fifth floor. It only occurs to me *after* we're joined by a second guard—who stands too close to me—that I realize I am not being escorted for protection. I'm being escorted so I don't run. The blood drains from my face, and sweat pools at the base of my spine. There's only one reason Lord Magnus would send his guards to take me to his study.

He knows that I know his secret.

The walk to Lord Magnus' private study seems to go entirely too quick. We pass the portraits of ancestors and landscape paintings of the Obsidian Mountains. A wall covered in portraits of bears of different sizes and colors lines the hall that leads directly to Lord Magnus' study. The foreboding large black door comes into view as soon as we turn the corner, positioned strategically next to the conference room. My eyes focus on the knob to the conference room door—taking notice of the 'U' engraved in it. It's pulling a memory that won't quite reveal itself, and I instinctively rub my palm.

The thump of my heart tells me to turn back. If he suspects my suspicion, it puts me in danger. I know what my father would do if someone found out a secret like this. He'd silence them, in the most permanent of ways. My hands shake, and I wrap them around my arms. Maybe I can run. The service lift isn't too far. I can figure out how to work it and one of the transport pods. They'd find me before I got far enough away though, which could be worse.

Lord Magnus is a kind man. I know he loves me... like a child of his own. He's said it himself... he won't harm me.

Lord Magnus wouldn't, but Mikail certainly would.

"Lord Magnus, you called for me?" I say as I approach the opened door.

"Yes, Aislinn, child, come in. Close the door behind you." He sits behind his ginormous black desk with ornately carved drawers and a sheet of obsidian glass sitting delicately atop. A desk crafted to show strength and power.

His calm voice soothes some of the anxiety, but my veins still feel ice shooting through them. Not because of Lord Magnus. Because standing behind him are Mikail and Hyacinth. Their dark beady eyes are fixed on me.

"We need to talk." Lord Magnus' voice holds none of the tender notes he usually carries for me and his other children.

I raise my chin and silently command my nerves to steady themselves.

"Yes, we do."

"It is to my understanding you have a theory about my children?" Lord Magnus doesn't dance around the subject. He is a born and bred politician through and through and has no need of small talk.

"I do." I fix my glare directly at Hyacinth who reveals no emotion on her small round face.

Lord Magnus folds his hands under his chin and leans forward.

"Would you like to know the truth?" he asks with softening eyes.

"Will you tell me the real truth?" My brows raise in accusation.

"I'd like to think that telling you the truth is far better than any alternatives." He pauses to look at Mikail whose scowl deepens. "It is obvious there will be no peace in this house until we can all get along and trust one another." His thumb and forefinger rub the bridge of his nose as if he is lecturing bickering children. "What I am going to tell you is of the utmost secrecy. It will ruin *all* of us if it gets out."

I nod and take a seat in the over-sized leather chair opposite him, leaning forward a bit, eager for the answers I've been craving.

"I married my wife for love. We were not betrothed to each other at birth as you and Rett were. In fact, I believe my father had been hoping for a match on the southern shores of Stellera if your grandfather, Lord Ralph, produced no daughters. Lyrica and I loved each other most of our lives. Our parents served on a small council together and would gather at one of the eight members' houses twice a year for two weeks. We were inseparable in those days and would write to each other as often as we could. When I suggested the marriage, my mother was overjoyed." A small smile dances on his lips at the memory.

"The match happened to be a favorable match for our parents. Uniting Obsidian and Thaus. If our parents hadn't given us their blessing, we planned to run away to Daillota together and strip our titles. We meant that much to one another. Shortly after we were married, my father passed, leaving me Lord of Obsidian far before I was ready and instilling all the responsibility that comes with said title. Which, of course, made Lyrica the Lady of Obsidian. Bestowing her with the responsibility of the lady of our house. Responsibilities I am sure you are well aware of. The most important duty—furthering the bloodline."

I shift uncomfortably in my seat, which squeaks at the movement, but I continue to remain quiet and let him continue.

"Try as she might, Lyrica could not produce a viable child. They'd die within months in her womb, or they would die at birth. Twelve times we tried. Twelve times we failed. All of them came out covered in thin green vines. Some thought the side effects of living near so much oxidous gas. Others thought it might be a curse if you believe in such things. Each loss took its toll on Lyrica. I couldn't see her go through another one. When Rett was born...well, he didn't make it either. I still remember his sweet face. He had my chin—I could tell even with the vines running up it." Lord Magnus takes a sharp inhale and clears his throat as a tear gathers in the corner of his eye and threatens to fall.

"I asked Mikail to find a healthy boy to swap him with. I did it for her...for my Lyrica. Hyacinth is trained in special medicinals from Rousse. She gave Lyrica a tonic that made her sleep for days after the birth. When she awoke, she had a healthy baby boy, *her* healthy baby boy. It was just going to be him."

"One was enough for me, but Lyrica loved being a mother. She kept wanting more. Then she got pregnant with the twins...and they made it. If I ever suspected that she'd be able to carry, I never would have...well...I hoped when she had Orynn that he'd make it too, but he didn't. Again, we'd had to make the switch. You see, my dear girl, I did it for love. I did it all for love. I couldn't bear to see my wife's heart break again. It would break me too. After Orynn's birth I asked Hyacinth to make me something so I could no longer impregnate her. I've taken the sterilization tonic everyday since. So we'd never have to do it again. Mikail and Hyacinth have helped me. I trust them with everything." Lord Magnus finishes filling the blanks in the story I'd already guessed, looking at his two comrades and smiling a thankful smile.

I'm staring at the three of them with my mouth hanging open. They're acting so casual. Like switching babies is something everyone does. While I admit his intention may have been...sweet...it is still so clearly wrong. I can't imagine how he is able to sleep at night knowing he has stolen children from their families.

"What of their birth parents?" I ask, cutting the silence with a sharp tone.

Lord Magnus looks down. "I've never wanted to know the answer."

"You can't just steal people's babies!" The disgust rises with each passing moment of being in their presence. "And what of Iris and the ivlodeas? You just excuse him poisoning your son because he's not really *your* son?" The built up rage is getting harder and harder to hold down.

"Rett *is* and always will be *my* son!" Lord Magnus slams his fist on the desk, and a darkness I've never seen washes over him.

Mikail puts his hand on Lord Magnus' shoulder to calm him.

"That was part of a plot but not what you think. Stellera is at an unrest. All over the nation servs are assassinating their house families. The people are rioting in the streets all over. It is a matter of time before it starts happening in Ashe and into the mountains. It's already begun in the Capital."

"I already know of the unrest. What does that have to do with poisoning the son of your lord?" I cross my arms.

Mikail's jaw clenches at the interruption. "Iris and Rett had already been so taken with each other. We could see the love our daughter had for him, and Rett is a good and honorable man. He'd make a fine husband. We are sure of that. Aside from not being titled, we had another major obstacle—you. Rett's sense of duty to honor you. He'd never break the engagement. He has love for you. Hyacinth and I thought if we could just remove that love from his head that he'd fight to marry Iris and could show unity in Obsidian, unity to show this house is different and that they'd show the disgruntled commoners we can all live happily together. We didn't think the ivlodeas would change him so drastically. We've never seen it used." Mikail seems bored. Like he'd rather be shoveling oxen manure than explaining himself to me.

"We weren't trying to cause harm to anyone. We love Rett," Hyacinth adds, nudging her husband.

"And you *knew* what they were doing to him?!"

He shakes his head. "Not until after. Believe me, I was angry about it. Once they explained, I understood their reasoning though. Aislinn, if you knew how dire the situation was.... I fear titles may soon not matter entirely. Stellera seems to be moving to anarchy. There have already been attempts on King Carrigan's life and that of his family." Lord Magnus meets my eyes, and they hold sympathy but for what or whom I can not tell. "It's madness I'd hoped we'd be spared from living in the mountains. I believed I could hide it."

His face falls sullen, obviously thinking of matters far beyond this room.

"Why tell me now? After going through all the lengths you have. Why tell me of all people?" I wonder how much Rett knows. Surely not of his true parentage.

Mikail answers, "Because you're terribly perceptive. You're smart and persistent. I knew you were close to finding the answers on your own, but when I heard you talking to the serv, Elinor, it became clear now was the time we tell you everything before you let the entire realm know our secrets."

His words aren't particularly insulting, but the way he says them makes me want to curl into myself.

"You *heard* me talking to Elinor?"

"My ears." He taps his own ears and then points to the ceiling, already knowing I know of them.

My fist tightens to keep from shaking.

"So, what happens now? Now that I know everything that will surely ruin this house? Will you kill me? It's what my father would do." I keep my voice from wavering, but each syllable causes my heart to drum louder.

"We will trust you." Lord Magnus offers the words with a weary smile that doesn't reach his eyes. "All I ask in return is that you trust us...and for the love of the gods, stop talking to servs about your theories and suspicions. It's hard enough to find good help here.

You mustn't ever tell anyone else. The only people who know are in this room, and it will remain that way until the day the reaper takes our shadows to the Afterlands." Lord Magnus' voice is so measured I almost miss the fear he conceals in it.

I roll my eyes. *Right, like any of them would go to the Afterlands. They're destined for the Shadows for sure.*

"And Elinor," I add.

The men look at each other. Hyacinth looks down with pity.

"You said the only people who know are in this room...and Elinor also knows. Well maybe not *knows,* but obviously, you know I talked to her. She's the only person I verbalized my suspicion to."

I'm met with silence.

"She's not in this room," I add.

"She will no longer know," Mikail says flatly. "You will be assigned a new serv. Immediately."

The room starts to spin as it registers what he is implying. I gasp. "No...you wouldn't."

"I do what I must to protect this family. If this house falls, so does my own family." He speaks without emotion or remorse.

My mouth hangs open, unable to form words.

Lord Magnus claps his hands loudly, bringing the attention back to him. "Now everyone is on the same page. No more secrets. No more lies. Ailie and Rett *will* be getting married." Lord Magnus pointedly looks at Mikail who scowls at the defeat but nods in compliance.

I get out of my chair, ready to make a break for it...to go find Elinor.

Lord Magnus stalls me for a moment longer. "Oh, and Aislinn dear, stop taking secret meetings with servs and trips in the tunnels. It makes Mikail's job more difficult trying to keep track of you." He doesn't look up from the paper on his desk. "Now, run along and join Lyrica and the twins for lunch. I'm told they have quite the surprise for you." He gestures for the door, finally dismissing me.

As soon as I hear the mechanisms of the door knob click back into place, I let the tears fall. I didn't want Mikail to have the satisfaction of seeing them. They run down my cheeks in hot steams as I run through the halls.

I have to save Elinor.

TEN
LITTLE EXPLOSIONS

I'm running through the halls toward the east wing in search of Elinor. I have to get her out before it's too late. My vision is blurred with tears, and I run into a serv who is clearing the morning dishes from chamber rooms. The cart turns sideways, and dishes shatter to the ground. Falling back on the floor, I collapse into myself. I'm breathing too hard. My lungs burn as if filled to capacity and ready to combust.

"We have to stop meeting like this," DeLuca says with a smirk. His face quickly twists into concern when he sees the tears flowing down mine. "What happened, Aislinn?" He grabs my elbows and helps me back to my feet. He looks me over. Forgetting his place, his large hands come to hold either side of my face as he searches my eyes.

I can't breathe. I can't speak. I'm trying to tell him. But the words stick in my throat. "Aislinn"—His voice deepens—"what happened?"

"There's—No—Time—We—Have to—Find—Elinor!" I'm hyperventilating. I know time is of the essence. Surely, Mikail's next step will be to go to her himself. "Now, DeLuca, we have to find her now."

Something snaps in his mind. The impassive expression he usually wears is gone. Here is a man on the brink of war. It was a mask. His compliance. This is the real DeLuca. I can tell. The one he kept hidden away. The one I need. He nods and abandons the mess I made in the hall. Taking my hand, he leads me to the lift.

"She's usually in the laundry room this time of day. We will start there," he says while working the gears.

The lift jerks sideways and then up. I can't stop shaking. My breath is uneven. I feel as if I may pass out at any moment, but I try to hold myself together for Elinors sake. DeLuca hesitantly looks at me as if weighing options. His features are severe, and his fist is clenched. When he finally pulls me to his chest, I feel him relax. I'm surprised by the gentleness of his hold and melt into his heat.

"They're going to kill her. It's my fault. It's my fault." I sob, burying my face deeper into him. The scent of smoke and river stones provides me with a small comfort. I take a long inhale, letting his calming scent envelope me.

For a moment, he is entirely still. Reminiscent of one of the statues dedicated to the gods. Then he lets out a pained breath. "I know a place she can go."

I nod without lifting my head, thankful for him. This serv who has every reason to despise me but has been a lifeline these last few weeks.

'No more secret meetings with servs in tunnels.' Lord Magnus' last words barrel through my mind.

They know about DeLuca too.

"You're going to have to go with her. They've been watching me. They know we've met in secret." I quietly say the words that fall to ashes on my tongue.

"Then I will go with her." He puts a finger under my chin, beckoning me to meet his blue eyes as they flicker with an unrecognizable emotion. He whispers so low I think I'm imagining the words. "Come with me."

I break my chin from his grip. "You know I can't do that."

The lift doors open to the laundry. I breathe out a sigh of relief. Elinor is here. She's okay.

"Miss Aislinn, what in the realm are you doing here?"

"You must come. Now. There isn't time to explain." I frantically motion for her to join us in the lift.

She drops the linen she's folding and hurries to meet us. DeLuca immediately works the gears and the lift moves down, to the side, and then down again.

"What's happened, Miss?" Elinor asks.

"They're coming after you. Because of what we talked about last night. They heard. I'm so sorry, Elinor. I'm so sorry." I sob.

She looks at DeLuca who nods his head.

"Oh, I see. Well, I suppose I'm off to find new adventures then, aren't I?" She places her hands on her hips and wears a reassuring smile. In return, I hug her with such force I fear I may crush her fragile bones.

"DeLuca has somewhere for you to go. I trust him to keep you safe... I am so sorry, dear friend. I never meant to put you in danger," I say, still holding her tightly. She smells like citrus. I've never noticed before, but I linger in it as long as I can.

The lift opens to a tunnel I'm not familiar with. I look at DeLuca in confusion.

"This one goes to the Capital." He answers my unvoiced question.

"The Capital? Won't that be *more* dangerous?" I ask.

He shakes his head no. "There's a safe place for outcasts and refugees." He hesitates before adding, "They know me,"

This tunnel is similar to the one we took to Ashe but much better kept. The walls have no cracks in them and are formed of well masoned bricks painted black.The transport pod looks much newer. No rust in sight. It's sleek and pitch black. I grab Elinor's hands with both of mine. She silently squeezes them one last time and climbs into the pod, offering a last sweet smile over her shoulder before disappearing within.

With a debilitating pain in my chest, it occurs to me I'll never see either of them again. I'll never see DeLuca again. As he goes to follow Elinor into the pod, I grab his arm and bring him back to me. Before either of us can stop—before I can overthink it—I pull his face to mine, claiming his lips with mine. They're soft and warm, and I never want to pull away. For a moment, everything else disappears. It's just the two of us. We aren't in a tunnel under the manor. We aren't in the Obsidian Mountains. We aren't in Stellera. We aren't even on the continent of Katova. It's just me and him. Nothing else matters but us and this moment. Little explosions set off beneath my skin.

He weaves his hands into my hair, pushing me further into him and deepening our kiss. My hands wrap around him, begging to be closer. Our breath tangles as he breaks the kiss but rests his forehead against mine.

"Please, Aislinn." His voice breaks and is full of agony. "Please, come with me."

My only reply is a slight shake of my head.

We don't speak.

We can't.

The words dissolve in my throat.

He lets out a hard breath and closes his eyes as he releases me from his grasp.

I bite my bottom lip to keep it from quivering as DeLuca climbs into the pod. The shiny black doors close, and the magnets above screech as they release. The pod takes off toward the Capital.

There is a hole eating through my heart. I'm not sure there will ever be a cure to this ache, but they are safe.

I slide down against the brick wall, pulling my knees up to my chest and stay in this position for what feels like hours. The same thought repeats over and over.

I should have gone with them.

*There's shouting. I'm in the conference room on the fifth floor
overlooking the main gardens. They're on fire. There is thick purple
smoke, making it almost impossible to see below, but it swirls where
there is movement. Some people are running toward the woods, others
toward the manor. The fire from the garden is spreading rapidly,
reaching the outerbanks of the forest and the western wall of the
manor. I hear explosions, but where are they coming from? The
manor shakes. It knocks me down. I'm on my hands and knees on
the floor. There is smoke creeping out from under the door. I crawl to
it. The smoke is cold. I go to open it but the door knob is so hot it burns
me. I retract my hand and examine it. A 'U' is burned into my palm
from the engraving on the knob. The door swings open, and a man
made of eternal darkness steps in. He's shouting at me.*

*"What have you done? You stupid, stupid girl. What have you
done? Stupid girl, what have you done?" His voice is sharp and loud.
Full of loathing.*

*Did I do this? Did I set the fire? No, I couldn't have. I've been here,
haven't I? Why am I here?*

*A slithery voice wraps itself around me. "Wake up, pet. Wake up,
or he will kill you."*

*There's an earthquake. Everything is blurring. I can't stand up.
No, it's not an earthquake.*

Someone is shaking me.

"Wake up!" The slithering voice hisses cold breath into my ear.

My eyes fly open.

Mikail is standing over me, shaking my shoulders.

The back of my head is sore from repeatedly hitting the brick
wall.

Coming out of the dream I realize it had been Mikail shouting and violenting shaking me. Rage boils beneath my skin.

"Get your hands off me, Mikail! You may have Lord Magnus entrapped with devious secrets, but he will not allow you to harm me!" I shout, sure my words are true.

"Who do you think sent me after you?" He smirks. "When we couldn't find Elinor or the serv boy, we knew you warned them. Do you have any idea what you've done? Any idea how dangerous it was to let them go? You're an idiot, girl."

"I don't care. I will not allow you to go around killing innocent people. There are no secrets worth a life."

"Lord Magnus does not share your opinion." His cruel smile sends a patch of ice behind my neck.

"When I am Lady of Obsidian, you and your family are out of the manor, secrets be damned." I threaten him with the only thing I can.

The veins in his neck grow thick, and his jaw clenches in a fury that makes me instantly regret my words.

He slaps me across the face and leans in so close our noses almost touch. "*If* you ever become *Lady of Obsidian*."

My hand holds my burning cheek while I look at him in shock.

Mikail is pulling me by the elbow to the lift. My legs drag behind us.

He doesn't loosen the grip the entire ride up. He doesn't speak. He just clenches his jaw tighter—his teeth grinding.

When we arrive at the east wing, Mikail drags me down the hall. My legs sting from being pulled along the floor. He won't even give me the chance to stand. Mikail throws me into my room. I barely catch myself before my face hits the floor.

"You will not leave this room until Lord Magnus and I have decided what to do with you. If you should try, I *will* know." He scowls, slamming my door.

I let out a soft sob, muffled into my arm. Crawling over to my mirror, I examine the bright red hand print plastered on my cheek. I've never been hit before.

It still throbs.

So does my hand.

I open it to reveal a '*U*' burned into my palm.

ELEVEN
FLICKER OF FURY

There's a knock at my door.

I consider the speed that I would be able to lock it to stop Mikail from entering—probably not quick enough. Before I can let out a word, the door swings open, bashing the knob against the wall.

"How rude of you to stand up a lunch invitation." Audrina places hands on her hips and a forced scowl across her face.

"Audrina!" I run to her, nearly toppling her over with a hug. "I don't understand. How did...when did...what are you doing here?"

"Well, you couldn't be expected to have your engagement party without your maid of honor, could you?"

My happiness at the surprise is quickly replaced by a full force of anxiousness. "At this point, I don't know if there's going to be an engagement party, let alone a wedding."

She strolls to my bed and pats the dark blue duvet, inviting me to join her. "Let's talk about it. Catch me up since you couldn't be bothered to write." Her face is riddled with concern, but I can't tell her. I can't put her life in danger like I had with Elinor and DeLuca.

"I can't. There's too much and it's not safe. Someone is always listening. I'm just glad you're here," I say, resting my head on her shoulder.

She bends her neck down and whispers in my ear. "Tell me everything."

I shouldn't...but I can't stop the words as they roll out, one incriminating admission after the next. The words spew like vomit. I tell her everything. Even the bits about DeLuca that I wanted to keep for myself.

When I've finished with the last bits of Mikail dragging me to my room, she taps her chin. "So, these *ears*...he probably is listening to us now?"

I nod. A sharp pain shoots up my spine.

She uses the back of her finger to trace the outline of Mikail's hand, still prominent on my cheek. "Mikail, if you're listening, would you please come join us in Aislinn's room." She calls into the air rather loudly, to my shock and horror.

"What are you doing, Audrina?!"

"I can fix some of this, but you'll have to trust me," she says with a wink.

"How?" I don't understand what is happening.

"Just trust me." She puts a finger to her mouth to shush me.

Mikail enters not too long after. He doesn't bother to knock. "You called?" A chill runs up my spine. He cannot conceal the annoyance, raising his eyebrow at the two of us.

"Ah, Mikail. Will you perhaps join us on this side of the room as we have much to discuss, and I do believe that it is best done with hushed voices as you no doubt know the sensitivity of the topic." Audrina smiles deceptively.

My brows knit as I try to understand her angle.

He comes closer, closing my bedroom door behind him.

Audrina gets off the bed to meet him in the center of my room. She uses her index finger to motion him to bend down as if to tell him a secret and whispers loud enough for me to hear. "You know nothing of Aislinn and the servs. Aislinn knows nothing of swapped babies. Everything is just as it was. You will tell Lord

Magnus and your wife everything is fine. You've handled it and leave it at that. When they try to discuss Aislinn and the secrets, you will refuse to talk about it. Instead, you will discuss how excited you are for Aislinn and Rett to be married. You are so happy for them. You will remain loyal to them over anyone else, including your own blood." She pauses and looks back at the red print on my face. A flicker of fury ignites behind her amber eyes. "Now, when you leave this room, you will slam your hand into the door as hard as you can. Try to break some fingers, because you should never hit a lady and will never do so again. Once that's done you will forget ever coming in here. You will continue the rest of your day as though nothing is out of the ordinary." She pats his arm, telling him to go.

Mikail doesn't respond. He walks to my door, slams his hand in it so hard we can hear the bone crunch, and then gently closes the door while letting himself out. The sound of his footsteps fade as he places distance between us.

My mouth hangs open. "What the Haile was that?" I ask, unable to wrap my mind around what I just witnessed.

She smiles proudly. "Haven't you ever wondered before how I always get away with everything? How I never get into trouble? How do I always have a way of convincing people of what I want?"

"I thought it was your charm."

"Hmm. Charm is one way to describe it, I suppose. I discovered it when I was nine. Something small at first, when one of the servs told me I couldn't swim until after I'd done my lessons. I told her, 'I can do whatever I please,' and after that, she always let me do as I pleased. Well, for a time. The effects seem to wear off after a few weeks."

"But how? Ivlodeas?" I ask in disgust, remembering the effects it had on Rett.

"Iv-lod-e-what-ass?" She laughs. "I've never heard of that. Eventually, my dear mother caught on to what was happening and confessed she, too, could influence people with her words. And her mother as well. We call ourselves *Whisperers.* Our family must have remained hidden during the Trinity War where they'd executed anyone with abnormal abilities. Mother sent me to the academy because I wouldn't stop using my whispers on the staff. The only person it doesn't work on is my mother, who believes we shouldnt use our gift so frivolously, that it's *wrong.*"

"But, Audrina, it *is* wrong. You're messing with people's free will."

"But think of how helpful it was just now?" She flashes her signature mischievous smile.

I do admit that it has proven to be helpful at this moment.

"Wait, have you used it on *me?*" I ask, feeling the sting of betrayal. I already know the answer but hope that I'm wrong.

"Only for little things, like when you didn't want to watch the Tears of Astoria that last night you were at the academy and to make you believe you'd find happiness here...small things like that. I'd never change your opinion on something that matters." Her voice is too casual. She truly doesn't see how wrong it is to fiddle in other people's minds.

"Audrina! It all matters. That is so violating. It poisons every memory I have of our friendship the last six years!" Angry tears begin to burn as I fight them off.

She rolls her eyes.

"You are okay with my abilities. In fact, you are thankful for them. You are so very glad to have a friend with such an awesome gift and so happy to have your truest friend here at the manor to help prepare you for your wedding. We are going to have the best time, just like at the academy," she whispers.

Audrina is right. I am so happy for her. What an amazing gift she has. How lucky am I that she'd share it with me. We are going to have the most amazing time. Just like at the academy. She's a true friend.

"Miss Delphia! Miss Soleil! Please. The Lord of Riverstone will be here on the hour." The new serv's plea forces me awake.

My mother is on her way.

Gods. I forget they were due back today.

Audrina spent the entire night with me. Partly so that we could talk until sunrise like we used to and partly because I was afraid to be alone—even after she worked her whisper magic on Mikail. We stayed up far too late and are feeling the repercussions of it now. Audrina responds to the serv by kicking me out of the bed with her freezing toes.

"Rude." I nudge her.

"Apologies, Miss Delphia. I would have let you sleep longer, but Lady Lyrica insisted you needed to be ready to greet our guests." The serv says in a small voice. She is clearly uncomfortable. Her short brown hair barely touches her shoulder and noticeably hasn't been washed in some time.

"No apologies necessary." I yawn. "What is your name?"

"Philomena." She curtsies.

"Philomena?" I raise my eyebrow. She doesn't look like a Philomena to me. Much too young for such an old-fashioned name.

Her cheeks flush at my response. "My friends and family call me Mena."

"Mena. Much better." I nod approvingly. "And you may call me Aislinn. Miss Delphia never feels right to me."

She smiles and looks down. Her skin still has a youthful glow despite the permanently purple sunken skin below her eyes.

"Should we start with your hair?" she asks, pointing to the chair stationed at my vanity.

"Sure." I wrap my robe around me and sit in front of her. "How old are you, Mena?" I stare at her face through the mirror in front of me. She still has a fullness in her cheeks that leads me to believe she is still a child.

"I just turned sixteen," she says proudly.

"I remember when I was sixteen." Audrina snorts from the bed, eyes still closed.

"Ignore her." I try to make her feel at ease. "How did you come to work at the manor?"

A haunted look enters Mena's eyes. "My uhm...my parents died...in the factories...exhaustion." She grimaces. "Now, I take care of my sister and brother. My sister, Winifred, is eight. My brother, Castiel, is five. He was born without arms, a side effect from the gasses in the factory I guess."

I look down, chewing on my lip. "I'm so sorry. That is awful. No one should have to live with that, especially so young. Where are they now? When you work?"

"Oh please, don't be sorry! We manage just fine. We live at our Aunt Dela's house. She's too old to work, so she watches Winifred and Castiel while I am here. I was in the laundry service until today. The promotion is a huge honor. I am so grateful."

"And I am grateful to have you." I smile with all the warmth I can muster and try not to let her see the pity I feel.

"And I'd be grateful if you would both stop talking," Audrina interjects.

"You know, you have a perfectly good room right across from mine." My words come out with a bite.

"Good, go use it." She flips the pillow over her head.

"She's not a morning person." I give Mena an apologetic look on behalf of my cranky friend.

"Not to worry, I'm sure Hilde will be up any moment to tend to her. Lord Urson has set an amazing breakfast to welcome the Riverstones."

I can't help but giggle. "The Delphias of Riverstone," I correct her.

Her face turns. "I thought they were Riverstone?"

"Riverstone is what they call the manor. The Delphias govern Vallae from Riverstone." Audrina sighs and kicks her feet over the side of the bed—giving up on tuning us out.

"I don't understand," she says as she tugs a knot out of my hair.

"Well, like how the Ursons live in Obsidian Manor but govern over Ashe and the towns surrounding it? We formally call him Lord Magnus Urson V of Obsidian. That is how he's addressed and how he signs his name."

"But we call him Lord Magnus." Mena's nose scrunches. I can see the confusion deepening.

"He prefers Lord Magnus because his father was called Lord Urson."

"Oh. Okay, I think I understand. So, what do I call the...Delphias?"

Poor girl, so young to be elevated to a position where she will have to work with highborns regularly.

"You will address my father as Lord Phillipe Delphia or just Lord Delphia and my mother Lady Secily Delphia or Lady Delphia. You can call my sister *Lady Witch*."

Mena lets out a snort that reminds me of a hog and quickly covers her mouth in embarrassment, but I smile at the slip.

"I wouldn't call Lorella that if you like having a position...or a life. She is the most insufferable of all of us. Lady Lorella or Lady Lorella Delphia will be fine." Audrina rubs her temples, clearly uninterested in the lesson we learned as children.

The serv, Hilde, knocks at the door and requests Audrina follow her to her guest room to get ready.

After the formal greeting out front of the manor, we all head to breakfast in the smaller banquet room, the one with the giant obsidian glass window as a wall. It is lined with servs as always. I find myself scanning the faces, forgetting I won't find the one I wish to see. I wonder how he's doing...if he's alright.

I bring my attention to the wall of food. Eggs cooked in six different ways, breakfast meats, fruits of all varieties, and freshly baked pastries cover the table in abundance. A scene that has been so consistent in my life, something I've taken for granted. A scene that now fills me with a sense of guilt after having visited Ashe. I allow myself to watch the faces of the servs. All keep stoic expressions, but if I watch long enough, I catch their quick glances at the food.

My heart sinks.

I'm relieved to see my place card set between Rett and Audrina rather than near my sister or parents. I give a silent look of thanks to Lyrica. She returns the smile but gestures to the twins with a wink—telling me that they were the ones who made the alteration in seating. They shrug their shoulders and flutter their lashes, claiming the credit. Before we sit down, I hesitantly make my way to Lord Magnus, whom I haven't spoken to since he made his confessions to me...and since I helped the servs escape.

"Uhm...Lord Magnus?" I tap his broad shoulder.

"Yes, Ailie?" He breaks away from his conversation with Rett with a smile.

"I was just wondering what happens to all the food we don't eat?"

"Some go to my pets, most of it the waste, I suppose. Why do you ask?"

"I think it should go to the servs in the manor. Maybe we could even invite their family members sometime."

He shrugs. "I don't see why not. Now go take your seat so we can begin. Busy day today!" He nudges me toward my seat. I'm thankful for the normal interaction and feel like we just took a step in the right direction for change.

Mikail, Hyacinth, and Iris enter. My eyes fall to the wrappings around Mikail's hand. The sight tugs the corners of my lips upwards, and I give Audriana a sly side-glance. She raises her brows and smirks. His bandage is a little secret amongst friends.

We all stand near our assigned seat, waiting for Lord Magnus to sit first. As he does, a symphony of chairs scooting against the hard floors sounds. Rett pulls my chair out for me and gives me a big goofy smile.

"After you, *my lady*." He bows mockingly.

I follow the joke and curtsy. "Why, thank you, *my lord*."

He kisses my hand before taking his seat.

I don't have to look to know Iris is staring. Her glare cuts like glass.

"Who's that?" Audrina leans in, keeping her voice low.

"Iris," I say— hopefully low enough that Rett doesn't hear. He has already engaged Evander in conversation as he stands guard nearby.

"*Her*?" She doesn't hide the shock from her face. "You didn't say she was the help?"

"Well, technically, *she's* not. Her parents are. She really doesn't do much of anything as far as I know."

"Well, she does a lot of *something*." Audrina elbows me, and I have to bite both lips together to keep from cackling.

My mother scowls at us from down the table and we straighten up.

"And that's the guard?" Audrina nods to Evander.

"One of them, Evander, just got out of the King's Army. I don't know the others."

"Cute."

"Which one?"

"Evander!"

Lysette is glaring in our direction. We notice more eyes on us, realizing she'd said his name too loud.

Evander looks our way expectantly.

"I- uhm-" Audrina stumbles over words. "I was wondering about your tour. How was it?"

Evander's brows pinch. "Oh, it was well...well enough. We were called to a few of the border towns for the riots, but it hasn't been anything we can't handle."

Lord Magnus clears his throat and shakes his head subtly at Evander telling him to stop talking.

"We don't speak of politics at the table," Lyrica says sweetly. "Audrina, how fares the Astoria Academy without the presence of our dear Aislinn?"

Audrina was about to take a sip of her juice but sighs and sets it down. "It definitely feels less like home without her, if I'm being honest, but everyone else is doing fine. Just another day."

"Very good. You know, my sister Liliahna, went to the Academy too. She's done quite well for herself. She married Lord Raicen of Port Harholde. You no doubt have met them being in such close proximity to Sutton, have you not?" Lyrica has her most polished etiquette out.

"Oh yes, I've met the Lord and Lady of Port Harholde many times. Lord Raicen has been the cause of many headaches for my mother." Audrina finally takes a sip of her juice. I watch the bubbles fizz— realizing it's spiked.

"If I know Guiliana as well as I used to, surely, she is the one providing the headaches." Lyrica muses with a smile.

Audrina almost spits out her drink. "You know my mother?"

"Of course. We grew up together and were friends."

"*Were?*" Audrina asks.

Lyrica's cheeks show a faint hint of a blush before she controls it. "Well, you know how it is. You grow up. You grow apart. Isn't that right, Secily?"

My mother politely agrees but offers nothing more.

"Ouch!" A tailor-serv sticks me with a needle during my dress fitting, causing me to squeal out.

"Apologies, Miss Delphia! Apologies, it won't happen again." She's young but older than me. Her straw colored hair is pulled into a neat bun so it doesn't fall into her face while she works hunched over.

She looks terrified.

"You careless thing! If you can't hem a gown without sticking it's wearer you shouldn't be working as a seamstress! Perhaps they should send you to the cleaning crew," my mother scolds her.

The young seamstress' eyes widen and she looks as if she may cry.

"It's fine. It just surprised me is all. Don't worry, we are not sending you to the cleaning crew," I assure her while shooting my mother a look. She rolls her eyes and focuses on her own gown, ordering the serv working on it to make changes and acting as if this was a party in her honor rather than mine.

Lorella strolls in with the twins and Audrina.

"Don't you look dazzling!" the twins exclaim in unison.

"You dont think it's too modern?" my sister shows her obvious distaste as her face scrunches.

"It's incredible!" Audrina chimes in.

"You're early girls," Lyrica says without turning toward them. She's fumbling over different fabrics.

"We wanted to see Ailie's gown," the twins explain.

"Good thing we did! The neckline plunges much too low!" Lorella marches over to me and pulls my dress inwards trying to hide my exposed cleavage. "Is it too late to sew this in?" she asks the serv who is stitching the hem below me.

"I like my dress the way it is, thank you." I huff at my sister. Lorella looks to my mother waiting for her to back her up.

"It is Aislinn's day, if she wants the attention let her have it." My mother's answer perplexes both me and Lorella.

I look over at Audrina who smirks and winks. She most definitely had something to do with Mother's defense of my choice in apparel. I bite back a laugh.

"Done, Miss Delphia," the serv says, sticking a pin in a cushion as she stands.

I step down from the podium and walk to the mirrors arranged in a half circle in the far corner of the room.

"Oh gods. Have you ever seen such a dress?!" I gush at the serv who looks down— turning red.

I hardly recognize my own reflection. The dress is a silver satin with a neckline that dips low between my breasts with long sleeves made of a delicate lace and open back. It hugs my curves but has a slit running up the side to the middle of my thigh allowing me to move comfortably. My favorite part is the diamonds cascading down the entirety of the dress. A homage to the beauty of the Tears of Astoria.

Astoria herself would be envious of this gown.

"It is really something," my mother says, which may be the nicest words I've ever heard come from her.

"Oh Ailie, I'm just so happy you're finally joining our family after all these years." Lyrica beams with her arms out to embrace me.

"So are we," the twins chime in.

Lorella rolls her eyes and Audrina looks back and forth from me to my sister as if silently asking if I want her to do something about Lorella's attitude.

I subtly shake my head 'no' and she shrugs.

It feels nice to be surrounded by friends and family after all the darkness the summer has brought, or rather, that I have brought to this summer.

I'm still standing in front of the mirrors when Hyacinth enters. I see her reflection and my smile instantly drops.

"Lord Magnus has an announcement once your fittings are through. He asks all Ursons and Delphias to meet him in the banquet room," she says.

"Thank you, Hyacinth." Lyrica smiles at her with far more warmth than she deserves— especially because she poisoned her son. I wonder if Lyrica knows that part. I'm guessing not if Lyrica is able to be in the same room as Hyacinth without tearing her head off.

My father, Lord Magnus, Rett, Orynn, Mikail, Hyacinth, and Iris are all seated around the obsidian banquet table when we arrive. Evander stands guard at the door along with an older officer. The rest of us take our prospective seats. Audrina right beside me, her hands hugging mine reassuringly.

Our attention is on Lord Magnus. It is apparent that no one in the room knows what announcement he has to make with the exception of my father who is tapping his foot— his eagerness is overwhelming his propriety. A part of me wonders if he will come clean about swapping the babies. It seems unlikely but not impossible now that the secret is slowly seeping out from hiding.

Lord Magnus clears his throat. "Tomorrow evening we will finally celebrate the betrothal of my firstborn son, Rett, and Aislinn— the uniting of houses Urson and Delphia at last! A dream of my own father's now being realized. We have waited decades for this union." He pauses for dramatic effect and smiles appreciatively to the people gathered before he continues. "I've decided enough is enough! We wait no longer. Tomorrow with all our family and friends we will solidify this union. Tomorrow Magnus Everett Urson VI and Aislinn Theodora Delphia will be married! Tonight we dine for the last time as friends. For tomorrow, we become family!"

No one can hide the shock. His speech is met with open mouths and gaping eyes from all except my father who is clapping wildly and shouts "Hurrah!" beaming with excitement.

I'm glad to be sitting because my head feels light and the room spins.

Rett looks down at his lap, brows furrowed.

Iris looks at him with an unspoken accusation.

"Hurrah." Audrina laughs at the development— shooting Evander a flirtatious smile from across the table.

My mother quickly composes herself. "But Lord Magnus, the wedding has not yet been planned. We don't have the preparations for the ceremony... we were planning on a winter wedding, after the first snowfall." She speaks with little emotion but I can see her mind spinning.

"I'm sure between you and Lyrica that the engagement party you planned will be far more grand than any wedding in Stellera. We will call an officiant, they will recite the words of old. There is nothing more to be planned." Lord Magnus waves his hand, shooing my mothers words away.

I look at Rett, and he looks at me. When our eyes meet I know for certain, *neither* of us want tomorrow to come. Iris slams her fists on the table and gets up, running out of the room with dramatic steps.

Rett moves to follow, but when his father shoots him a look that says '*sit down*' he sinks into his chair.

Hyacinth apologizes for her daughter and follows after her.

Orynn fidgets and slips a piece of candy from his pocket to his mouth, careful to not let his mother see him sneak the sweet and completely unbothered by the chaotic energy spitting through the room.

"Well, now that the news has broken, let's celebrate!" On cue eight servs come in with trays of celebratory drinks, the likes of which I've never seen. Some are multiple colors, some on fire, some adorned with flowers. They are exquisite. I grab three and swallow each in one gulp.

We stay in the banquet room for hours. The air has improved with good spirits the whimsical drinks have provided. Audrina and the twins are laughing at gossip about other girls in the great houses, especially ones at the Academy.

Father, Orynn, Rett, and Magnus are discussing going on a hunting trip following the wedding, *real male bonding* they call it. My mother, Lorella, and Lyrica are scrambling trying to go over every detail for tomorrow now that it is to be a wedding instead of an engagement party.

I slide out of my chair and find the one beside Rett who has moved closer to his father. I scoot until the sides of our chairs touch and my arm brushes his.

"Hello *husband*." I slur and laugh.

He snorts. "How many have you had, *wife*?"

"Enough to feel good," I respond, feeling my eyes squint.

"Do you want to get some air?"

"I'd love to get out of this prison." I place both hands on his shoulder and rest my head atop it. "You're going to have to help me." I whisper, earning an amused smile.

He gets up and offers his hand for me to hoist myself out of the chair, which I do with a lack of grace that I'm thankful my mother is too preoccupied to witness. "Come on Ailie-cat, lets walk it off."

We walk out to one of the smaller courtyards. This one was full of exotic potted plants covered in thorns and dark blooms of thick flowers. Vines creep up the walls reminding me of the Astoria Academy. There is a large fountain in the center of the courtyard and the sound of the water cascading in rhythmic motion fills my ears like a sweet melody. I take a deep inhale; letting the mountain air that is so crisp and refreshing sober my mind.

Rett leads me to the fountain and we sit on the edge. There is a small breeze which would've felt nice if I had on thicker clothing. My thin dress provides little protection from the chill.

"You're cold." Rett observes the goosebumps rising on my arm.

"I'm fine, I could probably use the cold air." I laugh.

He stands to his feet, taking off his shirt and revealing his naked hair-covered chest. For the first time I notice his tattoos—a portrait of Helena, the Reaper of Shadows, on his right bicep and the Urson family crest, a 'U' with a bears head centered and a ribbon baring the words 'loyal, honest, and strength', over his heart.

"Here." He offers the shirt to me.

I shake my head keeping my eyes low so I don't look at him, it feels too strange... too intimate; but he is too insistent, throwing the shirt at me. I catch it just before it hits the water. Pulling the warm shirt over my head I am suddenly very grateful for his persistence. It swallows me whole and still holds the warmth from Rett's body. I sink into myself pulling his shirt tighter around me with a large goofy smile plastered across my face.

Rett lets out a throaty laugh. "You look like a turtle!" He points at me, still laughing.

"I do not look like a turtle!" I pout.

He's doubled over in hysterics. "You do, you do." He snorts, barely able to breathe.

He looks down and begins to laugh even harder. "Well... if I'm a turtle you're a bear!" I point at his hair covered chest.

"Well then, I *am* a bear." He slaps his knee.

I look in the water at my reflection. The large bow on the back of my dress is puffing out his green shirt around me and my neck is hidden in the collar.

"Oh my gods... I *do* look like a turtle." I laugh.

The two of us laugh for so long my sides and cheeks hurt.

When the giggles fade we sit silent for a moment, listening to the sputtering water drip from the fountain behind us.

"You know Ailie-cat, I need to come clean about something."

"You and Iris never stopped seeing each other?"

He bites his lip and shakes his head.

I nod my own head and take his hand into mine. "Rett. We have known our entire lives we are *supposed* to be together. *Supposed* to be, not *meant* to be. I love you with all my heart, I truly do, I will always love you; but I'm not sure I will ever be in love with you. I could be... I don't know. I am not saying it is impossible, just that right now I'm not. So if you did find love with Iris, I'm happy you got to experience it."

The smile I give is genuine but quickly fades as I'm flooded with thoughts of DeLuca. I'm not sure if I love him, it would probably be crazy if I did considering I haven't known him very long. All I know is that he infiltrated every inch of my mind. And the way my body responded to him. And his eyes that have haunted my dreams even before our meeting. I sigh, "If only things were different. If we didn't have these titles and responsibilities."

"Ailie— do you *want* to marry me?" he asks, his eyes searching.

I look at my feet and shake my head no. "If I *have* to marry someone, I'm glad it's you... I'm just, I don't know if I am ready to be married at all. I've hardly lived."

He lets out a relieved breath. "I feel the same! When I kissed you in the sitting room I was just trying to see, well if I felt anything, the way I do with Iris."

"And did you?" My eyebrow raises into a question mark.

He scrunches his nose and shakes his head.

I can't help but laugh. "Good, because I felt nothing."

"Ouch, I'm offended." He holds his chest like I've just punched his heart. I swat his arm, which honestly hurts me more than him.

"I meant it though, I do love you, and if I have to marry someone I'm glad it's you, Rett."

He dances his fingers in the water and asks in a small voice, "Do you still think Iris was giving me the ivlodeas? Because I've been clear of it for weeks and still feel the same about her."

I bite my cheek. As much as I don't want to— I tell him the truth, "No, I don't think she knew about it."

We are not guilty of our parents' mistakes.

"Good." He smiles.

I inhale the mountain air.

"This is it, Rett. Our last night as our own people."

"Yup, this is it." He looks at the moon just starting to become visible in this part of the courtyard.

I look up too. I see the stars through a small clearing in the trees and I let their light wash over me. While my eyes are closed Rett pushes me into the ice cold fountain catching me completely off guard.

"What the Haile! What did you do that for?!"

He shrugs. "I don't know, the moment seemed a little too tense."

I jump up behind him and pull him backwards into the water with me.

When he comes up gasping for air I spit fountain water back in his face.

"Oh you're in trouble now!" he says while tackling me under again.

"Hey, don't have all the fun without us!" Audrina rushes from the doorway to the fountain, waving a bottle of wine and kicking her shoes. The twins and— to my surprise— Evander follow close behind kicking off their shoes as well.

They hop into the freezing water with us. The spirits in our system warm our blood so that the water isn't so shocking. We spend the next hour or so splashing, playing, and living care-free while bathing in the moonlight.

One last night.

Once the spirits have lost their effect and we are effectively frozen to the bone; we go back inside to the sitting room closest to us. Evander starts a fire and we all strip out of our soaking clothes and wrap ourselves in quilts and furs kept in a chest that sits in the middle of the room atop a foreign woven rug. We call for the servs to bring us hot tea and laugh at memories and stories. I've been craving a night like this since my arrival. A night with my friends, no worries, just us living in the moment. It's perfect. A perfect way to end my last night as a free-women. As free as any of us who hold title ever are.

"May I join you?" a small voice from behind us asks.

Iris.

She stands there holding a cup of tea and looking so out of place I actually feel sorry for her.

Everyone freezes and looks for my reaction.

Rett's eyes are pleading, the deep brown endless.

I shrug one shoulder and mouth *go ahead.*

He pulls Iris onto his lap with the biggest grin I've ever seen him wear.

She glances at me and I smile with encouragement.

Her returning smile is timid as she turns back to Rett and hands him her cup of tea before nuzzling against his neck.

I look over and Evander and Audrina who are snuggled up next to the fire. *That was fast.* The surprise is slapped across my face as I shoot the twins a look slightly nodding towards their household employee and my best friend, Linnea giggles but Lysette turns beet-red. Looking around the room at the warmth, the joy, the prospect of love brings my thoughts to a heavy place. It's not fair that we can't be with who we want.

Maybe the Liberators are right, it *is* time for change. Rett and I shouldn't have to marry to please our parents and a nation that doesn't care about us because of silly outdated laws that wont allow us to be with whom we truly desire.

To be born with title is to be born in restrictive chains... but Rett wasn't born with title... not really. He can be with who he wants without breaking any laws.

"Let's play a game," I say abruptly, interrupting the calm.

"What kind of game?" the twins ask with intrigue.

"If you weren't born with a title, what would you do?" I raise my eyebrow at Rett.

"I'm out of this one." Iris rests her head into Rett once more and he pats her thigh.

"I wouldn't ever want to change my life. I've already refused my title duties so I guess the question doesn't really apply to me either." Audrina shrugs.

"Well, I know what I would do. I would get myself a cute little cottage in Astoria and travel around all of Katova." I say smiling at the thought.

"Not that I have a title... but if I had the means I'd move to an island and sail everyday. Maybe even sail to the edge of the world and see what lies beyond." Evander says.

"That's something I can make that happen." Audrina smiles at him dreamily from her position nestled between his thighs, using him as a backrest. He leans down and kisses her softly on the temple. Her hands pull his head down further— to her lips, kissing him back enthusiastically. The rest of us turn away from their affectionate show.

Lysette clears her throat and rolls her eyes before saying, "I'd move to Dailotta and become a librarian at the great Library of Millena, in their capital city, Beine. I could learn all about the old gods. They intrigue and baffle me. I don't understand how all three nations on the continent worshiped the same deities with the same stories from the beginning of recorded time."

"I think I'd move to mother's home, Thaus, and get to know our lands and people," Linnea adds, shocking us all that the twins have such different answers.

"I'd marry Iris," Rett says quietly while stroking her cheek. Her long black hair covers her face but between strands I can see tears falling.

Everyone turns toward me, waiting for some kind of reaction. I just shrug in response. It's the answer I expected.

It isn't fair.

None of it.

I'm going to tell Rett.

What he chooses to do with the truth is up to him, but he deserves the truth and I'm running out of time.

TWELVE
IT BEGINS

The manor is bustling with excitement. There is a plethora of servs moving through the halls, carrying trays and decorations, bringing to life the vision they've been ordered to fulfill. Guests have started arriving from all of Stellera and have been given rooms throughout the manor. Typically, the household would greet them on the steps, but when there is a large-scale event such as this, the formal greeting is saved for cocktails in the ballroom. The clock is ticking. If I'm going to do something to stop this wedding, I am going to have to do it now.

I have to go find Lord Magnus and stop this wedding.

Mother has insisted I wear an all white dress she had made while still in Vallae. It is plain yet elegant and so constricting I'm unsure how I will move about without toppling over. Mena attends to fixing my dark hair into a braided up-do that makes me look every bit the lady I pretend to be. I sit in my vanity chair, impatiently tapping my nails against my lap, waiting for the serv to finish painting my face.

"There we go. All finished. What a beautiful bride you make." She smiles, putting down the small brush she used to add color to my lips. I make a face at my own unrecognizable reflection and force a smile of thanks while I dismiss her.

Try as I might, I can't move more than an inch at a time. The dress my mother sent for me is tight around my knees, forcing my legs together and making it nearly impossible to walk. I'm sure the choice was calculated. Mother knows me well and probably wanted me confined and subdued in front of her peers.

I don't have time for this.

A serv is clipping florals in a vase as I pass her. I politely ask for the shears she is using. When she hands them to me, I cut a slit from the bottom of my dress to my mid-thigh, freeing my legs from captivity.

"Much better, thank you." I hand the shears back to the serv who stifles a giggle and curtseys. Now that my legs have regained their mobility, I move as fast as my feet will carry me without breaking into a run, heading straight for Lord Magnus' study.

I am unstoppable.

There is no changing my mind.

There will be *no* wedding today.

We will be free.

I swing open the door to the study and open my mouth to begin the speech I've repeated over and over since last night, but Instead of Lord Magnus, I find Mikail sitting behind the desk reading some kind of report.

"Oh, it's you," I say with disappointment. My hand instinctively holds my cheek even though it no longer burns.

"And it's you...what a glorious day for a wedding. I am very excited for you and Rett to be married today." Mikail's unnatural enthusiasm has me biting my lips together to hold back the laughter.

Audrina's Whispers are clearly still at work.

"I am looking for Lord Magnus. It's of vital importance."

"He's with your father in the conference room. I'll take you."

"No, that won't be necessary, Mikail. I know the way."

Considering it is just one door over and I don't want to spend any more time with this abusive manipulator than I have to.

"Very well, Miss Delphia. I am just very excited for you today."
He claps his hands below his chin and dons a broad grin.

I can't hold back my own smile this time.

How lucky am I to have a friend like Audrina.

As I reach to open the door with the '*U*' engraved knob, I rub my
palm, tracing the place where the '*U*' had been burned into it with
my finger in my nightmare. It flares like a flesh memory.

Hearing Lord Magnus' booming voice on the other side of the
door brings me back to *this* reality. I push open the door, not
announcing myself beforehand.

"Aislinn, you shouldn't be here," my father says with his face
twisted in worry.

I've never seen my father look worried before. It's disarming, and
I have to gather my thoughts again before I speak.

"I need to speak with Lord Magnus...*Alone.*"

"Speak freely, child," Lord Magnus says, waving me inside.

I close the door behind me.

"I'm not sure if that's best, Lord." I look from him to my father.

"It doesn't matter anymore." Lord Magnus' expression is grim.

Confused, I clear my voice and begin the speech I'd been
preparing all night. "Lord Magnus, Rett deserves to be happy. We
must tell him of his true parentage. He wants to be with Iris, and
I believe we should let him. He was born without title and is not
subjected to the laws. Let the twins inherit your lordship...Lord."
The words sound more juvenile now that I've spoken them aloud,
and I wince as the two men stare back at me with lips pressed into
hard lines.

"That's not possible," my father says.

"Why not?"

"You must marry Rett. It has to be you. It has to be today. You
must solidify our bond by marriage for the good of our family."

"If it's about securing bonds, I can marry another. There are
a plethora of suitors across Stellera that can still benefit Vallae. It

doesn't have to be Obsidian...Lyrica's nephew, Trysten Raicen, in Port Harholde can help broaden our resources. It doesn't have to be Rett just because of a pact your fathers made."

"It does, because it has to happen *today,*" Father says, unwilling to look at me.

Lord Urson puts a hand on my father's shoulder and continues for him. "Vallae has been taken. They must've known of your family's plans to travel. It was under siege within an hour of their departure."

"Taken? I don't understand. By who?" Blood drains from my face, tingling my spine.

"The so-called *Liberators.*" Lord Magnus spits their name like a curse. "No doubt spreading like a plague in Stellera...I bet they'll soon have the entire continent of Katova"

"You see, you must marry Rett, for your mother, sister, and I have nowhere else to go. We no longer have a home. It's been taken. If you do not marry, we will lose all titles...four hundred years the Delphias have held Riverstone, and I am the one who loses it. *The lord of nothing.*" Father slams his fist on the table.

"Once you're married, I can send an envoy to help your father take back Vallae, but you must be married first. Our houses must be entwined. Otherwise, it will be a declaration of civil war in the king's eyes," Lord Magnus explains.

"You mustn't tell your mother or sister. Not until after. I do not want them to worry themselves with this matter when they should be celebrating."

Looking between the two, I can see the anger and despair written all over their faces. They're afraid...and they need *me.*

For the first time, my family *needs me.* I am wanted. I am useful. *I* can save them.

With a sigh I nod.

I want Rett to be happy—I really do, but sometimes, there are more important things than happiness, and this alliance is one of them.

I hope you can forgive me, Rett.

The formal banquet hall has been transformed into a party fit for the gods. There is a long table at the far end of the room covered in refreshments. On the center of the table stands a tall fountain spitting champagne. The servs are dressed in all black formal wear and carry trays of the same drinks we had the night before. The tables that usually sit in the room have been cleared out to make room for the entertainers who stand in various areas amongst the crowd. There's one juggling fire. A set of them are balancing off each, other doing tricks and flips. Some are wrapping themselves in the black and silver silks that hang from the ceiling and dance above us in fluid movements that a mere mortal could never replicate.

Our guests are happily chatting among themselves. Each governing house has sent an emissary on their behalf. The room is filled with music and laughter as old friends reunite. None of them are concerned with the civil unrest that has already claimed my childhood home. None of them believe the threat of the Liberators is real.

I grab a drink adorned with red flowers and make my way to where Audrina is standing. She's holding Evander's arm and speaking with an emissary from Rilysse. I can tell from the badge she wears on her sash containing their sigil: a storm cloud with a lightning bolt. Audrina appears completely unbothered by the emissary's stares at her hand wrapped around Evander. In fact, a lot of the highborns in the room keep staring and whispering about the two. Even Lysette seems to be giving them looks from across the room.

My mother steps in my path.

"What have you done to your dress?" She hisses her words through clenched teeth disguised as a smile.

I forgot about the thigh-high slit I'd cut.

"I couldn't walk, Mother."

"You don't *need* to walk."

I open my mouth to retort, but she walks away, plastering a fake smile on her face, greeting another guest who has entered the room.

I gulp my drink and grab another as I reach Audrina.

"Are all mothers so exasperating?" I ask her, staring at my mother who is now across the room.

"I think the mistresses said it's part of their required duties?" Audrina shrugs.

I let out a small laugh.

"My mom died when I was a toddler. I was raised by my uncle who had never taken a wife, so I guess I wouldn't know." Evander says grimly.

I take another fast gulp of my drink.

Rett finds his way to us. He's wearing the official black Obsidian uniform decorated with full medals and honors. I never knew how much a uniform could elevate someone's level of attraction until now. I have to pinch my elbow to stop staring.

"Hello you three." His hair is slightly disheveled.

I wipe a little red from under his lip with my thumb and shake my head.

"You know this has to stop, right?" I ask him in a harsh whisper.

"I don't know what you mean." He grins playfully.

"*Iris.* Look I get it, she's beautiful and you two have had a lot of time up here together but it has to stop now, Rett. We're getting married...*today.* You had your fun, it's over now."

"I think that's our cue," Evander says awkwardly, ushering Audrina, who's raising an eyebrow at me.

Rett looks down to meet my gaze, clearly confused by my change in attitude. It's my fault for indulging his behavior in the first place.

"I'm sorry, Ailie. I thought that you'd be okay with it, the way you've been. I shouldn't have...I apologize for disrespecting you."

"I wanted you to have your experiences before we got married. That's true, but today is the day. You can't be a true husband to me if you're bedding another woman. I *need* you to be a true husband," I say through clenched teeth.

He looks wounded, devastated even. I'm sure he is filled with an overwhelming flood of emotion.

Guilt. Heartache. Confusion.

His face. It's a punch in the gut. I feel sorry for him. I wanted us both to have what we wanted from life. But this is our role. This is what we were born to do. We both know it...have known it all our lives.

"Good, now let's greet our guests and get this day over with," I say, putting my arm in his. "Smile," I whisper as we approach our first guest, the emissary from Thalia.

I grab another drink to take the edge off.

We spend over an hour making small talk with the emissaries. About nothing that matters. The weight of responsibility hangs heavily over me like a cape made of stone, and the drinks make me dizzy.

I can't wait for this to be over.

Lyrica finally relieves us of our social duty and ushers us out of the room, toward the stairs to get ready for the ceremony. I couldn't be more thankful. We reach the bottom of the grand entryway staircase. Rett is to go left to the west wing, and I'm to go right to the east wing. I stand at the bottom for a moment, taking deep breaths and trying not to panic. He's already made it to the top.

"Oh— I uh, Aislinn— hello," a small voice says next to me.

My eyes are closed, but I already know who I'll find when I open them.

"Hello, Iris." I make no attempt to hide the irritation in my voice.

She steps back at my tone.

"I was going to—uhm—see Rett," she confesses. I look her up and down, she is wearing a tight white dress that pushes her breasts up so high she could use them as a chin rest. The sight of it has me clenching my jaw.

"Yes, *you* would go see him, dressed like this, just *hours* before he gets *married*." Her eyes widen as she takes a step back.

With a sigh, I change my tone. "You can't see him anymore, Iris. I know last night I may have seemed to accept your...*relationship*...but I don't. I can't. It *has* to end."

Iris looks me up and down slowly, eyes narrowing as she studies my face before she exhales and softens her features. "I understand, Aislinn. I never should have expected you to accept it." She turns to walk away back toward the party.

Something about her movements rubs me the wrong way, and I feel the need to add, "Oh, and one other thing, Iris—after today, you will address me as *Lady Urson*."

"This way, Miss Delphia." Mena ushers me out of my room. She is shaking with nerves but still does a fair job of her duties. Especially for someone so young. We walk down the stairs to the second floor to meet my bridal party and finish getting ready. I feel out of my body, just moving through the motions of the day, willing it to be finished.

We enter a huge powder room lined with rows of vanities. A multitude of sconces provide more light than in any other room. There is a wall made entirely of mirrors beside the large window showing the main garden below where our guests are starting to gather. Lyrica and my mother had the servs light lanterns to line the paths. Little lights flicker in the trees, resembling stars. The fountains are filled with white flowers and orbs containing candles. There is a silver aisle running down the center, leading to an altar adorned with more flickering lights and dark flowers speckled with white—lunalillies. I smile at my favorite flowers. It's more than I could've ever imagined.

The sun is setting behind the mountain, signaling it is almost time to begin. The servs put the finishing touches on our hair and makeup. Lysette, Linnea, Audrina, and Lorella all have matching dark blue gowns that flow to the floor but are loose below the hips so they can walk without constriction. Lyrica has a long black and silver skirt with a silk silver top. Mother's gown is a form fitting dark blue that hugs her neck and has a revealing slit cut along her spine.

My gown, my beautiful silver gown with diamonds cascading down my curves, fits just right after the alterations. Mother comes and places a delicate veil with silver embroidery over my smooth curls that hang loose at my back.

"I had the serv up all night making it," she says smiling. "You look beautiful, my daughter." The acceptance I have craved from my mother all my life almost brings me to my knees.

"I too have something for you." Lyrica walks toward us with a small rectangular box tied with a black ribbon. She opens it to reveal a necklace made of sparkling black diamonds. It takes my breath away.

"Thank you, thank you both." Tears sting my eyes.

"You will not cry today. It will ruin your makeup," Audrina whispers in my ear.

The tears instantly dry before they can fall. I shoot her a thankful look.

Even Lorella pays me a compliment. "You look less eccentric than usual." It is most definitely the only kind thing she's ever said to me, and it looks as if it pains her greatly to say it.

Down below, we hear the tempo of the music change, signaling the start of the ceremony. I look out the window and see Rett take his place next to the healer, Sylvie, who agreed to officiate our wedding on such short notice.

I take a deep inhale.

It begins.

The seven of us make our way downstairs together, along with our servs, who keep looking between each other as if silently communicating and have been acting strangely most of the day. Perhaps they know about DeLuca and Elinor. Perhaps they hate the idea of me becoming their lady.

The twins each hold one of my arms. They sense my nerves and are repeating encouraging words and telling me how they can't wait to call me sister. It doesn't have the calming effect they're hoping for. Not because of what they're saying, but because the nerves aren't caused by the marriage so much as the importance it has to my family...and to Vallae.

We arrive at the main garden doors. The servs hurry away after giving us our flowers. More lunalillies.

Mena leans in and says in a hushed tone, "Wait a beat before walking down the aisle," before following the other servs.

What a strange thing to say to someone before their wedding.
They must have the music timed perfectly or something.

Lyrica and Mother pin a flower onto each other's dresses. The music hums a whimsical melody, and the moon has risen in the sky, providing a beautiful silver glow that accentuates each of the carefully placed decorations. It is absolutely perfect. My stomach begins to flutter as I prepare to walk down the aisle. The twins, my sister, and Audrina each grab a bundle of lunalillies tied with silver ribbon. I grab my bundle which is so large it covers both my arms when I hold it in its place. The long, dark blue ribbons holding it together hang so low they almost touch the floor.

It's time. Lyrica walks first. Then mother. Then the twins. Followed by Lorella.

Before Audrina goes, she turns back and whispers, "You're not afraid. Hold your head high, and don't trip." She smiles and walks over the threshold.

I wait and watch as they walk gracefully towards my future.

At the end of the aisle, Rett is looking toward the doorway I stand in. He smiles encouragingly when our eyes meet. Despite everything, I *am* happy it's him and not some stanger.

Standing next to Rett are our fathers and Orynn.

Swallowing the lump in my throat, I take a deep inhale, and once all the air has been exhaled, I finally step a foot out the door.

Boom.

A loud noise similar to a meteor breaking through the atmosphere rattles the floor below me.

Purple gas fills the gardens.

Someone screams.

Another boom—the trees are aflame.

More screams.

I must be dreaming.

This is another nightmare.

Wake up, Aislinn.

Boom.
But I know...
I know this is real.
This is happening.
Boom.
Another. This one is much closer. It sends me flying back into the manor.

The back of my head makes an impact on the hard obsidian floor.

Everything goes dark.

But I can still hear their screams.

THIRTEEN
Everyone You Know is Dead

The ringing in my ears almost drowns out the cries around me. My vision is blurry as I reach under the veil to where my head collided with the floor. It's wet and sticky. My fingers are covered in blood. My blood. I struggle to sit up. I'm so dizzy.

I'm not afraid.

I blink away the dark spots clouding my vision. Through the open doors, I see the gardens engulfed in flames and purple smoke. There are people running in every direction. Complete chaos. Some of them are on fire. I can smell their flesh burn from here. Shadows of people start appearing out of the perimeter of the woods.

Hundreds of them.

They have on gas masks—the kind the people of Ashe were issued when the mines exploded.

The purple smoke—it's oxidous gas.

Our guests are panicking.

I should be too, but I am not afraid.

They don't know where to go.

My father is pointing people inside, as are the Ursons. The panicking guests run in, trampling over top of each other, clawing their way past the others.

Many of them are bleeding from their noses and eyes. Their skin is already turning purple.

There are catapults being pulled to the tree line. They load an orb made of fire and let it fly through the sky. It makes contact with my father's back. He lets out a chilling scream as his flesh burns and engulfs him entirely in flames. He runs erratically before succumbing to the pain and falling still. My father, the great Lord Phillipe Delphia of Riverstone, buckles at the knees before collapsing.

The flames continue to devour his body.

More balls of fire are hurled toward us.

I'm not afraid.

"Inside now! All of you get inside. Its oxidous gas! Run!" I shout, running out to the gardens to help as many people as I can.

The people coming from the woods are getting closer. We are surrounded. I can already feel the effects of the gas as blood dribbles from my nose.

Ignoring the blood, I continue pulling people to their feet and ushering them to the doors.

Lord Magnus pulls a small whistle from his pocket and blows it, but there is no sound.

I am not afraid.

Four large black bears emerge through the woods. Lord Magnus shouts something toward them. The bears charge through a section of the intruders near the woods. They knock into them as if they weigh less than the wind. One of the bears groans in pain as it is struck with a long spear through its giant paw. He falls when a second finds its way through its head. A larger bear snarls, and using its teeth, rips the arm of the man who'd been holding the spear. The distraction is all the archers need. They let loose a series of arrows into the biggest bear, and he falls with such force that he flattens another intruder who was standing too close.

In the distance, a woman, judging by her frame, throws a sphere at the other two bears. One curiously goes to sniff it, and upon contact with the sphere, it explodes in a puff of purple gas. Both remaining bears are motionless on the ground.

I push people toward the doors, searching for familiar faces but trying to reach everybody. There are bodies scattered across the once enchanting garden. The pond now flows red.

I trip over one of the bodies and land face to face with Orynn Urson's little lifeless body. His eyes are wide and pooled with blood.

The vomit comes instantaneously.

Someone picks me up and throws me over their shoulder—running while carrying me to the manor. I try to wiggle out of their grasp until I see the people from the woods have reached the garden. Lyrica walks toward them unafraid. She lifts her hands, and roots from the trees sprout out of the ground, tripping some of the invaders. She waves her hands from side to side, and vines whip back and forth, tangling around limbs of attackers.

I rub my eyes, sure that the gas is playing tricks on them. Lyrica's hands dig into the earth, and it starts to quake beneath her, making it hard for them to keep upright. She's not enough to stop them. Not alone. They're cutting down the vines and roots with axes and swords. Some shoot arrows from crossbows, still hiding along the treeline like cowards. One of the arrows lands in Lyrica's left eye. I let out a scream as I watch the arrow come out the back of her head with a burst of crimson. She drops in an instant. Her body jerks like the fish we used to catch in the Vallae rivers.

The roots and vines return to below as her body hits the ground.

"We have to go back!" I yell and kick whoever has me.

He doesn't stop.

Mikail runs straight for the attackers with a sword. His hand is still bandaged, but he doesn't waver in his charge. An arrow grazes his shoulder. He doesn't stop. Another hits his thigh. He doesn't stop.

Finally, one slides through his jugular. The tip of the arrow finds its way through his brainstem. He drops.

Hyacinth's scream curdles through the air, and she rushes to him, covering his body with her own. The attackers are upon them, and one of them swings his axe in a swift, fluid motion. The blade lands in Hyacinth's back. When he pulls it back out, her blood blankets both her and her husband.

We pass my mother and Lorella's bodies. Blood pools in their eyes and slides out their noses down their cheeks. They have a purple tint to their skin, and their faces are frozen in expressions of fear.

I'm sobbing, but the tears are red.

The people from the woods are close behind us now. There are too many.

We are all going to die.

Whoever has been carrying me through the carnage finally jumps over the threshold of the manor. Lord Magnus shuts the doors and barricades them along with a few others who are still able bodied. There are still people trapped in the gardens, banging on the doors and trying to get in. We hear them scream as they burn and are slaughtered like animals caught in a hunter's snare.

The man carrying me sets me down against a wall. *Evander.*

"Go find Audrina." My voice is hoarse, but he nods and follows the command.

Rett pushes through the crowd when he sees me and takes my head in both hands, examining it. "Are you okay, Ailie?" he asks. He uses his sleeve to wipe the blood from my nose and eyes. His voice is muffled by my still ringing ears. I assess the blood on my gown. The pain from my split open head. The toxic gas festering in my lungs. But, everyone in this house bleeds.

"As okay as anyone is." I gesture to the room full of frightened people.

He stands, scanning the room with the deepest furrow between his brow bones.

"Go." I nod. "Go find her. I'm okay. I can get up."

It doesn't take him more than a blink to go search the crowd for Iris.

The barricaded door is being hit from the outside by something heavy.

The wood is starting to split. With each crack, my heart beats more wildly, telling me to run.

"Everyone needs to move!" Lord Magnus booms over the cries and screams.

Hundreds of people, blood soaked and burning, move through the halls in all different directions. It's every man for themself.

Strangely, the servs have all disappeared.

The tunnels.

"The tunnels! Head for the tunnels below Obsidian Manor!" I shout, not bothering to see if anyone listens to me. It won't fit everyone, but it could be a while before we are caught.

There's a chance.

I need to find Audrina. The twins.

I need to help as many people as I can.

I am not afraid.

I run up four flights of stairs, yelling for Audrina. Lysette. Linnea. Mena. Evander. Any of them. Anyone familiar. I find my way to the fifth floor corner conference room. The one that overlooks the gardens. With the U engraved into the knob. I'm not even sure why, but an invisible force is pulling me toward it. There's a loud explosion from the first floor that rattles the manor, followed immediately by another. I brace myself as I look out the window. It's hard to see anything at night. There are swirls of purple smoke where people are moving through the flames. With an angry cry for all the lives lost, I tear my blood soaked veil off my head and rip a piece off, throwing the rest in a corner. I use the shard of fabric to tie back my blood matted hair and wince as it pulls the skin of my wound.

Boom.

Another explosion.

I need to get down to the tunnels.

They're trying to take the manor down.

The handle of the door turns as I reach for it.

A large man, whose face is hidden behind a gas mask and wearing a proudly bloodied apron, pushes his way in. His eyes squint wickedly behind the mask when he sees me.

"We've taken this castle, *princess*. Everyone you know is dead or is going to be. No one to save you now." He runs a dirty-fat finger down the length of my exposed arm.

I look at him with disgust and spit in his face. It lands on his uncovered forehead dripping frothy and red.

I *feel* his smile as he rubs it off.

"Ain't you afraid, little girl?" He brings his face as close as the mask will allow to mine. He grabs a lock of my hair and rubs it between his dirty sausage fingers.

"I am not." I lift my head stubbornly.

"I've always wanted a highborn." He pushes me to the ground and forces my legs open. My gown tears as he roughly pushes it up. Every instinct screams at me to run. I'm trying to fight him. I try to keep them closed. I pull my knees together as tightly as I can. He's so much stronger than I am.

I scream. Not out of fear, but out of frustration.

I'm hitting him. Slapping him. I tear his mask off. He's laughing. His hand slides up the inside of my thigh. I feel sick.

Suddenly, he stops. He's not laughing. He's not moving.

Warm liquid trickles from his belly, soaking me in a puddle. He falls forward and lands on top of me, pinning me to the floor.

I can't breathe. His body is crushing me.

An unseen force kicks him off of me, and I cough repeatedly as I try to fill my lungs with the oxygen they desperately crave. A man pulls me into him. Wrapping me completely in the warmth of his chest. I fight him. I'm hitting him and kicking and thrashing. Desperately trying to get away despite my growing fatigue. He holds me tighter, crushing my to his chest.

"I'm so sorry. I'm sorry I didn't get here in time. I'm so sorry. Are you okay? Aislinn, say something!"

I stop fighting and pull my face away—still dizzy—to see who has come to my rescue.

"DeLuca?" My voice is small and weak. My eyes start to flutter close.

I must be hallucinating.

Or dead.

That's it. This is a last gift before the Reaper takes me.

It's a good gift.

I'm glad his eyes are the last I'll see.

"No, no, no, no, no. Fuck! Aislinn, stay with me. Open your eyes, Aislinn. Aislinn, open your eyes. Please, for the love of the gods, open your eyes!" He's shouting at me.

I try to listen. I do. I try to open them but can't. It feels so good to keep them closed. So peaceful.

The blood is steadily trickling from my eyes and nose, sliding down either side of my face in red streams.

DeLuca's mouth finds mine. Not in a kiss like I expect. He parts my lips and pinches my nose. He's sucking the air from my lungs, taking the poisoned breath into his own.

With a gasp, my eyes fly open. I cough out a large clot of blood, and a cloud of purple smoke puffs from my lips when I finally exhale. I take a large, jagged breath.

No longer do I feel the oxidous gas. My head is clearer. It still hurts like Haile, but it's not foggy. DeLuca lets loose a large sigh of relief.

I hug him with all the strength I can and search his eyes for answers when they start to bleed.

I gasp. "DeLuca! Your eyes!"

He smiles and pulls me into him.

"It doesn't matter." He kisses the top of my blood soaked head.

Boom.

Another explosion.

DeLuca looks at the door. "We have to go."

"We *need* to find my friends."

"Aislinn...everyone is dead. If they're not, they will be. I have to get *you* out."

"You can't expect me to leave them behind?! We have to at least try."

He holds my face, searching my eyes. Realizing I won't budge, he sighs and nods, helping me to my feet and leading me out of the room.

We move carefully through the halls.

The fifth floor has no one on it.

We still hear distant screaming through the house.

The fourth floor is clear.

The third too, aside from the odd bodies scattered about. The guest quarters are all on the third floor. They must have been trying to find sanctuary in their rooms.

Once we get to the second floor, the bodies start increasing. It makes my stomach turn with each life lost. My limbs shake so severely it's a miracle I can walk at all.

We stick to the shadows in unlit halls, making no noise.

I have always found a sort of comfort in the dark, but this...this is something different. This is insidious. The kind not even nightmares could replicate.

The thunderous sound of my heart pounding fills my ears, and I fear each staggered breath will be the cause of our discovery.

Our search for survivors begins to seem pointless. The large doors at the front entrance have been blown off. The stained glass is shattered and covers the entire entryway.

Below, Lord Magnus' lifeless eyes stare back at me. Next to him lies Evander, arm in an impossible position with bone sticking out. He lies face down, surrounded by a pool of blood. My heart stops when I look beside him. At the twins. One atop the other.

A whimper escapes before I can cover my mouth at the sight of the people I called family.

DeLuca pulls me by my jaw to face him. "Don't look at them. Look at me. Breathe, Aislinn."

I shake as I nod, but this grief is overwhelming. I'm not sure I remember how to breathe.

"Let's go to the third floor and take the lift. There is no possibility of saving anyone on the first floor, and I don't want them to hear the gears on the second. It's too close." He grabs my hand to go back up when we hear a cry from below. DeLuca peers back down over the banister. He mutters a curse under his breath and tells me to stay against the wall before carefully walking down the grand stairwell.

I obey, letting him take command, unable to form coherent thoughts or gain control over my chattering teeth. I slide down, wrapping my arms around my legs and dropping my head to rest against my knees.

"No, no!" A girl sobs hysterically from below. Then muffled screams replace her cries.

DeLuca comes back up the stairs holding one of the twins who is fighting him. When she sees me, she immediately stops fighting and runs into my arms. We share an embrace that's only broken by voices below.

"It came from over here," one says

"You check up the stairs. I'll check down the hall," the other replies.

DeLuca motions for the lift down the hall. We can make it. It will expose the lift, but we can make it to the tunnels before they figure out how to work it. DeLuca silently counts to three on his fingers. We run on three.

The lift doors shutting alerts the men below of our position.There are very few servs who know how to operate the gears correctly. Even if they do, they won't know where we take it to. The lift can go virtually anywhere in the manor.

We have time.

DeLuca works the series of complex gears. "Anyone who's grown up here would know to go to the tunnels in case of an emergency." He pauses. "Aislinn, I'm sorry, but I don't think we will find anyone else alive up here."

Biting my lip, I nod. He's right. There are too many of them. I hold the twin I'm sure is Lysette while she sobs and continues saying, "She's gone. She's gone," repeatedly.

We approach the tunnel. DeLuca puts a finger to his lips telling us to be quiet. When Lysette doesn't stop her mantra of *'she's gone'*, I have to put my hand over her mouth.

The lift doors open. DeLuca motions for me to stay and pokes his head around the corner. His shoulders relax, and he motions for us to follow him.

At the end of the tunnel, we see Rett, Audrina, Iris, and Sylvie. I breathe out in relief at the sight of them.

We rush toward each other and embrace.

"Anyone else?" Rett looks at me.

"I don't think so. Not anyone we could get to in time at least."

His eyes harden while he no doubt mentally takes stock of the body count. "Okay, we go now."

I look around and realize we are not in either tunnel I'm familiar with. "Shouldn't we go to the Capital? To King Carrigan?" I ask.

Rett *and* DeLuca both shake their heads.

"The first Lord Magnus built this one for a moment such as this. We're going to cross the border. We're going to Dailotta," Rett says, pushing the door to the transport.

"It's only a matter of time before they take the Capital, and King Carrigan is losing more and more people every day," DeLuca adds.

Rett turns toward him, realizing for the first time he is there. "I'm sorry, you are *who* exactly?"

"DeLuca. I used to be a serv here."

"*Used* to? And what would bring you back after you no longer work here?"

DeLuca's only response is to look at me.

Rett's pupils dilate with something primal.

Lysette is still sobbing. "She's gone."

Iris is in tears. Her dress is torn, and the bottom is coated with blood and filth. Audrina is bleeding from a gash on her forehead and looks catatonic. Sylvie is rubbing her fingers to her ears, looking off in the distance. The bottom of her dress and braid are crusting over with drying blood. And Rett and DeLuca choose *now* to square off.

"We don't have time for any of this," I snap at them. The lift starts rumbling as if to add emphasis.

Rett stares at it. "Everyone in the pod. *Now*," he orders.

We all pile in the small pod that couldn't fit much more of us if we had them. Rett starts fumbling around, trying to figure out the levers. DeLuca scoffs, rolling his eyes, pushing him to the side and working the levers with ease. The magnets at the top of the track slide into place, and the pod zooms off, knocking us all off balance.

Rett gets up and starts pulling up all the empty cabinets that line the pod.

"What are you doing?" I ask

"My grandfather was an extremely paranoid man. I'm sure he would have left some kind of supplies in here." After searching the entire pod and coming up empty, he punches the metal wall in frustration.

"Who were those guys?!" he shouts.

I look at DeLuca.

"They call themselves the Liberators. Their leader's name is Pierce Decatur. He was a serv from Nylen. He worked in Lord Earth's house and eventually broke from the treatment he and his wife received. After his wife was killed in one of Lord Earth's hunts, Pierce left for the Capital. He started preaching to crowds about equality and the evils of the high houses. His following soon was big enough that they were being noticed and arrested for treason. It only made matters worse. Their numbers grew from there. They started attacking high houses...."

"They took Vallae just after my father left," I add.

"You knew this was happening?" Audrina asks, speaking for the first time.

"Kind of. I only found out this morning about Vallae. I did know there was unrest. I didn't know the extent," I reply.

"How does *he* know.?" Rett directs his glare toward DeLuca. Everyone follows his gaze.

"Leave him alone. *He* is the reason I'm still breathing. The reason I wasn't—" I can't finish the sentence. I tremble thinking about those dirty, fat fingers on my thigh.

Audrina pushes me aside and sits close to DeLuca. She whispers, "*Tell us everything.*"

He looks at her with confusion.

"After we've found safety, I swear I will tell you everything. We need to re-group though. You have a nasty gash on your head. Aislinn's bleeding. We need to assess ourselves and our injuries while we have a moment to breathe."

Audrina and I look at each other in surprise. He should have answered right away. She *whispered* him.

Rett looks as though he may argue, but after checking between his sister and Iris, he deflates, nodding in agreement.

"How did you do that?" Audrina asks DeLuca.

"Do what?" He raises his eyebrow.

Sylvie interrupts them. "Perhaps I may be of service. I can tend the wounds to the best of my ability." She pats a bag she wears across her body. The sound of glass vials clank within. "Aislinn, you first. Your head wound is pretty dire, I'm afraid." She pats her lap.

Unsure of how she could know of the gooey wound on the back of my head, I comply and rest my head on her lap.

She pulls out a vial. "Apologies in advance, Aislinn. This will hurt."

With those words, DeLuca rushes to my side to hold my hand as she drips the liquid on my wound. A burning sensation sets in as my skin melts. I hear it bubble and sizzle while it pulls itself back together. There is no holding back as I scream in pain and squeeze DeLuca's hand.

He puts his forehead to mine. "I'm here. It's almost done. I'm here. I won't leave you." He tries to comfort me, but his voice is pained. Like it hurts *him* to see me hurting like this.

Rett is staring at us. His brows furrow at the implication of our familiarity. I don't care anymore. Everything is different now.

The burning eases, and I slowly sit up with the assistance of DeLuca.

"Now drink this." Sylvie hands me a little purple vile with little silver specks floating in it. "Here, one for everyone. Yes, yes, drink it up."

"What is it?" DeLuca asks.

"Manugolous, an antidote to the oxidous gas."

"Save it for someone else. I don't need it." He hands it back.

She holds her fingers near his ears, rubbing them. "No, no, you do not. Audrina, your turn." She pats her lap where my head lay only moments ago.

Audrina complies, and I go to hold her hand.

"I'm here," I say quietly, knowing firsthand the pain she is about to feel. As Sylvie drops the liquid, Audrina shrieks. I watch her skin pull itself back together, erasing any evidence of the wound.

"Anyone else?" Sylvie asks.

Everyone looks at each other and their own bodies but can't find any more serious injuries.

"Hmmm," she says, listening to the air, "what about your eye, Lysette?"

"Her eye?" I look and realize her once blue eye has turned completely white.

She shakes her head no. "It was Linnea's...she's...she's gone." Her sobs turn into shrieking wails.

The pod screeches to a halt. The doors open, filling the pod with the smell of wet dirt and clay. One by one, we exit carefully. DeLuca holds his hand for each of us girls while Rett treks ahead to make sure it is safe. We are in a dimly purple-lit dirt tunnel. There is a large hill with a small opening at the top. Against one of the dirt walls is a series of wooden crates covered in a thick layer of dust.

Rett immediately starts to open them.

His shoulders relax with relief.

"Supplies."

FOURTEEN
SOMEONE IS COMING

"Supplies? For what? Where are we going?" I ask him. A small panic floods through me as I realize we are in another nation with no plan and nowhere to go.

Rett ignores me while digging through the boxes.

"Rett!" I try to get his attention.

"Hang on, Ailie!" He snaps at me as if I'm a small child interrupting an important conversation between adults. Iris walks over to him and puts a calming hand on the back of his shoulder blade.

He visibly relaxes at her touch and sighs. "I don't know. I don't know where we are going or what we are doing. I don't know if we are being hunted down or forgotten. I don't know if we survived a slaughter just to die in this tunnel. I don't have the answers. I'm hoping something in these boxes will help us." His fists clench so tightly around the lip of the crate his knuckles turn white.

"Then we will all search. We are in this together, and we will work together. No matter our histories or background," I assure him. The others nod in agreement.

Rett exhales and begins to unstack the dusty crates, setting them out for each of us to dig through. They were built to survive. The wood has hardly splintered even though they have to be three hundred years old.

"This one has empty packs and thin blankets." Audrina pulls out a rolled blanket and a leather carry pack. "Looks like there's enough for each of us, maybe more even." She starts laying them out.

"We have sealed nuts and empty canisters to use for water." DeLuca is setting out supplies from the box in front of him.

I push the top off the box nearest me. When it opens, a large plume of dust enters my airway, causing me to cough uncontrollably. Once the dust settles, I examine the contents.

"We have honeyed whiskey and wine." I hold up two bottles from the crate and shake them.

"Well, if we're going to die, at least we will die drunk." Audrina shrugs.

I can't take it. I'm in hysterics and can't stop laughing. Rett tries to stop himself, but he can't hold it back. He spits as the laugh escapes his lips. The saliva lands on Iris' shoulder. She looks at it before she topples over in a laughing fit as well. We are soon all in uncontrollable hysterics except DeLuca who is looking at us as though we may have lost our minds entirely and Sylvie who is listening to the wind. The laughter causes tears to escape my eyes. The tears flow steadily, and the laughter turns into wailing cries. I'm sobbing now. There are no magic words of comfort. The loss has been too great, and now that we're not in immediate danger, it's all catching up.

The emotions.

The loss.

Lord Magnus. Lyrica. Mother. Father. Lorella. Evander. Linnea. Orynn. The hundreds of emissaries who came from all over Stellera. Even Mikail and Hyacinth.

There is a heaviness that fills the cavern and a thickness in my throat. The unshed tears.

We continue digging through the crates.

We have to keep going.

"Hmm."

"What is it, Lysette?" Rett asks his sister.

"I'm not sure. A small rectangular box of some kind, but it wont open." She holds it up to show us.

"Let me see." He takes the small, hand carved box from Lysette. We all circle them to see what they've found. There is a small hole dug in the front of the box. Rett blows the dust off the box to reveal carved letters above the hole and reads aloud. "What in the name of Helena? 'Ukulsi Urson'? Is that a relative of ours?" he asks Lysette.

"I don't think so. I think Ukulsi is Old Daeil...it sounds similar at least."

"How do you know what it sounds like? No one has spoken the god's tongue in hundreds of years," he replies.

"I read." She deadpans.

"What does it mean then?"

"I don't know. No one has spoken Old Daeil in hundreds of years." She puts her hands on her hips.

"It looks like you need to put something in the hole. Like a key." DeLuca points to the opening.

Rett sticks his finger in the hole, inspecting it. "Fucking gods!" He jumps back, dropping the box and holding his finger which now has a fresh drop of blood at the tip.

"I get it. Only an Urson's blood can open the box." I pick up the still closed box and run a finger over the engravings.

"Some good that box is. It's still closed. Must be too old. Let's try smashing it," Rett says, reaching to take it from my hands. I pull it away.

"Hang on. Let Lysette try." I face the hole in the box toward Lysette.

She gives me a pleading look.

"Go on. It's just a finger prick. After the night we've had, it will be nothing." I attempt a smile.

Reluctantly, she sticks a shaking finger into the opening. Her face twists with nerves.

"Ouch!" She quickly pulls out her finger and sticks it in her mouth. I feel a gear inside the box, and it pops open with ease.

Rett stares in confusion, examining his bleeding finger and his sister's.

A later conversation will need to be had.

I turn the box back toward me. Inside the black velvet lined box lies a rolled piece of parchment. I carefully unfold it, taking extreme care with its old age.

A map.

"It's a map!" I place it on the ground so we can study the map of Dailotta.

"Look! Here." Iris points near the Obsidian Mountain range. There's an X to mark where we are. "Thickett Woods." She traces the woods with a delicate finger and finds another X northeast of us. "Safe Haven."

"Thank fuck for that. He left us a map to a safe place," Rett says with relief.

"It's time to go." Sylvie is looking toward the tunnel that leads back to the manor. Utterly still.

The magnet on top of the track shifts. There's a loud vibration, and the pod we arrived in flies back the way it came, rattling the entire tunnel and sending flecks of dirt raining from above.

They're coming for us.

We all grab a pack from the ground and fill it with as much supplies as we can, as quickly as we can. Within minutes, we are climbing uphill toward the opening of the tunnel. It's steep. Too steep for the heeled shoes Audrina, Lysette, Iris, and I wear. We have to leave them. Rett climbs out first. He has trouble fitting his broad body through such a small opening, but after some wiggling, he is able to make it. After a few moments, he tells us we are clear to come up. Iris goes first, then Audrina and Lysette.

DeLuca and I help Sylvie up, and Rett pulls her through. I follow close behind her. The compact dirt feels smooth and wet beneath my bare feet. I slip, but DeLuca is right behind me and pushes me forward. I smile back at him, and he returns the smile but nods me forward. I make my way through the small hole, throwing my pack through the opening first, then pulling myself through. It is tight, but I'm able to make it without trouble. Rett pulls me to my feet.

The air smells so clean and crisp compared to the smell of smoke and burning bodies. I take a deep inhale, letting the clean air fill my lungs. They sing in appreciation. Trees are woven together for as far as I can see. The sky is covered by the canopy. We can't see the mountains or stars. I grab my pack off the ground and throw it over my back. The hole DeLuca is crawling out of looks as though a small animal could've made it. It's hiding in plain sight.

Rett is holding the map. He and DeLuca are arguing over which way is north. They're pointing in opposite directions. We are lost and blind.

My ears start to ring, and Sylvie's head turns toward me so fast I think her neck may break. She stares at me with her empty eyes. "Which way, Aislinn?"

I look at her with confusion as does the rest of our party.

"I don't know, I've never been in these woods before." I rub my arms as the cold air sends shivers through them.

"Don't look with your eyes." She rubs her fingers through the air.

"That doesn't make sense."

"Feel it, Aislinn. Which way to Safe Haven?"

My ears are still ringing. Her questions are hurting my head. Not thinking, I point in a direction. She smiles and nods approvingly.

"Hold on, I'm not just leading everyone in an unknown direction because Sylvie told Aislinn to point somewhere!" Audrina can't hide her skepticism.

"Aislinn has a gift, Audrina. She knows things others do not because, like myself, she *sees* things others do not." Sylvie smiles as though she had provided an adequate answer.

"Aislinn's right. Look there." Lysette is staring at a tree in the direction I pointed. A sliver of starlight breaking through the dense foliage shines on a U carved high into the trunk.

"We can't stand here all night and argue. Let's just go that way. It's the best we have right now." DeLuca shrugs his pack over his shoulder.

Rett opens his mouth to argue, but Iris pushes the bottom of his chin, closing it for him.

The ground below us rumbles.

We wasted too much time.

We all feel it.

A quick moment of us looking at one another is all we have before we take off in a run deeper into the unfamiliar woods.

My feet are cut and bleeding. They are carrying me as fast as they can. DeLuca stays close by my side. Though I know he could be at the front if he wanted to be. Everyone else is in front of us. Sylvie is ducking in and out of trees with greater ease than the rest of us. Rett stays close to Lysette and Iris. Audrina is the fastest of us and is out of sight.

If there are gods, please let us find safety.

My chest is tightening, and my throat burns from running, but we can't slow down. We can't stop. Not with who's behind us.

Trees blur past, branches catch pieces of clothing, and twigs snap under our feet.

We keep going.

After what feels like an hour of running, Audrina stops. "I can't anymore," she says, showing us her bloodied feet.

"We-can't-stop," I say between labored breaths. "They-won't."

"Let them come. We're going to die anyway," Lysette says, collapsing to the ground. She's breathing heavily and drops her head between her legs.

Iris sits next to her and leans her head against a tree. "I don't know how much farther I can go." She pulls a huge thorn from the heel of her foot.

"We need to find somewhere to stop," Rett says to DeLuca, who nods in agreement.

"Perhaps we shall follow the wind?" Sylvie says.

"I'm getting tired of your riddles, *Healer*," Rett says. His emotions must be heightened by the predicament.

"We should listen to her. No one else knows what to do anyway," I say, exhausted.

DeLuca squeezes my hand. "I go where you go."

I smile at him despite everything.

Rett rolls his eyes. "Alright, Healer, where does the wind go?"

"Follow me." Sylvie leads us over a mile further.

We come to a hill. She walks us around it. On the other side is a small cave. The entrance is concealed by a bush, making it an optimal resting place. Well hidden. Protected from the elements.

Once inside, we have just enough room to lay out and catch our breath. Sylvie repairs our wounded feet with the serum she closed my head wound with. We bite sticks to keep from screaming. The pain. It's agonizing. Much worse than the wound itself. Even after the skin is repaired to perfection, I find myself unable to stop shaking.

Shock...I think I'm going into shock...

DeLuca's hand entwines with mine, silently telling me he's here—he's not leaving.

"This is as good of a place as any to try and get some rest. We can move again at first light. When the sun rises, we will know what direction to follow," Rett says. He's checking over Iris with a panic flare in his eyes.

Everyone murmurs in agreeance, feeling an exhaustion unlike any other.

Lysette's head rests on Retts lap. I'm lying next to Audrina, who is now snoring in my ear. Sylvie lay flat in the middle of the cave with her head toward the entrance. Iris is, of course, beside Rett. The two of them lean their heads together against the wall of the cave. Soon, they are sleeping. I find myself glad for them. Out of the tragic events of the night came an opportunity for them to be together.

I look over at DeLuca who's resting against the opposite wall.

I slide closer to him.

"Are you awake?" I whisper to him.

"Mhmm," he murmurs sleepily.

"Thank you for coming back for me." I lay my head into his lap.

He puts a hand in my matted hair, his eyes still closed. "I told you I would protect you. I'd walk through a thousand miles of fire if it meant I could keep you safe."

A warmth swells in my chest. I sit up to kiss his cheek and then lay my head against his shoulder.

I'm in a white palace. It's unlike any I've ever seen. It smells like a field of wildflowers in spring. Everything glistens as if painted with diamonds, and there's an ethereal melody humming through the air. Walking past the grand entry way, I see a series of enchanted instruments playing at their own volition. The sound is perfect. Almost perfect. Under the music, I hear a woman's sobs. Following the noise down a long corridor, it gets louder. Louder. Louder. Until I'm upon a slightly open door. I push it open further. A woman lay

on a chaise embroidered with stars, actual stars. A man towers over her holding something. There is another figure in the room, but I can not make out their details because they're mostly hidden on the other side of the door.

"Please, just one, just one. We can keep one," begs the woman. Her body is painted silver that matches the tiara that is banded around her head. A head of a remarkable white that shines like it's weaved from diamonds. Little droplets of intricate beading and diamonds hang from the band over her forehead. In the center lies a crescent moon.

"Not this one. Not any. You do this to yourself. Each time is the same," a man replies with an edge of annoyance in his tone. He has on a red cloak, hiding his face. In his arms is a bundled baby. The baby is cooing and reaching for the man, staring up at him with electric sapphire blue eyes.

"Please. I promise to always do as you ask. I will raise him in the mortal realm. Just let me keep him. Name your price, and it's yours. Please let me hold my son!" She reaches for him.

The second figure, a man, shoots an arm toward her, throwing a chain made of shadows that pulls her to the ground, binding her in place. The shadow chains wrap around her completely until she is unable to move. Tears fall from her eyes as she cries out in anguish. The tears are so bright they can pass for stars.

She stops crying. Her head turns toward me in an unnatural jerking motion. Her silver flecked eyes find mine, but it's as if she is looking through me.

"Go now," the woman commands.

My eyes fly open. Day is breaking. Sylvie is sitting at attention near the front of the cave. Someone is coming. We both feel it. I nudge Audrina's foot with mine and pat DeLuca's shoulder.

I put my finger to my lips when they wake and look at me in question. Audrina does the same to Rett, Iris, and Lysette. We're sitting in complete silence, listening to the wind outside. I grab a sharp rock and hold it close. The sound of a twig snapping outside makes Iris jump. Rett's hand is over her mouth. Lysette is breathing heavily, holding her hands over her own mouth and nose to try to keep quiet. We hear footsteps rustling the leaves on the ground.

Audrina slowly moves to the opening of the cave. A fat hand covered in blood moves the bush aside, and a dirty face looks into the cave. His eyes widen as he sees us, but Audrina is quicker than he is. She's in his ear and whispers, "You see nothing. Go back the way you came. Your search is over."

He ducks his head back out, and we let out a collective sigh. Rett, Lysette, Iris, and DeLuca are looking at Audrina with bewilderment as we hear the man call out. "I see nothing. I'm going back the way I came. My search is over."

Audrina mouths the word "later," and we wait to be certain no one else is coming.

I drop my rock after it feels as though enough time has passed. Rett emerges from the cave, signaling for us to follow him out.

The sun is shining through the trees, illuminating the dense wood. Now I know why it was named 'Thickett Woods'. I have never seen so many thick trees so close together. Their trunks are double—even triple—the size of the ones on top of the mountains. There is hardly room between them, and it obstructs any view of what lies beyond. We are all just as blind as Sylvie.

Stretching my arms overhead, they get caught in something. A rope. Before any of us know what is happening, there are four men upon us. All of them covered in the blood of our family and friends. All of them look at us as though we are the game and they are the hunters. My arms are tied to Audrina's and Sylvie's, the three of us toppled to the ground, the situation made worse by every effort to detangle ourselves. There is a man sitting atop DeLuca with a knife to the back of his skull.

One holds a knife to Iris' throat, and Rett looks as though he is debating whether or not to pounce on him—if he can get to her before the knife cuts her jugular. The fourth man is chasing Lysette, who managed to escape the initial attack. The man holding the end of the rope that binds me is laughing wickedly.

"Your bloodied footprints led us right to you, fools." He laughs until he turns purple.

With all the force I have, I kick his shin. He falls over, his face landing near mine. He laughs harder, spit launching from the back of his throat and hitting my cheek. I gag.

Audrina turns toward him from underneath me.

"You want to let us go," she whispers.

He gets up. "Hey, I want to let these ones go," he calls out to his comrades.

The one who is on top of DeLuca responds in shock, "Are you crazy?" The distraction is all DeLuca needs. He rolls out from under him and jumps onto the man's back. He then pulls the man's hair back and bashes his head into a nearby rock. DeLuca grabs the knife from the man's hand and stabs him in the back repeatedly. He then throws the knife toward the man who holds our rope. It spins impressively until it finds its mark in the man's throat with acute accuracy. He falls with a heavy thud. DeLuca runs toward us. He rips the knife from the man's throat, causing the blood to sputter out, hitting him and us. He wipes the blood from his face with his elbow and uses the knife to cut us free.

Two left. One has Iris.

The other is making his way back with a knife pressed to Lysette's side. As he approaches, a fiery rage builds in Lysette's one good eye. She's been pushed too far. She shouts, "No!" at the top of her lungs. As she does thick roots push up from the ground, impaling the men right beside her, leaving her unscathed.

DeLuca throws the knife beside Iris' head, leaving a small cut in her cheek. The man behind her drops with the knife wedged between his eyes.

Iris cries out from the small cut and falls into Rett's arms while he stares at his sister in disbelief and is unable to speak. Lysette collapses, and DeLuca races to catch her. I help Sylvie to her feet, and Audrina spits on the man who'd captured us.

We hear movement ahead of us and position to prepare for another fight. Weak as we are, we will not let them take us alive. From behind a large tree, a small man with graying hair and a cropped beard appears. He's clapping, it's a slow clap that makes my spine straighten. The seven of us look at the man.

"What do you want?!" Rett shouts

The man smiles. "You."

PART TWO

Safe Haven

FIFTEEN
SAFE PLACE

I am not afraid. Picking up a log near my foot, I charge after the man. DeLuca, Rett, and Audrina follow suit. I yell a war cry, ready to strike. I've had it with these men. They stole our home. Our loved ones. Our future. I'm tired of running. Just one more in our way. I raise the log over my head, ready to strike the man as he remains stoic, an eyebrow raised by what appears to be amusement. I'm about to make contact with his head with the log when he swishes a hand in front of him, keeping it in a straight line in front of his chest.

I can't move.

The log is still in my hand, an inch from the man's face. I'm frozen in place. My eyes shift to my left and right.

We are *all* frozen in place.

But it doesn't feel like ice in my veins. It feels like rock.

Solid rock has replaced all the blood in my body.

Surprisingly, it isn't painful, but rather—claustrophobic.

Like being in a straight jacket or bound.

I can't even speak.

There is movement in my peripherals. DeLuca. He's still moving. He jumps on the man who's stoic composure has been replaced by surprise. DeLuca straddles the man over his chest and holds the knife to his neck.

"What did you do to them?" he demands.

"Nothing that can't be undone. You must let me go first."
There's not an ounce of fear in the man's voice.

"How about I plunge this knife through your throat instead."
DeLuca bares his teeth and looks more like a feral creature than a man.

"You can—but it may not fix them. You don't know."

"He can be trusted." I hear Sylvie's voice and the crunching of leaves as she walks toward us.

"How can you be sure?" DeLuca questions her.

"I trust his energy," Sylvie responds.

"Fix them first," DeLuca snarls at the man.

"I will. As soon as you all swear not to attack me. I just want to talk."

DeLuca looks around, making eye contact with me. I blink to tell him it's okay. He takes the knife from the man's throat and gets off of him. The man gets up, dusts off his strange gray clothes, and then waves his hand in the opposite motion as before. We unfreeze, and the log falls from my hands and lands on my toe. A yelp escapes my lips and I jump back, holding my foot, tripping backwards, landing in the leaves and dirt. "Son of Erebus!" I hold my aching foot.

"We don't say such things here!" The man shoots me a look of warning.

DeLuca is instantly at my side, looking me over.

Rett walks toward the man. "Talk, stranger. What do you want with us?"

"I want to help you," he replies with a friendly smile as if he hadn't just magically froze us.

"How?"

"By taking you to Caeliss, to a safe haven for people like us."

"What do you mean people like us?" I ask.

"People with *abilities*. I watched you fight those men. I've seen your abilities, your gifts." He looks at Lysette.

She examines her own hands in confusion.

"You watched us as we fought for our lives and did nothing when you could've stopped them with a simple wave of your hand?" Rett looks seconds away from going feral. His jaw is clenched tight, and he has a hardness in his eyes that even has me inching back from him.

"I had to be sure of you. We can't let everyone in. It's not so long ago our people were hunted down and slaughtered for our abilities."

"Our entire family was just slaughtered by those men." Lysette fights tears and anger.

The man nods, noting our appearance. Covered in dried blood. Our formal clothing ripped to rags.

"I am a friend. Let me help you."

Sylvie walks toward him. "What is your name, friend?" she asks, rubbing her fingers together in the air around him.

"They call me Alec."

"Who are they?" Audrina asks suspiciously.

"Our people. Your people too."

She gets closer and whispers, "Tell me, what are your true intentions?"

"To help you." His response is immediate. Alec claps his hands in excitement. "My days! A Whisperer. We haven't had a Whisperer in ages. I thought they'd gone extinct. Dear girl, where are you from?"

"Erm, Sutton Isle, The Islands of the Sons. How do you know about my gift?" Not a lot surprises Audrina, but I can tell she is completely taken aback by his knowledge.

He nods his head. "Yes, yes...that makes sense. They were the most coveted. An island would be the safest place."

"Excuse me, does anyone else have no idea what's happening here?" Rett blurts out.

"Oh, yes, this all must seem strange to Stellerans. Come, come. We have much to discuss." He motions his hands toward the trees behind him.

Rett's face contorts as he tries to work through what's happening. Iris puts a hand on his arm and calms him. We're all looking between one another, debating if we should follow. Except Sylvie.

Sylvie smiles and follows behind the stranger, blindly.

"I believe him." Audrina shrugs and follows, Lysette close behind her.

"What are our other options?" Iris says, grabbing Rett's arm and leading him to join the others.

I'm about to follow when DeLuca pulls me back. "Don't you think this is strange? How did he know we'd be here? We are still at least a day's walk away from the Safe Haven marked on the map. We can't trust anyone." Concern is written in the crease where his dark brows knit together

"What other option do we have? We are deep in the Thickett Woods. Woods none of us have ever been in that stretch for hundreds and hundreds of miles."

"We can find our own way. I can protect you...provide for you. Find somewhere safe on our own. We don't need him."

I smile and squeeze his arm. "I'm going with my friends."

He sighs. "I'm going where you go."

I nod with a soft smile, and we follow after the others.

It's nightfall before we find a clearing near a stream to make camp for the night. The stream is the first bit of water we've found

since the manor, and thank the gods it is the clearest I've ever seen. It seems almost enchanted. Once we have filled all the empty canisters, I wash my arms and face.

The clear water runs in lines of red where the old blood touches it. So much blood. It takes several attempts before my arms are clean. I do the best I can with my face, but without a mirror it's impossible to know if I've gotten it all. I soak my sore feet, again bloodied from miles of walking without shoes.

Sylvie is mending both Lysette and Iris. I can hear their pained moans from behind me. Audrina comes and sits beside me, dipping her already mended feet in the water with mine.

"Some wedding." She grimaces.

I let out a small laugh. "Yeah, some wedding."

I have all but forgotten that I am supposed to be married to the man whose arms are currently wrapped around another woman just ten feet behind me.

"So, *DeLuca*?" She raises an eyebrow in accusation.

My cheeks burn as the blush rises to them.

"DeLuca." I nod, biting my lip while glancing his way. He's helping Alec build a fire.

"He's the one you told me about before, the one who took you to Ashe?"

Again, I nod.

She taps her fingers on her chin. "His sister is pretty hostile you said...and he's immune to my whispers. I don't like that. Are you absolutely sure you can trust him? He was a serv. He lived in Ashe. He has a million reasons to hate us."

"I trust him. He saved me from...something unspeakable." I shudder at the memory of my attacker, and my legs instinctively pull closed.

"Mhmm. Tell me, Aislinn, why do you really trust him?" she whispers.

I answer without thinking. "Because he has been protecting me in my dreams my entire life. Chasing the shadows. Providing me with hope. Each night...when the nightmares became too much to bear, he was there. He was there so I was never alone. I don't know how. I don't know why. But I think my whole life has been guiding me to him, like we are bound together by an invisible string. "

Audrina's eyebrows furrow with consideration.

"Stop using it on me!" I push her over.

"Okay, fine, fine, but what do you mean you've dreamt of him your entire life? That was...deep...and weird."

"I don't know...I didn't realize I had. Well...there was always someone...with those intense blue eyes, but I could never see him clearly. I didn't know it was DeLuca. Maybe suspected but never dared to really hope for it, to hope I found the man of my dreams."

Sylvie appears beside us, holding an almost empty vile. "Your turn, Aislinn. I'm afraid this will be the last of it. I pray to the gods we make it to Caeliss with minimal injury."

"We should save it, just in case. I can manage." I hide the severity of the injuries below the water. I don't want to walk on my split open feet for another day, but the fear of losing another friend outweighs my discomfort. Sylvie nods and returns the vial to her pouch.

As she leaves, DeLuca takes her place.

Audrina makes a timely excuse to leave. "I'm going to go see what Lysette is doing."

"You should have let her heal you. Alec says we still have half a day's journey to go." DeLuca eyes my battered feet as though they have gravely offended him.

I offer him a small smile. "I'll be okay. If we have half a journey left, there's a high possibility someone else could get seriously hurt. I don't want to use the rest of the only thing that would help them." I swirl my toes in the water.

DeLuca stills. I'm not even sure he's breathing. He is just looking at me in the way I've only caught glimpses of in the manor. The way that makes my heart race and time stop.

"That's the reason," he finally says, almost too quietly for me to hear.

I cock my head to the side and look at him. "Reason for what?"

He looks down at the stream. "The reason I—the reason I've—" He searches for the words, but they seem to slip from him. "Look, Aislinn, I've never met anyone like you. I'm pretty good at reading people, and yet you surprise me all the time. You're kind and good and just have this fierceness in you that is trying to break to the surface." DeLuca swallows hard. "I tried. With everything in me I tried not to like you, not to fall for you, but I couldn't stop myself."

My mouth is dry, and I feel like I may cry for some ridiculous reason. "I...thought I disgusted you. I thought you hated me for being born into the family I was." My voice is so small I don't even recognize it.

"How could you possibly think I hate you? How could anyone hate you? You are a light in this world that is overrun by darkness."

My lip quivers. "But you could hardly look at me."

"I couldn't look at you, Aislinn, because each time I did, I lost all sense of time. Of surroundings. I was crawling out of my skin just to be near you. To breathe your air. I couldn't look at you because the hole it opened in my chest knowing you were marrying a lord...marrying anyone who wasn't me. I couldn't look at you because I knew, *I fucking knew*, the second your hand accidentally brushed against mine and you turned those gorgeous green eyes to me that I would let all of Katova burn for you and that if you were ever hurt, *I'd* be the one burning it. Because in the depths of your gaze I saw my future. I saw my home."

Before I can respond, his lips are on mine. His hand finds its way to the side of my neck, fingers curving upward to hold the weight of my head. At first, the shock stills me. Then his lips part mine, furthering the kiss, caressing my tongue in the taste of him. And I process his words—process that *this* is real—he is real. I wrap both arms around him. My hand slides through his hair. Every inch of me is screaming—*More. More. More.*

I wish Alec would freeze us here for eternity.

"Okay, that's enough of that, Ailie-cat." Rett is standing over us, his face twisted in disgust.

We break apart, embarrassed at our disregard for the camp behind us. Rolling my eyes, I stand to my aching feet and push Rett's shoulder as I pass him. He smiles in a teasing way, and the three of us walk back to camp together. The fire is roaring. Little embers flying off in the wind. A wind that seems to follow DeLuca. I plot down on a large broken log next to Audrina. DeLuca sits beside me, sliding his fingers through mine, effectively sending a flutter through my belly.

As Iris walks by, Rett pulls her to his lap while staring directly at me. He pulls her face to his and kisses her. One eye on me while he does so. Audrina and I look at each other, laughter bursting at the childish display.

"Alec was telling me his people have been here since long before the Trinity war," DeLuca says, trying to tear through the tension arising.

"Well, yes, but they aren't *my* people. We are all the people of the gods."

My eyebrows raise, and I try not to insult the man who is inviting us to safety. Audrina does it for me. "The gods, hah. I didn't think anyone still believed in them."

I give her a look that says *be quiet.*

"I find them fascinating," Lysette chimes in.

"Yes, the disbelief planted by *scholars*. No matter, you will believe. I have no doubt about that," Alec says, unphased by Audrina's outburst.

"Can someone explain to me what has been happening with everyone's sudden emergence of ability? Or am I the only one who has been surprised by them?" Rett looks at Iris and continues. "What about you? What's your *gift*? Flying?"

She shakes her head. "Not that I know of, but wouldn't that be something?"

"It sure is!" Alec exclaims excitedly. "I've seen it. What a truly incredible gift."

"Are there really people who can fly?" Lysette asks in wonder.

"Oh yes, we have seen a variety of gifts come through Caeliss."

"But how?" Rett asks.

"Boy, you have many questions. They will be answered when we arrive tomorrow. Do not fret."

Rett is clearly insulted. "I am no boy. I am a lord."

"You are the lord of nothing," I mumble grimly, remembering my father's words in the study. Was it just yesterday morning?

Rett opens his mouth and then closes it again, sinking into himself.

Iris rubs his back in comforting circles.

"I can't believe they're gone." Rett's voice breaks. "All of them. Even Orynn. Who hurts children?"

DeLuca's hand tightens around mine.

The haunted look in the eyes of my companions tells me they are doing just as I am and replaying the horrors of last night on a reel.

Watching our loved ones die over and over again.

Seeing all that blood and fire.

The purple gas.

The lifeless eyes.

The people we love...loved.

And just like that, my chest feels as if it has been cracked open all over again. The ache. It chases out any fleeting happiness I felt moments ago, and now guilt fills in the gaps.

Lysette whimpers and hugs her legs, her head falling into them.

In the long moment of silence, Alec is respectful but clearly uncomfortable.

"Well, it's time I retire for the evening. We have a big day tomorrow," he announces

"Might I follow you?" Sylvie asks him.

"Of course, my dear. I'd like nothing more." He offers his hand. She happily accepts it, and they walk off into the night.

"You know what pairs well with a fire?" Lysette says, raising her head at last.

We look at her, waiting.

She pulls out a dusty bottle from her pack.

"Wine." She smiles.

"I'm more of a whiskey girl myself." Audrina pulls out a bottle of her own.

She takes a swig without making a face and hands the bottle to me. I gulp it. The liquid burns as it slides down my throat. I cough and fight the urge to vomit. DeLuca bites his bottom lip, trying not to laugh. Rett has no such courtesy and cackles at my expense. Audrina and Lysette follow. Even Iris lets a giggle escape but looks down immediately, not wanting to make eye contact.

"I think I'll stick to wine." I hand the bottle to DeLuca and grab the one Lysette is hoarding.

DeLuca can't hold back the laughter any longer. I realize this is the first time I've ever heard him fully laugh. It's deep and heartfelt. I love it. I take a large gulp of wine as if to prove a point, and he throws his hands up in surrender. DeLuca chugs from the honeyed whiskey, then passes it to Rett. Once he has had a drink, he skips over Iris and passes it to Lysette. We swap bottles around until the fire starts to die and our bodies go numb from the spirits.

"We should all get some rest. It's been a long few days," I say, feeling light and heavy at once.

Murmurs of agreement follow. As everyone gets up, Audrina grabs my hand.

"Sit with me another minute." She pauses and adds, "please."

I tell DeLuca to go on. He raises a suspicious brow to Audrina but gives me privacy with my friend.

"I've been thinking...Sutton is probably still safe, considering it's an island and isolated from the rest of Stellera. We could go there. All of us."

"Even DeLuca?" I look back at him as he walks further away.

"He can come...but he wasn't born to be one of us, Aislinn. He's not like us."

"There is no us and them anymore. Don't you understand what just happened? My province and Rett's province are gone. Taken. We are no longer highborn. Who knows how many governing houses still stand?"

"Just think about it. I'm going to go home though. I am not cut out for a life in the woods."

I laugh, imagining Audrina living a simple life in the woods. "No, you are not. I'll think about it." I squeeze her hand and get up. "We might really like Caeliss. Let's wait to make any big decisions until we've had some time to consider our options. We don't know what tomorrow holds," I say over my shoulder.

DeLuca is spread out on a scratchy blanket with a pack under his head. There's very little moonlight breaking through the trees, but what little does shines upon him, and I swear he's glowing. When I approach, he turns to me and smiles, patting the space beside him. I nuzzle myself under the warmth of his arm. My head rests on his chest.

"Everything okay?" He breathes against my hair

"No...I mean yes...but also no."

"I understand." He trails the back of his hands along my arm. The motion is soothing and has me completely relaxed. "I'm so sorry, for all of it."

"It wasn't your fault," is all I can muster before the steady rise and fall of his breathing lulls me to sleep.

The buildings that surround me are so close together they trap in the heat, making this sunny summer day all but unbearable. That and the crowd standing shoulder to shoulder. I'm in the middle of a gathering of people standing outside the palace gates. How did I get to the Capital? The people around me are shouting. Not in anger but in excitement and agreeance. They are demanding change. They are waiting for something. The palace gates creak open, and the crowd cheers. They rush into the courtyard. Men, women, and children. They are celebrating. Their cheers are near deafening. I can't see what. I'm pushing forward through the crowd. Moving toward the front of the palace to get a better look. I weave in and out of people, none of them bothered by my presence. I can finally see the front of the palace and gasp in horror. Hanging from the archway are seven bodies. The entire Carrigan family. Even Elianna who was only nine. The people rush through the gates and ransack the palace.

A royal family has been slaughtered.

The king is dead.

And his people are cheering.

SIXTEEN

ULDOAKA

"Who's dead?! Aislinn, who is it?"

Someone is shaking me. My face is wet with tears. I blink and adjust to the light shining through the sparse holes where treetops weave together. Forming a circle around me are the seven faces of my companions. All of them share the same grim expression.

"What's happened?" I ask sleepily.

"You were screaming 'They're dead. They're all dead' over and over. You were crying. I tried to hold you, but you were thrashing around violently." DeLuca's voice is full of concern while holding his cheek—a fresh red handprint upon it.

"Did I do that?" I point to his cheek.

"Don't worry about it. What were you dreaming about?"

I look down and pick at the dirty skin around my thumb nail. "It was just a bad dream. It doesn't matter."

"On the contrary, my dear. Your dreams matter most of all," Alec says beaming.

"How is that?" I ask in confusion.

"You are the *Isoot,* the Seer. The one who led me to you."

We all look at him in confusion, except Sylvie, who nods in understanding.

"I see...you have much to learn, all of you. Aislinn is what we call an Isoot. We have four others in Caeliss. One of them saw you and your friends running through the woods. She said she felt you specifically in the vision. They're the ones who sent me to find you. Aislinn, as an Isoot you can see the past, present, and future."

"No," I whisper, feeling the truth in his words. The words confirm a suspicion about myself I never wanted to breathe truth into, for fear of persecution...for fear of what the visions showed.

"It's true." He nods excitedly.

"If that's true, then the king is dead, and so is his family. If that's true, then Stellera has really fallen into anarchy."

Silence.

Alec is the first to speak. "May Helena guide them to the Afterlands."

"What...what do you mean the king is dead?!" Rett asks in alarm.

"That was my dream...my nightmare...vision? I was in a crowd looking at the palace. I made my way to the front, and the people were all cheering. They were celebrating. The bodies were hung from the arches. All seven of them. King Carrigan, Queen Calista. The princes, Vincente, Leopold, and Giddeon. They even...they even hung the princesses, Marisol and Elianna. And the people cheered." A tear tracks down my cheek. DeLuca catches it with the back of his finger.

"It was just a bad dream, Ailie. You're okay. You always have them. They don't always come to pass," Rett says. He's trying to comfort me, but I think he's also trying to comfort himself.

"Actually"—I bite my lip—"it doesn't always happen exactly like the dream...but there is always truth to them."

"They wouldn't hang a nine year old girl...." Rett's temper flares.

"With all due respect, *lord*, you don't know what they'd do." DeLuca makes the word '*lord*' feel like an insult.

"Yeah, and how do you know, *serv?*"

DeLuca and Rett are inching closer to one another, their shoulders back, fists clenched.

"Okay. That's enough, boys. Off to your own spaces with you." Lysette steps between the two.

"Come, let's make haste. Should we to leave now, we can make it to Caeliss by supper. I'm sure you all could use a hearty meal after nothing but those old nuts."

My stomach rumbles in agreement with Alec.

We begin packing up camp. My head spins as it tries to make sense of every dream...every vision...I've ever had. All the what ifs. The tragedies I could've prevented if only I'd stopped ignoring a piece of myself. Trying to hide it in shame. DeLuca comes to rescue me from my downward spiral.

"I made something." He shows me the ripped cloth he wrapped around his feet.

My head twists as I look at them sideways. "That's...uhm, very nice."

"So you can wear my boots." He hands his own shoes to me. It's now I realize he tied the bits of cloth together in place of shoes so that I wouldn't have to continue the journey on my still bleeding and bruised feet.

"Oh, no I couldn't. I'll be fine."

"I insist. Don't be stubborn. It's either my boots or I'm going to carry you the rest of the way."

I smirk. "Is that a promise?"

"Aislinn." He breathes my name low and demanding, stirring something deep and unexpected within me.

I look at my battered feet and nod. "okay, I'll wear them."

He bends down and lifts my leg from the knee, his hands ever so gentle as he slides the muddy boot on. It's cold and wet like maybe he had tried to clean them in the stream. They are so old and ragged. Much too big on my own small feet. But they are all he has to give, and he wants me to wear them. So I will. After he firmly ties the laces, he rises to look me in the eyes.

"I will still carry you if you'd like me to." He kisses me on the cheek before heading off to grab our supplies.

I hold my hand to where his lips were just moments ago. There is a glow in my heart and dumb smile plastered to my face.

"A bit forward, isn't he?" Rett says, pulling me from the moment.

"Oh shut it, Rett. And you're one to talk. Where is Iris anyway?"

"Don't be like that, Ailie. I just don't want you to get hurt. You're moving too fast. You don't know him, and ...well...he's beneath us."

Rett's eyes fall to DeLuca's boots on my feet with a disgusted scrunch of his nose.

"Look me in the eye and tell me how me and DeLuca are any different from you and Iris? She has no title either. Her father was *employed* by your father, lest you forget. I was *happy* for you, Rett. When you were supposed to be *with me,* I was still happy for you. Can't you show me the same kindness? Can't you give him a chance?" The words come out with bile.

"I'm just trying to watch out for you. We're all we have now." His voice is small, and the realization that he is right feels like I've been struck across the face. *Our* families were just blown into oblivion. Both of ours. This small group...this is all we have.

"Just, give him a chance, for me, please." I sigh.

He nods and squeezes my shoulder.

It's been hours since the noon sun held its peak. Surely, we are getting close now. The density of the wood hasn't let up, and the undergrowth grows thicker by the step, coming up to our knees. I try not to imagine the creatures crawling around near our feet, and I am infinitely thankful for the shelter DeLuca's boots are providing from them. We are entering a bog. It smells like death itself has entrapped us all. The green juices bubble and pop, releasing plumes of putrid smoke. There is a wide tree knocked down...no...not knocked. Cut down. The break is too clean to have been by accident. It creates a narrow bridge for us to use to cross over the ghastly bog.

"Careful here, the Aeikpo Bog is quite dangerous. It only takes one toe to be sucked in completely. This is the home of one of our many guardians, Vristra. She has been a fiercely loyal ally of ours since the beginning." Alec proudly gestures to the sickly goo around us.

"Home? How could any person live in this?" Audrina's nose is upturned.

"I did not say Vristra was *a person*." He smiles.

My shoulders shake at the implication.

"I can hear her below the bog," Sylvie says, her fingers fidgeting with the air. "She is watching us."

"How much farther?" Iris desperately calls ahead. I notice she now has large shoes on her feet; Rett no longer has any. The sight provokes a small smile of amusement..

"Not far, not far at all," Alec calls back to her.

"I don't think I can take much more of the smell," she says, holding her stomach.

"Ah yes, but it does well to ward off unwanted visitors. Don't you agree?"

"Ye-" she starts but something grabs the large boot covering her foot, trying to pull her down. Rett grabs hold of her just as a slimy, webbed hand reaches back to grab at her ankle. He grunts in effort to keep her on the log. DeLuca is quickly at his aid.

"Vristra! Yutalo uldaoka! Yutalo uldaoka!!" Alec shouts. The creature's body is long and eel-like with the head and torso of a naked woman covered in green scales and gills. Her eyes are pitch black matching her long hair perfectly. She bares her razor sharp teeth.

"Ku uldaoka! Dauteiol!" she snarls at him

"Goloeiyu, Vristra. Dasi uldaoka." It sounds like he's pleading with her.

Vristra hisses at Iris but lets her go. The creature swims, flaring her needle-like spine.

Iris is gasping with a hand to her chest the other on her stomach. "I never want to do this again."

"What is Vristra?" Lynette asks.

"I told you, a guardian," Alec replies.

"But she wasn't...well, she wasn't anything I'm familiar with."

Alec laughs, shaking his head. "You Stellerans really think you know everything, don't you?" He gets to the end of the makeshift bridge and pulls a veil of vines from the path, revealing a solid silver ruin of a temple.

"We're going in *there* now?" Audrina says in a whiny voice fit for her station. "Are there going to be any more...guardians?"

"Just one or two more this way. Do not fret; you are friends. You are safe." Alec helps lead Sylvie, his hand splayed on the small of her back.

"Hmph. Safe. Sure, just a bog monster trying to drown me in her sea of rank." Iris scowls, kicking off the remaining boot. It shoots directly into the bog and begins to sink.

Suddenly, the boot flies back through the air and hits Iris in the back of the shoulder. She turns, her face red with anger, looking around wildly to figure out who's thrown the boot.

"I think you made the bog monster mad." Audrina laughs.

When we make it to the otherside of the bridge. There's a small ruin of a temple. Cracks threaten to dismantle it entirely. Of course, that's our heading, a crumbling temple that will surely crash down on us the second we enter because such is our luck.

Once inside, Alec sticks his hand in a cobweb-covered hole in the wall. "Ah, here it is." He pulls out his hand, and the ceiling starts to come down on us.

"He means to kill us all!" Iris shrieks.

"Dear girl, whatever do you mean? We are only going underground." Alec looks at her, amused.

It's an illusion. *We* are going down. The ceiling isn't.

When the room stops moving, Alec calmly walks down the dirt path in a silver bricked tunnel. The only light comes from flickering sconces along the wall. There are images of gods painted along the tunnel. Each image appears to be a scene from the stories of old we grew up with—the stories about the gods. Most of them seem to depict Astoria, the Goddess of Beauty and Night.

"What does *uldaoka* mean?" I ask Alec. "You said it many times. What language is that?"

"Uldaoka means 'friend' in Daeiliot. I was telling Vristra that Iris was my friend. She could smell that you are mortal. We do not usually welcome mortals." Alec acts as if everything he said makes perfect sense.

"Daeiliot...you mean Old Daeil? The language of the gods? No one has spoken that in...centuries." Lysette can't hide the excitement in her voice.

"Aren't we *all* mortal?" Rett asks.

Alec ignores them and smiles, refusing to provide further explanations, as he has since we've met.

We finally get to the end of the tunnel.

Two statues of silver soldiers standing over ten feet tall are guarding a large door. Their long spears cross in front of it, forbidding entry.

"Uldoaka."

As Alec speaks the word *friend,* the tunnel rumbles around us. The two statues slowly pull their spears to an upright position, allowing us to pass through the door behind. As we walk under the statues, Alec thanks them, and they nod in response. They're not statues. They're giants painted silver.

"More guardians?" Audrina asks with a barely detectable tremble.

Alec nods yes. "Edwige and Ismat."

"Thank you, Edwige and Ismat." Lysette bows to them as she passes the doorway.

Sylvie stops. Her gray eyes fill with tears. "It's beautiful."

I walk up to her, anxious to see what a blind woman finds beautiful.

"Oh my gods," I say as my jaw drops in disbelief.

We stand atop a large grass covered hill. On either side of us are the most glorious waterfalls that cascade down around us before joining with a river. The sky above us is clear, and the sun shines down, making everything glisten. The whole of the safe haven is encompassed by high cliffs, as if it were built in the remains of a fallen star, only much bigger. You could fit Ashe twice over. On the side of the valley opposite us, water flows from the river, over the edge, into the ocean below. I suspect from the outside it would look like no more than a waterfall. There are marble statues of the gods surrounding the outskirts of the village, like protectors. The farmlands, meadows, streams, multitude of fully matured trees, and gardens all seem to be thriving. I smell their freshness wafting through with the gentle breeze. Birds sing as they soar above us in welcome. The buildings are all crafted from stone and wrap within the village like a circular maze. The rush of the waterfall throws the familiar scent of wet stone through the air. It reminds me of Vallae—if Vallae was a part of the gods' realm.

"I've never seen anywhere like it."

"Welcome to Cealiss." Alec spreads his arms in pride. "Home of the Children of Astoria."

SEVENTEEN
KATALVIA UL ASTORIA

We are met with a mixture of excitement and suspicion by the people of Caeliss, the so-called Children of Astoria. They stare in silence as we pass their brows, either furrowed in suspicion or raised with smiles of greeting. Alec leads us through the maze of a village to the center, where a temple sits elevated above all else, showing the devotion the people have for their gods.

"Priestess Alis will be most excited to meet you; we haven't had new arrivals in some time as we can be difficult to find." Alec chuckles as he turns another corner with Sylvie on his arm. He whispers something to her that makes her blush.

The stone buildings are in perfect condition. It's as if they were built only yesterday. The rows of homes are quaint but in a charming way. Each identical to the next, aside from the front yards, which are decorated to the inhabitant's taste. Some with potted plants. Some with sculptures. They each have a little something added to give the cloned homes a personality.

Some of the people start lining the path toward the temple. They applaud as we pass. It makes me feel unsettled. I don't enjoy this much attention. I'd much rather stick to the shadows than be in the spotlight. Now, I'm all too aware of our appearance. Crusted in blood and dirt. Positively battered, barefoot, and dressed in rags. DeLuca, likely sensing my unease, offers his hand. I'm instantly more calm with his fingers between mine. Whatever this next chapter of life holds, I want to begin it with him at my side.

The steps are deceptively steep. The ache in my feet makes itself more evident with each one we climb. Now closer to the top, I make out the engraved portrayals of the gods and prayers covering the entirety of the circular silver temple. The woman I take to be Priestess Alis stands at the top, patiently awaiting our arrival. Her wildfire hair is blowing in the gentle breeze, and her hazel eyes glow against the harsh sunlight that burns brighter against the silver temple behind her. She's wearing a floor length white robe that swallows her petite form. A serene expression lies atop the lines of wisdom etched into her soft features.

"Welcome, Children and friends," she says, greeting us. "Come, let us find answers to questions and then we can find you homes of your own." She eyes our blood stained and tattered clothes. " I am sure you are anxious to get into some clean clothing." Noticing our feet, she adds, "My, and shoes."

When we enter the temple behind her, I find myself completely and wholly awestruck. The temple is crafted purely from stone, maybe left over from whatever created this massive crater. The way it shimmers against the sun gleaming through the glass ceiling is otherwordly. There are soft hand-sewn cushions spread around the entirety of the floor. At the center of the room stands a podium, lifted up by a platform that is built into the stone floor. There's a wall made entirely of shelves which are lined with stacks and stacks of books.

Priestess Alis assesses the awe registered on each of our faces and smiles triumphantly. "Yes, it is quite something, isn't it?" We nod in silent agreement. "I am sure you all have many questions. Let's just get right down to it. It's been a long few days for you all. You are familiar with the story of old surrounding the 'Tears of Astoria', yes?"

We nod. Even though Stelleran's don't *believe* in the gods, their myths are still very much alive in our history lessons.

"I'm not," DeLuca says quietly.

I never considered what kind of education the children receive in Ashe...or, perhaps, lack of education. My heart aches for a younger version of DeLuca.

"It's a long story. I can tell you later, but essentially the Goddess, Astoria, married the God of the Shadows, Erebus, to create a peace in the god's realm. She wanted children. Erebus didn't want to share her attention, so he got rid of all of their babies. She weeps every night for the lost children, which is why the stars fall in the town, Astoria, where the academy was that Audrina and I went to." I try to explain quickly and run out of breath in the process.

Priestess Alis bobs her head in approval. "Fantastic. The stories are true. Astoria has had hundreds of her children taken from her by her husband, Erebus. He brings them down to our mortal world, and they grow up as orphans, unknowing of their true origin. These children soon discover they have abilities, and the children of these children, too, have abilities. As the family line grows, the abilities grow weaker. For example, the first Child of my line was able to teleport to any location, even between realms. As time went on, their grandchildren could teleport between nations, then their grandchildren only a few miles, and now me. I can only teleport my mind. My body stays in place. Does that make sense? The first in your line always has the greatest ability, and all who follow only have a shadow of that ability."

"So, one of our parents had to have an ability in order for us to have one?" I think about my own parents and their cruel attitudes toward my nightmares. They made me feel less than while I was crying each night, terrified to sleep. Told me to quit acting so childish. To just...get over it.

Priestess Alis nods. "Yes, that is correct, and it never skips children. All children born to a Child of Astoria will have an ability. Without exception, even if said ability is weak. There will always be a hint of it."

"What if both parents have one?" Lysette pipes in, keenly interested in the surprising turn of the day.

"Then the child will get the stronger ability, the one closest related to the first born Child of their line."

I feel my head start to spin at the possibility that the stories I've long thought to be fiction may have a morsel of truth. I want to fight it. To let my logic win. But it would fill so many holes in my life...answer so many questions if it is true.

"Wait...does that mean anyone with an ability is related? Because they all come from a Child of Astoria, technically Astoria is all of their great-grandmother?" Audrina asks.

"Only in the same way all people are related, I suppose. We were all made from the gods in some way or another. The only ones who share a true bloodline relation are those who have the same ability. God-blood mixed with god-blood creates an entirely new line of god-blood. Unlike mortals, the Children of Gods are not a mixture of the two parents but rather an entirely new being. But mortal blood mixed with god-blood acts as you would expect, half of each parent. You can trace all those who share the same ability to the same original Child." Priestess Alis speaks slowly so we can follow.

You can trace anyone with the same ability to the same original Child.

"Alec said that you have four Isa—uhm—Seers here, that I am one. Does that mean...Do I have family here?" I ask. I feel a wave of unrecognizable emotions at the thought of having a second chance of having a family.

Priestess Alis smiles and nods yes.

"Do you have some way to test the bloodline? To see who we are? Who we come from? If we have any ability at all?" Iris voices the questions we all share.

"We do. That's why you were brought here. To find out how pure your blood is. I'm a tenth generation. The Trinity War wiped a lot of our kind off this realm's existence. Most who escaped had muted abilities, more contaminated blood. They were able to pass for mortals. We have a serum that can tell the generation of Child you are. You simply prick your finger, squeeze a droplet of blood into the dish, and add the serum. Very simple, the redder the blood, the more mortal you have. The bluer the blood, the closer to our mother-goddess, Astoria. We have a chart to match the color, too, to get an approximation. It could be off by two to three generations but overall has been very accurate. Once we do this, we can catalog you as new arrivals and get you comfortable... And clean. How does that sound?"

"You can stick me with, whatever you want, as long as I can get out of the remains of this cursed dress." Audrina offers her hands, palms up, waiting for a stick.

DeLuca is biting the inside of his cheek. I grab his attention and offer him a smile of reassurance. He returns with a half smile, but I can see his mind working. It is a lot to take in. I get it. I sense something is heavily weighing on him, and I wish we could get a moment alone, so he could unload whatever plagues his mind so.

"Ah, here we go, here we go. Sylvie, my sweet. Would you care to go first?" Alec says while wheeling over a cart. On the cart sits a carafe of clear fizzy liquid, a large leather-bound book, a small dish, a dropper, and a silver handled knife. Carved into the greenish metal of the blade, I can barely make out the words *Katalvia ul Astoria*.

Sylvie offers Alec her hand without hesitation. He takes it gently and digs the tip of the blade into her index finger with a careful precision. She doesn't flinch. Alec pinches Sylvie's finger over the dish, releasing only a droplet of blood from the fresh wound before he wraps her finger in a torn cloth and kisses it sweetly. Once she smiles, communicating that she is absolutely okay, he uses the dropper to extract a small amount of the liquid from the carafe and drops it on top of the blood.

I hold my breath and lean in as we all watch the blood change from the deep red to a bluish-purple.

Priestess Alis dabs the blood with cloth and then swipes the cloth on an empty page of the book. She pulls another small book from her robe pocket. It has depictions of different shades of red, purple, and blue on each page. She flips through the book while Alec cleans Sylvie's blood away to get it the little station sanitized for the rest of us.

"Ah," Priestess Alis exclaims as she finds the shade that matches exactly. "Sixteenth Child, Sylvie, very good. Would you mind writing your name and ability into the book next to your blood swatch please?" She hands Sylvie a quill.

"We don't have names for our abilities in Rousse. I do not know what to call it," Sylvie replies.

"What does your ability allow you to do?" Alec asks her with a kind smile.

"I can read energies, the energy of people, of places, of things. I can sense vibrations and disturbances. I can see in vivid color. Where others may see the whole image, I see the intention."

"Yes, we have two others like you here. We call you Aurors. You're purer than the other two. They're younger. Also blind. Intriguing." Alec examines Sylvie with appreciation.

Audrina goes next as Sylvie writes her name in the leather bound book. Her blood tells us she is an eighteenth generation Whisperer. The only of her kind in Caeliss. They had assumed all Whisperers were annihilated in the Trinity War as they were some of the most sought after.

Next, Iris gives her blood. Priestess Alis clicks her tongue as the blood remains the same shade of bright red. "Mortal, such a shame." Iris looks down at her finger, clearly disappointed.

When she writes her name next to her blood, she is told to write "Uldaoka" instead of an ability.

I go next. The blade stings, but its incise sharpness makes quick work of it. The warm blood flows easily into the dish. As they test it, I stick my finger in my mouth to stop the bleeding.

"Curious." Priestess Alis cocks her head to her side.

"What is?"

"Your blood, take a look, it indicates somewhere between ninth and twelfth generation."

"Well, that's good, isn't it? It means I am closely related?"

"Yes, but look here." Priestess Alis points to the swatch of blood she's smeared. It's an ombre, going from red to a deep blue-purple.

"I don't understand." I furrow my brows.

"Neither do I." Priestess Alis looks intently curious, not frustrated as one would expect.

"It could be because she is Isoot. We should look for the blood of the other Isoots later on," Alec suggests.

Priestess Alis enthusiastically agrees, like they've just stumbled upon the most intriguing of mysteries. I am less intrigued, more upset with myself, not wanting to be an outcast here as well.

Lysette winces as Alec digs into the tip of her finger. He beams at her. "A sixth generation! How exciting. You must be exceptional!"

"I don't know, I never knew I could do anything until the woods…I was so angry about, well, everything, but especially losing Linnea, my twin. My other half. The rage boiled over and in my mind. I thought if only I could call the roots from the ground and impale them…and it happened as I wished." Lysette wipes a stray tear from the corner of her brown eye.

"The loss of a twin, you say? We haven't had many twin Children. The ones we have, their ability is usually split between the two. We've never had one die…I do wonder if the twin's death transferred the rest of the ability to you…hmm, we may experiment later, if you are up for it. I've never seen such a strong Bottinial," Alec says. Lysette twists her fingers and bites her lip.

"Don't you think that's insensitive of you?" Rett snaps when he sees the discomfort written on his sister.

"Not at all. Would you not like her sister's death to have meaning? Knowing we can not change the past?" Alec looks curiously at Rett.

The air shifts uncomfortably at the tension, and Priestess Alis motions for DeLuca to change the subject. Sylvie smiles wildly like she knows something the rest of us do not.

DeLuca seems nervous as he offers his finger. With good reason. The color changes so swiftly from red to blue I think it may jump from the edge of the dish. Pure deep blue. Not a hint of red. His eyes are just as wide as the rest of ours as he stares at the smudge of blood in the book and the color that matches it.

"Praise be to Haile...He's pure," Priestess Alis mumbles in disbelief. "He's pure." She speaks a little louder, looking him in the eye.

"Pure? What does pure mean?" Rett practically spits the words.

"He's a first generation Child," Alec says in wonder.

"But that would mean both of his parents are gods. Wouldn't that make him a—"

"A god." Alec and Priestess Alis finish for Rett, their eyes not leaving DeLuca with a kind of fear and admiration present in their gazes.

"That's not possible," DeLuca says. His brows deeply knit together, and his lips press in a hard line. "That can't be possible."

"It...it is," I say quietly, remembering my dream about the women painted silver. "I saw it...I saw the day you were born in a dream or a vision? Although, I didn't know it was you...I didn't know what any of it was...Astoria, she begged to keep you. Erebus wrapped her in chains of smoke while you were taken away...DeLuca. The baby I saw, he had your eyes. I'd know them anywhere. It's true...you're a god."

Everyone keeps quiet. We stare at DeLuca, unsure how to act. It's suddenly hard to breathe. I don't know why I am afraid...I'm not afraid of him...maybe I am afraid *for* him.

"I thought the explosion caused some kind of mutation," DeLuca finally says.

"All mighty DeLuca, please tell us, what is your ability? How may we honor you?" Priestess Alis asks while bowing as you would to a king. Alec and Sylvie follow suit.

"You can treat me as you would anyone else here. I do not feel like a god. I guess my ability would be that I can't die. Or rather that whatever tries to kill me, I can control. When the mines exploded and I was trapped as a child; the fire, smoke, and gas were all around me. I could feel the burning, and I just wanted it to stop. I imagined it all bouncing off me like light off a mirror, and it did. I've been able to manipulate some elements ever since, mostly fire and air...occasionally light...I haven't really learned the extent of it...I can not create, just control what's already there." DeLuca looks at his hands, studying them as if they are strangers.

Priestess Alis gasps. "An Elemental. You're most rare, DeLuca. Your abilities are near limitless."

"Okay, it's my turn now," Rett says, bringing the attention to him.

I'm still staring at DeLuca, waiting for someone to wake me up.

Alec goes to collect Rett's, blood and I feel a small surge of panic knowing it won't match his sister's and the truth will come out.

"Rett, Lysette already did it; you don't need to." I try to spare him the pain I know will come from testing his blood.

"No, all who enter Caeliss must sign the book in blood. It is a rule we do not break," Alec firmly states. I bite my lip and bounce my foot. I'm begging the gods for just a small hint of blue. Any.

My heart sinks as Rett's blood stays the same crimson shade it was when it left his body.

"That can't be right," he says to Alec.

"Are you, perhaps, half-blood siblings?" Alec questions him.

Lysette and Rett both shake their heads.

"They're not siblings at all. Not biologically," I say softly.

Rett's eyes shoot to me like daggers of accusation. "What do you mean by that?"

"Your father confessed it to me... Your mother had a hard time bringing pregnancies to term...or delivering live children...Lysette and Linnea were the only children by the blood of Urson."

"No, that can't be. I remember my mother being pregnant with Orynn. I remember the night he was born!" Rett shouts with a hand gripping his hair.

"Don't raise your voice to her!" DeLuca bares his teeth in warning.

I put my hand to his arm. "It's okay, DeLuca. Mikail swapped them the same night, with a babe from Ashe. Hyacinth gave your mother something to make her sleep the hours after. She never knew. The only ones who knew were your father, Mikail, Hyacinth, and me... and my serv, Elinor...well, and Audrina. She whispered it out of me.... But otherwise, no one else knew."

"*You* knew," Rett says, venom filling his voice. He won't meet my eyes. "You knew, and you didn't tell me? What about you? Your parents did this? Did you know? Is everyone in my life a liar?" He yells at Iris whose eyes begin welling up, and a look of horror rests soundly upon her face.

"She didn't know, Rett. She was in the dark about everything." A ball of pity forms in my belly from the way her body language changes with his tone. She looks like she is seconds away from breaking down.

"Well, at least I have one person," Rett says with a biting anger.

"You have me too. I don't care what the blood says; you're my big brother," Lysette says, hugging him. He softens as he hugs her back.

"But *you*"—His voice is nothing more than a hiss between his teeth—"You are not my family and not my friend. I want nothing to do with you. Either of you. Any of you. I want to leave."

Alec interjects, "You can't leave Caeliss. It would put the rest of us in danger."

"Can't leave?!" Audrina shouts.

He shakes his head.

"Come, lots of feelings are being felt. It's been a long few days. Let's all get cleaned off and let our emotions settle. I will show you to your new homes. We've already picked some out for you...." Alec pauses. "Although, with DeLuca's elevated status, we should probably move you to the Priestess' estate...." He looks at Priestess Alis for permission.

"No, thank you. I'm sure whatever you've picked will be more than enough," DeLuca says humbly.

Priestess Alis relaxes her shoulders.

"I'm good anywhere as long as it is as far away from them as I can get." Rett points at me.

EIGHTEEN
WHOLLY DIVIDED

There is nothing special about any of the houses. Rows and rows of homes cut from a opalescent-stone—Alec calls it imperialite—create a maze around Caeliss. Each house is two stories tall. Both floors are small enough to fit into the bedroom I had at the Obsidian Manor. The lower level has a small kitchen, dining area, and sitting room. The upstairs has three small bedrooms, each holding only a small bed and chest of drawers with a mirror set above it.

The only powder room is located between the two smallest rooms upstairs. It is very simple and has a strange contraption instead of a bathtub. Alec made sure to show us how to use it. We pull a chain and water shoots down from a tube above with a sprinkling of holes. It creates an effect similar to a warm summer rain. They call it a shower and say it is much cleaner as we do not have to sit in our own filth.

Laid out on each bed are three sets of clothes and a pair of strappy shoes. Audrina takes the first shower, rushing in before DeLuca or I can protest. Lysette, Iris, and Rett are all bunking in a house on the opposite side of the village, at Rett's request. Sylvie has decided to stay with Alec. She seems absolutely smitten and at home here already.

"So, a god, huh?" I smile at DeLuca. We're sitting at the small table set for four in the dining room.

"I guess, but it just feels so weird. Like it can't be true. After everything I've experienced...everything I've seen. It doesn't feel real. I don't even know where to begin to understand or accept it." He shakes his head. "I don't want it to change anything for us. I just want it to be us, to be Aislinn and DeLuca."

"It won't change. I promise. I've waited too long for you."

"Don't make promises you can't keep." DeLuca shifts uncomfortably and again can not bring himself to look me in the eyes.

"Why wouldn't I keep it?" I pull away, sensing a confession coming and not entirely sure I want to hear it. His presence grows heavier by the second. He's growing distant and curling within himself.

"Hey." I cup his cheek and gently pull his gaze to mine. "Talk to me."

"I never expected someone like you to be...you. You're so different, but before...Aislinn, I've done so many things I wish I could take back now." He drops his head in his hands. Wisps of black hair fall around his fingertips.

A prickle of sweat forms at the back of my neck, sensing the truth but praying to the gods I'm wrong.

"What did you do?" I ask hesitantly.

"Before you arrived...my sister was so distraught over her husband's death. From losing a baby to deformity. She blamed the Ursons, all of the Ursons. She hated them with every broken piece of herself left. She started going to Pierce's sermons in the Capital. I went with her to keep her out of harm's way. She told others in Ashe about him and they'd go too. Pierce, he's so convincing." He swallows once, twice, then continues.

"I was *so* sure he was right. That all we needed was to overturn the governing houses and other highborn families, and we could live in a peaceful and prosperous Stellera, where *everyone* could thrive and be happy. After seeing so much death and hardship my whole life, it sounded like a godsdamned dream. I worked in Obsidian Manor as a spy. Actually, many of us did. I'd report things that went on daily to Pierce. I didn't know how far he'd go.... I told them about the engagement party. They knew to take Vallae because I told them of your family's travels. I'm the reason they knew to go on that day—the engagement party with all those highborns in one place."

He stops talking, biting his top lip while searching my face that betrays the horror I feel. After taking a sad, staggered breath, he continues, "After you sent me to the Capital with Elinor, I went to Pierce. I told him to call it off. To find another way, to spare you. Because you are good and kind and just. But when I had to explain about Elinor and why I had brought her to the Capital...I had to tell them about the babies being swapped. About how they stole babies from Ashe. It's all he needed, Pierce needed, to fan the fires of rage in the people of Ashe."

I feel a pang of guilt. Elinor wouldn't have known about the babies if it weren't for me. I gave them that.

"He quickly recruited more to his cause in secret. I'd never seen anything like it. His numbers doubled, then tripled. Pretty soon, he had an army. In just a few days, Aislinn. I knew if an attack were to happen, it would be an absolute massacre. I tried, again pleading with Pierce. I made my case. He told me he'd wait. Now that their numbers had grown so rapidly, he needed to reevaluate. It was a lie. He didn't want me to warn you. Or the Ursons. Everyone kept me in the dark, even my sister...even Elinor. They went as far as to tell the house servs, the ones ignorant to the Liberators' plans. I didn't know until it was already happening. I should've come to warn you. I should have known. Should have told you that day in Ashe about Pierce planning to take the Manor. I wish I'd never gone. It is my biggest regret in this life. I didn't know they were going to kill everyone like that...maybe just the Lords. I didn't think they were capable of killing women and children. It makes me sick. I am so sorry, Aislinn. I'm so sorry."

The color drains from my face as the words scream in my head. *He's the reason your family died. He's the reason your friends died. He's the reason your home was lost.* Another voice tells me to forgive him, says it's my fault too for telling Elinor about the babies and then letting her escape. They argue back and forth. The voices are too loud. My ears ring.

I am wholly divided.

I need space. I need to catch my breath.

I need the room to stop spinning.

"I'm going to take a shower." I get up abruptly.

"Please, Aislinn, stay. Stay with me. Talk to me." His voice cracks. "Stay with me." By the brokenness in his eyes, I know he's asking for more than just this moment.

"I don't have anything to say to you right now." The words turn to ash on my tongue. My insides are still twisted, still fighting about what I should do. How could I do that to my family? Betray their memory by staying with someone who aided in their slaughter? I can't. I have to go. If I stay in his presence a second longer, I will crumble and cave. So, without a second glance, I leave him alone at the small table.

I'm in a daze as I climb the short, small staircase. I enter the bathing room and relish in the first moment of being alone in days.

How could he betray us like that?

Wouldn't you if you lived the same life he had?

I begin to strip off the torn wedding dress I've been wearing for days. It falls to my feet. My eyes fixate on the diamonds that no longer shine, remembering how beautiful they were. How they glistened like starlight. They now resemble dark garnet, and each gem is coated in a brown coating. It looks like dirt, but I know it's blood. The blood of my friends and the blood of my enemies, probably my blood too.

The once silver dress is also completely coated in blood and dirt, so much that no silver remains of it. I have half a mind to throw it away and be rid of the reminder of my tragic almost-wedding, but as I go to place it in the bin, it occurs to me this dress, this bloodied dirt laden gown, is all I have left of my old life—of my family. So, I fold it nicely and decide to put it away for safekeeping. I place the scrap of veil neatly on top of the pile after pulling it free from my hair.

As I step into the shower, the water feels like a warm embrace and massages my scalp, chasing off the dirt and blood held within the tangles of my hair. The brown murky water circles around my bloodied and bruised feet. The water soothes them, but their appearance is another reminder of the realm shattering events of the last few days. The weavers of fate have a sick sense of humor.

Why did *he* have to be one of *them?* Rett was right. I moved too fast. I fell too fast. And now, he won't have the satisfaction of rubbing it in my face because he's determined to never see me again, despite not being allowed to leave this small village. Maybe I am the monster he believes me to be. Everywhere I go, darkness follows. Like I draw it in, or maybe, *I am* the darkness.

I feel alone.

The weight of so much loss and change suddenly feels more than I can bear. My legs weaken, and I slide down the wall of the shower, folding myself like a babe in the womb and letting my tears fall in rhythm with the water. Mother. Father. Lorella. Evander. Linnea, Lyrica, Lord Magnus, Orynn. Their lifeless eyes haunt me. My body is shaking. My tears turn to full sobs that I try to muffle into my arm.

After I finally run out of tears, I turn off the water by pulling the same chain. When I step out, I study my own reflection. I look more like myself now that I've washed away the evidence of the tragedy. But I have been stained by it...marked. I feel as though I've aged. My eyes are rimmed red and puffy. I have bruises in places I never knew you could get bruises. But that's not it. It's the burden of knowledge that's aged me.

I dress in the soft cream colored tunic and pants set that was provided for me and head for the only comfort of familiarity that I can right now. I tap the door with soft little knocks. When there's no answer, I lightly push it open.

"Can I come in?" I say, my voice is still raspy from crying.

"Of course."

I make my way to the bed and put my head in Audrina's lap.

"Is it that bad?" she asks.

I nod. She sighs, grabs the brush off the dresser near her small bed, and combs it through my hair.

"I could make it go away?" she offers.

I consider letting her whisper away my troubles. Make me forget my feelings for DeLuca or forget what he told me. It's so tempting. But I don't want her messing around in my head, tainting it.

"I'd rather just talk about it."

"Interesting. Okay, which of the life changing events from the last week would you like to talk about first? We have no shortage."

The corner of my mouth twitches with the shadow of a smile but fades quickly into a snarl.

"How about that the first man I've ever had any kind of romantic feelings towards contributed to the annihilation of our family and friends...and probably that of other great houses...and the loss of not one but two of my childhood homes...or that the man that I have these feelings for also happens to be an *actual* god. A real life, true and in-person god. What kind of cruel joke is that? It was only yesterday that we believed the gods to be fairy tales. Oh, or that I guess my nightmares have been visions all these years, which is pretty godsdamn terrifying. The stuff I've seen...Audrina. I can't even begin to describe what I've seen. To know that it has passed, or will pass, or is currently passing. Is the king dead? Or Is he going to die? I don't know. I've only *seen* it happen. I'm so useless. I can see all these things but can't tell you anything helpful about them. And! And! One of my parents apparently also gets visions...and made me feel like I was less of a person for mine! And Lorella too. Ugh, the nerve of them. But they're *dead,* so I can't even confront them about it. It's all—It's all too much, and what I really want to do is walk across that tiny hallway and lie in that stupid god's arms until I fall asleep, but I can't because of what he did."

I'm huffing, breathless. My chest feels like it will implode at any second. The anger burns red hot through my entire body.

"That's ugh, that's a lot to unpack. Are you sure you don't want me to whisper it away? It definitely seems to be our easiest option." She cocks her head to one side.

I glare in response.

"Kidding, I'm kidding."Her hands lift in surrender.

"Why couldn't it have been simple?"

"I don't know." She's tapping her fingers above her knee, trying to decide what to say next. "But with all you've lost in the last few days, I'm surprised you're willing to lose any more, despite mistakes that were made. All of us have made mistakes. Who's to say ours haven't gotten people killed."

"What do you mean lose any more?"

"Well, losing another person you care about. It's obvious you care about DeLuca, and from what I saw the last few days in the woods, he definitely cares for you."

"That was actually insightful, Audrina."

"I have my moments." She flips her hair behind her shoulder and lowers her voice. "Okay, now me. I am not staying here for the rest of my life."

"I'm trying to just get through until tomorrow. I wasn't even thinking about the rest of my life."

"I'm going to stay for a few days, maybe a few weeks. But I *am* going home. I don't care if I have to whisper all of Caeliss. I'm going back to Sutton, and I want you to come with me."

I consider my best friend's proposal. Like she said, I can't lose someone else I care about. "You may be all I have left now. I'll go because I couldn't bear it if I lost you too."

"Well, that's decided. We will be leaving. Keep your wits about you, watch the people, and we will make a plan. Now go back to your bed. This one is hardly big enough for me, let alone the both of us." She shoos me off the edge of her bed.

I kiss her forehead and wish her a goodnight.

How lucky I am to have a friend like Audrina.

Slowly, I walk across to DeLuca's door and hesitate while listening to see if I can hear him breathing beyond the wood. I *almost* push it open, feeling heat radiating from the otherside of the door. Maybe it's my imagination, but I swear I can feel him pressing against the door as well. My index finger lingers on the knob a moment before eventually letting it go and walking past it to my own room.

The bed is soft, just as soft as any I've had. The pillows are filled with feathers. The sheets are buttery smooth, the quilt warm. I haven't had a good night of sleep in longer than I can remember. Yet I find myself tossing and turning, unable to will my eyes closed. I keep staring at the door expecting DeLuca to sneak in and hold me. To tell me he was mistaken. None of the blame lay with him...or with me for what I told Elinor.

I don't want him to, or maybe I do.

I'm ashamed of my desires.

Every bone aches for him.

My lips burn at the memory of delicious kisses under the moon.

My heart and body betray my mind.

With an exasperated sigh, I throw the quilt off and wander to the window. This majestic valley has an incredible view of the night sky. Every star is accounted for. The moon hangs centered in the sky, painting Caeliss with a dusting of silver light.

Maybe I *should* stay here.

There's really nowhere else for me to go. Sutton Isle, the Islands of the Sons. How long will they remain unaffected from Pierce and his 'Liberators'? We *know* Caeliss is safe. Protected by guardians...and gifted people...demi-gods? I don't know the right name for them other than the Children.

Down below, on the cobblestone path near the meadow, two dark figures of a man and women pull me from the labyrinth my mind holds me prisoner in. They're far, and only the night sky above is lighting the way, but I can make out a familiar long-silvery braid. Sylvie. And I think Alec, though, it's hard to say for sure. They're holding hands. A twinge of jealousy unintentionally forms in my gut, but I push it off. I am happy for them. Happy for anyone who can find any happiness in such a cruel dark world.

They stop by a large tree and share a tender kiss. I feel as though I'm invading their privacy by watching and quickly return to my bed, but I don't want to sleep for fear of what I may see. I make a mental note to ask Sylvie for more Rutide. The vial she gave me still remains at the manor—or what's left of it. I wonder what *is* left of Obsidian Manor. *If* there is anything left at all. After long hours of staring at the stone ceiling, my eyes flutter closed.

"That's it, pet, come to me." A voice slithers the second my consciousness fades.

Nineteen
A Prize

In the nine days we've been in Caeliss, I haven't seen
Rett—except when I spot the back of his head walking away from
wherever I am, Iris and Lysette in tow. Audrina and I have ventured
out and discovered the Children have a very organized way of life.
The Bottinials care for the gardens to ensure hearty harvests. The
Eikvidalis, who can communicate with animals, take care of the
livestock and ensure they're happy and healthy. The Children who
can bend the will of water, the Vodas, ensure we have pure clean
water for drinking and bathing. There are Children who can move
the ground beneath us and manipulate its resources. They're called
Grounders and are in charge of creating new development in the
village. It feels like there is a balance here of everyone working
together in harmony, complimenting each other's strengths and
differences.

Once a week, the Children of Astoria join together at the temple
in holy worship of the gods. They'll also share any news of interest
and hold a large feast in a hall below the temple. It has been the
only time they've required our presence. Otherwise, the people,
including the Priestess and Alec, have left us to adapt to our new
surroundings on our own. For the most part, Audrina and I have
kept to ourselves.

I am told Lysette has been studying the many books in the
temple as well as learning from the other Bottinials—distant

cousins, I suppose, if we were to trace the lineage. They're helping her to understand her gift and teaching her how to control it.

There are four other Isoots here. I have yet to meet them. Part of me is afraid they won't accept me because of my undisciplined visions. Part of me is afraid they will, and I will betray my dead family for a family I've never known.

Audrina has been searching the barriers trying to figure out a way out without alerting anyone of our departure. There appears to only be one real way out, the guardian laden path we arrived on. We could go over the falls, but even if we survived the five hundred foot drop, it would be a long swim to the Islands of the Sons. It doesn't stop her from sneaking off at all hours of the night. Never bothering to tell me where she has gone. I think she hopes to find a weak point somewhere on the outskirts.

DeLuca and I have skillfully avoided each other. Well, he's skillfully avoided me. He leaves before Audrina and I are up for the day. He comes home well after we've gone to bed. I find myself staring at the door, willing him to walk through it, to see him. So much time has passed. I miss him. I fear that it has been too much time now. Maybe he's found another woman, one with an incredible gift, one who's in control and knows who she is. One who wasn't born to a family he despises.

Acid rises in my throat. I was stupid. I should have talked to him that night. Audrina was right; how many mistakes have we made that ended the lives of servs? My mistake with Elinor was monumental, and no one has said a word about it to me. Perhaps I am the villain in this story.

I know he's been spending his time with Priestess Alis. She's been teaching him about the gods, about his birth parents...about his ability, so I'm told by Alec, who's been spending every waking moment with Sylvie.

It's worship day today. Each week, the Children focus on a different god or goddess, to ensure they all feel the love and devotion of their people. If you told me a month ago that I would regularly be attending worship, I would have thought it an impossible jest. Yet here I am, sitting in a meadow, weaving flower crowns with Audrina for the Goddess of Art and Love, Edwissa, as well as her muses; Evonie and Desaris. She is never depicted without her muses, and it is said during the War of Gods, Egon stole away her muses and kept them locked in the Shadows when she refused to join his side. During this time, Edwissa became a shell of herself. She became dark and cruel and declared there to be no more love and no more creation until they were returned. Without love, both realms descended into chaos—to Egon's pleasure. Without art, the world had no outlet for emotion other than *against* each other. Helena, the Reaper, collected many souls of the newly damned and brought them to be judged. Some were sent to their eternal bliss in the Afterlands, some to be tormented until the end of time in the Shadows. Both ruled over by Egon.

All seemed to be in favor of the God of Death, but without love, Egon's wife, Kaliel, grew to hate him. Kaliel would undermine him in any and all of his schemes. Out of spite, Kaliel freed those Egon kept hidden away in the Shadows. She laughed at his anger. As the Goddess of Fury, all that rage just made her stronger.

The moment Evonie and Desaris returned to Edwissa, love once again returned to the hearts of men and gods. Unfortunately for Egon, this was the same moment he pushed a blade made of aietal, the only material known to kill a god, through Kaliel's sternum. She collapsed in his arms just as he remembered his love for her. The cruel irony brought so much joy to Edwissa that she filled the mortal realm with more love than ever before. Too much. Everyone was in almost a trance of happiness and love for months. Needless to say, the population tripled the next year.

Today, we show her our appreciation for love and art in the silver temple of Caeliss. The weather is idyllic. A soft breeze blows while the sun weaves in and out of wispy clouds. The gentle motion of the stream lulls away the crowded thoughts that have set up residence in my mind.

"Pass me that purple one by your leg, would you?" Audrina asks without looking up from her weaving of stems.

I hand her the flower and continue on my own. My fingers work quickly to braid the stems tightly together but not so tightly that they break, a perfect balance between strong and delicate.

"Can you believe it wasn't so long ago we were doing this on the cliffside meadow in Astoria? Thinking gods were all but fairytales. And now, here we are with Astoria's Children, making offerings for a *Goddess*. Much has changed in such a short time," I say.

"Mhmm," she says, half-listening, entirely focused on her task at hand.

"Maybe we will see Rett and Lysette at worship today...or maybe at the feast after. I'd like to know how they are. I'm not used to so much tension between us. It's strange."

She stops what she's doing to give me a look of surprise. "Are you joking, Aislinn?"

"About what?"

"You knew his entire identity, his entire life, was false. His parents weren't his own...or his brother and sisters for that matter. They were *kidnapped* from his father's people, the very people his father was supposed to protect. He stole their children. And you knew and said nothing. You can't blame them for feeling hurt and betrayed. You have to let people feel their feelings. It's not up to you to decide definitively between right and wrong." Her eyebrow raises as she speaks a harsh truth.

"I didn't really think of it from that perspective. It didn't feel like my secret to tell."

"What if he'd kept the same secret from you?"

"I'd probably never speak to him again." With a sigh, I lay back in the smooth patch of clover beneath me, staring at the clouds as they morph shapes.

Her tone changes close to sympathetic. "You know I'm always on your side, but also, you were wrong this time."

"Why didn't you say that when you found out?"

"I was kind of busy trying to protect you from Iris' dad, lest you forget."

"Okay, that's true." I think back, remembering the day that Audrina revealed her gift to me. Her gift was so incredible...but was it really? The memory feels tainted somehow. It feels false.

I shake away the thought and focus on a fluffy cloud that reminds me of little sheep on the farmlands in Vallae.

"Do you really think they're up there?"

Audrina lets out a deep exhale through her nose, seemingly annoyed by another interruption to her work. "Who?"

"The gods."

"After everything we've seen the last week, I think it's safe to say that they're real."

"Yes, but are they up there?" I point at the sky.

"Who knows."

"And why don't they engage with us? Why doesn't Astoria come visit her children?"

"You know, I've grown up with the same information you have. Why don't you ask someone more knowledgeable on the subject, like a *Priestess?*"

"I don't know. DeLuca has been spending all his time there...." I look across the field to the top of the temple, visible above all else in the village.

"And don't you think it's about time you talk to him too?" she asks, her tone sharp.

"Maybe.... I don't even know what I'd say."

"Well, what better day to try than one where we are honoring a Goddess of Love?" She holds up her flower chain, which looks infinitely better than mine.

"Come on, let's go before we're late. We don't need to give them anything else to talk about."

We take the cobblestone path back to the village. As we cross a fork, I see Iris, Lysette, and Rett walking ahead of us. If they've seen us, they don't let on. DeLuca is coming from the opposite side, surrounded by the elders. I only know Alec and Priestess Alis by name. The others haven't bothered with introductions. I'm suddenly too aware of my body. What should I be doing with my hands? Am I walking as oddly as I feel? Why are my hips so wide? What does my hair look like? It feels frizzy. Why is it suddenly so hot? I'm certain I'm sweating through the soft tunic I'm wearing.

Oh gods, please don't let him notice me walking.

He does.

I feel like I'm going to melt in place the moment I see his blue eyes examine me. He looks away quickly, his eyes hard and straight as he heads into the temple. It reminds me of my first day in the manor. When we were strangers.

"Please kill me," I whisper to Audrina.

"Just talk to him before I whisper you together," she jokes. At least, I hope it's a joke.

We trail in with the last of the Children, putting our offerings on a large table placed in the entryway that's already overflowing with flowers, poems, baked goods, and art of all kinds. When Rett spots me, his entire body tightens. Lysette puts a hand on his shoulder, and Iris slides her hand through his. None of them look my way again. DeLuca sits nearest to Priestess Alis. Alec and Sylvie are close by them, and the group of Elders sit on the other side. I haven't taken the time to get to know their names. If they don't care enough to introduce themselves, I don't care either. Not since Audrina and I plan on leaving anyway. We take seats in cushions on the outside of the circle. Someone closes the doors, and all the pleasant chatter in the circular room comes to a halt.

"Welcome, Children." Priestess Alis moves to the podium in the center of the room. "Today we bring offerings to the Goddess, Edwissa, and her muses. We hope she will accept them and in turn bless us with creativity, and of course, love. Love for each other, the Children. Love for the gods. Love for those who need it most, the lost and confused, and, of course, romantic love." She smiles and gestures to Alec and Sylvie.

"Our cousin, Alec, is from one of the oldest families in Caeliss. He is the last of his line of Sanguists. It is not uncommon knowledge that Alec had thought to never take a wife nor father children *until* he met Sylvie in the woods. No two souls ever entwined so swiftly and completely as theirs. So, what better way is there to honor the Goddess of Love than with a wedding?"

Gasps, cheers, and applause erupt in the temple. Priestess Alis holds the hands of both Sylvie and Alec. Their smiles radiate joy. A man brings Priestess Alis a dagger and a thick line of white ribbon.

She clears her throat and begins the nuptials. "Dearest Children, today we gather and honor our Goddess Edwissa by thanking her for filling these hearts with love. We bind them together for eternity, to follow each other in this life and the next. We combine their blood, never to differentiate between the two again." She slices through their palms with the same dagger they used to test our blood, the one that reads, *Katalvia ul Astoria,* on the blade. Neither Alec nor Sylvie winces, their smiles still plastered and un-moving.

Their palms drip, weeping and red over the thick ribbon. Priestess Alis then ties their wrists together. "We bind these two shadows before all the gods so they may lay witness to its truth. We bind them before our neighbors and friends so they lay witness to its truth. No longer two but one. It is done. Praise be to the gods.

Praise be to the union. And, of course, praise be to Edwissa!" She shouts.

A roar of cheering follows as Alec takes Sylvie in a deep embrace. He dips her, letting the entirety of her weight fall into his deceptively strong arm, then kisses her. The sun's rays sparkle down on them through the glass ceiling. It's almost like a blessing from the gods.

"Much better than the last wedding I went to." Audrina nudges my side.

The sheer morbidity of her joke is too much, and I let out a snort.

The two of us fly into a stitch of giggles.

The cheers are too loud for anyone to notice.

Except DeLuca, whose face is turned to us, eyes locked on me with a twitch of amusement tugging at his mouth.

The feast below the temple could rival one thrown at Obsidian Manor. A plethora of meats, fresh fruits, baked goods of all kinds, and, of course, wine. The room is filled with laughter and cheerful chatter. It has been years since the last wedding in Caeliss, and the Children are celebrating to the fullest. Audrina has even been taken with the mood and talks to one of the Vodas that has caught her attention. Her cheeks are flushed while she laughs too much and continually touches his arm. From the way he's been looking at her, I'd be surprised if she comes home tonight.

While everyone has a good time, I've been sitting at the end of one of the long tables within the hall, biting the skin around my nails, trying to think of an excuse to talk to DeLuca, who has yet to leave the side of Priestess Alis. The longer I sit, the weirder it feels.

I'm staring at him.

I hope he sees.

I hope he makes the first move.

He's deep in conversation, giving lazy smiles to all the Children Priestess Alis has paraded him too.

A prize. She treats him like a prize.

He hasn't looked at me once since the temple.

I watch as a woman I believe to be a Gale—someone who commands the wind—walks up to him and introduces herself. They're out of earshot, so I can't be sure what she's said, but it brings a true smile from DeLuca. Not the lazy ones he offered the others. This one reaches his eyes. I hate that she made him smile like that. I want to make him smile like that. She's beaming at him with a brightness unparalleled. She is a beacon of light, radiating warmth. She flips her long honey blonde hair over her shoulder.

She's flirting.

He's smiling.

I stab the knife I was using for meat into the wood of the table. Taking a chug of wine for courage, I get up to interrupt whatever conversation they're having. As I scoot my chair back, fully prepared with an epic speech in my mind, I am stopped by a small group of people I haven't seen before. A young man about my age along with a woman I take to be his mother. A girl aged around seven or eight years with wild dark brunette curls follows closely behind the woman, and an older man stands stiffly beside them.

My ears start to ring as the boy around my age speaks.

"I'm Heidon. This is my mother, Maegora, my grandpapa, Demetrius, and my little sister—."

"Hadleigh." The young girl interrupts him and puts out a hand to shake mine.

"A pleasure." I try to look around them, keeping my sights on DeLuca.

"I'm the one who saw you!" Hadleigh exclaims loudly. "My first vision! I called to you in it, but I don't think you found me." Her mother, Maegora, smiles down at her proudly and puts her hands on her shoulders with a loving squeeze.

Realization hits me that the members of this family are the other Isoots in Caeliss...my lost family. "Oh!" I exclaim, bending down to her level. "I am so very glad you did because I can't imagine where we'd be if you hadn't seen us!"

She giggles and hides into her mother's skirts.

"We have wanted to give you your space. What an adjustment it must be coming from out there...especially Stellera." Demetrius makes a face when saying Stellera, like it's a curse.

"It certainly has been. Many things are different here. Not to mention...well, how we came to need refuge." I don't want to say too much in front of young Hadleigh, though. If her visions are anything like mine, she probably has or will see much worse. My heart breaks for this little girl full of sweet innocence. It may be that I know what her future holds, but I feel this instant need to protect her. It's like we are somehow bound together by the threads of fate, and being near her completes a piece of me that I didn't know was empty.

"Heidon can introduce you to the younger crowd, if you need any company," Maegora offers on behalf of her son, who smiles and nods enthusiastically.

"That would be lovely." I'm only half paying attention as I spot DeLuca leaving the hall with the blonde Gale girl. My shoulders drop. I turn my attention back to the family of *Isoots*.

"How long have you been settled in Caeliss?" I ask, trying to be polite. They clearly aren't as ready for the conversation to be over as I am.

"Oh, I'd say it's been around twenty-five years now," Demetrius says, scratching the side of his neck. "Yes, that seems right. It was difficult after the Trinity War for any new Children to find their way here, but there are some trusted to safeguard the information, a small council of some kind. I used my sight to locate one of the keepers after I saw the creation of Caeliss in a dream. Maegora was so young. She had an older brother who refused to join us. He stayed behind. We haven't seen him since. It is a shame we have to remain so secretive. I'm sure there are so many others like you who have no idea how truly special you are. If only we could smoke out the mortals with evil in their souls and bring a second coming of gods."

"That may be too much at a first meeting, Grandpapa." Heidon shoots me an apologetic look.

I give a half smile in return. "This is nothing. You should have been at my house whenever we entertained a new diplomat."

"Come on, Mama! I want to get to the sweets before they're all gone." Hadleigh pulls on her mother's hand. Maegora flashes a smile of apology as she is pulled away by the impatience of her little one.

"It was wonderful to meet you!" I call after the two.

"So, Aislinn, right? Where do you come from?" Heidon asks

"Well, mostly Astoria, I suppose." I let out a small laugh at the irony. "I mean the province, not the goddess. I went to an academy there. Most recently, I was in the Obsidian Mountains, but I grew up in Vallae."

Demetrius pales. "Vallae, you say?"

"Yes, Vallae, in the center of Stellera. It's very beautiful. The majority of it is built along the rivers. Everything is lush and green. Have you heard of it?"

"Yes, I know it. It is where our family lived before we sought out Caeliss." The ringing in my ears is getting louder.

"That's interesting. I guess to be expected though. We share some kind of bloodline somewhere," I say, brushing off the nagging feeling in my gut.

He shakes his head. "No, we moved there after my wife passed. I am an excellent fisherman and thought I'd make a life there. The rest of our family came from the west, Thaus mostly and beyond...as far as Rilyse." He comes closer and examines my hair between two fingers. "My wife had hair like this. Hadleigh got it too."

Heidon is looking back and forth between the two of us with furrowed brows. Suddenly, I realize where his thoughts are going.

"Sir, it's not possible. My mother is Sescily Thermaline of Ezolle, and my father is Phillipe Delphia of Vallae. Somewhere down, one of their lines is who connects us."

"Tell me, *Aislinn*, were there any signs of the visions in your parents? Siblings, perhaps, if you have any?" Demetrius is searching over every inch of my face.

"Well, no. Not that they'd let on. It was a large house though; I don't know if I would have heard them at night."

His eyes zero in.

"Aislinn, my son, my Draydon, he went to work as a serv in the Delphia Manor. The coincidence...it's too great."

"If you are insinuating that my mother, that *Sescily Delphia*, would ever have an affair with a serv, you're greatly mistaken, sir." I almost laugh at the notion.

"My son was murdered twenty years ago. By your father. I never...I wouldn't have guessed the reason." Demetrius burns a hole into my eyes with his own of the same emerald hue.

"We can find out," Heidon says, his voice too chipper for the severity of this conversation.

"Good, good idea, boy. Yes. Aislinn, do you know how to search for moments in time?"

"I'm sorry, search for moments in time?"

"Isoots can focus on any point in time and see it as though it's happening."

"I'm not very good at it. I have to really focus all my energy into the search. Sometimes I feel as though it will split my head open," Heidon offers.

"No, I can't do anything like that. I don't know how to control any of it. They usually just come disguised as nightmares and bleeding daydreams." I look down at my hands with embarrassment.

"I'll do it," Demetrius says. In an instant, his eyes go completely white.

His appearance is unnerving. "Are you okay?" I ask.

"He's fine. He's searching for a moment," Heidon explains as if it's a regular occurrence.

"He can do it while awake?"

"Mhmm. It took him decades, but he was able to figure out how. Mama can't do it quite as easily. No one but him."

"Is it always so—"

"It is truth," Demetrius interrupts, his eyes returning to their usual emerald color.

"What is?"I ask.

"You, Aislinn Delphia, are my granddaughter," he says with a soft smile.

Heidon and I both look at him in shock.

"But...that can't be. Mother wouldn't...well, her and Father, they never liked each other much...but I don't think...."

As I contemplate more, it could be possible. It isn't unusual for married highborns to stray as they often have no say in who they are to be married to...but the thought of *Mother* with a serv. It seems so unlikely.

Maybe as unlikely as you and a serv. Or as you and a god.

"*Cousin* Aislinn." Heidon smiles and bows after a moment.

"Can I...I need a moment...I'll find you...both of you after I process."

"Take your time. We will be here whenever you're ready. We're here for you anytime, granddaughter or not," Demetrius says. He puts a hand behind Heidon's shoulder, leading him away.

I sit in place, too stunned to move. Suddenly understanding how Rett must have felt. Except how he felt must've been infinitely worse...because I knew. He trusted me, and I knew and didn't tell him.

I wonder if there's anyone who knows about me.... *Your father had him beheaded.* The words fight through like an earwig. *He* knew. My father. My false father. The animosity I faced all of my childhood now makes sense. I wasn't one of them. I was a walking reminder of a mistake. *Where's Audrina?*

I scan the room. She's not here. I'm pretty sure my heart is stopping. I don't think I'm breathing anymore. Wait, no. I'm breathing too much, too rapidly.

Air.

I need air.

The fresh breeze sobers my mind. I'm standing just a few feet from the grand doors to the hall, close enough to hear the merriment but far enough from prying eyes. I take a deep inhale and let the clean Caeliss air fill my lungs. I count to three before releasing. I repeat this until I feel like I can breathe normally again.

"Are you okay?" I hear Lysettes familiar voice. "I saw you run out. You looked...uhm...pale."

"Do you believe in karma?" I ask without turning around.

"No."

My voice breaks. "Well, I'm starting to."

"Hey, what happened?" She puts a gentle hand on my arm.

"Phillipe Delphia was never my father. All of us, all highborn children, grew up in houses of lies."

Lysette pursed her lips and nodded. "Well...now we know how the priss-genes skipped you."

I *almost* smile at that.

"Do you know your actual father?"

"No. He was a serv...Draydon. His father and sister are here. My fa-uhm, Phillipe...he...had him killed. I think it's because my mother became pregnant...with me."

"Well, at least we know where you got your love for servs. I would have never guessed it of Sescily though. I didn't take her for a rule breaker."

I let out a sad half-laugh. "Yeah, neither would I."

"Well, none of it matters anymore. They're all dead. We aren't. This is where we are. These are our people now. We can't look back."

"How can you say that?"

"Because if you linger in the past, you might as well forget about having a future. You of all people should know that, considering you can see both."

I sigh. "Not very well."

"Maybe not. But well enough. If you'd known what it was all these years I'm sure you'd have much more control, would've known what you were seeing and how to use the information."

"I suppose...." I take this opportunity to ask the burning question I've had since our arrival. "How's Rett?"

"Not ready to talk to you yet, but in time, I think he may be. He grows less angry every day. Did you know Iris has started studying with the Healers? Aside from Sylvie, there are two others. She wants to become a midwife like her mother. She's quite gifted with making remedies. I've been helping her grow herbs. You can maybe come by sometime to see?" Lysette asks with a hopeful voice.

"When Rett is ready to see me, I will. It's been so strange having him not speaking to me. There's so much I want to talk with him about. It feels as though I've lost a part of myself."

"He's not lost. He's just...finding himself. His life has been torn from the inside out too, you know. Let's go back inside. The party is really heating up now that everyone is good and drunk." Lysette smiles and offers her arm.

I graciously take it, and we walk into the hall together once again.

"Dance with me?" she asks.

It's been so long since I've danced. Just for tonight, I decide to free myself of the weights that bind my heart—if only for tonight.

Lysette and I hold hands, and our feet move in rhythm across the floor. We're twirling and clapping. Laughing and forgetting our burdens. The Children around us are all alive with song.

The song changes, some sweet melody that is not fit for two ladies to be jumping around like lunatics. Standing against the far wall, I drink my wine and fan myself with my hand, waiting for a livelier song.

It's across the room that I spot him.

A beautiful mop of black hair. Electric blue eyes fixed on something. It takes a second to register that they're fixed *on me*.

He looks wounded, like it physically hurts to look at me.

I offer a small smile, a peace offering.

It's all the encouragement he needs to walk forward.

And without thinking, I'm walking toward him.

We meet somewhere in the middle.

"Aislinn." He breathes out my name like a secret, one he wants to keep forever.

"DeLuca."

He offers his hand as an invitation to dance.

I accept.

He uses one hand to lift my arm around his shoulders. The slow movement is strangely intimate. The other hand finds its way around my waist, causing a sensation of tiny lightning bolts to fan out below my skin. I'm following his steps as he leads me around the hall as though I'm weightless. I don't hear the music. It's as if everything else has stopped for everyone but us. We go around and around. His eyes never leave mine. There is fire behind them, burning a hot blue.

I wrap my other arm around him so that both my hands rest behind his neck.

He lets out a long sigh. "Aislinn, I-"

"No, let's not talk about any of it tonight. I'm so incredibly tired of hard conversations."

"Okay, no hard conversations." His voice is gentle and comforting. I rest my head in the space between his shoulder and his chest. His heartbeat quickens, and his hands pull me in tighter. We stay like this awhile and let the realm melt away.

When he does pull away, it is to place a finger under my chin, tenderly tipping it upwards so I meet his intense gaze.

I'm suddenly very aware of the eyes upon us and feel a little self conscious. "Do you want to get out of here?" I ask.

"More than anything," he replies.

TWENTY
WE ALL BLEED

The moonlit sky shines bright, illuminating the stones on the path home. There are no words, but so much hangs in the veil of the unspoken. When we approach the door, I reach for the knob, but he stops me by sliding a hang down my arm. It sends a delicious shiver racing down my spine. His hard body is pushed against my back, and the warmth of him is so inviting I lean my head back into him. He bends down to trail kisses along the curve of my neck. His breath is close, so sweet, so intoxicating. With my arm in his hand, he turns me around so my back is flush against the wood of the door. He cups my cheek in his hand, staring at me as if he's memorizing every line of my face. I bite my bottom lip, craving his. He tracks the movement with hard eyes and gives me a savage smile before his lips find their place upon mine.

Before I can process anything other than the feel of his kiss, his tongue slides into my mouth, and in the same moment, he pulls me up by my thighs so I can easily wrap my legs around him. Electric currents race down to my belly. My grip tightens, and I dig into his skin. One hand splays around the small of my back, holding me in place. His free hand opens the door behind us, and he carries me inside.

I place small kisses along his jawline as he brings me up the stairs with ease. Carefully, he lays me onto his small bed and ever so gently moves his body over my own. His hands explore my soft curves as he kisses me fully and deeply. I let out a groan of needy desire that has me forgetting my own name as his hand begins to explore the curve of my breast.

It's hard to catch my breath, let alone catch a thought, but I realize where this is going and how rapidly it is getting there. As much as my body wants this, I'm not sure I'm fully ready for this step.

"DeLuca...I...I've never," I start breathlessly.

He puts his thumb over my lips. "Then we won't. Not tonight," he whispers behind my ear with warm open-mouth kisses. "I just want to be close to you, to feel you near me. I want to make up for every minute we were apart."

Good gods.

Once we are well past our limits of self control of exploring each other's bodies with our hands...*and mouths*...he stops before he surrenders into the temptation we both feel.

What comes next almost feels *more* intimate than what we just did. I feel like our shadows are fusing together as he holds me against him. His racing heartbeat calming under my head while he gently strokes my hair. I've never been held like this—like I'm treasured.

"What's your middle name?" he asks. My back is pressed into his chest and he's drawing lines along my arm with his finger tips that has me so completely and utterly relaxed.

"My middle name?" I ask sleepily.

"Yeah. I don't know it, and I don't like that I don't know it. I want to know *everything* about you."

I smile. "It's Theodora."

"Aislinn Theodora. I love it."

"What's yours?"

"DeLuca." He laughs.

I turn so that I'm facing him. "DeLuca? Then what is your first name?"

"It's Rainier, but no one has ever called me that, and I mean *never*. My mother found me in a rainstorm and thought it was clever. DeLuca comes from the blanket I was wrapped in. The name was stitched along the edge in Old Daeil...Delun, I think is what it said...but my family mostly calls me Luc."

"I like Luc."

He kisses my nose. "I like you."

"I like you too, *Luc*."

His smile is wide and infectious. "Do I get to call you *Ailie* now that you're calling me *Luc*?"

I shrug. "It is only fair, I suppose."

"I've always liked your nickname. That day on the transport to Ashe, I wanted to use it but was unsure how you'd react...."

"I probably would have been relieved. I did tell you *anything* other than *lady*, remember?"

"Trust me, I remember *every* word you have ever said to me." He pulls me closer so that I am laying in the crook of his arm. "So, *Ailie*, what is your favorite color?"

"Blue, but not bright blue. The darkest blue like the night sky. I like that in the dark in looks black but when you shine even the barest of light upon it you see the depth of color. What's yours, *Rainier* DeLuca?"

He chuckles low and throaty before he answers. "Green—like your eyes." I blush and he moves the hair falling in my face behind my ear. "Specifically *this* emerald color." His thumb strokes my cheek bone.

"Do you believe in fate?"

"Like the Weavers? Alec has been teaching me about them."

"I guess, but just in general, fate—Weavers or no. I'm honestly not all that sure I believe in five entities controlling everything." I shrug.

"Maybe. I don't know. With all that's happened lately, it's hard not to believe in it."

"Well, either way, I think we were fated to be together. I have been drawn to you since the first moment my eyes met yours, even when I shouldn't have. Even when I tried not to be. It was irritating as all Haile, but I *ached* for you, every moment of every day."

His grin changes into something a bit more devious. "Do you still ache for me, baby?"

I kiss him and answer against his lips, "More now than ever."

A cloud of strange smoke obscures my vision. Someone is under attack. I can't tell who through the smoke. I hear crazed laughter. The smell of sulfur is overwhelming. People are screaming. I close my eyes to try to tune my ears to find the screams. They're all around me. I can't pinpoint it because it's in all directions. The cobblestone path comes into view below the smoke. I follow it, finding the temple in the center of Caeliss. I'm running up the steps. My heart threatens to stop in anticipation of what I'll find at the top. There's a man standing there. He's the one laughing. I don't recognize him. He has salt and pepper hair, a thick mustache, and a murderous look in his eyes. Eyes that are wrong.

"You see, we are all the same. We all bleed. We all die." He keeps a tight smile as he bends down to someone chained against the rail of the steps.

I squint, trying to see through swirls of smoke.

Wildfire-red hair...Priestess Alis.

The man holds her face firmly between his hands, forcing her to look outward to the village.

I take a deep breath. I'm halfway up the steps and turn around. Smoke is clearing. And the bodies become visible in its wake. Bodies of the Children. Heidon. Hadleigh. Demetrius. Maegora. Lysette. Rett. Iris. I see them all and many more. Familiar faces I haven't bothered getting to know.

I'm sick to my stomach.

It can't end like this.

Suddenly, I have a dagger in my hand.

On the blade is carved Katalvia Ul Astoria.

"It's you. It has to be you," a voice hisses.

Me? Why me? There's nothing special about me.

The voice whispers again, "It has to be you."

"I'm afraid."

"You should be."

When my eyes open, DeLuca is staring at me with a worried expression. He's still holding me, but he's now propped on one elbow with his body contorted sideways. The sun glistens against the olive color of his skin, and whatever troubled me a moment ago seems to have disappeared entirely as I melt further into him.

"Aislinn?" The concern in his voice irritates me. I want to stay in this moment.

"Mmm?"

"What has to be you?"

"What?"

"You were saying 'it has to be you'. What did you see?" He sits up gently, sliding his arm out from under me.

Letting out all my breath I follow the action.

"A lot of deaths in smoke. Again. I'm so tired of seeing death and smoke." I sigh.

"Where?" He's biting the inside of his cheek.

"Here. Everyone here."

"What else?"

"There was a man." I scrunch my face trying to remember the details. "He had graying hair...."

"A mustache?" DeLuca seems to grow more worried.

I nod.

He lets out an angry breath. "Pierce. We need to tell Priestess Alis and Alec."

I grab his head and whisper, "Later" in his ear. I proceed to climb on top of him and put my hands through his hair, pulling his head back slightly as I kiss him with a savageness that takes him completely by surprise.

"That's how I want to be woken up from now on, *Luc*." I breathe against his ear. I climb off of him and walk across the room, opening the door and giving him my sweetest smile as he stares at me with a devious hunger.

"Well, isn't this a surprise?" Audrina is waiting for me on the other side of the door. I put my finger to my lips and nod her across the hall to her own room.

We both fall onto her bed, giggling like school girls.

"Did you?" she asks with eyebrows raised.

"No, but it was so much more. He's so much more. I could never explain it. But just being around him makes me tremble in the best way. It's maddening and wonderful." I hug her pillow. "Wait...did you? And that water boy?" I ask, remembering the boy from the feast.

She gives a half smirk and pretends to zip her lips shut before turning an imaginary key.

"Oh, come on!" I plead.

"Okay, yes. Yes, I did. His name is Dover. I just got back as I ran into you."

We both explode into another giggle fit. Suddenly, I am transported to the simpler days at the Astoria Academy.

"I think Edwissa liked our offerings."

"She did, indeed." Audrina smiles at what I assume is a memory involving *Dover*. "Tell me more about your night. I felt bad leaving you alone but saw you talking to another boy...the one with light brown hair."

"Ah, yes. Heidon." Thinking of yet another one of our parents' uncovered secrets sobers my mood. "My cousin."

"Cousin?" She raises a brow.

"Yes. *First* cousin. Two of them. An aunt and a grandfather."

"Wait." She counts on her fingers, trying to figure out how that's possible.

"I am not a Delphia. My mother lay with a serv, whose father and sister happen to be here. An odd coincidence. Fate? Destiny? A sick joke bestowed upon me by the gods? Who knows? Surely, I do not."

"Whoa. Go Sescily. Like mother, like daughter, I guess." She tries not to smile, biting her lips firmly together.

I give her a playful nudge. "Stop that! I just found out my life is a lie, and you're making jokes!"

"Well, the upside is that you thought your family was dead...but you actually have a whole other family...possibly one that treats you like their own, perhaps?"

"I can always count on you to find the brighter side." I shake my head.

A knock interrupts our schoolgirl laughter.

"Come in!" Audrina calls.

The door creaks open, revealing a fully dressed and ready for the day DeLuca.

"I made breakfast." He smiles. "It's ready whenever you are."

I smile and thank him as he closes the door.

Audrina pretends to swoon. "Oh my gods...he cooks too?"

We make our way downstairs after we've gotten ourselves ready to greet whatever this day offers us. On the table, DeLuca set out plates full of eggs and smoked ham with bread that he toasted in the oven. The center of the table holds a vase full of wildflowers he must've gone out and picked while we were upstairs. I smile at the thoughtfulness. He's still in the kitchen washing the pans he used.

"You're going to have to teach me how to cook someday."

He smirks over his shoulder. "I'll teach you anything you want, baby. All you have to do is ask."

Audrina mouths, *'baby?'* with a raised brow. I answer with a shrug. The smile that has been glued to my face turns into a frown as I realize there are only two place settings.

"Are you not joining us?" I ask him.

He turns off the water and wipes his hands on a towel draped over his shoulder.

"Not this morning. I have to go meet with Priestess Alis. I'll be back in a few hours though...or you can come meet me there, and we can talk about your dream last night?"

I shudder thinking about the discussion of what my dream could mean. Maybe I should go meet with my *grandfather* instead. He can probably help me understand it more than Priestess Alis.

"No, that's okay. I have somewhere else I need to be," I say after a moment in thought.

He nods, plucking a flower from the vase. He sticks the small white flower behind my ear and kisses the top of my head, letting his lips linger near my ear. "Until later then, *Aislinn Theodora.*"

I've *never* liked my name as much as I do right now. He says a polite goodbye to Audrina as he walks out the door.

"Okay, you're right, we *have* to take him when we leave," Audrina says with a mouthful of eggs.

"Maybe we should stay." I watch through the window as he strolls down the cobblestone path.

She drops her fork.

"Aislinn, no, we talked about this. I am leaving."

"But what if we didn't. We could be happy here, away from everyone and everything. Our own place in Katova. I kind of like it here. Sure, the people are a bit quirky...but they're better than the majority of highborns I've met."

"No. I want to go back to Sutton. I have to see my mother. My people. They're probably worried about me."

"Maybe we can send them a message. What about Dover?"

"What about him?! I just met him. I can't leave everyone I know about for a boy I just met!"

"You don't understand. I just found out I'm not who I thought I was, that no one is who I thought they were. I have questions, and the answers are all here in Caeliss. We are Children. This is where we belong."

"I don't belong in a crater nestled deep in the middle of the woods. I belong by my mother's side in Sutton."

"I thought you didn't want the responsibility?"

"That was before." She looks away.

"Before what?"

"Before I witnessed the slaughter of someone from each high house in all of Stellera." I see something in Audrina I've never seen before. Fear. Her amber eyes flicker as the ghosts from the manor haunt her mind.

I gently put a hand on her arm.

"Everyone was so focused on the family *we* lost, no one checked on you, how you're doing. Do you want to talk about it?"

She shakes her head, a single tear sliding down her cheek.

"No. I just want to go home."

TWENTY-ONE
CHILD OF MOON AND SHADOW

Audrina said she needed to go relieve some stress...with Dover...and headed out after we finished breakfast. I gave my friend an extra tight hug as she left. I had no idea how much pain she had been carrying. I was too wrapped up in everything that had been happening to me. I'd never considered how surviving the massacre at the manor impacted her. Seeing all that death. Being so afraid. She was supposed to have gone back to Astoria Academy after the wedding. Her whole life is just as upside down as mine...and I'd never considered her. I've been a bad friend. A selfish one. To all my friends. Especially Rett. I've been so wrapped up in solving mysteries that have nothing to do with me and in DeLuca and his...DeLuca-ness.

My gods, that man is delicious. I could wrap myself in him for eternity and forget the realm around me.

No, focus, Aislinn.

I shake my head, trying to focus, and continue down the path, trying to hunt down my new family of Isoots...Seers. I don't know. All the Old Daeil words are starting to confuse me.

While I follow the cobblestones, it occurs to me I don't actually know which of these identical houses winding around the village my new family members call their own—or where they spend their days. I'm walking blindly, just praying to any gods listening I'll run into one of them.

The gods are gracious today.

Across the meadows, I see wild brown curls whipping in a flurry of wind on a small body. *Hadleigh*.

She's playing in a field of wildflowers with that *Gale* girl. The blonde one I saw with DeLuca. A pit forms in my stomach as I remember the genuine smile he wore. Her slight blush. The way she touched his arm while telling him some kind of story. The way her golden locks bounced as she walked away with him. I swallow a mouthful of bile and the memory makes me want to turn away.

Hadleigh's giggles bring me back to task. The Gale girl is floating flowers around my tiny cousin. They tickle her as they brush against her skin. I take a calming breath and force a smile before striding towards them.

I smile and ignore my feelings towards the ray of sunshine, focusing my efforts on the small girl who I feel a deep connection to already. "Good morning, Hadleigh,"

They stop whatever game they're playing.

Hadleigh's eyes brighten, and her smile stretches wide across her small face. "Hi, Aislinn!"

The blonde grins. It's annoyingly radiant with perfect teeth behind pouty rose bud lips. "Good morning, Aislinn! I've heard so much about you already! I feel like we already know each other! My name is Cassandra. Everyone here calls me Cass. I'm a Gale"—She gestures to Hadleigh,—"and this one's cousin on her father's side."

Even her voice is irritatingly beautiful. She has deep brown eyes with little flecks of gold that are only made brighter by her flowing gold hair glowing under the sun. I'm decidedly not a fan of Cassandra.

"Aislinn, also her cousin, mom's side," I mumble. The green in my eyes has surely deepened.

"Ah! That makes us almost-cousins!" She pulls me into a forced embrace. Of course, she smells amazing. My arms just hang loose at my side, and my face turns into one that amuses Hadleigh, judging by her expression.

I clear my throat and try to hide the contempt from my voice. "I was wondering if Hadleigh could show me where her family...our family, I guess...where they live. I had a vision last night and could use some help untangling it."

"A vision! Lucky. I've not had any since I found you." Hadleigh frowns and kicks a small patch of flowers in front of her. I don't have the heart to tell her she is truly the lucky one. "Was it a good one?" she asks hopefully.

"It was not." A little light turns out in her eyes that cracks my heart. "But, sometimes, I dream of the gods. Those are pretty cool. I saw Astoria once."

Her eyes brighten again, and she grabs my hand...and to my dismay, Cassandra's. The latter offers me a heartfelt smile as though we've always been the best of friends.

Hadleigh drags us through the cobblestone paths. Their small home is located three rows down from mine. Given the way the rows of houses are formed into a maze, I'm sure I never would have come across it without Hadleigh's help. The entire way, she and Cassandra point at homes, telling me who lives in it and what ability they possess.

My mind begins to wander, tuning out the pair entirely as I reminisce on last night's vision. There was something about that man—the man DeLuca believes to be Pierce—that didn't seem entirely human. Aside from his cruelty and the wicked look he wore with pride, his eyes glowed in a familiar way that I can't quite place. It could have been part of the nightmare. They're not always exact. It could have been an omen. There are so many possibilities. I pray to all gods who will hear me that Demetrius can help me decipher it.

"Mama! Grandpapa! I've brought Aislinn." Hadleigh calls as she opens the door. The house is a copy of my own inside as well as out, though there's more evidence of life lived. Quilts are thrown across the top of the sofas. Handmade placemats are set on the small table. There is a basket of hand-carved toys I take to be Hadleigh's resting in a corner of the sitting room. It actually feels like a home. What I always imagined a home would feel like, or rather, what it *should* feel like.

"It's just me, Haddie. Grandpapa and Heidon went into the center," Maegora calls while coming down the stairs.

"Aislinn, darling, I'm so glad you've found your way to us." She greets me in a warm embrace and does the same to Cassandra and Hadleigh.

"You have such a lovely home." I smile.

"Mama! Aislinn had a vision. A *not good* vision."

"This is probably best left to the Isoots. I'll show myself out. I'll see you later, Aunt Maeg...Aislinn." Cassandra heads back for the door, and a wave of relief crashes over me.

"Wait for me, wait for me!" Hadleigh runs after her.

"I'll start some tea." My new aunt gestures me to their dining table.

She glides through the kitchen with ease. This is her domain, and you can tell it's where she's comfortable. I've never seen my own mother near a kitchen unless it was barking orders at servs.

As the water heats up, she comes and pulls a seat next to mine. "So, you've had a vision?" She props a hand under her chin and gives me her undivided attention.

"I have. Well, I always do, if I'm being honest. But the one last night..." I bite my lip and stare at her vibrant green eyes, remembering the hollow look in them as she lay on the cold ground. "It was here," I finally say.

The kettle behind her starts to whistle, making me jump in my chair.

"Just one second, Aislinn." She generously fills two mugs over a strainer filled with loose tea leaves. I take a deep inhale of the herbal aroma as she places one of the steaming cups in front of me.

"Tulsi, for clarity and calm. It's what I drink when I'm having a hard time sorting through a vision. So, what happened here in your vision that has you so worried?" she asks, blowing the steam from her cup.

"Everyone died," I reply grimly. "Pierce Decatur... the man who started the rebellion of so-called Liberators in Stellera, the man responsible for the murders of men, women, and children—entire family lines. He was here, standing at the top of the temple. Laughing like mad. Priestess Alis was in chains. Everyone else was dead. Your whole family. Everyone."

She places her mug gently onto the placemat. "I see. Did anything else stick out? Did you see what season it was?" If she is afraid, she doesn't let it show.

"Um, I'm not sure what season it was. There wasn't snow, but it did seem there was a chill in the air. It's hard to say. There was smoke everywhere.... His eyes, they kind of glowed." I pause while remembering something else. "And the knife that was used to test our blood suddenly appeared in my hand. A voice said 'it has to be me.'"

She nods, taking in the information I gave her. "I see why you are concerned. I will discuss this with my father and Priestess Alis. I believe we are safe here. Caeliss has been a safe haven for hundreds of years. No one has even known to look for it, and I heard that the only men chasing you were...no longer a concern."

I grimace remembering the men who attacked us in the woods. Thankfully, they all died in our place.

A bead of sweat rolls between my shoulder blades, and ice chases it down my spine.

They all died... except for the one Audrina whispered.

I must look sick because Maegora rushes to my side and immediately begins examining my face.

"What is it? What happened?" she asks frantically, looking for signs of ailment.

"Not all of them died," I say under my breath.

"What? But Alec, he watched. He said you and your friends used your abilities, that they were taken care of." There's an undeniable flash of panic in her voice.

I shake my head. "One got away. Audrina, she used her whispers. Told him he never saw us and made him leave. He did.... But Audrina's whispers are not permanent."

She sucks in her breath. "How long? How long does it last?"

"I don't know. It's not exact. But not for long. A few weeks at most."

She starts mumbling to herself and tapping the table with her nails. I can make out 'need to fortify' and 'it will take them time to find', but the rest is too soft to catch.

Maegora finally straightens. "We need to go to Priestess Alis, *today*. Please gather Audrina and meet me there right away. I need to find my father." She's already moving for the door, holding her arm out, beckoning me to follow.

A few feet away from their home, we run into Demetrius and Heidon, as though it was the will of the gods. Maegora pulls her father aside and speaks to him quietly enough to not be overheard.

"Cousin! I'm glad to see you!" Heidon smiles in blissful ignorance of the heavy energy pouring from both me and his mother. "Have you met many people yet?"

"Uhm, no, just a few. I met your cousin, Cassandra, today." My words are directed at Heidon, but my eyes remain on his mother and his...our...grandfather. A vein starts to protrude from Demetrius's forehead as concern settles in.

"Ah, Cass, I bet you hit it off. She's really friendly. Have you seen her fly yet? She can blow gusts so strong tha—"

"I don't mean to be rude, Heidon, but I need to go find my friend Audrina." I'm growing impatient with idle chatter...or maybe the mention of the enigmatic *Cass*.

"Oh, the Whisperer? I saw her and Dover not too long ago walking towards the river on the other side of Caeliss. I can show you?"

"That would actually be great."

"Maybe on the way you can tell me what's gotten Mama so on edge." He gestures to his mother.

I nod, grateful for a guide in this labyrinth to save me some time. If my vision has any truth to it, we have precious little of it.

It takes us less than twenty minutes to find Audrina and Dover. I caught Heidon up on our concerns during the walk. He's now biting the skin around his thumb, and the carefree spirit he wore at the start of our journey has quickly dulled and been replaced by an overwhelming sense of anxiety. I feel guilty for being the cause of his snuffed light. It seems no matter how much I try, I always end up bearing this darkness.

Dover is standing in the river swirling the water around him into dancing orbs while Audrina watches in awe. Though, I'm sure the look on her face has more to do with the drops of water glistening in the sunlight dripping between his naked and absurdly muscular shoulder blades.

"Audrina!" I pull her attention away from the half-naked man in the river.

She turns and glares, telling me to go with her eyes.

"We have to go to the temple, now," I say, ignoring her silent request.

"Why?"

Dover's attention falls to us. He drops the balls of water and joins the conversation, grabbing a shirt off a nearby tree branch.

"Hey, what's going on?" he asks, looking between the three of us. Dover's brows crease slightly as he notices Heidon obviously not acting like himself.

"We have to go to the temple. It's about the man in the woods that you Whispered...and a vision I had. I can explain on the way, but can we please go?"

"Okay, fine, but I'm bringing Dover." She flips her hair behind her back.

As if queued, Dover comes and puts his hand around her shoulder and outstretches the other in greeting. "That would be me, Dover, Voda."

I shake his hand. "So I've heard. I'm Aislinn, best friend. Let's go."

Audrina stares icily at me for my harsh tone. I am unapologetic.

All these people might die. And it's our fault.

We've compromised the safe haven.

I'm all but breathless once we've climbed the temple steps. A drop of sweat falls from my hairline and drips down my neck. I've kept a quick pace that the other's followed. I feel a sense of time running out and increasing worry with each minute the chance of oblivion becomes more likely.

Not again.

Pierce will not murder an entire village full of innocents. Someone has to stop him. Even if I have to do it myself.

"Gods, it's hot. Next time we should send for Priestess Alis. These temple steps are going to be the death of me." Audrina pants as we finally enter the magnificent archway leading into the silver temple.

Demetrius and Maegora are already inside near the center near Priestess Alis. Alec and DeLuca stand on either side of her. My heart jumps as a flash of memories from last night invade my head. His hands on my body. Lazy kisses as our eyes grew heavy. Falling asleep in his arms. He sees me bite my lip and gives a knowing smile. He's thinking about it too. Then he looks to Heidon and Dover and his face twists in question. I make an expression that I hope he reads as 'I'll fill you in later'.

"Greetings, Children. Maegora and Demetrius have told us to expect your arrival."

I feel the pressure of the moment. I'm not sure why but I feel like the course of Katova, will change from this one conversation. My mouth goes dry. My palms are slick with sweat. This moment is too important.

"Priestess Alis, last night I had a vision-"

"Yes, DeLuca has told me just this morning. A terrible vision to be sure," she says, interrupting me.

"It's not just the vision.... One of the men from the woods that attacked us.. Still lives."

"That's not possible. I saw it myself. You all cut them down," Alec says.

"Not all. One came before the others. I whispered him to leave. My whispers don't last more than a few weeks. Six weeks at most. When he remembers, they will come looking for us. Aislinn's vision could bear truth," Audrina explains.

Dover's hand slides into hers.

A flash of worry creeps into both Alec and Priestess Alis, but they are quick to mask their emotions well.

"I see. This must be discussed with the other elders and all of Caeliss as it affects them all. Next Worship Day we will use our time to figure out what we will do about this information." Priestess Alis says as if it's the only option.

"With all due respect, Priestess, Next Worship Day is almost a week away still. We don't know that we have that kind of time."

She arches her brow. "What would you suggest, Aislinn?"

I'm not prepared for the question. I don't have a plan. I only know *something* must be done.

"I don't have a plan. That's why we came to you. I know we don't have the time to spare. I feel it."

"If I may suggest. Perhaps, Priestess and I should look into the situation?" Demetrius asks Priestess Alis.

She looks and considers, then nods. Simultaneously, Demetrius and Priestess Alis' eyes roll white. Their bodies remain, but their minds do not.

"What are they doing?" Audrina asks, her voice shaking—betraying her unease.

"Grandpapa is searching through the ripples of time," Heidon explains.

"And Priestess Alis is likely searching for the man from the woods, or Pierce. Perhaps both. To see what they're currently planning, what they're currently doing." Alec explains. "She may be gone for some time."

After a few minutes of waiting for Demetrius and Priestess Alis to come back to our reality, Audrina interrupts the heavy silence. "I've been meaning to ask, DeLuca, what have you been doing here all these days?"

"I've been learning. Alec has shared many stories with me about the gods that I'd never heard. Stories about the first Children of Astoria. He's been helping me to understand my ability. Priestess

Alis has been trying to convince me to succeed her as Priest of Caeliss... but I do not want it. I lived my whole life in a constant battle for survival, my own and that of my family. I wouldn't know the first thing about leading. Despite what my blood says, I am not special."

"And I've been telling him he's very wrong. There's a prophecy that hails from one of my earliest books," Alec says as he browses through his shelves. "Ah, it's in here." He opens to a page. " 'Ei katalvia ul dauuk eika istaleia yviol l'too eioll'— *A child of moon and shadow will free all*. I believe the child is DeLuca."

"A prophecy?" Skepticism contorts my features into an unsavory look.

"Yes. DeLuca being an elemental, he can control fire. He can actually control all the elements. He can harvest them, manipulate them. It is quite fascinating. He is probably the strongest new god to exist since the originals were created."

DeLuca scoffs. "I might be if I ever figure out how to control it."

"Time, time is all you need." Alec rests a hand on DeLuca's shoulder.

"Time, we do not have." Demetrius comes out of his trance. He looks as though he may faint. Maegora quickly grabs a bit of cloth from a shelf in the room and asks Dover for a few drops of water on it. She begins dabbing her fathers brow with the wet cloth.

Priestess Alis comes to a few moments later.

"A war is brewing," she says eerily. "The man from the woods, I don't believe he remembers anything...yet. I did look in on Pierce. He has captured some of our people, other Children who've never found safe-haven. He calls them abominations, riles up his followers with claims of unfairness. He says it is unfair that they possess an ability that others do not. He will publicly burn them. I don't know when. They have small children, babies, families. They're locked in the dungeons beneath the palace in the Stelleran

Capital. It would appear as though it has become the base for the now massive army of Liberators Pierce has collected."

"He doesn't just have the army of Liberators. He has the army of Stellera. Most of the soldiers were common. All they needed was the smallest whisper of betrayal, and they slaughtered their generals. This war that is brewing...it's one we can not win," Demetrius says grimly. "Aislinn's vision is the same as I saw. Everyone will die if we wait. The man from the woods will have men looking through the Thickett Woods in no more than three weeks. If they should search, they will eventually find us. There are too many of them."

A silence blankets the room.

Unable to stand the heavy quiet, I finally speak up. "So, what can we do?"

"Well, we can't leave. Caeliss is far safer than venturing into the world," Priestess Alis says. "We do not have the numbers of people able and willing to fight. We are not an army. We could try to have the Illusionaries cast our city out of sight, but their illusions are finicky. They do not always work as intended."

"We can kill Pierce." A look of hatred burns in DeLuca's eyes. "Before he slaughters another village. Before he kills another innocent."

All heads turn towards DeLuca.

"How would we do that? Not all of us are essentially immortal...I don't think," Audrina says. She looks at Dover, who shakes his head no.

DeLuca doesn't hesitate. "I'll do it. I can go alone."

"To the Shadows you will!" I shout. "If you go, I go."

"Aislinn," his voice deepens and the tone has my nerves igniting. "If you go, I will only be able to focus on your safety. It will compromise the entire mission. Stay. Stay where it's safe."

"*You* are my safe place." I cross my arms.

"I'll go," Dover volunteers. Audrina's head whips around and she stares at him for a moment then at me before offering to go as well.

"We have an air-transport. It can fit ten. You will need an illusionary to help conceal it, and a Gale to help steer," Priestess Alis says. "Can you see the possibility, Demetrius?"

His eyes go blank and within a minute he's back.

"It is possible. Many variations, this seems the best course to avoid slaughter." My grandfather looks at me with sadness in his eyes. "Aislinn *needs* to go."

DeLuca rises to his feet. "Absolutely not!"

I jump up and even though he towers over me, I lift my head and look him in the eyes, "I'm going!"

He glares down at me. Fire flashes in his eyes as the rage within him builds. I stand my ground. I do not like him treating me like a useless child.

"I will be going too. My ability could be of use," Alec says while looking at his hands.

"Freezing time could definitely be useful." Audrina nods.

Alec turns to her in confusion. "Freeze time? No, no, dear Child. I'm a Sanguist."

"What is a *Sanguist*?" she asks.

"Blood. Audrina. He can manipulate someone's blood while it still flows through their veins. He can slow them down. Stop them completely. He could burst someone's organs apart with a simple look," Dover explains.

"That is the truth. It is a gift I believe no one should possess. It's why I chose to father no children. I am the last Sanguist," Alec says with repulsion in his eyes.

Priestess Alis puts a comforting hand on his back and offers an encouraging smile.

"So we have DeLuca, Alec, Dover, Aislinn, and Audrina. That's five."

"And me," Maegora adds. "Aislinn will need help with her ability from someone who knows how to use it."

"No, Mama, you have to stay with Hadleigh. I'll go. I know everything that you do," Heidon insists.

Aunt Maegora smiles sweetly at her son. "Only if you promise to take *every* precaution." He nods, and she places a kiss on his temple.

"So six. Plus we need to find our Gale and Illusionary." Priestess Alis taps her chin.

"I can ask Cass. She's as good as any Gale we've got," Heidon says.

DeLuca nods in agreement. I scowl but keep quiet.

"I'll ask Leighra. She's quite the accomplished Illusionary," Alec adds.

"Okay, let's spend the next day preparing. The sooner the better. You'll leave at sundown tomorrow and let Astoria guide you through the night." Priestess Alis claps her hands to signal our dismissal.

Priestess Alis, Alec, and Demetrius stay behind to discuss other matters when we leave the temple.

I try to go to DeLuca but he brushes me away. His eyes are still alight with the flames of anger. In the brief moment of close proximity I feel an inferno radiating off of him.

"DeLuca!" I call after him when I realize he won't slow his pace.

"Not now, Aislinn." His voice is abrasive and rattles my core.

"DeLuca, stop, don't push me away. Talk to me."

Heidon, Audrina, and Dover sidestep around us— no doubt feeling the tension rising.

He sighs in exasperation and runs his hands through his hair. "Do you want to die, Aislinn? Do you have a death wish? Why is it that whenever danger is near you run right for it?" His words are angry, but I hear that hint of fear he desperately tries to hide.

"I can't just do nothing! I am just as much a part of this as any of you!"

"Don't you understand?"

I throw my hands up, "understand what?!"

He snarls and searches for the words. When he can't find any he pulls me hard against him and takes my mouth in a claiming kiss. I lose whatever frustration I was holding and melt into his lips. The kiss turns ravenous, savage, possessive. It's exactly what he needs at this moment and I'm more than happy to let him have it.

His shoulders relax and his temperature drops. When he breaks away his face has softened. He traces my cheek with the back of his finger.

"Don't you understand that if something happened to you, I'd have to burn the whole damn realm to ash?"

TWENTY-TWO
How Unexpected

"He said that?" Audrina asks with eyes wide.

"Yup, kissed me then said if anything happened to me he'd burn the realm down. The way he said it, the look in his eyes. It was so dangerous. I think he meant it," I say while lying on Audrina's floor. We're meant to be packing for the Capital but we have nothing to pack. So we are just waiting out the clock at this point. I do want to go say goodbye to Lysette... and maybe Rett.

"I don't know if that is the hottest *or* the scariest thing I've ever heard." Audrina laughs. "I'm going to go with *hot*. I can see it now, his stupid blue eyes getting all dark and serious the way they do *every time* he's around you. Let's make sure nothing happens to you so we don't have to test him."

"Yeah, I'd rather not die this time." I let out a small laugh. "Do you think it's a mistake that I'm going? That I might just get in the way?"

"Probably. But we're going anyway. It's the only chance we have of getting back to Sutton."

"Audrina, what if he's taken Sutton already?"

She shrugs. "Then we come back."

"Why don't you ask my surprise-grandfather to look?"

"If he looks and sees that I'm planning to leave I don't want him to tell Alec. I don't want them to stop me."

"I don't know him well enough to say if he would or wouldn't. I'd like to believe in him. He's family after all."

"Well, with your track record of family that doesn't mean much."

"How rude, yet alas, how true."

"I almost want to ask Dover to go to Sutton with me... but I don't know. He's lived his entire life here.... And his family is here... but, there's something different about him... How did you know you could trust DeLuca?"

I stare at the ceiling thinking about how I had trusted him, prematurely. He had already been working with Pierce... as a spy, but I'd trusted him. I would have told him anything he'd asked. I let out a long dramatic sigh. "I trusted him when I shouldn't have. I'm not sure why, but he always made me feel safe. Probably because I've been dreaming about him my whole life. Ever since I was little. There has always been a darkness lingering in my mind, but each time he appeared in my nightmares, my visions, he chased away that darkness."

"Is that true, baby?" DeLuca says, leaning against the doorway.

"Were you eavesdropping? Very unbecoming of you, DeLuca." Audrina huffs.

"I wasn't eavesdropping. It's a small house. I just came up to go to my room." He gestures to the staircase just behind him. "Have you dreamt of me your whole life, Ailie?"

My heart pounds and a blush creeps up my neck. "I think so. It's your eyes. It's like I've always known them."

His expression changes to a boyish smile, exposing the softness in his heart. I feel myself melting into the floor I lay on. He definitely has too much hold over me. Not that I care. He can hold me for eternity.

"I was just going to try to find Lysette and Rett. Do you want to join me?" I ask.

The softness in his face instantly hardens at the mention of *Rett*.

"I think that's best left to you. I was going to meet up with *Cass*. She's been trying to help me manipulate the wind. So far I can only do small whisps. I need as much practice as I can get, and Dover actually said he'd help me connect to the water as well."

"Ooh, I'm going to go with DeLuca." Audrina straightens and looks much more enthusiastic then she had moments ago.

"Cass huh?" My voice grows sharp.

"Yeah, she's a great teacher. I'm glad she's coming. I think she will be really helpful."

"Oh, you're glad Cass is going. But I'll just get in the way. Okay." I feel my green eyes flare.

DeLuca looks to Audrina for an answer to explain my sudden outburst.

She laughs and shrugs. "You're on your own."

"I'm just going to go find *Rett*. Have fun with your *lesson*." I brush past him in the doorway. He calls my name but I block out his voice. I know I'm acting childish. He really probably has no idea why. The cluelessness of men, but I am sure of Cass' feelings for DeLuca. I saw it in every movement she made toward him in the hall. Hot bile returns to my throat. The jealousy I feel is consuming.

I slam the front door as punctuation to my departure.

After a few steps in the soberingly fresh air I wish I'd just stayed and talked to him. Tomorrow we are going to be flying in a contraption none of us have ever been in before, flying into a hostile nation, and assassinating the leader of a movement. We shouldn't waste time on petty jealousies.

But then I see her sunny blonde locks bouncing along the path toward *my* house, toward DeLuca, Dover in tow. The toxic bile returns. They try to say 'hello' but my gaze is fixed in front of me. If I stop, I'm afraid all the emotion inside me will explode.

Maybe I shouldn't see Rett right now...

You know what, no. I'm going.

He is my oldest friend and he will talk to me tonight whether he wants to or not. The world as we know it is in chaos and I may never see him again. I'm going.

I'll at least just say goodbye. Even if it's quick.

In the midst of the battle within my own mind I realize that I don't actually know where to find Lysette or Rett. I kick a few pebbles in front of me just willing one of them to appear like Hadleigh had when I needed to find her house. After several minutes of nothing happening except the sun setting and a cool breeze blowing my hair into a sea of tangles I decide to just walk the direction that feels right like I had in the woods when Sylvie asked me which way to go. It's an unexplainable feeling, almost as though there is an invisible rope tied around my waist and someone is pulling it to where I need to go.

I still my mind, clearing the way to follow and not lead. It's working; the invisible rope is being pulled. I'm walking to the outer edge of the village. There's a building with a large carving of a hand. Inside the hand is a spiral in the shape of a crescent moon. The sigil of Sana, God of Healing and Inner Peace.

Healers.

"Okay, interesting choice," I say under my breath to whatever mystic entity is guiding me.

Maybe I'm being led to Sylvie.

The healing quarters are not what I expected. Whenever highborns are in need of a healer they come to us. Mother said that their places of business are too dirty for us and that we were likely to get sick with something we'd not had before going. I assumed it would have been slightly musty with an old scent of blood hinting at the tragedies the walls had seen. I would've thought there'd be lines of beds to take care of the sick. Walls of concoctions to treat all sorts of ailments.

This place of healing is actually quite pleasant. Serene even. When you enter there is a soothing fountain and an herbal scent

I can't place. The walls have been painted a calming light blue. There is a desk at the front and behind it is a hallway with lines of doors on either side. The adjustment from the dusk outside to the well-lit room causes me to blink.

Once adjusted I see her behind the desk.

"Oh, Hello, Aislinn. How unexpected," Iris says with indifference.

"Iris, you're not who I expected either."

"Were you looking for Sylvie? She already left with a bag of vials to give to Alec."

"Actually, I was looking for Lysette... and Rett. What are you doing here Iris?"

"I'm training to be a midwife. I can take you to Lysette in a few minutes but Rett isn't ready to see you."

"I just want to say goodbye to them, to both of them. I'm going tomorrow. On their flying transport. It may be the last time I see them... Rett was... is... my oldest friend."

Her expression softens with pity. She slowly gets up from behind the white stone desk. My gaze is drawn to her hand that lays low over her belly. The way it's held it's... protective.

"You're pregnant." The realization hits me like a meteor dropped from the sky.

Her eyes widen but she doesn't deny it.

"How far?" I ask, feeling my chest constrict.

She looks down at her hand on her small belly. "About three months," she says quietly.

My eyes shift to the space above her head as I gather my thoughts. "That's why your parent's really gave him the ivlodeas. I never thought that part of their story made sense."

"I had nothing to do with that!" She gets defensive.

"I know. But your parents probably didn't want you to be with a married man's child. The scandal it would bring, even if you weren't titled... especially because you weren't titled. You'd never have any decent marriage prospects. That's why Mikail would risk betraying Lord Magnus, to protect his daughter." I sigh. "Did Rett know? Was he just going to marry me while your belly grew with his bastard?"

"He didn't know until we got here. My mother told me to keep it a secret. She was afraid we'd be thrown to the streets or sent back to Rousse. Mikail was loyal to Lord Magnus but Lyrica was always suspicious of my parents. She sensed they were hiding something. Turns out she was right I guess."

I nod as the pieces fall together. "Well, I hope I make it back to meet her."

"Her?" Iris asks.

"Just a suspicion. But I've never been wrong."

A smile sits on the bow of her lips.

"Emberlin. If you're right her name will be Emberlin. Our ember of light after all the dark that has led us here."

"It's beautiful, as I'm sure she will be. Despite everything, I am truly happy for you and Rett. That you are able to be together and raise your daughter together. I know it was supposed to be me and him, but the love I share for him is the same love I'd share for a brother. Substantial but not at all romantic."

"He's said the same about you... I've loved him from the moment I met him." She loses herself in thought.

I reach for her but she recoils with a flash of fear. So I step back and out of her space, "look Iris, I'm sorry for how I acted at the manor... so hot and cold with you. It was probably confusing."

She lets out a laugh, "I expected you to be much worse if I'm being honest. Don't hate me for saying this but I wish you *were* a bitch. It would have made ruining your life so much easier."

"You didn't ruin anything Iris. I promise. Will you help me say goodbye to him, ask him to give me a chance to?"

Iris nods her head. "I will try."

I follow her out onto the now dark cobblestone path. There is an abundance of flora ruling over the front yard and vines creeping along the walls. Flowers of every color bloom throughout the entire yard. I smile at Lysette's progress.

"She's been busy." I nod at their foliage.

"Lysette has gotten very good at controlling her ability in such a short time. I think she focuses all her emotion into it. All the memories of—" she shudders, "that night."

"How different everything is now."

Iris gives a bleak smile and pushes open her door.

Rett is already rushing towards her beaming with pride at the future mother of his child. His face sours when he sees me.

"Maybe you should wait out here." Iris gives an apologetic look before sliding into the house, leaving me outside.

With a sigh I sit on the half wall serving as a border between houses. I can hear the faint tone of a raised male voice but not at all what they're saying. Probably for the best. The front door creaks open and Lysette comes bouncing out.

"Hey, Ailie! *I* for one am very happy you've come to visit," she says, shooting a dirty look towards her house.

"I'm leaving tomorrow. On the transport, one that flies," I say quickly.

"I know. Word travels quickly in these small villages. It's the most interesting thing to happen here... ever... supposedly."

I look down and bite the inner corner of my cheek. My brows furrow.

"What's wrong?"

"We're going to assassinate Pierce."

Her mouth hangs open.

"I had a vision, either he goes... or everyone in Caeliss does... maybe the whole continent of Katova. Who knows when he'd ever stop. The people blindly follow him. They think of him as a savior. He has already started rounding up people with abilities... He thinks it's unfair they have them and others don't. Men, women, children, babies... no one is safe from him. DeLuca volunteered to go alone... so naturally, I have to go with him." I shrug.

She closes her mouth, gets lost in thought for only a moment, and nods. Her one good eye sparkles with mischief. "What time do we leave?"

"We?"

"Yes. We. That son of a bitch killed my twin." Rage flickers over her features.

"Are you sure?"

"Haile yes I'm sure! I can't think of a better way to honor my sister... my family... my home. Let's watch him bleed."

I've never seen Lysette so passionate about anything. The entire air around her has changed. All around us the vines start growing rapidly. They're answering her war cry.

"We leave at sundown tomorrow."

Rett never comes. He will have nothing to do with me. Now or ever. Lysette and Iris both apologized profusely. But I understand.

After everything that's happened... I understand.

So I'm walking home. The moonlight is my guide. It's peaceful. I bask in her glow while she chooses to shine on me. I feel as though I'm being recharged. Something about the night has always had that effect on me. Even the air feels more crisp with the slight chill tonight brings.

I'm lost in a moment, and then that moment is gone.

A flash of light hits me and knocks me back. When I come to, I am no longer in Caeliss.

I am again in the god's palace.

The gold one with the fountain flowing in the grand entryway.
The same melodic symphony sweeps sweetly through the air.

How did I get back here?

Chatter cuts the noise of the ethereal music coming through one of
the halls. Two men round a corner. Erebus, I recognize him from my
previous vision... and another tall man. A man who is most certainly
a god. Tall, dark, full of mystery and wonder. He only wears golden
pants that hang just below his hip bone. His muscles are cut deep and
look to be made of stone. I want to taste them. Just gazing upon him
fills me with desire. It's strong... too strong. It makes me want to claw
my own skin off.

What is this magic?

They walk through me and are unbothered. They can't see me.
This is a vision. A waking one.

"Why do you torture her this way, brother?" the half-naked god
asks.

"You know why, Cintamarri. I need her. She can't remember our
love. Not how she has been. Your influence is the closest I get. Even
if it only lasts a short while. Those precious hours are worth twenty
million shadows." Erubus sighs.

Cintamarri. God of all desires, known mainly for lust.
Half-brother to Erebus. He's said to bring people to madness just by
being in their presence, causing even the smallest cinder of want to
erupt into a roaring blaze.

"Is it not cruel though, brother? Using my influence on your wife?"
Cintamarri's words drip like honey.

"It is the only way!" Shadows explode off of Erebus like wicked
tentacles. To Cintamarri's credit he does not recoil, but rather stands
motionless with a bored expression.

Erebus calms himself before speaking again. The tentacles
dissipate as he gets hold of his mood. "I would give her what she
so desperately wants. I would give her a child if it weren't for the

prophecy of those damned Utikalos. That a child of moon and shadow will deliver freedom to all those imprisoned in the Shadows and ultimately destroy it. Without the Shadows I have nothing. If they are let out of their cage, chaos will reign. I can not let this pass. You know what it would mean— the end times."

Their voices become mumbled as if speaking below water. My ears ring as I try to tune into what they're saying. The two gods blur, like someone has pulled a veil over them. I feel a tingling sensation throughout my entire torso. I'm wrapped in a rope of shadows. It's restricting my breath. It's crushing me. Erebus floats to me, his movement unnatural, jerky. His face is inches from mine.

"And how, pray tell, did you get here, pet?" His grin is perverse.

This isn't right. He can't see me. This is a vision. He shouldn't be able to touch me. Something is very wrong.

"Well? His shadows squeeze tighter.

"I uh... can you see me?" I stutter, struggling to breath.

"Yes." He hisses.

His shadows squeeze harder, constricting my airflow completely. I'm floating above the ground. He's pulling me along behind him. I don't know where. A single tear escapes the corner of my eye. My ears are ringing so loud they feel as if they will burst.

Please gods, please let me wake up.

A light floats toward me.

His shadows screech in retreat. It's ear splitting. I drop to the ground when they lose their hold. The light flashes and blinds me.

And I'm back on the moonlit cobblestone. Surrounded by faces. It takes a minute to adjust my eyes. Alec, Priestess Alis, Demetrius, and DeLuca are all staring at me with horrified expressions. The back of my head is pounding. I place my hand on the source of my agony and rub it. There's a tender lump. My spine screams as I try to get up. The fall must've been hard. I cough as I struggle to breathe. My lungs feel as though I've been holding my breath for hours.

"Don't get up too fast," Demetrius instructs.

He places one hand on my own and his other on my back. DeLuca mirrors the action. I'm grateful for the assistance, much too dizzy to have done it myself.

"Are you hurt?" DeLuca looks like he could break at any moment. Worry completely takes hold of his features.

"It's tender. I was just enjoying the night and then I saw a flash of light. When it disappeared I was in a vision... but this vision was different... At first it was the same... But Erebus, he touched me, his shadows did. He shouldn't be able to do that." My brain threatens to splice open. I turn to the side and vomit, narrowly missing Demetrius's feet. The vomit is black.

"Erebus?" Priestess Alis sounds shocked and is looking at Alec.

DeLuca is holding me against him, sitting on the cool ground. He's rubbing the space above my ear. It's so soothing. I don't ever want to leave this spot.

"You saw a god?" Demetrius asks.

I nod. "Two. Erebus and Cintamari. Last time was Erebus, Astoria, and a hooded god I couldn't identify. Once when I was a child I saw a whole party of gods, more than I could count."

"You see gods? *In* the god's realm?" Demetrius asks.

"Yes. Don't you?"

He shakes his head no. "There's a blockade of sorts between our realm and theirs. You shouldn't have been able to get through, especially on accident..."

"When you said you saw DeLuca as a baby... I assumed you meant when he was brought here. I was so distracted by the excitement of the day... I'd never thought you'd seen through realms," Alec says.

"So what does that mean?" DeLuca asks.

"Either Aislinn is the most powerful Isoot since the first Child of her line or-" Alec stops and looks at Priestess Alis.

"Or what?!" DeLuca snaps.

"Or a god has been sending her visions," Demetrius finishes.

"Why would a god do that?" DeLuca asks.

The three look between each other with a mixture of concern and curiosity. None of them have an answer.

"I can't breathe," I mumble.

They don't hear me.

My vision starts to get spotty.

"I can't breathe." I try again, going limp.

DeLuca must feel the change in weight. He lays me flat and presses an ear to my chest.

"A healer, now!" he demands.

The others scurry off. My eyes won't open.

DeLuca stays. He's rubbing my head. He's repeating, "it's okay, Ailie, you're okay." I think he's trying to reassure himself. He leans his forehead against mine. "Stay with me, baby."

I want to stay with him. But everything is so dark and cold... I start to shiver so hard it feels like a vibration. DeLuca puts his hands under my shirt. They're so deliciously warm. I wish I could wrap myself in him. His hands move. I think he notices something. He lifts my shirt over my ribcage, careful to not expose me. He curses angrily. His fingers trace something along my ribs. I wince in pain. It's too much. It's too hard to breathe.

Everything hurts.

I succumb to the darkness.

TWENTY-THREE
TRUSTED

The way the morning light hits his face it's a wonder I'd never suspected him a god before. His eyes are closed and his breathing even but I can't begin to understand how he fell asleep sitting in the hard wood chair he'd dragged up from the dining room.

Was it all a dream?

I go to feel my head. No bump. I roll slightly. There is still pain in my ribs but my breath is no longer constricted. DeLuca's eyes open swiftly at my movement. Before I get a word out he's kneeling beside my bed. His hands clasp around one of my own.

"Ailie. Thank the gods. How do you feel? Are you okay?"

"I think so... it's all kind of... blurry. What happened?" I wince while sitting up. The tenderness of my rib cage screams in protest.

DeLuca puts his hands gently around my waist and behind my back and helps me sit fully before joining beside me on the bed.

"You had a vision. Of gods, which apparently doesn't happen to anyone else... and uh-"

"And what? What else happened?"

"When we found you... you were floating... as if being carried by something we couldn't see. I kept trying to wake you but nothing worked. Your eyes... they weren't yours. They were black. Then you started to fall. I caught you but somehow you still had a lump on your head and bruises as if you'd fallen. It was bizarre... and then you were cold so I tried to warm you... that's when I noticed it."

"Noticed what?"

"Noticed you'd been marked."

"Marked? What are you talking about?" I look all over my exposed skin. When I don't find anything I lift my shirt while walking to the standing mirror in the corner of my room. I let a gasp slip. Starting from my right shoulder and ending at my belly button a bruise spirals down my body. Or not a bruise... It's gray. Like the remnant of a shadow. I rub at it gently with a finger. Beneath my finger an icy chill erupts, spreading the entirety of the mark. It feels... hollow. Cold. Foreboding.

DeLuca watches me examine the mark. The fire in his eyes returns. Anger. I see it consuming him. The temperature rises in the room.

"W-what does it mean?" I turn around to face him.

"Erebus wants to lay claim to your shadow. He will always be watching you. Always be able to find you. You will never be safe from him... until I kill him." There's a dangerous edge in his voice.

"I'm sorry, did you just say kill Erebus? How do you plan on that? Walking into the God's Realm and giving a good tussle? You're both immortal."

"There are ways to kill immortals. Certain blades are the easiest. Aietal blades. There are very few in this realm. Luckily, one happens to be here in Caeliss and Alec has already graciously agreed to let me borrow it."

"Katalvia ul Astoria." I suck in my breath as he nods.

"The Katalvia Blade, The Child Blade."

"DeLuca, you can't challenge a god... you don't know enough of your ability yet."

"You will never be safe until he's dead, not while you wear his mark. I once told you I'd walk through a thousand miles of fire for you. It wasn't a figure of speech. I will kill Erebus and set you free of him."

He rubs his fingers over the exposed flesh along my side, carefully avoiding the shadowed places. The sensation leaves little explosions beneath his touch. I want his fingers to explore further but the look on his face tells me there's more.

"What else?"

He bites his lip. He doesn't want to tell me. "Erebus is the god of shadows... and trickery... with his mark, you might not always be able to trust what you see. He could send false visions. Both when you're awake and asleep." The air around him is impossibly hot now.

"Is that all? It's a good thing I've been having un-trustworthy visions most of my life, what luck." I smile in an attempt to alleviate some of his anger. It works; he settles a bit.

"I hope you don't think this means I'll sit out of the mission? Near death experiences are kind of becoming our thing," I kiss his cheek.

He lets out a genuine laugh, running fingers through his mess of hair. "So it would seem. There's not a chance I'm letting you out of my sight with that thing on you. Now you *have* to go." He points to the Mark of Erebus around my still exposed middle.

"Good, because there was no way I was letting you go without me." I move closer, straddling him while he sits on the edge of the bed. My weight rests on his lap. I kiss him ever so gently. In return he firmly presses me into him with one strong arm and gently tugs on my hair with the other.

His body radiates a heat that transfers to my own and I feel every nerve stand at attention wanting more. I want all of him. I pull away from our kiss and drag my lips to his ear. I kiss just below it.

He groans against my lips and carefully rolls me onto my back, doing all the work so I don't agitate my rib-pain. "You scared the shit out of me. I thought we were going to lose you and that thought was unbearable. I wasn't alive until you... *living*... but not *alive*. You stoked the flame that now burns fiercely inside of me."

"I'm not going anywhere."

The open kisses he plants on my neck cause my body to quiver. It pleads more, more. To my agitation he abruptly pulls away.

"My emotions are all over the place... I'm not sure I could give you what you deserve right now. Not to mention, your ribs." He takes my hand and kisses it as he helps me off the bed.

But I *want* his fire.

I let out a disgruntled groan. I know he's right, my body screams from the movement it takes to rise even with his help.

He smiles at my discomfort with a darkened gaze. "Unless you *really* want to?"

I sigh, "no, the moments gone."

"Probably better. We need to keep our wits about us today... and once we start, we won't be stopping." He gives a devious grin as I melt into a puddle of desire, ribs be damned.

This boy... god... man... *Rainier DeLuca* will be the death of me.

The two of us make our way down the creaking small stairwell, his hand in mine. Audrina and Dover's voices carry from in the kitchen.

"There's absolutely no way I'm wearing this," Audrina says.

"I, for one, can't wait to see it on you," Dover replies, a hint of seduction in his deep voice.

We round the corner of the small dining room to find Dover sitting at the table gazing up at Audrina with a look of utter amusement. Audrina is making a face of disgust while holding up a deep blue full bodysuit. Without taking her eyes off the suit she turns toward DeLuca and I, shaking the suit wildly at us. "Flight suits. We are *required* to wear them." Her distaste is obvious. "They brought one for each of us." She drops the one she's holding over the dining chair and picks up two others of the same color that had been folded neatly and placed on the table. A small piece of parchment lay atop each. Labeled with exquisite handwriting one reads *Aislinn* the other *DeLuca*. As she hands them to us she eyes DeLuca's ruffled black curls. Her eyes shift to the tangled mess atop my own head. Her eyebrows shoot up as she looks me up and down with a knowing smile. Heat rises to my cheeks and I quickly grab the suit from her and hold it over my body like a shield from her conjecture.

"We've also been invited to a *mandatory* farewell feast this evening before we are set to head out. We're to lay offerings for Soren for favorable skies, Felix for luck, and Agnar... in... just in case," Dover adds.

We examine the stretch of our suits, they're soft and light weight. I have no doubt they will fit our bodies like a second pair of skin. Thinking about DeLuca wearing something so form fitting brings back the heat I had only moments ago cooled. "I don't think they're so bad." I smile slightly. My face feels hot. He nudges me gently with his elbow and has a wicked gleam in his eye. His nudge brings me to focus.

A farewell feast. *Soren, Felix, and... Agnar.*

The last one strikes a note of fear.

Soren. Astoria's most favored brother, God of Storms and Skies. Makes sense because we will be flying.

Felix. God of Luck. Also makes sense. We could use all the luck we can get.

Agnar. God of the Hunt... and War. In case we fail.

After taking what could very well be my last shower, I stand naked and alone before the mirror once more. My finger trails the spaces between the Mark of Erebus on my ribs. The soft skin between the swirl of gray still feels like me. But where I'm marked is hard and cold, like stone. When my fingers slightly brush against it I feel as if all the happiness in the world has been sucked away. All the desire. All the light. All the warmth. It's a hopeless endless void. A flash of memory impedes my mind. Erebus had me wrapped in shadows. He'd seen me in *my* vision. And he could touch me. Is that how I was marked? It begs the question of how... and why? My ears ring as I try to search within my memories of visions for answers. Nothing. I have no answers. *Stupid fragments of time.*

I kick the wall in front of me out of frustration. Of course all that accomplishes is a sore toe, but it felt like a good idea at the moment. I blow out a heavy sigh and slide on a robe. These questions need to be answered, but they can wait until after we commit a murder.

A loud repetitive rap strikes the wood of the door.

"If you're done, others have been waiting! In case you forgot we only have *one* bathroom." Audrina's annoyance cuts clearly through the door. I open it immediately and she falls forward slightly as if she'd been leaning against it.

"Finally." She pushes past me.

"You could've asked nicely." I stick my tongue out to her.

"I could've, but we both know that's not my style." She gives a fake smile that wrinkles her nose and scrunches her eyes as she slams the door in my face.

"She's in a mood."

I turn to find DeLuca leaning against the frame of his door, already dressed in his dark blue suit. Now that it's on I notice silver stars dusting across his broad shoulders. The sleeves end tightly in the middle of his bicep so the cut in the muscle is still visible. My eyes drift down noticing how the fabric hugs *every* indent of him. He tracks my gaze and then shifts his to the belt around my robe. A lazy half smile forms and I wonder what titillating thoughts he might be thinking. Judging by the electricity in his eyes, it's similar to thoughts I'm having. I take a step toward him. Heat is radiating off his body. He takes a step closer, closing the remaining distance but not daring to touch me, waiting for my next move. I smile sweetly as he looks down at my mouth. His breathing grows harder in anticipation. I pull him down to me by the back of his neck and plant a hungry kiss on his lips, just enough to make him want more, before walking away.

I reach my door and say, "she's always in a bad mood," before shutting it, hoping I've left him just as on edge as he'd left me earlier.

As I pull the suit out of the drawer I catch a glisten. Opening the drawer further, I pull out my once silver now deep-ruddy-crimson gown that is still folded neatly where I left it. I run a finger along the trail of diamonds, feeling the little pricks of the claps along the way. A scrap of bloodied fabric lay tangled in one of the clasps. I pluck the embroidered fabric. The piece of my veil I had torn to tie my hair back. An unbearable sadness washes over me like a sobering rain. Truly the only piece of my family I have left. Our relationship was... strained, sure. But they were my family. Another glisten catches my eyes... The necklace. The black diamonds Lyrica gave to me just moments before she died. My face feels like fire. The burn isn't from tears. It's anger. I'm angry. The inferno of fury stirring within me is directed at one person. *Pierce.*

I slide the suit over my body, wincing a little at the pain in my ribs. As expected it fits perfectly and leaves little to the imagination. It's surprisingly comfortable, and the fabric breathes well, almost as if I'm not wearing anything at all.

The same dusting of stars that is on DeLuca's suit glides along my collar and shoulders though my sleeves go down to my wrists instead of ending at my bicep. I give an extra pull on the laces of the boots and braid my hair. My fingers moving swiftly to tame the wet strands into their secured place. Once finished, I take the scrap of fabric from my veil and tie it around my bicep before grabbing the necklace as a reminder of why we are doing what we are.

I'm ready, Pierce.

"Ready for war I see." Audrina salutes me when I arrive downstairs. She is dressed in her suit with her hair tied back, prepared for whatever may come. "DeLuca and Dover went to try to work on his water skills some more. They're going to meet us at the feast."

I feel a rush of disappointment. I'd been secretly hoping DeLuca would be down here waiting for me.

Audrina notices the turn of my face. "Wow, I didn't realize my company was *so* terrible."

I give an apologetic smile. "It's not that, I just-"

"Wanted your lover-boy to look upon you in an eternal yearning?" She bats her lashes teasingly.

"When you put it that way it makes me feel ridiculous."

"That's because it is ridiculous. You're losing yourself."

"Maybe I'm finding myself."

She shrugs her shoulders. "Time will tell. Are you ready?"

I exhale. "I'm ready."

For all of it.

We walk together to the feast, again located below the temple. On our walk I notice flowers, ribbons, and candles dripping around some of the statues of gods. There are four but I can't make them out from this far away. If I had to guess I'd say they are Soren, Felix, Agnar, and perhaps our Mother Goddess, Astoria.

"They're really going big with the offerings today," I say, nodding my head to the closest of the statues.

Audrina follows my movement and smiles. "Praise be the gods. We need all the help we can get, especially from them."

I hear the music from the hall just ahead of us. The light flickers as bodies dance in front of it. Laughter fills the air as well as the savory scent from whatever grand meal they have prepared. Above all the dancing and merriment I make out the figures of Alec and Sylvie. His arm is around her and her head rests on his shoulder. What short lived happiness they've shared. How hard it must be for them. To have only found each other just to say goodbye soon after. I pray the goddess Edwissa will reunite them, in this life or the next.

"Come on slowpoke." Audrina grabs my hand and together we are running mad like the carefree girls we once were. A smile quirks up my lips as a fast tune starts. Audrina pulls me straight into the center dance floor and spins me around. As I spin out I bow toward her, mocking a gentlemanly gesture. She grabs my hand at once and puts it around her waist, taking my other hand in her own. We twirl about in this manner for a few moments, but our uncontainable laughter makes it impossible to focus on our steps. We must be quite the spectacle. Those around us give a grand applause for our benefit when our dance has finished and we take our bows.

Someone taps my shoulder. "May I have the next?" My spine straightens. Demetrius holds out a proper hand. I nod and accept.

"I wanted to speak with you before you left... especially after last night." His tone is serious and low.

A shudder shoots through my Mark of Erebus.

"Well it would appear as though this is the perfect chance to do so." I swallow down the unease.

"With gods, nothing can ever be trusted; nothing will ever be exactly what you think. The gods can be wonderful. They can also be cruel. Their moods change as swiftly as a mortal's, but when a mortal's mood shifts it doesn't end civilization."

"Well, that's rather cryptic, *Grandfather*."

I catch him off guard by calling him Grandfather. He looks at our feet as they stride around the room, hiding a look of pride with a hint of sadness.

The energy between us feels unspoken, as if he wants to tell me something but can't, or isn't sure how to. He sighs. It's as if he is deciding against whatever he truly wanted to say. "Someday, I'd like to get to know you... and tell you about my son and the family we have." his eyes turn from emerald into a foggy jade as unfallen tears invade. "Live long enough for me to tell you. Come back to us." He squeezes my hand and leaves me on the floor, confused with a patch of ice behind my neck.

I move through the slew of dancers to the refreshment table. There is an array of drinks set out, adorned with fruit or sprigs of herbs. I chose one that is mostly clear. It has a slight green hue and a mint leaf floating at the top. It is delectable. The drink is crisp with the slightest tang. There is a freshness to it that slides down my throat like a cool mountain breeze. I finish it and grab another, before making my way to the other side of the table where the food is laid out.

As I go to grab a plate my elbow knocks into someone. My new drink splashes over my legs. To my surprise the fabric doesn't appear wet in the slightest.

I curiously examine the dry material until interrupted by a sultry voice blowing against my ear, "we have to stop meeting like this."

I know it's him before I turn. A smile forms but I quickly conceal it with a mask of frustration.

"Why must you insist on always spilling my drinks? This makes... three I believe?"

DeLuca's smile is warm. "Four, if you count the knocked over cart."

"Right, four times. tsk tsk." I lift my nose in the air.

"If we're being honest, you've always been the one doing the spilling. I'm just always there to clean it up." He grabs my glass and kisses my temple. "I'll get you another. You finish making your plate. They've sat us all together at the head table." He nods toward the long table at the back of the room.

I stack my plate with a little of everything. Meats, cheeses, fresh fruit from the garden, warm breads. I don't know what my next meal will look like but I doubt it will be anything like this so I plan on overindulging in every bit of it.

I'm carrying a roll in my mouth heading to the table. Audrina is sitting on an end with Dover. Lysette is beside them wearing a suit that matches ours. There's an empty chair beside Lysette and I head for it. The dinner roll is still secured between my teeth as I set my plate on the table. It isn't until I sit down that I hear the honey-sweet laugh belonging to a certain golden-haired Gale. She is wearing the same blue flight suit as everyone else at the table but somehow looks *so much* better in it.

Two chairs down Cass is talking with Heidon and a girl who has shoulder length auburn hair, maybe the illusionary... Layla... or Lila maybe, something like that. They are in the midst of conversation when they spot me and say hello with the widest smiles I have ever seen. I swiftly remove the dinner roll from my mouth and curse the gods for this moment. I nod a friendly hello and DeLuca, drinks in hand, settles himself in the seat between me... and Cass. I mutter a few more curses under my breath before grabbing my drink and promptly chugging it down.

"Easy there. I've been told the altitude change in flying could get you drunk faster," Lysette warns.

"Well, it's a good thing we're not flying yet." I grin.

"Suit yourself." She shrugs and turns back to the conversation she is having with Audrina and Dover.

DeLuca casually slides a hand to my thigh. The thin fabric can't hide the feel of his callouses. I can't help myself from imagining them all over my bare skin. He leans in and whispers low enough that only I can hear, "I like your suit."

He watches the blush creep into my cheeks with satisfaction and rubs small circles with his thumb on my inner thigh.

Sweet merciful goddesses.

That tiny motion is enough to send me over the edge. My breath starts to get a little more rugged and DeLuca presses a smile between his lips.

Alec clears his throat, interrupting whatever moment we were having. "Good afternoon people of Caeliss. There has been much chatter about what we are about to do. I'm here to tell you it is not pretty, but what we are doing is for the protection of everyone here, and the Children of Astoria who are not here. For anyone who is different. And—" Alec's eyes travel to me and my friends, "for those who have already lost so much, lost everything. We go to cut the head of the serpent. We're going after the man in charge so that all the death and destruction in our sister nation of Stellera will halt. We fight for the future. We've already offered our lanterns to Soren and hung chimes for him. We've offered Felix our clovers and herbs. And now, in case our mission fails, in case tomorrow brings war, we will make an offering to Agnar!" A thunderous applause waves through the room.

Wondering what we will offer to a god of hunt and war, I continue piling delicious food into my mouth. DeLuca squeezes my leg, hard.

"Ouch." I stare bitterly at him.

"You might not want to watch," he says under his breath.

"Watch wha-" My eyes shift to the center of the floor and prickle with tears. I quietly gasp. "No, they wouldn't."

With a blade in hand, Priestess Alis brings a large buck before us. "Oh God of War, Agnar! We call upon you, that should we befall battle. We will be victorious in our strides! Bless us mighty Agnar, in return for this gift of offering." As she utters the last words her hand glides the blade across the creature's throat so swiftly I barely see the blade at all. Neither does the buck, who I'm sure is kept calm by a Eikvidalis. The blood pools around Priestess Alis and the poor beast she offered falls limp to the ground. The puddle grows as the blood pours from the slash across the buck's neck. It just keeps going, growing closer and closer to where we sit. Priestess Alis dips a hand into the blood and smears it across her face like war paint. My eyes widen. The food I was chewing falls out as my mouth hangs wide.

Everything threatens to come back up again.

"I'll be back." I get up and move quickly to the opening of the hall.

All I can focus on is not vomiting.

Just keep it in Aislinn. Don't make a scene. Few more steps until you're out.

I collide head on with a large figure in a deep blue jumpsuit.

"Oh, I'm so sorry...." My eyes lift to the figure I bumped into. A new wave of nausea hits me.

Not him. Please, gods anyone else.

"Hey, Ailie-cat."

TWENTY-FOUR
SILVER HILLS

"You can't come."

"It's not up to you." Rett crosses his arms with a deep scowl upon his face.

"You have a *baby* coming." I lower my voice. "You can't leave them. We don't even know if we will make it back. It's not a risk you can take."

"If you think I'm going to let my *sisters* go on a mission like this alone after losing my entire family you're insane. Not to mention I'd love nothing more than to enact revenge on the man responsible."

"Sisters?"

"You and Lysette."

"...me?"

It was only yesterday he wouldn't speak to me. Now suddenly I am his sister?

"Yes. *You.* I may be mad at you. Maybe irreparably angry. I may never trust you again. It doesn't mean I want you to die. You are, and will always be, my family."

"That's the sweetest thing you've ever said to me. I wish you would've said it yesterday instead of springing it on me at the last minute." I roll my eyes.

"Yeah, well, I didn't know what was happening yesterday. I was also stationed near the Capital when I was serving. I know the layout. You'll need my information. Again I remind you, *it's not up to you.*"

"Is there a problem?" I hear DeLuca's deep voice from behind me. He's looking from my face to Rett's and back, obviously sensing the strenuous conversation.

"No," we both grumble, our gazes locked in battle.

"Come on you two, put it away for the time being." Lysette's sweet voice cuts through the tension.

DeLuca places a gentle hand on my upper arm to calm me.

"Fine." I turn on my heels. "But I don't think *mortals* should go." I throw the word out like an insult before heading back inside and taking my place at the table. The blood on the floor is no longer of any concern. I have a feeling I'll be seeing a lot more of it soon.

We've properly feasted and made offerings. We've said our goodbyes and packed the supplies. Priestess Alis is leading the ten of us away from the village, all in matching flight suits as if it were some kind of battle uniform. We are brought to the farest eastern side of Caeliss, near the cliffs where the water flows down and journeys back to the ocean. A statue of the sea goddess, Oonaugh, stands over eight feet tall and faces outward, as if to keep the tides at bay and watch over the lands.

We come upon the very edge of the rocks creating the protective crater around Caeliss. A statue of Soren stands guard here. Priestess Alis says a quick prayer to him before she walks directly into the rock wall and disappears.

"*Nothing is ever as it seems.*" Alec grins and follows.

Heidon, Cass, Leighra, and Dover follow without hesitation, used to the games and illusions played in Caeliss. The rest of us look at each other with skepticism when we hear Heidon's voice call to us from beyond the rock wall. "Come on guys, you can't be afraid of a little wall after what you've been through!"

Rett's jaw clenches at the mocking tone. He grabs Lysette's arm and they head through the wall.

"Well, we can't just stand around here." Audrina follows.

I reach for DeLuca's hand. He gives me an assured squeeze as we walk toward the wall. I hold my breath waiting to feel myself smash against the hard stone, exhaling in relief only when I realize I'm not walking into a wall, but a cavern. The wall is further back than it appears. On either side is a small tunnel that loops around in both directions. It is another designed illusion. Like the temple entrance.

Once I find my breath it again escapes me. My eyes fall to the enormous contraption hidden within the spacious cavern. It has an elongated dome made mostly of a metal so dark it could pass for black but in certain light has a purplish-blue sheen. There is a line of glass that encapsulates the entire circumference. The top of it has ship-like sails that match the color of the metal. It reminds me somewhat of a large whale ready to swallow us whole. As if the sky-ship has read my mind the half that faces us opens and lowers, providing a ramp for us to walk up.

"This is where I bid you farewell and good luck. We shall make offerings in your honor until your return." Priestess Alis bows to us. She and Alec place their hands on each other's shoulders as the two old friends part ways.

Our party steadily climbs aboard the strange transport. At the front are two oversized chairs looking out the nose. Through the front window we see the sky from an opening in the secluded cavern. Lining either side of the rounded walls sit eight more oversized chairs, four on each side, identical to the ones at the front. Centered between the rows of seats rests a large oval table, intricately painted with a map of Katova. The edges are designed to look as though water is falling off into nothingness mirroring the edge of our realm.

"This is it, strap in your seats. Leighra and Cass, you'll need to be at the front to see ahead and change winds or conceal the vessel if need be. Everyone else, make yourself comfortable." Alec gestures to the seats. He then turns and pulls a lever that squeaks as the ramp closes.

The moment it shuts my heart starts to pound. I never considered what it would actually be like to fly and now that the moment is here I realize, I'm terrified.

"Breathe. I'm right here with you, baby. " DeLuca gives my hand an extra squeeze.

I silently nod and we take two seats side by side. Alec and Heidon sandwich us. Directly across sits Dover, Audrina, Lysette, and Rett. We each pull our harness over our heads and fasten it into the buckle between our legs. A symphony of clicks disrupts the eager silence draping the sky-ship.

Audrina and I make eye contact. I see fear behind her composed mask. I try to offer an encouraging smile but the tightness in my face turns it to more of a grimace.

"Don't worry everyone. Cass' great-grandfather designed this vessel many many years ago with stealth, speed, and safety in mind." Alec assures us.

"He did, it's all he talked about according to my granddad." She looks back at us with a chipper smile. When she makes eye contact with DeLuca it sends a wave of anger over me, extinguishing whatever worries I had just felt.

"Well, let's go then," I say impatiently.

She shifts her gaze to mine. "Alright, if everyones ready!" Her hands reach out and simultaneously a strong wind pushes us forward.

My fingers grasp my harness in place as the transport shakes violently. The strong wind guides us through the opening in the cavern. I shut my eyes, not wanting to watch the vessel rise above the ocean.

Deep inhales, long exhales. I repeat my focused breathing until I feel the incline straighten out. When my eyes open, the windows above and surrounding us are all full of pink and orange clouds, like little tufts of dyed cotton. We're heading toward a setting sun. I feel weightless. In front of me Lysette has a wide smile plastered from cheek to cheek. She's loving every minute of this. Rett's eyes are hard ahead.

My brows furrow and my head tilts to the side when I notice Cass' and Leighra's hands... fingers laced between fingers. Leighra's thumb is rubbing small circles on the dip of Cass's hand. I look at DeLuca who has followed my gaze with an amused smile.

He leans in and whispers, "that's Leighra. She and Cass have been together for three years."

My face turns hotter than the sun blazing in front of us.

"Together... as in?" My mortification rises at the realization.

DeLuca nods yes. His face contorts as he tries to hold back a laugh.

"You've known."

"I've known," he says smugly.

I shove him awkwardly because of the restraints. "You could've told me."

"When? Anytime she's been brought up I can't get another word in." He looks sideways at me.

"I don't know. But you could have." Feeling upset with myself for letting my imagination get the best of me. DeLuca slides his hand along my arm sending goosebumps wherever his rough palm touches. He laces his fingers between mine and brings my hand to his lips for a gentle kiss.

"There's no one else I'd rather be with. No one in this realm or any realm. You never have to worry about that, Ailie," he says quietly.

I pretend to still be mad at him and bite my involuntary smile.

"You all should get some sleep," Cass says behind her shoulder. "It will be a few hours before we get there and you'll need to be rested."

"She's right, once we land we will make camp and come up with a plan," Alec adds.

"How can anyone sleep when we're in the sky?! The actual sky! Like *we're* the gods or something!" Lysette practically squeals with delight.

"Well one god, eight semi-demi gods, and one mortal." Audrina laughs.

"It is quite exciting isn't it?" Alec nods in agreement.

"Flying yes, probably dying... not so much," Dover replies, sobering the mood.

Despite the excitement, after an hour, the lull of the winds carrying us is enough to drive the crew's eyes closed. Only Cass and Leighra remain awake, keeping each other company and sharing small giggles. The sun has disappeared entirely paving the way for the mother-moon to watch over us. Through every window it appears as though we are sailing through an ocean made of stars. My head lies against DeLuca's shoulder. I wrap my arm around his, holding him in his rightful place beside me. My eyes drift close and sleep overcomes me.

Something is tugging me awake.

It's still dark. The stars are still out, but there's something wrong about them, like a gray haze. The moon has disappeared altogether.

I rub my eyes sleepily. "Are we getting close?"

Around me everyone is still asleep. I fuss with my buckle and finally unclasp it, walking up to Cass and Leigha. They're asleep, heads nestled against each other. I gently shake Cass' shoulder. Her head falls back. Her eyes are open, but they're black. It looks as though smoke is flowing out. I jump back from the sight and go to wake DeLuca. He's staring at me, his eyes also black and smoking. At the same time all heads turn toward me in an unnaturally fast manner with black-smoking eyes. The shadows seep out as their bodies slink, void of life. They slither along the floor and join together as one, forming the shape of a man. He bends in jerky motions, limbs in positions no man could ever recreate. He skitters toward me. I step back as far as I can until my back is flush against the wall. The shadow-man is so close I feel its endless abyss.

It reaches its hollow face close to mine. "I'm coming for you, pet." The ice-cold breath freezes my nose and cheeks. The man of shadow disappears while everyone aboard the transport starts chanting. He's coming. He's coming. He's coming." in unison over and over.

Frosty breath clouds from my lips as I gasp awake. I'm still shaking. My Mark of Erebus feels like it's been turned to ice, constricting around me like a coiling snake. Around the cabin everyone else is still asleep, with the exception of Cass and Leighra.

"Are you okay back there?" Leighra calls.

"I'm f-f-fine." I stutter the lie through chattering teeth.

"Are you sure? You're shaking up a storm. These suits were designed to hold in your body heat." She looks at me with concern.

"Just a nightmare." *Just a nightmare.* I tell myself the lie to try and calm my nerves but after everything, I know it's more.

Our voices wake DeLuca who's now staring at me with a fierce apprehensiveness.

"You don't look fine." He searches my eyes.

I shake my head, "I'm not. I had another dream about Erebus... I think." I keep my voice low so as to not worry or wake the others.

He sucks in an angry breath. "Tell me."

"It wasn't like a vision... I don't know what to call it. I've never had one like this before. We weren't anywhere else. We were still right here, but everyone was wrong. There were shadows... and a voice kept saying 'he's coming' over and over... it was so cold. When I woke up my mark was as cold as ice." I look down at the place where my mark is beneath my flight suit. My heart stops— my buckle is undone. DeLuca notices too.

"Why did you unclasp it?" he asks

"I didn't... Well, I did... in my dream..."

"In your dream?" Heidon pops his eyes open with keen interest.

"Yes. In my dream I went to check on Cass and Leighra; they'd fallen asleep."

"We did fall asleep, accidentally. Only for a few minutes though. It happened all of a sudden. We didn't even realize we were tired," Leighra says, looking at Cass in confusion.

"Right, we were completely awake one minute and out cold the next," Cass agrees. "We'd only just woken up a few minutes before we heard Aislinn rustling around."

"I don't like this." DeLuca grinds his teeth.

"I don't either." I lean into him.

"You don't think he's reaching out through her visions, into our realm? Is that possible, a bridge like that?" Heidon asks a now very awake and tentatively listening Alec.

He's searching through a sack for something. Its contents clink around like glass. "It is a possibility. With the mark a great deal is possible. There is much we don't know of the connections between realms. It may be best to take this until we learn more." He pulls out a familiar vial full of red liquid.

"You want to stop my visions?" *and render me utterly useless.*

"Just for now, we don't know what Erebus wants with you and if you don't have visions. I don't believe he will be able to access your mind... or get to those around you. It's just for now. We should all say a prayer to Raza to watch over your dreams."

DeLuca was right, I should have stayed in Caeliss, out of the way.

"We're almost to The Hills of Illyria," Cass calls.

"Now is the time to hide our vessel. Leighra, if you will?" Alec says.

Leighra's eyes roll back, turning white and milky.

"The Hills of Illyria? That's still in Dailotta, isn't it? I thought we were going to The Capital?" I ask.

"The Hills of Illyria are just north of the border to The Capital. East of The Capital is too much open land. South is Thalia then Vallae and the rivers which are currently occupied by the Liberators. West is Fort Vicanti, home to the rebelled army. Our best bet is to cross through the hills and pass through the river that runs under the border wall. There are grates throughout to allow the water to pass. It shouldn't be hard to get through." Rett explains as if it were the obvious plan.

"Okay, we're going down. Everyone, hold on," Cass says. The lull of the wind grows softer. We're dropping quickly. I re-clip my buckle and say a quick prayer to Soren. Cass pulls a lever and the sails above us fan out. She guides a gust through the fabric which directs us forward in smooth motion. Another wind forms below the belly of the aircraft allowing its descent to slow and gently float to the ground below.

Replacing stars and a night sky are hills of all shapes and sizes covered in trees. Cass steers us through them with ease. The Hopea trees are unique to this area. Nothing would look exceptional about them if it weren't for the silver blooms that appear at night. It's where The Hills of Illyria get their nickname from, the Silver Hills. As we glide through them they look like tiny mirrors reflecting the night's sky above. It's beautifully breathtaking.

The transport comes to a halt.

"We should take no chances. We leave immediately," Rett says, walking to the table and fingering the painted map.

"Shouldn't we take the day to scout it first? To learn the lay of the land and the movements of the people... Try to, I don't know, find Pierce first?" DeLuca says with a brazen edge.

"We don't know how much time we have. Every minute can be another life gone." Rett matches his tone.

"You were in the army; you should know better than anyone else here you need a plan of attack and to do that you have to gather information." DeLuca is now standing inches from Rett. Both their chests are puffed in a show of dominance that reminds me of two animals fighting over territory.

"Not all of us are accustomed to spying." Rett's tone is designed as an insult.

"We should vote," Lysette says.

"Okay. We vote." Rett glares at DeLuca. "Show of hands for going to The Capital tonight."

Lysette, Heidon, and Dover raise their hands.

DeLuca has a smug smile. "It looks like we are waiting."

"Okay, *Captain DeLuca*, since this is your team now, what is your master plan?" Rett has the enthusiasm of someone who has been asked to slash their own throat.

"We should send a small team into the Capital. Track movements, defenses, see if we can't find where Pierce is. Return after the day and come up with a movement from there." I raise my hand, afraid to get in between whatever is going on between DeLuca and Rett. DeLuca smiles sweetly at me, a drastic change in behavior. "Yes, Ailie?"

"Shouldn't the air transport be kept close... whenever we go in... in case we have to leave suddenly?"

DeLuca taps his hands on the map. "Rett, how many miles are we from the wall?"

"Somewhere between ten and twelve."

DeLuca traces his fingers along painted lines on the table. "Cass and Leighra, you should stay with the transport. We will come up with a time that you will meet us east of the city on the Stellera side of the border. You will need to keep it hidden. It will be out in the open. Can you do that, Leighra?"

"I can, but only for an hour at most," Leighra says. Her eyes have returned to normal.

"We will have to be sure we make it then," DeLuca says, biting the corner of his lip.

"Who's going tonight to scout?" Audrina asks.

"I will, and I think Rett should. We can use his mind and knowledge. Dover of course to get us through the river. I've gained some skills with water but I am nowhere close to as practiced as he is," DeLuca answers.

"You *want* me to go?" Rett can't hide his surprise.

"It isn't about *want*. It's what I believe is the best course" DeLuca hesitates and looks at me. "I think Audrina should come as well... if we run into trouble we can't leave bodies or evidence of our being there. Audrina can whisper it away."

She shrugs her shoulders as if he were sharing news on the evening weather. "That's fine with me."

"And you want me to stay..." DeLuca grimaces and nods.

He wants to bring Audrina. And not me. I can't pretend that doesn't hurt. I can't pretend it doesn't make me feel useless. It does. But I refrain from interjecting. What DeLuca said is true; it's not about *want*. I *want* to go. I *want* to be helpful. As much as I hate to admit, the most helpful thing I can do at the moment is stay out of their way. DeLuca's shoulders relax in relief as if he'd expected me to argue.

"Everyone else can stay here. Alec needs to stay. He's the best chance to protect all of you." As DeLuca says 'all of you' he only looks to me. "Heidon, you can work with Aislinn on strengthening her mind, the way your mother and grandfather have taught you. We will move out in one hour. If we aren't back by the time the moon is centered in the sky then leave us."

"We're not going to leave you." I roll my eyes. The notion is ridiculous.

DeLuca turns his eyes to Cass. "Leave us," his voice is steel.

To my horror she nods, yes.

"Okay, I suggest everyone say goodbyes and prepare as best they can." DeLuca dismisses everyone.

Alec opens the back of the air transport and I march off.

Leave them? How can we leave them? How can he even ask that of us? We are still in Dailotta. We're safe here. He's marching into danger and wants us to run and hide. I will not. I could never leave them. It's Audrina. And Rett. And DeLuca. The three most important people in my life. I kick a patch of dirt and specs of silver fly up, sparkling like something out of a fairytale.

"Hopea dust." Lysette comes up from behind me and admires the work of my frustrations.

"What?" I ask, a sharp edge in my voice.

"The silver mixed with the dirt you just kicked up, it's Hopea dust. Essentially pollen but is said to have medicinal uses, like the ability to remove poisons and toxins from a body." She puts out a hand and the silver dust separates itself from the dirt. The silver flecks fly into her open hand. Lysette pulls out a small vile and pours the dust inside.

"Just in case," she says.

"Are you upset they're leaving us behind?"

"No, why would I be? What good would either of us be if we went?"

"I know." I sigh. "I just wish that I could be useful. I hate to think of them going in alone."

"We all knew what we signed up for by coming. *All of us.* We have to get this right, Ailie, no matter the cost."

"Yeah, you're right." I unclasp the black diamond from around my neck and hand it to her. "Your mom gave this to me... the day of the... Well, the last day we saw her. I want you to have it. To have something from her."

Lysette's lip trembles and her face softens... she looks more as she did when I first arrived at the manor, save for the white eye. I hadn't noticed how she has hardened since then until this moment. I suppose we all have. Trauma will do that. She hugs me. Tightly. Barely breathing. And when she pulls away her features have hardened again.

"I'm going to say goodbye to my brother while I can. I suggest you do the same." She nods toward Rett who's fumbling around with a bag of who-knows-what near the air transport.

I start with Audrina who is sitting on a large boulder watching everyone else fumble around. "Don't work too hard," I say as I approach her.

"I never do." She flings her ponytail off her shoulder.

"Don't get hurt," I say a little quieter.

"Please, I am much too stubborn to get hurt. Not to mention I'm favored by at least one of the gods." She smiles. She's deflecting her worry. To anyone who didn't know her, she would appear calm and collected. But I do know her. The slight change in her tone. The stoic yet proud look she's using as a mask can't hide her true emotions from me. I give her a comforting hug. She melts into me, resting her head against my shoulder.

"I wish you were coming."

"Me too."

She breaks our embrace and quickly fixes her mask of indifference. "I'll be fine. Go, make your rounds."

I fondly squeeze her hand and Dover takes my place as I go to find Rett. I don't see him so I decide to trek back into the transport. The ramp is steep. I can't see into the vessel from the ground. When I reach the top Rett is lurched over studying the painted map. His face is more serious than I have ever seen him. The lines of worry root themselves into his forehead. I had wondered how anyone took him seriously in the army. Now I know. This Rett is one I don't recognize. He doesn't draw his gaze from the map. I don't know how to act. It's not easy as it once was between us. Too much has happened. Too much still lingers. Too much-

"Are you going to stare all night, or did you have something to say?" He interrupts my thoughts.

"I... uh... honestly don't know where to begin."

He stands up straight and rubs the bridge of his nose like he's warding off a headache.

"I'll start then. I don't forgive you. I probably won't ever forgive you for concealing such an important truth from me."

"Rett I-"

He puts up a hand to stop me. "*But*, if this is the last time we see each other, I don't want it to end the way it has been, the way I have been. We've all been through so much, lost so much. You are my family. And I love you."

Tears sting my eyes as I fight to withhold them. I run for Rett and wrap myself into him as if I were a child seeking comfort. I rest my head against his chest and hold my arms tightly around his waist. He hesitates only for a second before wrapping his arms around me too.

"I'm so sorry. I never should've kept that from you. I should have told you right away. You've always been there for me. I should've been there for you." The tears start falling in a steady stream and I'm thankful the fabric in our suits is water resistant so I can hide them. Rett rubs comforting circles on my back to soothe me. I'm sure he feels the shaking in my shoulders but is good enough not to comment on it.

"I'm scared."

"You should be... I am too." He pulls back to look me in the eye. A half smile forms, turning his face to that of my friend again.

"Ailie, I have something to ask of you... maybe too much to ask of you..."

"Anything, of course." I am eager to earn his full forgiveness.

"If... If I don't make it back... help Iris, with the baby... please. She doesn't have anyone. Her parents immigrated from Rousse before she was born. She has some family there. None that she knows though... only me... and our baby."

I touch his arm gently, "and she will have me."

A light of appreciation flickers in his eyes.

"Am I interrupting?" A deep voice that undeniably belongs to DeLuca calls from the opening of the plane.

"Yes." Rett's body instantly tenses beneath my hand that I only now realize is still on his arm.

"No!" I say as I quickly pull in back, a blush pooling in my cheeks.

DeLuca raises a questioning brow. "We head out in twenty. I was just coming up to tell Rett, but then I was actually going to look for you. Aislinn, can we go for a walk?"

"Of course" I nod and link my arm into DeLuca's.

Rett stares back with that same hardened look I'd found on him earlier.

"He really doesn't like me," DeLuca says. We walk between some of the Hopea trees away from the others.

"No, it appears he doesn't."

"I get it, we haven't exactly been discrete with our affection for one another." He wears a sly victorious smile.

I burst out laughing. Real doubled over uncontrollable laughter. DeLuca stares at me as if I've lost my entire mind. "Trust me, it has nothing to do with me. His dislike of you is something else entirely. Something primal."

"I don't understand, I assumed... because you were betrothed."

"Highborns don't ever get a choice in betrothals." I continue laughing. "They're usually made when we are children, or even babies! Rett and I were fortunate enough to care for each other. It was never romantic."

"But... that day in the sitting room, I saw you kissing." A flame ignites behind his eyes at the memory, and I think I see them turn a shade of green but it could be my imagination.

"Oh yes, when you not so inconspicuously crashed your cart interrupting us... He kissed me. He was seeing if it felt as it did with Iris... which it didn't... and I felt *nothing*."

DeLuca bites a smile but it doesn't conceal the relief that glosses across his face. "Nothing?"

I nod.

"All this time I thought that's why he was determined to argue with me at every turn."

I shake my head. "Men. I swear to the gods you're all clueless sometimes. No, I'm pretty sure he's resistant because he's not used to following someone else, especially someone who'd been a serv in *his* manor until said manor was annihilated by said serv's old friends."

DeLuca stops walking, he looks like he is pondering what I said. "I wouldn't trust me either."

"You'll have time to work it out on this mission together." An amusing image of the two of them trying to work side by side tugs at the corners of my mouth. The smile quickly drops as the images turn grim. "You better come back."

DeLuca raises my chin. "I told you I'd burn this realm for you. I meant it. I won't leave you. Ever. Besides, we still have this to take care of." He lightly rubs his fingers down my side.

I know he's talking about the Mark of Erebus but his touch sends a different kind of shiver through me. One that beckons him to touch me again. As if reading my thoughts he puts both hands behind my hips and pulls me into him. Our bodies lay flush against one another. My arms wrap around his neck. He leans down and brushes a soft kiss to my lips. At their touch day breaks through the trees. The silver blossoms atop quickly close at the first sight of light, leaving plumes of silver dust encapsulating us in our own sort of haven. The small flecks of sunlight reflect off the dust and glow around us, like magic. With the slow chirps of birds greeting the morning it feels as if the gods have designed this moment just for us.

I run my fingers through DeLuca's curls and part his lips with my tongue, tasting his sweet breath. His kiss hardens. The beat of his heart quickens. His fingers dig into my hips, hard, and I like it. My breath hitches and I run my nails down the length of his back. He lets out a soft groan against my mouth before tipping his head back, trying to pull away. I take the opportunity to kiss his neck. When he brings his gaze back down, his eyes have darkened with desire. Mutually shared desire. He takes a step back from me. My body already misses his warmth.

"Ailie." He breathes heavily. The want in his voice makes my toes curl.

"Luc." I smile seductively.

"We should go back."

"Oh," I say as a wave of disappointment washes over me.

"This just isn't the right place."

I nod, not wanting to look at him. I'm embarrassed and I don't want him to see it. I start walking back toward our transport. He grabs my hand, pulling me back to him.

"Someday, when the time is right, when you're ready and we're back home... in our home, or whatever home is to us, I promise you, I will give in to your every desire. I will touch you *everywhere* you wish to be touched. But not here, not in these woods. Not before we go on a mission that lives depend on. I want to be sure you're completely sure, and not just caught in a moment. I want to give you my undivided attention. There's no rush because I love you, Aislinn Theodora, now and always. That's never going to change."

I'm sure the butterflies in my belly are about to break free from how hard they're fluttering. He *loves* me. *Me.* Now that we've lived together, been together, I can't imagine a life without him in it. By my side. Forever. Whatever forever looks like between a god and an unimpressive Seer.

"I want to spend eternity with you, Luc." The words slip from my tongue like silk.

He smiles and I can see electricity dancing in his eyes. "Is that so, baby?"

"Without a single doubt. So you *have* to come back. Oh, and Luc?"

"Yes, Ailie?"

"I love you too."

With a smile that burns right into my heart he dips down and kisses me, lingering there for not nearly long enough.

When he breaks free he rests his forehead against mine. "It's time to go."

TWENTY-FIVE
DOMAIN OF MONSTERS

"I wish walking into certain doom was as exciting for the rest of us as it is for you," Audrina says as DeLuca and I return.

We look at each other and try to smother the smiles and prepare for the day ahead.

"Are you ready?" Rett asks with an edge of agitation.

DeLuca stares at me a moment longer. The sweet and playful look in his eye grows darker within seconds. He turns away. "I'm ready." He nods and looks to Dover and Audrina who nod in return.

His hand lets go of mine, my fingers reaching for as long as they're able. DeLuca walks toward Alec and gestures at me. His face is grave, protective. Surely he is threatening Alec of what will happen to him if something happens to me.

Men.

Rett hugs Lysette and goes to meet up with the quartett. I intercept him.

"Not before one last hug," I say. Before he can protest I wrap him in an embrace. "You can't leave me alone to take care of your mistress's child." I smile jokingly at him.

"I'll do my best, but at least I'll know they'll be well taken care of." He smiles and heads off.

"And me? Do I get a last hug?" Audrina dramatically sighs.

I wrap myself tightly around her. "Of course. I love you always, my sister. Give them hell and watch over these boys."

"You know I will. I love you." She squeezes me tightly.

From over her shoulder I mouth *'keep her safe'* to Dover who nods in return.

"I felt that," she says.

I kiss the top of her head. "Good."

Off they go, disappearing through the hills and trees. The most important people in my life. Walking away from me together into the domain of monsters while I sit here and imagine all the horrible ways they could die. With the visions I've had, I don't need much of an imagination.

It's been hours. The sun sits high in the sky directly overhead telling me it's mid-day. I'm thankful for the breeze that gives mild relief from the scorching heat. Every slight blow cools the sweat dripping on the back of my neck. Lysette has been practicing her control of the Hopea's. She is forcing the silver blooms on the surrounding trees to open and plume their silver dusts despite the daylight. She then swirls the dust around her and makes it rain from above. Once the dust hits the ground she places her hands in the earth and little Hopea sproutlings emerge. All around her are trees at different gestations. She's really quite talented. It's hypnotic to watch.

Inside the transport Cass and Leighra are napping, exhausted from the flight and in preparation for what we suspect will be another long night. Alec, Heidon, and I have been trying— and failing— to find some sort of control over my visions, trying to call upon simple ones like memories, to no avail.

"Clear your mind, Aislinn." Instructs Heidon. "Your thoughts are getting in the way."

"And focus on your breathing," Alec adds.

"How can I clear my mind and focus?" I am irritated from hours of practice and the blazing sun overhead. My head is fighting off a headache and I can't stop thinking of DeLuca, Rett, and Audrina. "I thought you didn't want me to have visions anymore because of my connection to Erebus?" I shoot a dirty look at Alec.

"I don't want you to have *dream* visions, ones out of your control. If you're purposely looking for them it's different. You will be in control of your own mind. Erebus shouldn't be able to reach them."

I snort. "*Shouldn't?*"

"Cousin, I know it's hard. You should've been learning this since you were Hadleigh's age. I have been and it's still difficult for me. I can't imagine how hard it has been for you. Having an untrained ability can be dangerous, most of all to you."

It's impossible to get annoyed with Heidon. He's too good, too optimistic. Watching his face fall tugs at my heart in the way a wounded small animal would.

"Okay, I'll try again," I close my eyes and try to clear my mind. *Clearing my mind. Clearing my mind. Rett's dying. No. Clearing my mind. Audrina's throat's been slashed. No. It hasn't. Clearing my mind. DeLuca's blue eyes looking back at me, void of life. No. He's fine. Clearing my mind. Clearing my mind. Clearing my-*

It's dark. I'm cold. There's nothing. Absolutely nothing. I spin around looking for any form of light. But there's nothing at all except the echo of my footsteps.

"Hello, pet." *A rough yet silky, male voice whispers against my ear. The hairs along my arm stand up and a chill rolls through my spine.*

"Who's there?!" I call out, still unable to see anything or anyone in the darkness. My mark starts to tingle. It constricts and freezes causing my teeth to chatter.

"I'm disappointed. You really don't have a guess as to who I am?" The voice sounds hurt. "You haven't been dreaming of me?" he asks, already knowing the answer.

"Erebus," I whisper. A gust of wind caused by movement disrupts my balance. I fall back but two ice cold hands splay behind my shoulder blades to steady me.

"What do you want from me?" There's a quiver in my voice.

"From you? You with such little control and no exceptional qualities? I want nothing from you. What could you have to give me? No, pet, I don't want anything from you. I simply want you."

"Me? If I have nothing exceptional about me then why?"

Icy breath blows against my face. "That is the question dear pet. Why? Why you? I am interested in finding the answer myself. What makes you special? I've been watching you. You seem so incredibly, most dully, mortal. Yet there is something. Something I recognize in you. You have something that does not belong to you." He runs an ice cold finger along my left arm tracing the back of it ever so gently. It makes me want to be sick and I pull my arm into me.

"Where are we?" I demand.

"Where are we? We are not anywhere. We are nowhere. The abyss that is the Shadows, land of the damned."

I feel the blood drain from my body and I feel weak. "The Shadows?" I whimper.

"Yes. Welcome home." I feel him smile with pride though his voice is anything but happy.

In the distance I see a small light. Holding on to any kind of hope I can muster, I run toward it, knowing the shadows can't touch it. It grows larger and larger, slightly illuminating the areas around it in a soft glow. I gasp as I see shadows moving violently away from it. Hundreds of shadows. They're afraid of the light. I feel them rushing past me. I can't stop until I get to the light. I beg my feet to carry me faster. I hear laughter behind me. Ice cold laughter.

"I'll see you soon, pet. Please, come again,"

As I reach the glowing orb, I jump for it and let it consume me. It blinds me for a moment but being blinded by the light is infinitely better than being blinded by complete darkness. At least it's something, rather than nothing.

"Aislinn!" Heidon yells as my eyes blink rapidly. My chest is rising and falling but I feel like I'm not breathing. I am lying flat on my back. Someone has placed a quilt behind my head.

Looking up I see that the sky is filled with pinks and oranges—sunset.

I steady my breath and try to rise.

"Slowly, slowly," Alec says, helping me to a seated position.

Cass, Leighra, and Lysette stare at me with worry etched deep into their soft features.

"The sun is setting," I say in confusion. "It was just midday."

"You've been out for hours. We couldn't wake you. Your eyes-" Heidon shudders. "They were gone."

"Gone? What do you mean gone?"

"They were black. Completely black, Aislinn. It was terrifying. I've never seen anything like it," Lysette says. She kneels before me examining my face as if she hasn't known it all her life.

"Where did you go?" Alec asks sternly. "What did you see?!"

I try to remember, but nothing comes.

"Nothing," I say quietly, "absolutely nothing. It's a blank place in my mind. I don't remember anything. Except for being incredibly cold. I've lost time."

A shiver spirals its way through the Mark of Erebus around my torso and on the backs of my shoulders. Confused, I wiggle out of the top of my flight suit and carefully slide my arms out to examine the tingling feeling. I hold the suit in place so as to not expose myself. Cass gasps and goes to touch something on my shoulder blade.

"No, don't!" Alec warns. "You must not form a connection!"

"A connection to what?" I ask.

"You've been marked again. This time though they appear as large handprints against your shoulder blades. Little veins of shadows fan out in all directions from the fingers. They look like wings. If wings were the very essence of darkness," Cass says with wide eyes.

"Marked again? I thought Erebus couldn't reach me in a controlled vision?"

"It must not have been controlled... and I said shouldn't not couldn't," Alec says. "It was my mistake to think training would be the solution. The best course now would be to try to suppress the visions entirely until we are able to sort all of this out."

"Fine by me." I cross my arms in front of me noticing for the first time another mark tracing the length of my left arm.

Alec turns away. A look of perplexion consumes his face.

"What?" I ask, growing more irritated by the minute.

"It just... it shouldn't be possible for him to get to you as he has. I want to know why."

The word 'why' shakes a memory that won't come to surface. It hurts to try to bring it forth so I let it go.

Cass scoffs. "Who knows *why* the gods do anything. They change the course of *our* realm on whims and mood swings."

Leighra places her arm over Cass who in turn leans into her. "Best not to anger them."

"I have an idea..." Heidon says quietly.

"Don't" Alec hisses under his breath.

"What is it?" I ask.

Alec shoots him a warning glance but Heidon inhales and continues, "It's possible that I can see whatever it is you saw... if I touch the mark."

"But he could get lost in the memory. He won't have any control because it's *your* mind and *you* don't have control. It's unsafe and there are no guarantees. Whatever it is you saw, it's not worth the risk." Alec's voice is harder than I've ever heard from him.

"I couldn't ask that of you, Heidon. What I do remember from the encounters from Erebus aren't pleasant. Any vision I've had of him isn't like the others. In fact, any vision of the gods I've had isn't like the others... they see me, communicate, even if only briefly."

"You didn't ask. I offered, and we should know what happened. His hold on you could affect all of us. We have to know what he wants."

Before I can further protest Heidon's hand is on my still exposed shoulder blade and his eyes roll white.

I go to remove his hand. Alec quickly intercepts my arm before I can. His large hands encase my small wrist and he shakes his head 'no'. "It would be *more* dangerous to stop him now."

"There *is* nothing." Heidon's voice drones. "It's very cold and there is nothing. It's too dark to see anything. I've never seen darkness like this. I hear voices. Aislinn's, I'm not sure of the others. I can't hear what they're saying. It's muffled. It's as though someone has tainted the memory. There's a flash of light... I can't hear Aislinn. Now there's nothing. There's nothing at all. There's no voices. No light. There's nothing. There's nothing. There's nothing." He repeats the words over and over again.

"Heidon! Come back, Heidon!!" I yell. I'm careful not to move my shoulder from his hand so as to not break the connection.

"There's nothing."

"Pull out, my boy! Pull out of the memory!" Alec cries.

"There's nothing."

"What can we do, Alec?" Cass kneels beside Heidon.

For the first time, Alec truly looks as though he is at a loss for words.

"There's nothing."

It's dark now. The sun has finally set but the starlight paints Alec's face and bounces off the tears rolling down his cheeks.

"Foolish boy." My head snaps to look at Heidon whose eyes are now black, and he wears a toothy smile that doesn't sit right on his face.

"Tricky, tricky, digging where he doesn't belong." Heidon's mouth moves but the voice is wrong. It is familiar, rough yet silky, and instills instant dread. "Did you miss me already, pet?" it asks.

And I know.

"Erebus," I say on a shaky inhale.

"My dear pet, you didn't have to get me a gift."

I feel nauseous, "a gift?"

All eyes fall to me.

"A new shadow for my collection. What a lovely shadow it is, so *pure*. I'll have to find you something equally as worthy."

"You can't have him."

"On the contrary, *pet*. I can have anything." Heidon's hand lifts from my shoulder and he falls back.

"No!" Alec cries out. He scoops Heidon in his arms and tips his head back examining his eyes, listening to his chest and breath. Searching for signs of life.

There are none.

His eyes are blacker than a moonless night.

His chest still, no breath, no beating.

Heidon is gone, and it's my fault.

Alec sobs, rocking him back and forth. Cass hides her face into Leighra, her shoulders shaking as she too sobs uncontrollably. Lysette falls to her knees in disbelief. I stare at the lifeless body of my newly found cousin in shock.

Warm wet tears fall down my cheeks and I let them. I don't try to hold them back. These tears have been earned. The grief and guilt are so overpowering I don't know how I will ever be able to fight through them. My head falls into my hands. Heidon had so much life. So much light. Now he's trapped in the Shadows and it's because of me. I am a harbinger of darkness. Everywhere I go I suffocate all the light, all the good. I'll never be able to face his family... our family again. They will hate me for what I've done. I hate me for all the trouble I've caused.

Something stirs deep within me. Something that has thus far lain dormant. A seething anger awakens. I feel it pulsate through the entirety of my body. Through my fingertips to my toes. Tipping my head back, I let out an angry cry that disturbs the birds around us. They fly off and I bring my head back down in time to see four figures emerge from the trees ahead.

They're back.

Once upon us, DeLuca looks at all the sullen faces, Heidon's body still being cradled by Alec, and the anger that writes itself over my features. His face contorts into one of rage that could equally match my own.

"What the fuck happened?"

TWENTY-SIX
LETS FINISH THIS

"I killed him." My angry eyes meet DeLuca's.

"You what?" His face falls, looking between me and Heidon, trying to make sense of my words.

"*I killed him.*"

"No, you didn't. Erebus did. We saw it. All of us." Leighra explains on my behalf.

"Because of me." My fist clenches at my side.

"Everyone be quiet!" Alec yells.

"Do—" I start to choke on my words. Literally. A metallic taste fills my mouth, and I can't speak. I look over at Alec and realize his hand is in a fist. He is filling my throat with my own blood. The blood drips from my mouth as I can no longer hold it in. DeLuca runs to me and holds my head, not realizing what's happening. He's frantic. Panicking. My eyes dart to Alec who has an ear to Heidon's throat. "There's movement. There's movement!" He releases his fist, and the blood stops pooling in my throat.

I spit the remainder next to me. "How dare you?!"

Alec ignores me entirely, as if he hadn't just invaded my body and choked me on my own blood. "He has a very weak blood flow. We must return his body home and keep it healthy. If we can return his shadow, we can save him."

DeLuca looks at the blood drying around my mouth to Alec's freshly unclenched fist. I see the realization hit him like a boulder.

A snarl curls his lip, and he grounds out a cold, "you." Flames rise in his eyes. The ground trembles. A gust of wind blows so strong it knocks down a nearby tree. Cass tries to fight the wind but is only able to redirect it around us so the debris doesn't come our way. DeLuca gently lets go of my head and stalks toward Alec.

He is going to kill him. There's a murderous look in his eyes. The movement, the wind. It's him. Everyone else backs away in fear of the god on a path toward vengeance. They can see just as I can that the DeLuca we know has been completely overtaken by something else.

"DeLuca!" I call out to him. "Stop. Don't do it. I'm okay. I'm fine. We don't have time for any of this." I stand on the shaking ground and try to reach him. I place my hand on his arm and immediately pull it away with a hiss. His flesh is so hot that it leaves welts on my finger tips. DeLuca snaps his head back to me and moves with inhuman speed to examine the burn on my hand. The ground stops trembling and the wind stops blowing.

"I'm so sorry, Ailie, I didn't mean to hurt you, I would never hurt you." He holds my injured hand. The anger flees his eyes in favor of remorse.

"It's...it's fine." I've never seen DeLuca use any of his abilities. I didn't realize just how strong he is. It's easy to forget that he is a god, a true god.

"I'm sorry too, Aislinn. I never resort to using my friend's blood against them. I don't know what came over me." I hear the sincerity in Alec's voice.

"Don't speak to her. You've lost any right you have to speak to her." DeLuca's tone is harsh and unforgiving while he gently rubs the blood from my face.

"Okay, everyone take a breath. It would appear none of us are quite ourselves," Lysette says warily, eyeing DeLuca.

"She's right," I say to him, drawing his attention to me and off her.

"We have to get Heidon home." Alec is carrying the nearly lifeless body toward the transport.

"We can't." Rett surprises us all.

"What do you mean we can't?" Cass scowls.

"I mean, we can't. We have to finish the mission. Otherwise, everyone we love, everyone *you* know, will die."

"We got here just in time. The man from the woods remembers," Audrina adds.

"It was easy to pass amongst them. We dressed the way they do. It wasn't hard to blend in. Their numbers are enormous and grow hourly. The bodies of the royals still rot on nooses in the front of the castle. You can smell the decay for a mile before you see them." Rett clenches his fists as he speaks. "They're preparing a team to search the Thickett Woods. They plan on using the pods below the Obsidian Mountains...from below my—the manor. To gain access. They have hounds. Dozens of them. They won't stop until we are found. They know about Audrina. The man described what happened. They want her."

"How did you find all this out?" Leighra asks, the skepticism revealed by her tone.

Dover interjects on Rett's behalf. "They're not hiding it. They're proud of their plans. They flaunt them. They rile up the people with them. Pierce parades the bodies of highborns and Children of Astoria—though he calls them *abominations*—before the people, and they cheer for it." His eyes seem haunted, as though the last twelve hours have attached themself to any happy memory and snuffed it out.

Audrina finally speaks out. "It was unbearable. They...they burned them in front of everyone...the families that they'd held in the dungeons. We thought they were going to show them as proof of the abilities...but they tied them to posts and burned them. I'll never forget the way they screamed or the smell of their flesh as it burned." Thick tears fall in monstrous waves down her face. I've never seen Audrina cry. Not once. She lets them roll down the curves of her cheeks and disappear at the neck of her flight suit.

"We have to destroy him. He's a monster," DeLuca adds.

"He will be a monster in a few days too. We don't know how long Heidon can survive this way. We have to get him to the healers," Cass says.

"We have to finish the mission. We also have to save Heidon." I draw their attention. "So, we split up. Cass and Leighra were never going into the Capital anyway. They have time to take Heidon to Caeliss and come back. The rest of us will finish the mission."

"I'm going with Heidon. I promised his mother I'd keep him safe. I failed. I need to bring him back and face her."

"Good. We only need people we trust guarding our backs." DeLuca scoffs. I place a hand on his chest to calm him, forgetting the burns and wince as they touch the fabric of his suit.

"Let me heal that for you." Alec looks to the burns with sympathy.

"You will not touch her!" DeLuca bares his teeth.

"Why don't you go for a walk and clear your head, DeLuca," I suggest, feeling his body heat rise.

For a second, I think he might argue. The way his pupils contract sends a splice of fear through me. DeLuca sucks in a breath and tightens his fist. He closes his eyes, and when he opens them, his pupils have gone back to normal. "Fine," he says, then stalks off towards the silver-blossomed trees.

Alec pulls down a long-board from the wall of the transport. He gently straps Heidon in, then grabs the bag of vials Sylvie gave him. He pulls out a familiar looking liquid, and I wince at the memory of it.

"Let's get it over with then." I hold my hand out to him.

He drops it all over the burns of my hand. It sizzles and I have to bite my lip from screaming out. I watch the skin pull itself back together and briefly think that cutting off the entire hand might be less painful. After the longest seconds of my life, it's finished, and the burns have been erased from existence.

"Here, you should keep this. Lysette knows what most of them do." He hands me the bag of vials. "Oh, and don't forget the red drops before you sleep. Every time, Aislinn, you mustn't forget."

I nod and accept the bag. "Alec, one more thing."

He raises his eyebrow.

"If you ever take control of my blood again, I won't stop DeLuca from killing you."

His eyes grow dark and sunken as the words hang in the air, and I walk out of the transport.

"Here, the medicinals. Alec said you knew what most of them were." I shove the bag at Lysette without even looking at her. She takes it and grumpily eyes me. I'm over pleasantries. I'm ready for this nightmare to be over and to start my life, safe and with DeLuca. Away from all of this.

"What's the plan?" I ask Rett.

"We go in through the river as we did before, tonight. Pierce sleeps in King Carrigan's bed. DeLuca will kill him as he sleeps. He insists you will not leave his side. Dover and Audrina will go after the man from the woods who sleeps in one of the lower levels. Lysette and I will go for his second in command. A woman named Maude."

"A woman?" The surprise catches in my voice.

He shakes his head grimly.

"*You* are going to kill a woman?"

"She's the one who makes the Oxidous bombs. She invented them. Hopefully, with her out of the picture, it will take care of the bombs...or at least drastically affect their supply," he says. His fists are clenched so tightly that his knuckles turn white.

Lysette's face goes wholly blank. "No, *I'm* going to kill a woman." Her usual melodic voice turns harsh and full of hate.

"What about after? We can't kill every person who has rebelled. They've turned the common-born Stelleran people against us."

Rett bites his lip.

"No, we can't fight them all. We can only hope that without direction they disband."

"And then what? Leave the entire nation in shambles? No governing of any kind? They'd turn savage."

"That's no longer our problem. They decided to overthrow the hierarchy; they can figure out how to survive without it."

"He's right, that's not our problem," Audrina says. "We just need to kill this psychotic bastard before he can harm any more innocents. Stellera is lost, but we can still save lives."

DeLuca emerges from the trees, sprinkled with silver dust, glowing under the stars like he belongs with them.

"We should go before we lose the night," he says, void of emotion. "Let's go talk to Cass and Leighra and make a place and time for pick up."

Rett nods and the two of them set out to find the Gale and Illusionary.

"Are you okay?" Lysette's worried hand finds my arm, and I shrug it away.

"No. None of us are."

"Fair." She looks down at her feet.

The sadness in her eyes worms through the wall of anger I've built.

"I'm sorry, Lysette. I'm not trying to be so sharp. I'm just so tired. Of all of it. Everything that's happened this summer. All the lies and betrayals. I'm tired, and I want to rest. We are so close to resting."

"Resting where? We will never be safe because of what we are." Audrina scoffs.

"Caeliss was safe until we showed up," I remind her.

"Right, *was*. Now it's been compromised. The nations are on the brink of imploding. Stellera has fallen. Who knows about the islands. It seems the only safe place may be the god's realm, but even the gods are always at each other's throats. There is no safety for us."

"I choose not to believe that," Lysette says, meeting Audrina's hard gaze.

"Well, then, you're an idiot. Or in denial. Or both."

"Stop it, Audrina," I warn.

"Or what? You'll send your attack god on me?"

"Audrina!"

"What?!"

"You are not yourself."

She leans in as if she is about to whisper something to me. I slap her face before she gets the chance. "Don't use it on me!"

"Fine. If you need me, I'll be over here throwing a knife into a tree, pretending it's Pierce."

"I have never seen her like that," I say to Lysette once Audrina is out earshot

"I think everyone's running a little hot right now. A lot of emotions are bubbling up for all of us. You heard what they saw. Can you imagine witnessing entire families being burned and being helpless to stop it?" Lysette stares in the direction of the Capital with a haunted expression.

I shudder. "No...I can't."

DeLuca and Rett are walking back together. Something has shifted in the energies between them. They seem more familiar...friendly even. My shoulders release some of the tension I hadn't realized they were carrying when I see them getting along. They're talking about something I can't hear. DeLuca nods and Rett gives a quick pat to the back of his shoulder. Rett goes to grab bags near the transport as the door lifts to close. DeLuca's energy has returned to its normal state of calm as he approaches me. He kisses my cheek and pulls my hand up to examine it. With a satisfied nod, he releases it again.

"I've never burned that hot before." The shame is apparent in the rough scratch of his voice.

"It's okay, we are all on edge." *But when the rest of us are on edge, we don't cause the ground to quake or winds that would make a storm envious.*

"You never have to be afraid of me. You know that, right?" He lifts my chin with delicate fingers and pulls my gaze to his.

"I know." And I do know. He would *never* hurt me—not intentionally.

"I have something for you." He pulls a wrapped object from his bag and hands it to me.

I unwrap the familiar blade. The moonlight glistens along the silver, causing the inscription to glow.

"Katalvia ul Astoria," I whisper.

DeLuca translates. "Child of Astoria. It's aietal and can kill gods. I want you to hold it...in case Erebus makes another appearance."

"Thank you." I stick it in my boot.

"Ailie, I—." He stops himself.

"What is it, Luc?"

He looks down. "I'm afraid."

"Of Pierce?" I touch his face and beckon him to meet my eyes.

"No, not him, of myself. My abilities have never felt so close to the surface before. Meeting you has unlocked something within me. I'm strong, Ailie. I can feel the strength rippling beneath my skin, begging to be released. It scares me because I don't know how to control it. I could've taken down all of the Silver Hills, and in the moment, I wouldn't have felt a thing. Thank the gods you were able to pull me back. Otherwise.... I don't want to think about what would have happened."

I wrap my arms around DeLuca. My head rests on his chest as his heart beats rhythmically. He rests his head on top of mine and pulls me tighter.

"I'll always be here to pull you back. I'm not afraid of you. " I say, enjoying his warmth. If I wasn't leaning against him, I might've missed his breath catch in the hollow of his throat. "and anyway, if you do end up burning, I will happily burn with you. When we are nothing more than ashes in the wind we can return to the stars together. Forever together."

"I don't know how I'd survive if I lost you, and that scares me too. I never knew how much I needed you until you fell into my life. I need you like I need air. Like I need water. Like I need fire. I love you, Aislinn Theodora, with everything that I am. Mortal or god or whatever else there is, I love you."

"I love you too, Rainier DeLuca, more than I can put into words. I am yours, completely." I plant a light kiss in the dip where his neck meets his shoulder, then breathe against his ear. "Let's finish this."

TWENTY-SEVEN
KEEP GOING

DeLuca leads us out of the hills. The six of us barely speak unless necessary. Tension and anxiety consume us while the weight of the task at hand makes each step more agonizing. We only have a few precious hours until the sun is up and no time for any detours. The silver blooms are now miles behind us. They twinkle and blend to the horizon, blurring the difference between ground and sky—creating an illusion of infinite space. It's a scene I commit to memory, and I silently vow to make a return visit once all has settled. Dover is now at the river. He parts the current to allow us to cross without getting wet but doesn't stop it completely as to not alert anyone who may be watching the waters.

We stay close together, and the waters continue to ripple in front and behind us. The reflection of the moon above sits on top of the water and gives off a glow that will make us visible to anyone looking, so we have to move quickly. The smell of wet river stones fill the air, and I find myself homesick for the rivers of Vallae and the days I spent basking in the sun and splashing in the shallows. I swallow hard at the memory and push it aside. There will be time to dwell after. As if reading my mind, Rett squeezes my shoulder, silently telling me he remembers too.

We are at the wall that separates Dailotta from Stellera. DeLuca removes a few loose poles from the brick half circle that allows water to freely move between the lands. Dover goes first to keep our path clear. Once we're all through, DeLuca places the poles where he found them and follows behind our pack. The shoreline is just ahead; we're almost out of the water.

A slow, steady hum of a transport sounds from atop the bridge. My heart pounds, and I feel faint. Dover points down, and we all quickly crouch on our knees. He pulls a layer of water over us, and we pray to Haile it's enough to stop the patrol from spotting us. Lights shine over the water. The air pocket has enough oxygen for us to breathe, but I still hold my breath in fear of making any movement. It feels like no one else is breathing either. Everyone stares blankly at one another. Small droplets of water drip from above us. They plop to the naked riverbed under our feet in a steady rhythm, like a clock counting down. The light disappears. We wait for a few more anxious minutes to be sure they're gone before Dover removes our cover. When standing again, I gasp for the air I deprived myself of.

Rett climbs out of the river first, careful not to disturb the water or make any noise. We follow him in silence. He offers his hand to help each of us climb out. Dover remains in the river until all of us have made our way to the dry land, and then he uses a wave to lift himself out of the river. Audrina smirks. "Show off."

Dover lifts his hands innocently and smiles back at her.

We find cover under some trees near the palace walls. Rett drops the bag he's been carrying and dumps it. A tumble of rags fall to the dirt. "Clothes. We grabbed some for everyone so we can blend. In case anyone is patrolling or roaming," he explains.

We dig through the clothes, trying to find some that fit. I pull out a dark gray peasant top and flowy black pants that will be easy to move around in. Not feeling a need for modesty after everything we've been through, I start to shimmy out of the skin tight flight suit. When my top is completely exposed, DeLuca's eyes quickly dart between Rett and Dover, who both turn around immediately—giving me privacy.

DeLuca is about to turn as well when something catches his eye. He pulls my left arm out and traces a line delicately from my wrist to my shoulder, careful not to go over the mark itself. A line of goosebumps follows his touch along my exposed skin. Standing behind me, he carefully sweeps my braid over my right shoulder and continues dancing his fingers up my arm and to my shoulder blades. I never want him to stop touching me. It makes the rest of the world fade away to nothing.

"Why didn't you tell me he got to you again." His voice carries a heavy sadness.

I turn around to face him, holding my suit over my breasts. "We have other things to worry about right now." I drop my suit, and like the gentle-god he is, he turns around before he can see anything more than a flash of skin. But not quick enough to hide the wicked gleam in his eyes.

As I peel the suit the rest of the way off, I silently thank the gods he's turned around. I am deeply struggling to get it off my legs and end up having to sit down and roll it off my ankles in a completely unflattering manner. Finally, I pull the cursed suit off and slide the pants on. The material is thin, but I like how they are tight at the waist and fall loose everywhere else, almost like a skirt but one that allows for maximum movement. I pull on the peasant top before turning to face the group.

Everyone is dressed in dark clothes that are easy to move around in, prepared for any range of motion we may need. The fabrics are unremarkable, and there is nothing to distinguish us between the common people of the Capital.

"This way." DeLuca leads us to an alley behind the palace. "We found a serv entrance earlier. It will be our best way to go undetected."

The door is in a dark alleyway littered with mounds of garbage that borders the castle. I try not to dwell on what the brownish-red discoloration along the stone walls could be. I'm relieved we aren't going through the front. Not because I'm afraid of being seen. Because I'm afraid to see the corpses of a family I once knew being displayed with morbid pride.

The door opens silently, no creaks. No guards. They are arrogant enough to believe themselves—*the rebels*—safe from rebellion. It's astonishing how these people were able to overthrow an entire nation on nothing but anger and numbers.

We enter a dark hallway. The sconces remain unlit, likely due to not having servs to light them. It reminds me of the halls the servs used in Obsidian Manor, when DeLuca had led me through them. It feels like a lifetime ago. There is staleness in the air and an eerie energy that I can't shake away.

"Ready?" DeLuca looks to Dover and Audrina who nod. Rett opens his pack and hands them knives. I suppose I should have known he had weapons—considering what we are here to do—but it still takes me back for a second. The pit forming in my belly as it really hits me that we are all about to kill people. I wonder if that makes us just as bad as them? There's a slight tremble in Audrina's fingers as she takes the knife offered to her. I watch her jaw clench and the breath she takes as she mentally prepares and then looks at me. We haven't spoken since our fight. I'm not sure she knows how. I shake my head and hug her. This isn't the time for grudges amongst friends.

She relaxes and lets out a long breath. "I'm sorry," she says softly.

"No need," I whisper back.

Dover grabs her hand and nods to us, leading Audrina down a different dark hallway. I try not to think about the possibilities of failure. We come to a large spiral staircase. The stairs go up at least seven floors. Each flight has a ledge and a door to access the rest of the floor. My heart starts to drum uncontrollably. There's no way to know if someone is on the other side of each door. Someone that will alert the entire palace of our presence.

I take a calming breath and try to remind myself that I am not afraid. Those words that brought such comfort a few weeks ago now feel like a lie. I move forward anyway, fighting the fear, and following closely behind DeLuca.

This is it. One last horror. I can make it through this.

We keep our footsteps feather-light and our movement slow. Once we get to the fourth floor, Lysette gives me a quick hug while Rett opens the door. I wait for the sound of guards shouting commands. There are none. I lose a relieved breath. No one is on the other side. DeLuca and I continue our ascent to the top. My legs begin to burn from the climb. But I push through.

One last horror. I can make it through this.

On the sixth floor, I pull on DeLuca's hand, silently begging him to stop.

His brows furrow. "We don't have much time."

"I know...I know...I just...." I take a deep breath, not knowing what to say. Instead, I look into his electric blue eyes that are dancing with an impending storm. I grab a fistful of his shirt into both my hands and pull him into me—clashing my mouth to his. Little sparks dance between our lips as they envelop each other. I let the taste of him wash away all the other emotions. It is only us and this moment...and one person standing in the path of our happily ever after.

This time, I'm the one to pull away. "Okay, I'm ready now."

"Are you sure?"

"Absolutely." I push all my courage to the surface.

DeLuca mouths *'stay behind me'* and lightly pushes the door on the seventh floor open. No one is there. DeLuca's shoulders relax. But I'm still uneasy. This hall is lit completely by sconces. There's nowhere to hide. We are too visible leaving us vulnerable, and I don't like it.

With quick steps, we make our way down the hallway until we reach a gold door reaching from floor to ceiling. A door fit for royalty. My jaw starts to shiver as the nerves light up throughout my body, causing my bones to go rigid. I try to breathe through them, to make them dissipate.

The sound of footsteps is almost my undoing. We freeze in place and slide flat against the wall. The footsteps grow closer. DeLuca nudges me to catch my attention. I turn to him, wide eyed with fear. He gestures to my boot where I had securely hidden the aietal blade. Already forgotten even as it digs with each step. I creep down and free it, offering it to him hilt first. He shakes his head and points to me, so I hold it close to my chest and breathe as best as I can. DeLuca reaches behind his back and pulls a rusted dagger that is tucked into his pants. He holds it up as the footsteps get closer. Each step causes my heart to stop.

The man finally emerges from the adjoining hall. He's dressed similarly to how we are, nothing to set him apart from any of the other rebels aside from a gold circle pinned to his chest.

I hold my breath as DeLuca lunges while the man's back is toward us. DeLuca covers the man's mouth and quickly pulls his dagger across the rebel's throat. I watch almost in a trance as DeLuca silently eases the man to the ground. The way DeLuca moves...like he's gliding through air. It's effortless to him. The way he slid the knife. The way he caught the man. It all happened faster than I found control over my breath. I haven't asked him much about what it was like to spy for the Liberators. Seeing him move this way makes me wonder what kind of training he had.

With the body on the ground, DeLuca turns to me with one side of his lip quirked. It drops quickly, and his eyes grow wide as he throws his still bloodied knife. I feel a piercing sting in my back that gets worse when something heavy falls upon me, toppling me over.

DeLuca is quick to get the body off of me. He pulls something from my back. I have to bite my lip to keep from screaming out. DeLuca shows me the small knife he pulled from me, the tip dripping with my blood. His fingers touch around the tender wound.

"It's not that deep. It will heal. When we find Lysette, we will have her disinfect it." He kisses above the wound with a gentleness that makes me swoon, despite just being stabbed...or maybe it is the stabbing that makes me feel faint. Either way, I lose balance and nestle into him until I find my ground again.

He kisses my head. "As much as I love holding you, baby, we have to keep moving."

I look at the bodies in the hall. The men are both middle-aged. I wonder if they had wives...or children. I feel a morsel of guilt until the sharp pain in the middle of my back reminds me they would have killed us if it hadn't been for DeLuca.

Please, Haile...Astoria...gods. Please let us make it out of here alive.

DeLuca carefully opens the door to what was formerly the king's quarters. It creaks slightly. We pause and wait to hear movement. When there isn't any, we both slide in the small opening, taking care to close the door behind us and turn the lock.

There is a window that takes up nearly the entire wall to the right of the entryway. You can see most of the scarcely lit Capital below us. Purple drapes adorn it, and gold ribbons hold them securely against the wall. The carpeting is also a deep purple, and set in the center is a large circular golden bed that is bigger than the entire top floor of my home in Caeliss. A purple canopy rises over the bed, and the drapes around it are drawn closed. We have no way of knowing what lies beyond the drapery. We just have to pray it's a sleeping tyrant.

My palms sweat as we make our way to the backside of the bed. DeLuca grabs his rusty dagger, holding it ready. I grab mine and do the same. We each grab the curtain and gently pull it.

"Hello, DeLuca." Pierce smiles viciously, sitting up straight as if expecting us.

"Pierce." DeLuca growls, his eyes alight with flames.

There's a woman in his bed as well. She's not facing us, but I know her.

I look at DeLuca with panic.

Has he noticed yet?

He hasn't. He's still focused on Pierce.

She turns to face him.

DeLuca's breath quickens. His grip on the knife loosens.

This isn't good.

"What the Haile, Val?" His voice shakes.

Valera grins with a wickedness comparable to the man sitting beside her.

"Valera has become one of my most trusted...*advisors*...in your absence, DeLuca. Though, we certainly miss you. All will be forgiven if you join us again and help locate the others. *Especially* the one who can influence with words. She sounds most interesting."

"I still think you should burn her too." Valera sneers.

"How could you?" is all DeLuca can manage.

"How could I? How could you?!" She snaps at him. "How could you betray your people for theirs?" She gestures toward me.

"She *is* my people. She is my person."

"And I am your *sister*. I practically raised you. I stayed when the others didn't. Come back to us. Forget the highborns and abominations. Come back to your *real* family."

"I am with my *real* family, Val...you have no idea. You could come with us."

"I would never, not when I'm so close to seeing this through. Not when I've finally found a smidge of happiness." She rests her head against Pierce's shoulder. It's the last straw for DeLuca. He pulls Pierce away from his sister and pushes him to the floor. DeLuca holds him in place by sticking a boot to his neck. The air grows dangerously hot, and I know he's close to losing it like he did in the woods.

DeLuca's voice shakes with anger. "Valera, I will say this *once* because you are my sister. *Run.*"

Valera rises from the bed. "And I will say this once because you're my brother. Release Pierce, or I will kill your highborn *whore*." She pulls me into her. A hidden knife jabs against my ribs, the pressure enough to make me wince but not enough to draw blood.

The Child Blade is still in my hand. My fingers tighten around the handle. I look at DeLuca. He gives the slightest nod—as if giving me permission—then looks away. Valera hisses angrily through her teeth as I slice the blade across her thigh. She backs away, leaving only a knick against my side. DeLuca rushes his sister and knocks her to the ground.

"Don't get up," he orders.

Pierce takes the opportunity to return to his feet. "Enough. Stop being ridiculous. DeLuca, come back to us. You can bring your prize. You should be with us. Your sister, she loves you. You only have each other since your siblings left."

Valera looks at her brother while stumbling to her feet. "Please, DeLuca, you belong here,"

As DeLuca walks toward his sister, I can't help but worry he may choose her, his last family member, over me.

DeLuca is looking down. Without seeing his eyes, I have no idea what he's thinking...who he will choose. My pulse quickens in the seconds that pass.

When he finally speaks, his voice is low but sends a nervous rumble to my core, "Valera...I *don't* belong here." He raises his eyes to reveal blue flames blazing. DeLuca reaches his palm out and calls forth the fire from the flaming wicks on the bedside table. A little ball of fire dances between his knuckles. "There's something you both should know about me," he says, flashing a devious smile.

Valera's eyes are wide in horror. "You're one of them? An abomination!" she shouts.

The fireball hits Pierce in the shoulder and Pierce retaliates with a shout of undignified curses.

"No, dear sister, I'm not an abomination." He gets close and grabs his sister by the throat, then turns her head and whispers in her ear, "I am a god." DeLuca throws his sister back, and she lands on the ground with a hard thud.

"Intruders!" Valera shouts.

While DeLuca's attention is to his sister and the door, Pierce attempts to sneak up behind him, dagger in hand.

No, you will not take him too.

The rage I've been storing returns, consuming and empowering. I release my fury and jump onto Pierce's back, pulling the Child Blade high over our heads to gain momentum. I bring it down with all the strength I have and plunge it repeatedly into Pierce's chest, not aiming for anything in particular but praying the wounds I inflict are fatal. With each thrust of my blade, I see the faces of loved ones I've lost and the ones I would have lost. The families he burned proudly and homes he destroyed. Orynn. Linnea. Lord Magnus. Evander. Mother. Father. Lorella. All of them.

Valera screams. Gurgles come from Pierce as he drowns on his own blood. I managed to slice open his jugular. The wound weeps into a river of red. DeLuca is too stunned to move. His sister makes for the door. "Stop her, DeLuca!" I shout.

He snaps back and lunges for his sister, sitting on her to keep her from moving. She fights him, but he is too strong.

"You bastard! We never should have taken you in! You have always been a freak! I bet Mama and Papa would still be alive if they'd never found you. You're a curse!"

"We can't let her leave," I say quietly.

She continues her profanities.

"You mean we can't let her *live*." I see his heart break as he utters the words.

"No...no... DeLuca...Luc...you wouldn't. You wouldn't right?" Valera's eyes grow wide.

"Tell me, Valera, did you aid in the capture and massacre of entire families? Of killing children?" I ask. A dark calm has flown over me.

"Why should they get to live happily with their families when I was robbed of mine!"

DeLuca's voice breaks. "Val." The hurt in the crack is enough to shatter me. It's a sound I never want to hear again.

I come up behind him and place my hands on his shoulder. "I'll do it."

He doesn't dare look at her when he gives me a slight nod.

"I'll haunt you from the Shadows." Her smile is predatory and sends a shiver down my spine.

Before she can hurl any more hurtful words at the man I love, I take the blade and slide it clean across her throat. Valera goes silent. I pull DeLuca's head into me so he doesn't look at his sister. The warmth of her blood coats my knees, and I pray DeLuca doesn't feel it.

"Let's go," I say into his hair.

He's silent.

"I thought it would be harder," DeLuca says.

I slide the blade back into my boot. "Well, I wouldn't say it was easy."

"It feels like it should've been harder. Like Pierce should have fought more." He puts a blood-covered arm around me and pulls me into him. I listen as he inhales my scent. It seems to calm him.

"He was probably just a coward. A coward whose only skill was talking louder than everyone else. I'm sorry about your sister." I turn my head up to kiss his neck.

The sconces suddenly dim, and the air chills around us. A voices hisses and says, "Well, isn't this the most romantic scene?"

The blood flowing through my veins turns to ice, in strong contrast to DeLuca who might as well burst into flames with the heat he's radiating. Pierce's head snaps backwards. His neck breaks with a bone chilling crack as it turns to look at us—blood pouring down from the stab wound deep in his throat.

"That's...not possible." DeLuca stares at the scene unfolding with his expression twisted in disbelief.

Pierce's eyes open and reveal themselves to have turned completely black. "Hello, *pet*." Pierce wears a smile too large for his face. While remaining in the same position, he lifts his arms behind him and pushes up with his legs. Everything about him is wrong. He skitters toward us as we back ourselves against the wall.

I'm going to be sick. It's so unnatural. So, so wrong.

"Pet," I say under my breath as it hits me. I harden my stance, and the anger flows rampant through my veins. "Hello, *Erebus*."

"Oh, pet. I like when you say my name with such *passion*."

"Don't speak to her!" DeLuca plunges the knife he's carrying into Pierce...Erebus...a dozen times. Each time, shadows seep out instead of blood.

"I grow tired of this game, *son*." He turns his body around to a standing position. It's full of holes, and his head is dangling to the side.

"I am no son of yours." DeLuca seethes.

"Oh, but you are, *Delun*. Your mother bares the scars to prove it"

He's baiting DeLuca. To what end? I do not know. But it is working. DeLuca seems moments away from combusting.

"Was it you all along? As Pierce?" I demand.

"Not all along. I would love to take credit for this one's corruption, but his shadow darkened long before our dealings. This mortal sold me his dark shadow—to serve me along with my other pets. He wanted what all mortals want. Power. He wanted the ability to influence. Imagine my surprise when I saw you in his company, son. Your power started to grow, unlike any child we've ever had. When you were young, I tried to crush your liveliness. Extinguishing your mortal family, accidents in mines, whispers and illusions driving your mortal mother to take her own life. It only served as fuel to your flame. A miscalculation on my part. I thought you'd be easy to break living amongst the mortals. I forget sometimes that the children I banish are *my* children. *Gods.*"

DeLuca's teeth grind, and I let go of his arm as it begins to burn.

"When I saw you at this nasty mortal's sermons I thought you'd finally been driven to a darker path...until you came to him begging for a girl's life. A girl high above your stature. A girl you should hate but claimed to care for. You claimed her as different. I've been watching. She is no different. She is the same. Mostly mortal, ruled by emotion, exceptionally unexceptional...yet, I, too, find myself drawn to her. There is something within her I'd like to explore. Something I want for myself. Soon, I will have your pet."

An icy chill wraps around my torso and spans out like wings behind my back.

I visibly shiver and Erebus turns toward me. "Do you feel me? Do you feel the caress of my shadows, pet?"

There's no holding it back now. I vomit. Everything in my stomach lands at his feet.

DeLuca bares his teeth. "Why? Why do you want her?"

Erebus wears a wicked smile. "Because I may find use for her. Not to mention, I am incredibly bored. The Realm of Gods is not what it once was, and I could use a new play-thing."

While Erebus' attention is on DeLuca, I grab the aietal blade from my boot, placing it in DeLuca's hand and stepping back. DeLuca wastes no time. He is upon the perverted body in half a second, stabbing what's left of Pierce's head in a smooth motion.

The shadows let off an ominous whine as the body deflates and sags to the ground.

I let out a breath. "Fuck."

TWENTY-EIGHT
BRED TO KILL

"I don't think I've ever heard you swear before." DeLuca frees the dagger from Pierce's skull. The blood from the wound sizzles and hisses. Using the gold sheets hanging off the bed, he wipes the blade clean.

"I'm not usually in the habit of doing so, but there weren't any other words that felt appropriate."

DeLuca has the ghost of a smile trying to break free before letting out a long exhale. He kneels before me, gently running his fingers up my leg stopping midway up my calf, lifting my leg and placing my foot upon his thigh. I cringe a little as he slides the dagger back into my boot. If I'm being honest, I would be glad to never see it again after all this. DeLuca takes this moment to breathe as he presses his forehead against my knee.

My fingers run through his hair in what I hope is comforting motions. I don't want to disturb him. I feel his exhaustion radiating in waves, but we only have a small window before sun up, and we have to get to our meeting spot before we miss Cass and Leighra with the transport.

We are so close to this being over.

"Luc," I whisper, "we have to go."

He kisses my knee before placing my foot firmly on the ground. "I know, baby. I know."

I didn't realize my hands were shaking until his warm fingers clasp around them and stilled the tremor. The body of Pierce—who is now folded in position that resembles a ragdoll tossed without care—is slumped in the corner. I watch for a second to make sure it doesn't spring to life again. Blood is seeping out from every part of him, but I still kick the lifeless sack for good measure. Erebus or not, this man was a true monster, and the realm is better off without him.

We pass Valera's body. DeLuca refuses to look. He keeps his eyes fixed at the door, but his hand tightens around mine like he's falling and I'm his only salvation. We make our way back to the serv stairwell, all too aware daylight will soon make its appearance. Our feet move quickly to carry us down the long flights that curve along the circular wall. I pause at the third floor. The door is shut tight. No sign of movement. Hesitating, I wonder if we should check to see if Rett and Lysette made it.

"They'd be downstairs waiting for us by now," DeLuca says as if reading my thoughts.

He's right. They'd be long done if everything went as planned. I try to swallow the lump in my throat and disperse the thoughts of plans gone wrong. We don't hear any commotion which tells me that no one has been caught...*unless they've been taken somewhere else...or immediately killed...or....*

I let out a sigh of relief as we set foot on the ground floor and I catch sight of four familiar faces waiting against the wall beside the stairwell. As far as I can tell, everyone has all limbs intact, though Rett is bleeding from his shoulder. The blood seeps the length of the sleeve. I can't see the wound, but he appears unbothered, and it isn't dripping, which is a good sign. Lysette, too, has been cut. Small strands of blonde hair that have escaped her ponytail are now dyed red. The bloodied strands cling to her face against a gash starting from her temple running diagonally along her cheek, barely missing her snow-white eye. Her wound drips crimson down to her neck and gathers along her collar, but it seems to be superficial, and the blood is coagulating, creating a dam against any fresh blood waiting to fall. My eyes roll over Dover and Audrina who are free of any wounds as far as I can tell. The relief hits fast and hard, making me feel lighter than I have in weeks.

We completed our tasks. We are all still alive.

"Reunions and celebrations later. We need to go to the meeting spot before anyone wakes up and realizes what happened," Rett says when he notices my lips begin to move. I close my mouth, silently agreeing with him. He leads us back down the same dark hallway we had come in through and back out the door. The sun shines in its first break of light. Clouds hovering in the distance are illuminated in glorious hues of gold and pink, meeting the dark navy sky above in a drastic contrast. We can see the twinkle of lights from the Capital just over the walls on the other side of the courtyard. I say a quick prayer to Haile to watch over the innocent that remain. The bystanders caught in the webs weaved by politicians and tyrants.

We keep our backs firmly against the wall of the castle to remain hidden from any eyes that might greet the morning from the windows above. Instead of going through the river, we follow it east and to a clearing that lay just a few miles outside of the Capital. It will be in the open but take half the time to get to rather than going back to the Silver Hills.

Thankfully, the palace sits on the border, meaning we won't have to go through the city. While we might blend in with our clothing, the blood would surely set us apart from the locals. Especially in the outer ring of the palace gates where the wealthier previously resided. All we have to do is make it to the other side of the wall without being spotted and we will have a clear shot to the river. It's easy enough. As of now, no one suspects anything is amiss. They're blissfully ignorant of our attack, but we are definitely on borrowed time. Felix has been on our side thus far, but even luck has its limits. We left bodies in the palace, bodies that will soon be discovered.

Once we reach the river, we wash away the blood on our hands and clothes as much as possible. Rett doesn't bother with his arm, but he does attempt to quickly clean Lysette's wound on her face. He clears away the old blood, only for new blood to replace it.

"It's going to need the serum," Rett says after the third attempt to clear the wound.

"No," Lysette says firmly, "I want the scar. I want the memory of retribution."

"Are you sure?" Rett asks. The hint of pride in his voice tells me he already knows she is.

"I am. It's only fitting for it to be on the side of Linnea's eye. I'll wear it with honor."

Bong.

The sound of bells carries over the palace walls and echoes throughout the land. Birds fly out from every direction, spooked at the sudden burst of sound interrupting the quiet of dawn.

"They found the bodies," DeLuca says. His voice is quiet and absolute.

Bong.

"They will continue for an hour. It's also to signal the army of what's happened. We always had a man at every mile mark in case they were rung." Rett looks to the wall as though he expects to see a dispatched battalion at any moment.

Bong.

"We will beat them to the transport," Dover says.

"We'd better go. They might send out teams to look for the assassins. We're still too close to the palace." DeLuca is watching the now distant palace windows looking for movement.

Bong.

We continue downstream the river, east.

Silently, I pray to Soren that Cass will find us in time. I pray to Haile we'll survive this day. I pray to Felix to continue our luck. I pray to them all. Except Erebus. I'd tell him to go to the Shadows, but he's already there. My marks grow cold as I think of the shadow god. Quickly, I push out any thought of him just in case it may somehow summon him.

We walk a good distance before we hear the noise we've all been dreading—rapid barking.

We freeze.

Eyes wide.

Spines chilled.

The hounds.

They released the damned hunting dogs. No doubt already tracking us.

"Run. Now," Rett orders through clenched teeth.

We remain still.

"Run, damn it!"

And we do. We run.

My legs carry me faster than they ever have before. The wall, trees, and buildings on the edge of the Capital blur together in my peripherals until all that's left is a vast unkempt field of weeds and wildflowers. The wind stings my face, bringing burning tears to my eyes. My heart thumps wildly, and my chest feels as though it will explode from a mixture of my lungs struggling to keep up with my motion and a climbing heart rate. DeLuca slows his strides so he falls to my side. His legs are considerably longer and more muscular. I know for certain he could be well ahead of us. Instead, Rett remains at the front, leading us toward the clearing that is now at last in sight thanks to our quickened pace.

Shouts accompany the bells and barking, followed by a familiar hum atop the border wall running parallel to the river.

Transports.

My heart drops.

I will my legs to move quicker. They miraculously obey, racing at a speed I never thought possible. I've never been known for my athleticism, but the adrenaline coursing through my veins makes it easy to ignore the ache in my legs.

We are fast.

The hounds are faster.

They are quickly closing the distance between us now that they've been let off their leashes. I can hear how they salivate as they grow nearer to their targets.

Where the Shadows is Cass?

We are a short distance from our meeting spot, a large clearing near the mile marker six-hundred, but the air transport isn't in sight. A panic begins to battle the adrenaline for control of my body. I'm suddenly all too aware of the aches in my feet and legs. My throat burns with thirst. I feel myself slow despite my brain screaming at my legs to keep going. DeLuca notices my loss of momentum and slows so he is behind me. He's shielding me from the dogs who are now only three long jumps from us. The hound masters struggle to stay on their tail.

"Get them," one commands.

A series of orders from the other masters follow, and the group of no less than twenty hounds charge at full speed, baring their teeth.

Without slowing pace, Rett calls back in warning. "They are bred to kill. Do *not* let them catch you."

Not today, Egon, I'm not ready.

Before my eyes, in what appears to be nothing more than an empty field, our transport shimmers into existence. It looks as though someone has pulled a veil sewn from the fabric of time to uncover it. The back hatch is open, telling me it has been here waiting all along.

Leighra is standing at the edge, waving us in, her other hand hovering over the lever, ready to shut it as soon as we are safely aboard. "Hurry! They're right behind you!" she warns.

Dover doesn't slow his stride but pushes a hand out to the side and over his head. The waves of the river swell and mimic the motion of his hand. I hear the yelps of some of the dogs as they are dragged into the water.

The hound handlers shout.

"Did you see that?"

"Abomination!"

"You will die!"

Ahead of me, Lysette's shoulders stiffen. In a violent and swift movement, she throws both hands back. A ripple shoots beneath the ground behind us, and huge roots shoot up, tripping the dogs with their handlers. A symphony of curses and yelps sound, and a proud smile tugs my lips up—Lysette is kind of a badass.

We finally reach the air transport. As I climb in, a hound lunges teeth first, sinking them into my calf. I shriek in pain. The hound is massive. He could pass for a small stallion made of pure muscle. The beady eyes attached to his large squared head stare at me with hunger as he rips into my flesh. I hit his head repeatedly trying to get him off, crying out from the searing pain. His bite breaks, and before he can get a second taste, a mix of fire and wind flies like an arrow, knocking him off the landing completely. Large hands scoop me up as I scream. A trail of my blood follows. After placing me down on the table in the center, DeLuca walks back to the opening. Dover and Audrina climb aboard, and Cass starts the winds below the belly of the vessel.

We make it in the air, but just as Leighra is about to close the hatch, DeLuca stops her. "Just a minute, Leighra." He stands dangerously close to the opening. I try to protest, but my words are drowned out by the restless winds below. We are angled at a point as the transport climbs altitude. DeLuca presses his hands firmly together and then jerks them open rapidly. The ground below the hounds and men splits in two, effectively trapping them all in a small canyon. DeLuca's eyes are frighteningly dark as he brings the ground back together, crushing them and leaving no trace of their existence. He then sends a violent wind to the border wall that knocks the transports off and into Dailotta.

"Okay, now you may pull the lever." His smile is vicious. Perhaps it should scare me. If my leg wasn't threatening to burst apart, it probably would. I scream in pain again, and bile rises from my stomach, burning the back of my throat. Not being able to hold back, I roll to the side and let go of the frothy spew on the floor beside the table.

"Lysette!" DeLuca's burning gaze flies to her as she fumbles through the bag of vials Sylvie prepared. Her hands aren't as practiced, and she has to read the tiny labels on each vial, looking for the right ingredients.

I sit up, gripping the sides of the table with both hands. Looking down at my leg nearly sends me into shock. The giant beast tore away a large chunk of muscle in my calf. I can see tendons and bone. There is so much blood. It's hard to see the true extent. Feeling faint, I fall back on my elbows. DeLuca is quickly by my side, rubbing the hair off my face.

"She's turning green. Lysette, hurry!" He yells to her, though the concern in his voice now rules over the command.

"I'm trying! Rutide. Furlious. Verticeptim. Manugolous. Found it! Parantaa!" She hurries over with the familiar serum.

The first few drops sizzle over the wound. It tries to pull itself together, but the distance between intact skin is too great. It just keeps pulling back into itself on the edge of the wound. I feel like lava is being over my opened flesh. It's agony, and I cannot bear it. My screams echo through the transport.

"It's not working!" DeLuca shouts. He's panicking, and the air around him jumps in temperature.

"It will. She just needs more."

"No!" I shout. "It's too much. Just take the leg! Take it off! It's too much, please!" I beg.

DeLuca's worried fingers continuously rub my hair back.

"The pain might be too much. She may fight the healing," Lysette says. "We have to sedate her."

"Just take it off." I cry, feeling delirium take hold.

"Do it." DeLuca nods.

"Rett, find the bottle with furlious as its main ingredient. It has a yellowish hue." Lysette gives the order to her older brother, who quickly complies.

He brings the yellowish vial to the table and hands it to Lysette. She shakes her head and points at DeLuca. He takes the vial.

"Her eyes. It goes in her eyes," Lysette says. She's breathless but remains focused on my leg.

"Well, looks like we're about to be even," Rett says as he holds my eye open for DeLuca. The liquid drops in. It's gritty like sand. I blink rapidly when Rett finally lets go of my eye lid.

"I'm here, baby, I'm here. You're safe." DeLuca repeats the words over and over again while rubbing my hair. He doesn't stop until my body finally relaxes and lets go of the fight.

I feel as if I'm floating then suddenly falling, and once I land, it's on a small island.

TWENTY-NINE
ISTALEIA VIISOLO

The shadow filmed sun hangs directly overhead, sitting mid-sky and casting a gray hue. I'm surrounded by sand and sea. The waves throw themselves around my feet violently before tumbling back to their mother ocean. This island is deserted. I am utterly alone. Fresh salty air fills my nostrils as a damp breeze combs through the wild tendrils of my hair. I sit down in the odd blackened sand and stick my hands in it. I expect it to be warm from the sun beating down, but it's cold, as cold as the snow that fell atop the Obsidian Mountains during the winters I spent there.

Strange.

Laying back, I try to relax. There is a tugging feeling in my gut that something is wrong. I can't remember. I can't remember how I ended up on this island. I can't remember anything other than this is not where I'm meant to be. It's the most infuriating thing, feeling the tip of a thought...of a memory and not able to pull it forth. My brain is fuzzy, and my ears are ringing. I go to rub an itch on my calf. My fingers slide through something warm and sticky. I pull my hand back to examine the substance. My fingers are coated red with blood. Quickly, I pull my leg up to look for the source of the blood. There's nothing there but my own smooth skin.

"What the Haile is going on?"

"Wrong god," a chilling and familiar voice answers.

I whip my head around, looking for the source. There is still no one I can see.

"Where are you?"

"I'm everywhere, dear pet." The voice comes from all around me, like it's the very air I breathe.

Pet. The word forces a memory forward. I try to grasp it, but it slips away, leaving a trail of goosebumps on my arm as it drifts off.

"Why can't I remember anything?" I whisper.

"A little experiment of my own, I suppose. It's been hard thus far to communicate with you, my pet. I wanted to see if we could talk civilly with one another." A man appears out of a burst of shadow.

He's tall...taller than any man I've ever met. I think even taller than Lord Magnus. Sturdy and strong, wearing a tight fitting suit of all deep gray. His jawline is squared and appears to be chiseled from stone. Lush full lips fall below his sharp nose. He may have been attractive if it wasn't for the look in his deep gray eyes. The look of a predator gazing hungrily at its prey. Every muscle tells me to run, but the fuzziness in my brain makes it impossible to command my own body.

"Who are you?"

"It is not of importance at the moment of who I am. I am far more interested in you, pet."

"Why?"

"Why, indeed?" He traces the back of his finger along my right arm. "I don't know what it is about you that draws me in. It has been all consuming. You may think you can't escape me, but it is I who can't escape you." The man moves his hand into my hair and brings it near his face, inhaling. The act makes my stomach turn. "Curious, you're not one of mine, but the scent is familiar."

"What are you talking about?" Rage forms beneath my skin, threatening to spill out through every pore. "How did I get here?"

"You're not here, pet. Though, I'd like you to be." He sighs. "I do wish we could stay on this island and get to know one another more. I fear it is almost time for you to wake."

"Why won't you give me any answers?" I demand.

His sharp features turn up in amusement. "I like your spirit. I shall enjoy you in my realm. You may yet prove to be entertaining"

"Your realm?" The dots start connecting in my brain. Wrong god. "A god...you're a god," I say as a fact. For once, the words pass my lips I know it to be true. Somehow, I know this god.

"Yes." His teeth flash.

A god...a terrifying god. For some reason, I can't remember any of the god's names. Curse this place and its mind games. I rack my brain for clues.

The god kneels beside me. In my ear, he whispers, "Come with me willingly. Find me, my pet, let's discover the secrets that lay beneath your skin together."

"Why would I go anywhere with you?" I ask, fighting the urge to pull my own eardrum out.

His smile deepens in a sick and twisted way that makes my teeth chatter. "Because, pet, if you don't, I will kill everyone. Starting with your so-called iseilo talewok...your safe haven."

Moving his hands up the back of my shirt, his long fingers splay along my spine. A cold and hollow feeling envelopes my abdomen and shoots around my shoulders like wings blooming. The feeling travels down the length of each of my arms. I wrap them around me and close my eyes, trying to fight the empty abyss that threatens to consume me. I breathe in ice cold air. With it, a flood of memories return.

"Erebus."

"Brava, pet. Before I go, I must make a request." He's now breathing against my neck, making my skin crawl like hundreds of spiders racing away from him. "Come to Isukis Viisoleika. I will

meet you in five days time, at Istaleia Viisolo. Dusk. I am confident you will find it, find me. Come alone, Aislinn Delphia."

He's gone. As is the island. I'm strapped to a board in the center of the transport, and I'm freezing. The high altitude causes the inside of the transport to feel like a capsule of ice. No wonder we'd been made to wear the special suits. I flex my toes, trying to return the blood circulation, and notice my calf that had been bitten by the murderous hound has been healed completely. DeLuca is standing by my side. I start to wiggle my fingers, and the small movement alerts him to my rising consciousness. He is quickly pulling off the leather straps holding me in place. DeLuca's warm hand slides behind the small of my back, a stark contrast to the cold hand that had weaseled its way to my skin just moments ago. My stomach turns at the memory.

"What is it? Are you hurt?" DeLuca asks, sensing my discomfort. He answers his own question when he notices a gray mark along my right arm that mirrors the one on the left.

"He got to you again.... How?" DeLuca slams his fist on the table beside me.

"Oh gods, I forgot," Lysette's small voice says from her seat.

"Forgot what?" DeLuca's head snaps to face her. "What did you forget, Lysette?!"

"The Rutide...the red drops she takes before sleeping. They stop the visions. She has to take them before she sleeps so he can't get to her. Everything happened so fast, and she was in so much pain...I forgot. I'm so sorry, Aislinn!"

"I'm okay, Lysette, truly. I'm fine. Thank you for whatever you did."

"We're about an hour from Caeliss still," Cass calls from the front of the transport.

I trace my fingers around the fine lines of the map painted on the table in the center of the transport.

"What are you looking for?" DeLuca's brows weave together.

I mumble, "Isukis Viisoleika."

"There's no such place," Rett responds with confidence.

Audrina argues. "Yes, there is. It's what the Islands of the Sons used to be called. It's in many of the original documents and buildings in Sutton."

"Convenient that you wanted nothing more than to go to Sutton, and now that's the place Aislinn says we *need* to go." Rett crosses his arms.

"We should go home and regroup. We need to check on Heidon. We need to see our families and let them know we succeeded," Cass says.

I look to DeLuca for backup.

"I go where Aislinn goes, and she says we're going to the Islands." His eyes are fierce and protective.

Cass gives a worried sideways glance to Leighra. "We're not supposed to take you anywhere else," she says quietly. "Alec got in trouble for splitting away from us. He was supposed to make sure none of you tried to leave. The safety of Caeliss largely depends on remaining a secret. The only reason it was allowed now was because it was under the supervision of an Elder Child, and the mission was for the safety of Caeliss. Alec made us swear to take you home and nowhere else."

"Going to the Islands of the Sons is for the safety of Caeliss too. Erebus—" I begin but am interrupted by DeLuca,

"Wait a minute, Erebus *told* you to come?"

"He did. He also said if I didn't come in five days, he'd kill everyone, starting with the safe haven...starting with Caeliss."

"I don't like it. It sounds like a trap." DeLuca chews the inside of his cheek.

"Is it worth risking all of Caeliss? I'd rather us go and finish it now. We have the aietal blade. We can make a trap of our own. I don't know why he wants me, but we can use it to our advantage.

Audrina knows those islands. We can make a plan." I try to sound more confident than I feel.

"I don't think you heard me. I can't take you anywhere but home," Cass says firmly.

Audrina unbuckles her harness and rises to her feet with a sigh.

"Sit down, Audrina." Leighra eyes her, but it is too late. Audrina is already in Cass' ear.

Her whisper is too low for us to hear, but when she pulls away, Cass says, "You know, I've been thinking we should go to the Islands of the Sons."

Leighra looks appalled, and I can tell she is about to say something, but before she can, Audrina is in her ear, and she suddenly looks much more agreeable.

"Anyone else?" Audrina asks as she walks back to her seat.

Dover looks uncomfortable but keeps his mouth shut.

"I wanted to go home, Audrina. I need to be with Iris," Rett says without hesitation.

She starts toward him, but I'm quick to intercept her.

"Don't." I stand between her and Rett. "You can't whisper your friends. It's not okay to mess with our heads like that. You've been careless with your ability. You have no idea how it affects us."

"You sound like my mother." She huffs but complies, strapping herself back in her seat.

I slightly lose balance as Cass' wind rotates us forty-five degrees to the south, toward the islands.

"I'm sorry, Rett, but if we want to keep her safe, keep everyone safe, we have to go."

His eyes are soft. "Okay, but this is it. I want to go back *immediately* after."

I sit and nod.

"Tell us about your vision." DeLuca inspects the newest addition to my mark with furious eyes.

"There wasn't much. I lost my memory in it, so when he was speaking, I had no idea who I was speaking to."

"Did you recognize where you were?" DeLuca asks.

"No, it was an island. As far as I could tell, it was isolated and uninhabited."

"Audrina?" DeLuca turns to her in question.

"There are many uninhabited islands surrounding all three main islands. It's hard to know which." She rolls her eyes toward the ceiling as if it should have been obvious.

I rack my brain, and my ears ring as I search for the memory of the vision. "Istaleia Viisolo," I say under my breath. "Istaleia Viisolo?" I ask Audrina louder.

She laughs. "Of course, he would. Istaleia Viisolo, Isle of Shadows. It gets its name for two reasons. One is because it's said to be haunted by the first people, the ones that predate any of our written histories, and two, because it only appears during the Shadow Moon when the tides change. I could see it from our house and would insist to my mother she had to take me to see it. She never did. She said no living being had any business with the Isle of Shadows."

"Comforting." DeLuca exhales, grinding his teeth.

"When's the next Shadow Moon?" I ask.

Everyone is quiet as we try to remember what day it is.

"Five days." Lysette breaks the silence.

Audrina claps her hands. "What a tricky bastard. Choosing a place we have no way of scoping beforehand."

"They don't call him the God of Shadows and *Trickery* for nothing," Dover adds.

"Soon, they won't call him anything," DeLuca promises.

The rest of the long flight to Sutton Isle is long and full of tension. No one can agree to a plan or course of action. All we know for certain is we are most definitely walking straight into a trap. DeLuca, of course, doesn't want me near Erebus at all. Rett thinks the entire thing is idiotic, walking into unfamiliar territory against a god. Dover thinks it's pointless to try and outwit a god at all but sees no alternative to luring his sight away from Caeliss. Cass and Leighra have been talking about how nice it will be to lay on the beach together and that the rest will happen as it should. I assume that has to do with whatever Audrina whispered to them. Audrina is just happy to be going home and has insisted several times she will be staying put. She's done with missions and gods. Lysette has been the only one who has had a helpful idea: to use the archive libraries in Audrina's childhood home. They should have information on the Isle of Shadows, possibly a map. They could have information on the gods as well. We plan to thoroughly scan any documents they may have. It's not a plan, but it's a step. We have five days to prepare, and I swear to the gods we will be victorious.

DeLuca stands behind me with his hands wrapped around my waist. His chin rests on my shoulder. "How are you, baby?"

I'm standing in the back of the transport, watching the moon rise from the window. Its silver glow seems darker than normal. Back here is the closest thing to privacy we get in this vessel built for ten. We've all changed back into our flight suits that Rett thankfully kept safe in his bag.

"How am I? There's a loaded question. My head is spinning. So much has happened. I can't stop and think about any of it. Otherwise, I'm afraid my brain will implode trying to process. All I can do is focus on the immediate next move. Not the past or future."

He laughs. "That must be hard for an Isoot."

I respond with a sideways smile, "And how are you, oh wonderful Elemental God of Vengeance?" I chuckle at the new title I've come up with, thinking it is befitting of the man.

"God of Vengeance, huh? I like it." I feel his smirk even though I can't see it. "I'm...it's complicated, I suppose. I am wary of the trap we are falling into and glad that Pierce is no longer a problem. I have more emotions than I can put into words about Val. Nervous about what will happen to the common-born people of Stellera now without any sort of leadership or purpose. Everything that's happened lately has been so tragic but...uhm...nevermind."

"What is it?" I turn in his arms to face him and cup my hands around the back of his neck.

"I shouldn't. It's terrible to say."

"You can say anything to me. I'd never think you to be terrible. I know your heart." I place my hand on his chest for emphasis.

He sighs and looks back at the sleeping passengers. "I don't regret anything that's happened," he quietly admits. "If none of the tragedy had happened, I'd never have grown close to you. You never would have loved me...and, Ailie, I didn't know what it was to live before you." I bite my top lip, and he runs his thumb over it. "Does that make me a monster?" he finally asks.

I shake my head. "No. I don't think anyone who's not us could understand it, but now that you're in my life, I can't imagine it any other way. I love you, Luc. With every inch of my heart and body, I love you. When you were still a serv, I would fantasize about a life without complications. About stripping my title and just being with you. It would be enough for me. A small house somewhere. I never wanted to be a highborn. I just wanted to be happy and loved."

DeLuca's soft lips brush mine, then trail my jaw. I suppress the tiny moan forming at the back of my throat. I'm aware of the other passengers aboard the transport but close to not caring.

I open my eyes in time to see a familiar sight outside the window and gasp. "Look out the window!"

He raises his head from the crook of my neck in time to see stars dancing across the sky. The windows surrounding the transport and that make up the ceiling give us a view even the gods would be envious of. Stars shooting across the night sky, thousands of them. They fall around us like a blanket of starlight.

"What is this?" he asks, his eyes alight in wonder.

"It's the Tears of Astoria." I grab his hand and kiss the back of it, then lace my fingers in through his. "I used to watch them almost every night when I lived at the academy. I always felt a connection to them somehow. Now I know why."

"It's so beautiful. I've heard of it, but there's no way for anyone to describe this and do it justice.... *My mother.*" His voice is a hushed whisper and he shakes his head in disbelief.

I lean my head into him. "She's incredible...but the greatest thing she has ever made is you. You are my favorite fallen star."

His arm wraps around me tighter, and he kisses the top of my head. "Do you think she's really crying? Every night?" The pain in his voice breaks my heart.

I want to say something comforting, but I also don't want to lie to him. He doesn't deserve that. I let out a sigh. "Yes. I do believe that."

His jaw flexes, and his eyes harden. "We have to kill Erebus. For her. For everyone."

I nod. "We do."

"Can you...tell me about her? I mean...I know the stories...Alec and Priestess Alis were very informative, but those are just stories written long ago, and who knows what has been lost to time and translation?"

His question takes me aback. How preoccupied we've been. I'm the only person in the entire world who can tell him anything definite about her, and I haven't. It's his mother. All I have shared with him was that he was ripped from her.

"You don't have to." He notices the change in my expression.

"No. No, I want to. It never occurred to me. You shouldn't have even had to ask. I'm sorry I didn't already. I don't know much more than you do. In the vision I had where you were born, she was painted silver. She wore a tiara that had a crescent moon and diamonds dripping down. She was the most beautiful woman I've ever seen. Her hair was white and glowing like moonlight. Her blue eyes were just a shade darker but just as electrifying as yours, and she had flecks of silver in them—kind of like scattered stars. Her voice was soft and hoarse, like she'd been screaming a long time"—I stop and gauge DeLuca's reaction. He smiles briefly, telling me to keep going. "—even through the hoarseness I could hear such kindness behind it. She desperately wanted to keep you. There was another god there, one I do not know and who wore a hood. It was Erebus who put chains on her. I think Erebus has her locked up like a pet." A slow realization runs like ice through my veins. Like a *pet*. He's been calling me '*pet*' all this time. "I think he wants to take me."

"Take you where?" DeLuca's hand tightens around mine as if begging me to stay with him.

"Take me to his realm, to his palace. He wants to keep me in chains like he has with Astoria."

"He can't have you." DeLuca all but growls as an animal would when fighting for their territory. The temperature in the transport rises by twenty degrees, making my flight suit unbearable.

"Some day you're going to burst straight into flames." I step back, remembering the burn I got last time he ran so hot.

"I can't make fire. Only manipulate it," he reminds me.

"For now." I shrug. "You're still fairly new to all of your abilities. You don't know what you're capable of. None of us truly do."

The temperature drops as he calms himself down. "You're right. Priestess Alis said it could take a hundred years to fully understand my abilities."

A hundred years. I don't think it has occurred to me yet that DeLuca is immortal. I swallow down the revelation and pack away that worry for a later date.

"Why do you think you get hot, like fire, when your emotions are strongest? Why do you have more of a connection to fire than the other elements?"

"I'm not really sure. Maybe because fire was the first element I connected to?"

"You split the ground with ease, it seemed." I flash back to how he caused the earth to swallow dozens of men and dogs.

"When I'm angry, it seems easier to control. When I'm angry, I just tell the element what it has to do, and it obeys. It recognizes my authority."

"Well, at least we know you'll have plenty to be angry about when you face Erebus." I smile.

"Yes, he has the full attention of my wrath now."

DeLuca and I sleep buckled in our seats for the rest of the journey to the island with our hands tightly entwined. A jerky motion causes me to jump at the sudden disturbance to my dreamless sleep.

"Sorry!" Cass calls back. "The island winds are a bit wild, and it's hard to move mine against them."

"Audrina, do you think we will need to hide the air transport?" Leighra asks.

Audrina thinks, tapping her nails to her chin. Her amber eyes are bright and rested. She has clearly been awake for a while now despite the night still owning the sky. "You probably should. My mother is suspicious of outsiders. She would have no way of knowing I'm aboard. She may try to shoot us down."

"Shoot us down? With what?" Dover looks at her in shock. His sheltered upbringing in Caeliss is showing.

Audrina smiles at him as though endeared by the ignorance. "Cannons, sweet boy. Cannons. The islands have them facing every direction to protect against threats."

"Do you have many threats on the island? I've always read that islands are peaceful places."

"They are. Mostly. We are often forgotten about. We're technically part of the nation of Stellera and officially accepted as one of their own provinces, but before the Trinity War, the Islands of the Sons were their own nation. We had our own government and had since the beginning of time. When Rousse attacked Stellera, they knew coming from the south would be their best chance of surprise. There are border walls running the whole of the Rousse-Dailotta border and the Dailotta-Stellera border, but there never has been any kind of defense in the south. So, the Rousse took over the Islands. Being that we were peaceful people, it was easy for them. There was no way to fight back. They used us as a stronghold and invaded the southern provinces from the sea. That's why Stellera has so many military forts along the coast now and they turned our smallest island, Isoie, into a naval port," Audrina explains.

"The beginning of the Trinity War is when my ancestors found Caeliss. They used to let people come and go back then, so it was easier to find more of Astoria's children. During the War, the Elders at the time decided it was too risky since we were being sought out," Dover shares.

"Mine came just before the wars," Leighra adds. "They had a caravan and traveled all over Katova performing magic tricks. The people loved it and thought the tricks to be very well done illusions...the mortal kind...until someone in one of the crowds recognized them for what they were, Children. Fortunately, they were uldoaka...friends...and told them about Caeliss. They never looked back. I have a whole load of cousins now, and for over three hundred years, there's always been one of us on the Elder council."

"Darling, it's time," Cass says to Leighra with a kiss to her cheek.

Leighra smiles in response. Her eyes roll back white.

The transport rocks unevenly as Cass fights through the strong winds.

"Do you need help?" DeLuca asks.

"Are you *able* to help? The last time we practiced, you couldn't even call a breeze." She laughs, but there is a strain in her voice as she struggles to keep us level.

"Did you not see me knock those transports off a bridge?"

"No, I didn't. I was too busy flying us away." She smirks.

DeLuca unbuckles himself and walks forward to see ahead of us, intent on restoring his dignity which from the look on his face and rigidness in his shoulders has taken a brutal hit.

"If you must help, you can try to block the island wind. That should be easier than calling upon it," Cass says, giving in.

"How?" DeLuca asks.

"Imagine a wall blocking them. That's what I do."

DeLuca closes his eyes. Lines form between his eyebrows as he scrunches in concentration.

Suddenly, we're dropping.

"Stop, DeLuca! Stop, that's my wind!" Cass yells in panic.

DeLuca opens his eyes, and Cass restores her winds with ease.

"Sorry," he says with a sheepish smile, "I'll try again."

She breathes heavily. "No, don't."

"It's okay, I can do it. I can feel the difference in the wind now, which one is fighting against you. I can almost see it as a string that needs to be unwoven," he says.

Cass looks shocked. "Yes, that's exactly right."

He smiles triumphantly, "Okay. Hang on." His eyes close again. His face looks more relaxed this time. His breathing deepens as if meditating. The ship stops rocking and slides with ease on the winds Cass provides.

"You actually did it," she says, impressed.

He opens his eyes, the triumphant smile still plastered to his face. "Don't sound so surprised."

"Considering a few weeks ago you didn't know you had any kind of ability, I am *very* surprised."

"There's a large clearing we use for entertaining in the courtyard facing the west. My bedroom overlooks it. It should be plenty big enough for you to land," Audrina tells Cass.

"I see it." Cass nods. "That will work."

"I should get off the transport before you uncover it as well. Go give my mother a warning before strangers in matching jumpsuits and an invisible transport march into her home."

"Good plan," Cass agrees.

Leighra keeps the illusion on after we have landed. We are all stretching out stiff muscles from the multitude of hours spent sitting. The sun is rising and paints the vast sea that surrounds us in its golden warmth. Salty air is filling the transport through the open hatch, and I can already feel my skin getting dewy from the moisture. I see why Audrina was desperate to get back to this place. It's beautiful. The courtyard we've landed in overlooks the ocean. It's serene, especially with the sound of the ocean lapping against the rocks below. I find it calming, and my heart slows to match the rhythm. Sea birds cry out to greet the new day while flying high above the enormous ocean palace in front of us. It could rival Obsidian Manor in size, but the architecture is vastly different.

There are white columns that raise the palace high above ground level in case of flooding. There is a wide marble staircase that leads from the courtyard to a large patio that seems to stretch around the palace. Large round windows arch along the wall facing us.

"I see her!" Lysette says from the back of the transport.

"Is she alone?" Cass asks, not leaving her seat in case we need to make a quick get-a-way.

"No, she has an older woman with her, and three men," Rett answers.

"She's waving," Dover adds.

"That's probably her signal." I grab DeLuca's hand and walk toward the open hatch.

"You can let it go now, darling." Cass kisses Leighras knuckles.

Leighra's eyes return to normal. The woman with Audrina gasps and steps back. The three men quickly flank her sides, and one walks in front of her.

"I almost forgot about servs and security," I say with my head to the side.

"I never could." DeLuca's tone is bitter. His grasp tightens around my hand.

"Mama, these are my friends, Cass, Leighra, Lysette and Rett Urson, DeLuca, Dover, and, of course, Aislinn Delphia." Hearing my family name for the first time in weeks feels strange, like it no longer fits. Or I no longer fit it—if I ever did. "Everyone, this is my mother, The Lady Guiliana Soleil of Sutton Isle."

Audrina's mother stands with her head high and brushes the guard in front of her, telling him he can move.

"Lady Soleil, an honor to make your acquaintance." Rett bows, falling back into the habits of our upbringing.

"A pleasure, Lady Soliel. You have a lovely home." Lysette follows suit and manages to return her face to resemble that of a highborn, even with the dried blood on it.

"Lady Soleil, at last we meet." I kiss both her cheeks.

Dover, Leighra, Cass, and DeLuca look uncomfortable and are obviously untrained in the art of proper introductions. Lady Soleil looks at them expectantly. An uncomfortable silence fills the air that feels as if it will never disperse.

Audrina breaks the silence when it's clear they don't know what to do. "Mother, we have much to discuss. It may be more comfortable inside."

"Ah yes, you simply must tell me about where you've been and all you've done. How you came to acquire such...unique...attire." She eyes our jumpsuits as though we stand before her in the nude. Without missing a beat, she turns on her heel and beckons us to follow.

Leighra pulls Audrina's hand so she will hang back. Her mother doesn't notice.

"What?!" Audrina's voice betrayes her annoyance.

"You can't tell her about Caeliss," Leighra warns.

"She's my mother. I can tell her anything."

Leighra's eyes narrow. "Anything, except about Caeliss."

"How can I explain where we've been, who you all are without it?"

"Figure out another way."

"She will know if I'm lying."

"Audrina, I'm telling you as a friend. If you try to tell her, I have instructions to stop you." She pauses and looks in Audrina's eyes so she knows she is absolutely serious. "By any means necessary.

PART THREE

Islands of the Sons

THIRTY
WHISPER IT AWAY

The breakfast parlor is decorated in creams and gold with exotic floral wallpaper and a large window overlooking the island's village. It is meant to feel light and airy as to greet the day with a fresh beginning, but the thick tensions in the room weigh heavily around us. Morning light catches on a large crystal chandelier sitting above a round glass table in the center, illuminating the room with the light bouncing off the delicate crystals. The table has room for twelve, though they've only set it for the nine of us this morning.

Lady Soleil has been staring icily at Audrina, waiting for her explanations. Though it is considered poor etiquette to begin conversation before the meal has started. We wait in loud silence for the servs to bring our breakfasts. Cass is fidgeting with her napkin. Leighra has her fists below her chin and is leaning forward with her elbows supporting her on the glass table. Dover is anxiously tapping his foot and sitting directly beside Audrina. She, Lysette, Rett, and I sit with our backs straight and heads forward, as we've been taught all our lives. DeLuca tries to move his hand to my own. I subtly shake my head no, and he quickly retracts it, doing his best imitation of our posture.

Finally, two of the men who had provided security to Lady Soleil earlier open the doors to the parlor to allow a team of servs in, each rolling in a cart filled abundantly with exotic fruits I have never seen, some spiky, some brightly colored. They also wheel in freshly baked pastries, juices squeezed moments before, egg dishes, fried potatoes, cured pig, and other familiar comforts. My mouth waters, and I realize it has been two days since we've had a real meal.

Servs surround the tables with their carts, and we point to what we want. They make our plates and fill our glasses without a word and leave with their carts as if they'd never been there in the first place. DeLuca's eyes slightly harden, and a muscle twitches in his jaw, but I'm the only one who notices.

Audrina piles fruits and pastries on her plate but looks like she might get sick when the meat cart rolls by, and she pushes her plate away with a scowl. The closing of the door signals that now is the appropriate time for conversation.

"Out with it, Audrina." Lady Soleil calmly slices through a spiky orange fruit.

"Out with what, Mama?" She tries to stall.

"Where have you been? Stellera has been completely overthrown by rebels. I feared the worst. You couldn't send word that you were alive?" She keeps her composure, but the worry in her voice is detectable to ears trained in a proper upbringing.

Audrina looks at Leighra, whose face is set in a hardline. Her body is angled in such a way that she looks like a big cat setting up for a kill.

"We were attacked at Obsidian Manor, during the Urson-Delphia wedding. They came from the woods. They killed everyone. Almost everyone. We escaped through a tunnel transport system built beneath the manor. We ended up in Dailotta...and"—She takes a breath as she looks between her mother and Leighra—"we were found by a man. He led us to a camp of refugees. That's where we met Cass, Leighra, and Dover. We wanted retribution and formed a team to assassinate the man responsible, a serv named Pierce Decatur. We came straight here after we accomplished it."

More or less the truth.

Lady Soleil's eyes lay suspiciously on her daughter. "*You* assassinated someone?"

"*We* did." Audrina's voice doesn't waver.

"Very good, welcome to the world of politics." Her mother's face warms as she accepts Audrina's story. The air lightens a little. Leighra's eyes turn to her food, and she visibly relaxes.

I'm sitting directly beside Lady Soleil. Once she notices Leighra's guard lower, she leans beside me and whispers so low it is hardly audible. "Tell me, is what my daughter says the truth?"

Fighting the words feels like a hot poker repeatedly being stabbed into my eardrum and pulled out. I try, though. I fight them until beads of sweat form along my forehead and I am trembling everywhere.

"Not the whole truth," I blurt, unable to stop myself.

"Aislinn!" Leighra looks horrified. "Don't." Her voice is full of warning.

"What, pray tell, has happened in *full truth*?" Lady Soleil whispers.

Leighra stands with a paring knife in her hand, ready to throw it at me.

My eyes are wide, and I bite my lips together to try to contain their secrets. DeLuca tackles Leighra just as the words start spilling from my mouth.

"What Audrina said about the wedding was true, up until we were found. We were attacked in the woods as well. A man named Alec found us. He took us to a Safe Haven in the Thickett Woods. It's called Caeliss and is guarded well and hidden. It's the home to the Children of Astoria. We're all Children...except Rett, who was stolen from Ashe as a baby. So was his brother. Lysette and Linnea were the only true-born Ursons. They can control plants. Dover is a Voda. Leighra can cause Illusions. DeLuca is a first-born, which means he's a god. Cass over there is a Gale. She can control the wind. It's how the transport works. She guides it. Her grandfather invented it. I have visions. I had one we're in danger of being found in Caeliss. We were dispatched to eliminate the threat. We're not supposed to go anywhere else or tell anyone about Caeliss in fear of compromising the location...like right now. And we've come here to destroy Erebus after he sent me a vision telling me to meet him...here...most certainly to trap me." The words come out fast and uncontrolled, toppling over each other.

If Lady Soleil is at all surprised, she truly hides it well.

DeLuca is still on top of Leighra, his knee digging into her back and his hands holding hers to her shoulder blade. She is yelling obscenities when her eyes roll back white. A storm swiftly replaces the calm morning. Thunder and lightning threaten to break into the room. A gust of wind strongly blows into the parlor, knocking down the crystal chandelier, sending it crashing through the glass table. It grows dark and cold. Our food and dishes and bits of glass are swept up in the wind, encircling the room.

DeLuca uses one of his hands to fight the wind surrounding Cass, who now floats above us.

The battling winds cause wallpaper to tear and pictures to fall off of their hooks. My hair whips violently in the storm.

"Enough." Lady Soleil slams a fist to what remains of the table.

Cass is distracted with DeLuca and doesn't notice Audrina slide out of her chair and crawl to where Leighra is still pinned to the floor. She whispers something to her. The storm immediately stops. The two guards who'd been standing outside the door barge in and grab Leighra. Cass turns her attention to them, calling back her wind, preparing to launch it at the men, but DeLuca quickly stands in front of her.

"Don't. It will only make it worse," he warns her.

The room is in shambles. Lady Soleil pinches the bridge of her nose. "Everyone sit," she commands. We obey, sitting around the circular frame that had once been the glass table. "Now, there is no need for such behavior." She brushes a bit of broken glass off her lap.

"Mama, she was sworn to keep the secret." Audrina pleads for the still restrained Leighra.

"I know very well *why* she reacted the way she did. I'm going to have my men let you go, but you must allow me to speak before trying to *murder* someone else in this room." Her eyes fall to Leighra and then Cass. They both nod, silently agreeing to behave.

Lady Soleil takes a deep breath. "I've always known about Caeliss and the Children." Audrina's jaw drops. "Most Children with a lineage that predates the Trinity War have been told there is a safe haven for us should we ever need it. While its location is secret, there are eight families who have been trusted with the location and handed down maps through generations."

"Why didn't you ever tell me?" Audrina demands.

"I would have on your twentieth birthday next month. I couldn't have predicted the discord in Stellera. You were supposed to come home from the Astoria Academy next month." She waves a hand as if this were obvious.

"Only Urson," Lysette mumbles. "We found a box that was hidden away at the end of the tunnel that could only be opened with Urson blood, my blood...but my gift, it comes from my mother."

Lady Soleil smiles. "Your mother is just of closer descent to Astoria. The Ursons are one of the oldest lines of Children we know of. It's entirely possible your father no longer possesses an ability strong enough to recognize, but long generations ago, the Ursons could transform themselves into bears. Huge bears, larger than any other known species."

"How do you know all of this?" Audrina looks at her mother as if she is a stranger.

"Ours was a part of the council of trusted families. The Guardians of Astoria. It's been two decades since we've met, but our family was on it, as well as the Ursons. Lyrica's family too. I believe it is how Magnus met her, through the connection of their grandparents. Our secrets are passed down to the new generation on their twentieth birthday."

"Why wasn't Rett told then? If both of our parents were on it, then why not Rett? He's two years past twenty," Lysette says.

Rett looks down. "Because I'm not a Child."

Lady Soleil sighs in pity. "Bottinials have historically had a hard time with conception. Seems with each generation, it gets worse. It's like with any botanical seed. You need seeds that are viable, that can germinate. Unfortunately, they also pass many dormant seeds. They may grow but will never thrive."

"Did my parents know about my true father? About the visions?" I ask quietly.

"I'm not sure of that dear. I didn't know any families with visions. I certainly didn't know Phillipe Delphia wasn't your true father. In fact, to think Secilly Delphia ever strayed is quite the surprise, and I am not easily surprised. Your parents had no knowledge of the Guardians as far as I know. Or Children. Are there any more questions, or can we get on without secrets and murder?" She stares at Leighra as she speaks.

"I'm fine. I'd never hurt anyone under this roof," she says. Her demeanor subdued as if she hadn't just tried to throw a paring knife through my skull.

Thank you, Audrina.

"As long as we aren't threatened," Cass agrees.

"Wonderful. So, what is your plan about Erebus? Send god on god?" Lady Soleil looks DeLuca up and down, an eyebrow raised in question. "That could very well destroy the island...perhaps this half of the realm entirely."

Audrina shudders.

Lysette speaks clearly, taking charge. "We haven't gotten as far as a plan. We were hoping to look through your archives, and if you have a map of the Isle of Shadows, we need that as well."

"Of course, but you'll want to see *my* personal archives, not the ones anyone could stumble across." Lady Soleil smiles mischievously.

Lysette's eyes flicker with excitement.

"Okay, you're all dismissed. I'm sure you need a few hours of rest, and we need to get the servs in here to clean this." The Lady of Sutton gestures around us to the remnants of the room. The table is nothing more than a gold frame, and beneath it lies our breakfast covered in broken glass and ceramics. The chandelier now rests on the floor. The wallpaper is peeling off, pictures on the floor.

I side eye Audrina, who returns with a grimace.

"I've had Aurelia prepare seven rooms. They're all on the same floor as Audrina's," Lady Soleil says.

"Mama, can we speak for a moment once everyone's left?" Audrina asks. Her voice transforms into that of a childs, and she pulls Dover closer by his hand.

"But, of course, Audrina." Her mother smiles at her with warmth.

We trek up two flights of stairs, following behind Aurelia. She is a small woman. She might even pass for a child if it weren't for the lines of age creasing her forehead and cheeks and the gray hairs that are held back in a tight bun. She is dressed modestly. Tan slacks paired with a white blouse, nothing special. She looks well put together and taken care of.

"These rooms are for Ms. Cassandra and Ms. Leighra." Aurelia points at two rooms side by side that are closest to the stairs we just climbed.

"We'd actually like to share a room." Cass, with a smile as bright as her hair, has a hand wrapped around Leighra's and leans into her shoulder.

Aurelia looks appalled. "Absolutely not."

"Because we are two women?" Leighra's hands come to her hips, a threat of violence in her gaze.

"Certainly not, no one cares about that. You are unmarried. No one may share a bed unless they're married. It is just so *improper*." She wags a finger at them. "Besides, the Lady of Sutton has sent for wardrobes to be prepared in each of your rooms." Aurelia scoots them off into their assigned doors. I have to suppress a giggle watching Leighra get bossed around by someone half her size.

"Ladies will be on the west side of the hall. Gentleman on the East. Here you are, Miss Urson." Aurelia points to a door a few feet from Cass and Leighra's. "And, Miss Delphia, Miss Soleil is the next one down. They thought to put you closest to her."

My door is just beside Lysette's. I stand in the doorway and watch as she assigns Rett and DeLuca. DeLuca's door is directly across the hall from mine. He looks back to me, a dare forming in his eyes before he disappears behind his door.

Shaking my head with half a smile, I walk into my assigned room. It's smaller than the one I had at Obsidian Manor, but it is still bigger than the top floor of our house in Caeliss. There are long cream drapes that hang from the ceiling and cascade down to the floor. A gentle island breeze ripples the fabric through the open windows and door that lead out to an impressive balcony overlooking the courtyard.

The furniture is all made from a light wood and wicker woven together. It complements the cream bedding and pale blue walls. Above the bed is a canopy with strips of blue that matches the walls and cream fabric delicately placed over top, falling to the floor on either side. They are tied to each corner of the bed by a ribbon, allowing me to see a dark blue dress lying delicately across the comforter. The wardrobe in the corner of the room seems to be fully stocked with gowns in my size, of all lengths and colors. The opposite corner contains a full length mirror beside a door leading to a personal powder room. On the two night tables lay a plethora of candles in various stages of use. Matching candles are scattered atop the dresser and on the vanity table. It is light and airy. It feels safe, despite being exactly the opposite of what I would have designed. Tension I hadn't realized I was carrying releases from my shoulders.

There is an assortment of bath oils set near the tub. I pick one that smells of wisteria. The flight suit sticks around my ankles again. I sit on the floor and give it a few hard pulls before it finally gives and throw it in a corner, anxious to never have to put it on again. Finally, I dip my toes in the warm water and lower myself in. Steam rises and swirls around me, filling the air with the sweet aroma of wisteria and fresh water. The tub is deep enough that I'm able to submerge myself up to my neck. Using a soap made of goat's milk and honey, I wash my hair and face and let the grime melt away. All my muscles sing from the warmth soothing them. I lean my head back against the tub and close my eyes. The sound of ocean waves and birds calling to one another lulls me into a deep relaxation. My hands gently fall to my belly, absentmindedly laying over the gray lines that wrap around my torso.

"Are you thinking about me, *pet*?" a familiar silky voice whispers in my head. "Do you wish I were there with you? Do you miss *my touch*? Do you wish it were my hand laying over your exposed belly?" He laughs sadistically.

Dark shadows replace the swirls of steam hovering over my bath. Dropping my hand from the mark, I quickly jump from the tub and wrap myself in a towel that lay near.

When I look back at the water, it's gone back to normal. Not a hint of a shadow. I shiver and pull the plug, cursing Erebus as it drains. I'll keep this interaction to myself. No use in worrying DeLuca. I think he feels responsible each time Erebus gets to me. I see it in his eyes, the way he internalizes the hurt of each encounter. We will deal with Erebus. Soon enough, he will be a distant memory.

Once I slip on the blue dress that had been laid out for me, I towel dry my hair, scrunching my waves upwards to preserve their natural shape. They fall like the waterfalls of Caeliss down my back. As I look in the mirror, I hardly recognize myself. Once again, I resemble the young lady of a highborn house. The dress fits perfectly, hugging my chest tightly and flowing out just below my breasts. It falls at my ankles, and every time I walk, it flows backward as if part of it is stuck in time.

My door flies open.

"You look like yourself again." Audrina leans against the doorway.

"So do you. Being home suits you." I smile.

A shadow crosses her face, and for a split second, she looks as though she might be sick before shaking it off and grinning wildly. "I introduced my mother to Dover."

"And?"

"She was accepting. Titles are of little importance now that the nation is in shambles. I'm free to marry whomever I'd like."

My eyes narrow. "Marry?"

"Not that we're planning to. It's just nice to know that if we did, he'd be accepted."

"Is he willing to leave Caeliss?"

She looks down. "No. He doesn't want to leave his family, but I could persuade him."

"*Whisper* him you mean. You can't whisper him if you want it to be real."

Her smile falters. "Yeah, you're right. Anyway, I ran into Cass and Leighra on my way to see you. They want to go home...now, not later...well, after they get a little sleep."

"But if they leave, they'll have to take the transport."

"Yes."

"Which means anyone who stays won't make it back to Caeliss."

"Right."

"Why won't they wait?"

"It probably has to do with what happened downstairs. Maybe they just don't feel at ease here. They finished *their* mission." Audrina shrugs and shifts her eyes to look out my window.

"The mission was to keep Caeliss safe. We haven't done that, not completely," I argue.

"You can't blame them for wanting to go home. They only came here because I whispered them. I told them how nice it would be to enjoy the beach together. They walked along the shore and that seemed to placate whatever control my words had. You and DeLuca can stay here, of course. You don't need to go back to Caeliss. We're just as safe on the island."

"What about Rett and Lysette? Do you think they will just leave Iris and the baby?"

"I don't suspect that they will, no."

I feel my throat tighten and my heart race. "Am I going to have to truly face him"—My voice breaks—"alone?"

She comes over to the bed where I sit and pulls my head into her.

"Aislinn, darling, I'm here and as long as I am here I won't let anything happen to this island. And there's also a certain raven-haired god I know would demolish an entire village before letting anything bad happen to you." She strokes my hair. "With them or without them, it doesn't matter. You're the one who's always telling me people have their choices. Let them make their choice."

"You're right, they do deserve a choice. I'm just...afraid. You don't know what he's like. The way he slithers, the way he speaks, his eyes. The hollow cold that comes with his presence." My breath becomes ragged.

"Shhh. It's okay, you're going to be okay. It's almost over." She keeps rubbing my shoulder, trying to comfort me.

"Audrina?"

"Hmm?"

"Can you whisper it away again? The fear?"

"I can...but are you sure? You've made it very clear you don't approve of it."

"I'm sure. I don't know how else I can survive him."

She nods and presses her forehead gently to the side of my head, just above my ear. "It's the very least I can do for you. You're no longer afraid of Erebus. You're brave. You feel strong. He has no hold over you." Her whisper gently envelopes itself around my brain. When I'm not fighting it, the way the words repeat over and over is almost soothing.

"Better?" she asks.

"Better. Thank you." I squeeze her hand as my nerves turn to steel under my skin.

A knock rapts on my door.

"Enter," Audrina says.

DeLuca opens the door, wearing a smile and finer clothes than I've ever seen him in. He looks every bit as highborn as the rest of us now. The fitted button down shirt has the sleeves rolled up to his elbow, revealing his muscular forearms and scars that swirl like smoke. His usual tousled curls have been cut back shorter on the sides and left a bit longer at the top, swooped sideways in a purposeful mess.

"What are you two chatting about?" He gives us a half smile, causing my heart to leap in my chest.

"Doom and gloom, our usual," Audrina answers.

"Can we have a minute, Audrina?" I ask her, my eyes scouring every inch of DeLuca.

She raises a brow at me. "Okay, but we're meeting downstairs in ten. Mama's taking us to her personal archives."

"We will be there." I motion her to leave with a nod of my head.

She takes her que with grace and closes the door behind her.

I don't give DeLuca a chance to say anything. I throw myself into him, pressing my body firmly to his. My hands wrap around his neck and pull it down to mine. As I kiss him, one of his hands finds its way into my hair, slightly tugging it, the other around my waist, his fingers curving into the skin.

"I don't want to wait any longer. I'm ready now," I whisper against his neck. Thanks to Audrina's whispers, I'm feeling braver than I ever have before, and I'm unafraid to ask for what I so desperately crave—DeLuca.

He groans before he pulls away, visibily struggling to catch his breath. "The first time we're together will not be a quick moment of stolen passion."

"And why do you get to decide?" I push my body back into his.

He runs his fingers through his hair in frustration, but there is a softness in his eyes.

"Because, baby, I don't want you for a fleeting moment." He kisses below my ear.

"I want you for hours." He continues kissing, lower.

"I want to know every part of your body." This kiss lands in the dip where my shoulder meets my neck, and I instinctively bite my lip.

"Each place you like to be touched." He gently moves the strap of my dress below my shoulder.

"Or tasted." He emphasizes his words by trailing his tongue along my collar bone, to the top of my breast. My breathing is ragged now. I feel like I'm almost panting.

My breath catches, and my body leans toward him, silently begging for more. He smiles wickedly, taking joy in this torment while using two fingers to return the strap of my dress to its rightful place on my shoulder.

"Damn you, Rainier DeLuca."

He kisses the top of my head. "You don't mean that, do you baby?"

I let my head rest against his chest. Freshly cleaned, he smells salty like the ocean, but underneath, I still smell his natural river stone musk. The scent of home.

"No. I don't mean it." I smile.

"Good. You look beautiful, Ailie. I like this color on you."

"You clean up very well yourself, for *a god*." I arch a brow at him, and he laughs in return. Gods, I love the way he laughs. It's so different from his usual serious demeanor. It's so free.

"Shall we meet the others?" He bows and offers his arm, mocking a gentleman.

"Mmm, yes, we shall." With a giggle, I rest my hand flat on his offered arm as a lady does when making an introduction.

THIRTY-ONE
ALL COSTS

"At last, welcome. I'm glad to see the clothing was suitable," Lady Soleil says once we've made our way downstairs.

"Thank you, Lady Soleil. You have been so generous. I am thankful for your hospitality." DeLuca's sudden grasp of etiquette catches me by surprise.

"You're most welcome. I do hope my humble home is enough for a god." She bows her head—a sign of respect.

Audrina and I can't control our laughter. If only the Lady of Sutton knew just months ago this god was a serv, a rebel spy, no less. The irony of a Lady of Province bowing is too much.

Lady Soleil glares at us while DeLuca ignores our outburst. "It is more than comfortable, Lady Soleil." He bends and kisses her hand. When he pulls his lips away, he flashes her his most charming smile, causing Lady Soleil to blush. Seeing this side of DeLuca is strange. He must have seen many interactions between highborns, but to act as one himself is entirely unexpected, and I am not entirely sure I like it.

Audrina is thoroughly amused at the whole interaction.

"And you, Lady Delphia, how dazzling you look in that color. It suits your complexion." Lady Soleil's attention turns to me, kissing both of my cheeks.

"You have wonderful taste." I offer a polite smile.

"I wish I could take credit, but Aurelia had the clothing brought in. She is truly wonderful. I'd be lost without her."

"Are we ready?" Lysette calls as she and Rett make their way down the stairs.

Lady Soleil looks at Audrina. "Are we, dear?"

Audrina nods.

"Will the others be down?" DeLuca asks.

Audrina answers with the faintest hint of agitation. "I don't think so. They wanted to rest. I'm sure we will be able to catch up with them later."

Rett and Lysette formally greet Lady Soleil with stiff idle conversation. After the pleasantries, Lady Soleil beckons us to follow her to another set of stairs on the other side of the sea-side palace. These stairs go up four floors but don't stop on any landing other than her own. At the top of the stairs is a large sitting area with tufted cream furniture wrapped in gold and adorned with engraved filigree. There are three doors and no windows. The farthest door is presumably Lady Soleil's private quarters. The door on the right is cracked open ever so slightly, enough so I can see rows and rows of books. Lady Soleil leads us through the left door.

The room serves as an office, not very different from my father's but with a feminine touch. Lady Soleil moves to the desk and opens a drawer. She digs around a bit, and we hear a click. The wall to the right of the door slides back, revealing a hole in the floor. I catch myself gaping at the secret she willingly uncovered. A quick look at the other faces in the room shows me everyone else is just as surprised by this latest development.

"After you." Lady Soleil invites us to the opening. "Oh Audrina, dear, lock the door behind you."

Audrina obeys, locking the office door to protect the secrets within. Rett and Lysette disappear into the hole. DeLuca places a reassuring hand at the small of my back. We walk together and discover the hole is in fact an opening leading to a metal spiral staircase. It is extremely narrow, hardly large enough for one person to venture down at once.

My body is halfway in the hole when I look back at Audrina and mouth 'Did you know about this?'

She shakes her head 'no' in response and shrugs.

The passage is dark. I'm exceedingly thankful for the rails that help guide us down. The stairs slightly shake and creak with each unsettled step we take. I'm unsure of how many floors we've gone down, but it feels like at least three before I finally see a light. A sconce on the wall illuminates very little, only a part of the exposed brick. Lady Soleil flips a large lever. A small flame travels along a wire from the lit sconce to another a few feet away. Another flame travels from the newly lit sconce to another the same way, and another, and another, until the room is fully lit.

There are books and scrolls overflowing from each shelf that line three out of four walls. The other wall has framed maps of Katova and the islands. It's musky and warm. There is no airflow down here as far as I can tell. A huge circular conference table sits in the center of the room. Quills and parchment are left in place from the last time the room was used. The layer of dust tells me it's been quite some time. I flash back to the secret room at Obsidian Manor, and it clicks into place. That was their secret archive. They were a part of the same council as Lady Soleil. I wish we could have uncovered the secrets held within before the manor had been overtaken. Maybe it would have saved us some trouble.

"This is incredible!" Lysette claps her hands. Her face is a mix of astonishment and excitement.

"Yes, incredible and dangerous. There's information in here that could destroy families...even the realm as we know it. Information is the most important weapon any man or god can possess." Lady Soliel looks around, appearing to reminisce. "It's been two decades since I've come down here." She sighs. "Of course, you're welcome to all of it. Nothing leaves this room though. Not even its secrets. Do you understand?"

We nod, still taking in the entirety of it.

"I'll leave you to it then. Come and go as you will. Always be sure to flip the switch upstairs to hide the room again. Let me know if I can be of any service. Aislinn, a word if you will." I cock my head in surprise, and she brings me into a corner while everyone else begins to carefully explore the archives.

"Yes, Lady Soliel?"

"Aislinn, I understand that the shadow god is involved with whatever is going on, specifically with you." Lady Soleil's voice wavers slightly. "Does he know much of Audrina?"

"I'm not sure what he knows and doesn't know. Any time we've spoken, he's been frustratingly cryptic. He threatened everyone though. I have to assume he meant my friends and Caeliss. I know he watches me. He's...marked me." I pull my hair to the side so she can see the shadow wings placed on my back.

She nods her head. "Yes, I saw this one." Her hand gestures to my arm. "Aislinn, I will be of any service you need...under one condition." Her voice is hushed.

"Name it. You've been so generous. I'd be happy to return the favor."

"If that is true, leave Audrina out of it. I don't want her anywhere near Erebus." Her face is stern, her voice quiet.

My heart stops for a moment. My list of allies grows smaller and smaller with every tick of the clock. I gulp. "What if she won't stay out of it?"

"Then find a way to make her. Lie to her. Anything. Don't let her go near that deranged god. Please, I beg you as a mother." The authority in her voice fades away, replaced by the plea of a frightened parent.

"I'll try." I place a hand on her arm to show my sincerity.

She puts her hand over my own and leans in for a hug, then turns her head close to me. "You will keep her out of it, at all costs," she whispers.

"Yes, Lady Soleil, *I will keep Audrina out of it at all costs.*" The words pour from my lips.

With a satisfied smile, Lady Soleil turns back to the stairs and makes her way up. I move to where Audrina examines the maps on the wall.

"What was that about?" Audrina asks.

"She's just concerned about Erebus," I say, not lying yet not wanting to reveal the full truth. If I tell her she can't come, she will fight until she can.

Audrina accepts my answer and continues tracing her finger over the map pressed behind a sheet of glass. "Look at this," she says when her finger stops. "This is Shadow Isle, but its written Istaleia Viisolo."

The small island is marked by a skull wedged in between Sutton and Driera. The key at the bottom of the page tells us the skull marks Istaleia Viisolo. There is a crescent moon with a smudge over it separating the two words. Underneath the key, it's signed and dated a hundred years before the start of Trinity Wars.

"This map belongs in a museum," I say, grabbing Lysettes attention.

She hurries over to us.

"Let me see!" She nudges me slightly to get a better view and starts tracing lines. "Amazing. This map is written in a mix of Old Daile and the common tongue. Look! Iselarra. That's what they called Stellera before most of Katova adopted the common tongue."

"When did you learn Old Daeil?" I ask her, impressed by her knowledge of a lost language.

"I was dabbling back in Caeliss. I don't know too much, but I did learn the nations' names and a few other places and phrases. For example, did you know they named aietal metal after the Daeliot word for death?"

"No, I never knew." I think about the Child Blade I have safely tucked away with my things upstairs. "How fitting."

The five of us comb through pages of old books and unrolled scrolls for a few hours. There is no indication of what is contained within the leathers binding the pages together. We search blindly. The table now holds piles of books atop of it. Nothing of use to us yet. Interesting secrets and scandals, sure, but they will have to wait until after we've dealt with Erebus.

"This is pointless." Rett throws another book in the pile. "Do we even know what we're looking for?" His legs are kicked up on the table with his chair tipped back and his hands folded behind his head.

I look to Lysette, hoping she has an answer.

She sighs. "Anything that might tell us more about Erebus or Istaleia Viisolo, maybe of Astoria...the God's War. Really, anything is better than what we have." She flings another book on the pile and rubs her temples.

"All that's in here is the lineage and histories of known Children," Audrina says in frustration.

"Let's take a break," I suggest, looking at the glaze in each of their eyes. We haven't taken more than a few minutes to catch our breath in days. We won't get anywhere if we're burnt out. "The archive will still be here tomorrow. We've had a crazy few days. Let's eat and come back in the morning with fresh eyes."

"We don't have time to play around." DeLuca's tone is stern.

"We're not going to be good for much longer." I gesture around the table.

He bites his lip to try to conceal his scowl, but the lines in his forehead give him away.

"Well, you don't have to convince me." Rett shoots out of his seat and stretches out his back.

"Yeah, I could use a break. There's a certain Voda I need to have a conversation with." Audrina grits her teeth, referring to Dover whose absence has become a bitter topic of discussion throughout the hours we've been down here.

Purposely, I close my book too loudly to signal the end of research. "Let's go then." I grab DeLuca by the arm.

He huffs and carefully sets down the large black leather book he has been reading. At some point, he unbuttoned the top three buttons of his shirt, teasing a hint of his chest.

I lean against him on my tip toes. My lips almost touch his ear. "I can think of some things that would be way more fun than flipping through hundred year old books." DeLuca's entire body shifts with eager excitement.

Now, he's leading me out.

THIRTY-TWO
BE CIVIL

Before we can sneak away, we run into Cass and Leighra. Audrina has already found Dover and took him for a walk along the shoreline. I can't help but notice how out of place they look, both in elegant day dresses that sweep the floor as they walk. Cass in pink and Leighra in a light yellow that does nothing to flatter her broad shoulders. They stumble over the gowns as they come toward us. A small rage bubbles to the surface. The memory of Leighra trying to throw a knife at my throat has not been forgotten. DeLuca's hand tightens around mine as he pulls me closer to him, slightly positioning his body between hers and mine.

"Cass." I smile and acknowledge her.

"Did you find anything helpful?" Cass' voice is hopeful while ignoring the tension between us and her lover.

"Not yet, there are hundreds of books in Lady Soleil's private archive. We just needed a break. We are gonna get back to it later," Lysette answers for me.

Cass fiddles with the fabric of her dress, her fingers twisting around the sheer overlay below her waist. Leighra nudges her, and she sighs. "We're going back to Caeliss. Tonight. We *have* to tell the Elders what has happened and what you're doing...and about Lady Soleil and the guardian council she mentioned."

"And we need to decide what to do about it." Leighra's eyes fixate on me.

"It wasn't her fault. She was whispered! You can't seriously hold her responsible," DeLuca says. His voice is deep and authoritative—ready for a fight if it comes.

"It's not for me to decide. I just follow orders. We never should have come here. If it wasn't for your whisper friend, I'm sure we never would have." Leighra folds her arms.

"You still have the option to return with us." Cass' deep brown eyes silently beg us to go with them.

"You know I can't. Not until Erebus has been dealt with. No one would be safe," I remind her.

"The Elders will know how to help."

I think of all the families in Caeliss. The vision I had of their deaths. Of little Hadleigh. It was Pierce in the dream, but now that I've seen Erebus, I know the eyes were not his, but the shadow gods. It was a warning.

"It's not worth the risk, Cass, but I speak for myself. I am the one Erebus wants. I *hope* to have my friends by my side, but I won't fault anyone who chooses to leave." I glance at Rett and Lysette so they understand I'm talking about them.

"I wouldn't leave you at a time like this, Ailie." Rett seems offended by the suggestion that he'd abandon me in my time of need, yet the struggle he feels is evident in his stance. It's rigid and full of agony. Torn by love for his growing family and his old one.

"You *should* go back with them, Rett." I place a hand on his arm.

Rett huffs. "I can't leave you and Lysette here, but I can't stay knowing I might not make it back and leave my child and future wife alone with strangers. You're putting us in an impossible position." He looks at Leighra and Cass before storming off. Lysette trails behind him. I want to follow, but DeLuca holds me back, shaking his head.

"You should let Lysette handle it." He turns his attention to Leighra. "The least you could have done was wait a few days. Even if you didn't go with us to the Isle of Shadows. You could have stayed here, comfortable and well cared for, which is more than you deserve after your attempt to *murder* Aislinn." His voice is scarily calm, but I feel him heating more and more with each passing moment.

"I have only done what I've been bound to do by oath."

"Okay, enough. The decisions have been made. If we start fighting amongst ourselves, Erebus has already won." I step out from behind DeLca. "We can be civil, for now. *If* we return to Caeliss, we can settle this bad blood before the Elders."

Cass agrees quickly, surely, she, too, is feeling the heat coming off DeLuca and probably wants to protect Leighra, who is more reluctant but does agree.

Audrina and Dover are noticeably absent at dinner. Lady Soleil looks at their place settings with a disapproving side-eye every so often but doesn't comment on it. We have to take dinner in the banquet room since the parlor is still demolished. We all sit at one end of the extravagantly large marble table meant to hold more than thirty.

The savory and sweet scents mix together as the island's fare wafts through the air, cutting through the stale tensions of the room. A succulent pig served with a glaze made of pineapples is the prized dish of the night, served alongside a sticky sweet rice.

"So?" Lady Soleil asks, tiring of the silence.

"Oh, it's delicious. I've never had anything like it," I say after a swallow.

"Of course, it's delicious. I have the finest cook in the nation. I'm more curious as to what the day has brought forth. Any form of a plan? I remind you he is a god...a strong and very old god."

"Oh, well, we haven't had much luck in the archives yet," I admit.

"We plan on leaving tonight, with the moon rise," Leighra adds.

Lady Soleil arches her brow. "Leaving? All of you?" She looks around the table.

Cass pushes food around with her fork. "No, not all."

"I see. Who will be going then?" She sits back in her seat, dabbing the corner of her mouth with a napkin.

"Cass and I. Maybe Dover, if we ever find him again," Leighra answers.

"And me," Rett adds, his eyes fixed at a spot on the table in front of him.

A wave of sadness crashes around me. My chest feels heavy. DeLuca's hand falls to my knee and gently squeezes, silently telling me, 'I'm still here.' I give him the best smile I can muster, but it isn't much.

"I see. So, you're leaving half your party behind. How noble of you." Lady Soleil's jab is directed at Cass who looks as though she is fighting tears already.

"You of all people should understand the duty we have to our people." Leighra's voice is harsh.

"Young lady, are the people you are about to leave behind no longer considered *your* people?"

Audrina and Dover burst through the double doors before Leighra can reply. Audrina slides into her seat near her mother while Dover chooses one on the other side of Cass, farthest from Audrina. The servs quickly create a new place setting for him and serve them their meal. Audrina has no intention of eating. She pushes the plate in front of her and crosses her arms. Her amber eyes are puffy and lined red. Dover wears a scowl that masks a sadness beneath. I don't need to ask to know what Dover decided.

We make our way to the courtyard. The moon has risen, signaling the sky is ready for the voyage back to Caeliss. Audrina retreats back to her room the moment dinner is over, not speaking to anyone. It must have been hard for her to want something so badly—and be able to have it with nothing but a whisper—but choosing to honor his free will. I couldn't be more proud of her. Despite how much her heart may ache, she did the right thing.

Dover climbs aboard the transport with little more than a wave. He, too, is feeling the ache of his decision to leave, and it's evident in his heavy steps up the transport. I hug Cass. I ask her to find a way to send word of Heidon whenever she gets back and to tell Hadleigh I miss her. She nods with tears in her eyes. Leighra is already aboard the ship and impatiently waiting for us to say goodbye to Rett, who has just finished thanking Lady Soleil for her hospitality and shared a long embrace with Lysette.

"And me?" I ask when he lets go. "Do I get one?"

He scoops me in his arms so tightly he pulls my feet off the ground. DeLuca, who has been by my side, walks back to stand with Lady Soliel, giving us a moment to ourselves.

"Don't hate me, Ailie-cat," he says quietly into my hair.

"I could never."

"Lysette...she is more useful with research—"

I interrupt him before he can ask. "I wasn't going to put her in harm's way, even if you had decided to stay."

"I couldn't choose, you know? Between you and Iris, I couldn't choose," he admits with raw emotion, "but the baby...my baby...I can't leave him."

"Her."

"Her?"

I shrug and smile.

His returned smile is impossibly large before a look of sorrow replaces it. "You have to come back. She needs to know her Auntie Ailie."

"I'll come back, somehow, someway. Or maybe you'll leave with Iris and the baby. This isn't goodbye. I know it." I reassure him, but if I am being honest, I don't know if it's a lie.

Rett nods and kisses the top of my head. "I love you, Ailie."

"I love you too, Rett. Be good to your family." My smile slightly wavers, but I hold my breath to keep it from falling.

He looks behind me and shouts to DeLuca, "If you let anything happen to her, or Lysette, I'm coming for you."

DeLuca nods in both understanding and agreement.

Rett turns and heads up the transport ramp which closes before he can turn back. Lysette slips a hand in mine, needing me just as much as I need her. DeLuca comes back to my side and wraps his arm around my shoulders, pulling me into him while we watch the transport lift into the air. Our hair whips around ferociously as Cass' wind grows stronger, and the transport disappears before our eyes.

Feeling completely mentally and physically drained, I take my red drops that Lysette conveniently left on my bedside table. I lay in the plush oversized bed and wait for the sleep I crave to claim me. The bed feels too big—too soft. To my surprise, I find myself missing the small bed in Caeliss. It felt safer, especially lying next to DeLuca.

I toss. I turn. I toss some more. I lay on my back and stare at the fabric carefully laid atop, obscuring my view of the ceiling. It has been days since we've had a proper night's sleep. Yet sleep evades me like an old enemy.

Giving up, I hop out of bed and slowly open my door, trying to quiet the creak of the hinges, and tip-toe across the hall to DeLuca's room. I can sleep in the safety of his arms and make it back to my room before Aurelia knows. She may be tiny, but she scares me more than all the mistresses at the academy combined.

My hand is about to twist the knob when I hear a soft whimper from the other side of the hall, next to my room. Audrina's room.

I hesitate with my fingers on the knob, debating between love and friendship. I sigh and let go of the handle, making my way to Audrina's door. I don't bother knocking, pushing my way in to find her sitting on a bench under her window, watching the dark waves crashing in the moonlight. She turns her face to me, revealing a steady stream of tears.

"Oh, Audrina." My arms are outstretched as I walk toward her.

She breaks into uncontrolled sobs and falls into my arms. Her shoulders shake as she releases her grief. I knew she really liked Dover. I guess I hadn't realized how much. There have been so many boys and infatuations over the years of our friendship, but I have never seen her this upset over the loss of one. I rub her back in soothing circles as she cries. We don't say anything for a long time.

"I've made so many mistakes." Her voice cracks after she runs out of tears.

"You did the right thing. I know it doesn't feel that way, but you did."

Her face twists. Then her eyes widen. "I thought he'd stay."

"Maybe he will come back. We don't know."

"He won't leave his family, and besides that...he doesn't trust me enough to stay."

"You did the right thing by not making him. I think that even with a whisper, part of him would always feel torn and, eventually, resentful."

"It doesn't feel like the right thing."

"I know, but someday it will."

"Will you stay with me tonight? I don't want to be"—Her lip quivers—"alone."

"Of course, I will, and you're never alone so long as I draw breath," I assure her.

"I don't deserve a friend like you." She sobs harder. "I don't, truly. You're too good for this realm, and I am not even remotely good. I'm so sorry. I hope you can forgive me."

I shush her, stroking her hair until she stops quivering. "Don't be ridiculous. You were the very first person to accept me wholly as I am. You're my chosen family."

We climb into her enormous bed that has room to fit six people. No wonder she complained so much about the beds in Caeliss. Her head lays on my shoulder, and I stroke my index finger along her hairline, tracing it behind her ear. I repeat the motion until she starts lightly snoring. The combination of waves crashing outside mixed with the heavily salted air and her steady soft snores lulls me into a deep dreamless sleep.

THIRTY-THREE
MORTAL

We spend the next few days following the departure of our friends in Lady Soleil's archives. So far, nothing useful has been revealed other than a full map of the Isle of Shadows, but the elusive island is as mysterious as the name. There are no known facts about it other than there are old world ruins and that it appears with the Shadow Moon and at no other time. This room is dreadfully musky and warm, making reading a tedious task that we've all grown tired of. I look down and read a passage from the book I've been flipping through for well over an hour. The handwriting is neat and precise, and there are tiny ink smudges, telling me the writer was in a hurry to write the contents.

Millena and Agnar conceived only once after their union before the goddess met her untimely death. Their child was born with three heads and one body. They named each head for they all presented their own unique personality and talent. Forbis could see events that had come before. Opari could see any place in the exact moment. Viitor could see events that had not yet come to pass but would, in time, to come. Together, the heads made the Utikalo.

During the God's War, the Utikalo was sought after between both sides. Haile and Egon both wanted to claim the knowledge it possessed. Taking after their mother, the Utikalo boasted amnesty and balance, choosing to aid neither of the brothers. The Utikalo renounced its godliness and abilities. It hunted for a way to become mortal and succeeded. Each head transferred its ability into a precious gemstone, hiding them so that they may never be joined again. No one has since seen the Utikalo. Once void of power, their three heads became one. It is presumed long dead.' I rub my temples as written lines blur together.

"If only we could make Erebus mortal," I say under my breath. The sudden noise in the quiet of the room grabs the attention of the others.

"What was that?" Lysette looks over the top of the book she is reading.

"I said, 'If only we could make Erebus mortal.' I was reading a story about Millena's child, the Utikalo. To avoid taking sides in the God's War, it turned itself mortal and hid its power away into some kind of stone."

"Ailie...that's our first viable idea," Lysette says, placing her book down and reaching her hand out, silently asking for mine.

"There's only one problem. We have no idea how they did it, and we only have a day and a half." I sigh, feeling the minutes tick by like quicksand trying to swallow me whole.

"I can ask my mother if she knows anything about it. It's the first promising lead we've had. There's nothing on Erebus in any of these. As if he's been erased from the history of gods," Audrina says, itching for an excuse to leave the dank room.

"Yeah, go ahead." Lysette, who has taken point as head of research, nods.

Audrina happily closes her book and flits up the stairs.

Lysette leafs through the book I hand her and sighs, closing it and about to add it to the large pile on the table.

"May I see that, please, Lysette?" DeLuca asks.

"Go for it. The rest is on the life and death of Millena." She stretches her arm over the pile and hands it to him.

He concentrates on the passage. The strong lines form between his brow, showing gears shifting in his mind. I carefully unroll part of a scroll to find it is written completely in Old Daeil, rendering it entirely useless to us. I roll it back up and place it carefully amongst the other scrolls.

"Aislinn." DeLuca calls me over.

"Yes?'

"I wonder..." He trails off in thought.

"What?" Lysette asks, her curiosity peaked.

"Do you think it's possible the line of Isoots comes from the Utikalo?" he asks, looking to Lysette, who is far more versed in the gods then we are.

"I'm sure it's entirely possible, especially if it decided to live the remainder of its life amongst the mortals."

"While wildly interesting, at the moment, it is of no importance. We have only a day and a half left. I can't go to the Isle of Shadows with nothing. I can't let him kill everyone. We have to find something," I say, irritated by the wasted time.

After another hour, Audrina stampedes down the steps waving a small book around frantically.

"It was in the main archives!" she shouts. "Mama knew it! She knew!"

"What did she know?"

"What did you find?"

Lysette and I speak at the same time.

"It's a *Siphon Stone*!" She lays the book open in front of us. "She's not sure it will make him mortal, but it will take his abilities!"

"Without his abilities, he's as good as mortal. We could finish it with the Child Blade." DeLuca looks hopeful, a light sparking the intensity in his eyes. I hadn't realized how dim they'd become over the days until witnessing the light return.

Lysette's finger traces the words written under a drawing of a long cylinder shaped stone, each side coming to a sharp point. "It could work," she says quietly.

"It could work?" I ask her, making sure I heard right.

Smiling, she repeats, "It could work."

"Yes!" Audrina pumps a fist in the air.

"Hold on, before we celebrate, where would we even find one?" I ask.

Audrina bites her lips and suppresses a knowing smile, practically jumping out of her skin.

"Yes, Audrina?"

"That's the best part! Mama has a whole load of them that have been passed down in our family! The Soleil line was gifted the stones to keep them protected and hidden. From the days of the *Secret Guardian Children* or whatever they were called. They kept them in case a Child went bad." She claps.

"It's too easy," I say.

"Well," she begins, "it's not that easy."

"Tell us what you know, Audrina." DeLuca's voice grows hard with impatience.

"You have to stab him with it. It must break skin, but I'm positive DeLuca can do it with all his fire and air and elements and stuff." She smiles at him.

He nods.

"He told me to come alone," I admit.

"In no way would we allow that," DeLuca says.

"I know you wouldn't. If he senses we've tricked him, he may leave...or kill everyone...probably both." I shudder.

Lysette snorts. "If only we had an illusionary to conceal us."

I look at her for a long while. "You can't go, Lysette."

"You can't tell me I can't come," she argues. "You are not in charge just because he's after you. We are a team."

"Exactly. We are a team. If it goes wrong, you have to warn Rett and Caeliss. You need to stay behind," I insist.

She goes to argue, but I interrupt. "DeLuca and I can go. He can conceal himself below the water...like Dover did in the river."

"And me. He can conceal me too," Audrina adds, her eyes twinkling.

"No. You have to stay too," I say, not meeting her gaze.

"Says who?"

"Me."

"Hmph. You mean my mother?"

I try to form the words, but the look on my face gives her the answer. She nods and grits her teeth, quickly turning on her heel and storming back up the stairs.

"We finally have something." I smile with relief despite the glare Lysette is sending my way.

"You know what we need to do now?" DeLuca asks.

"What?" Lysette and I both look at him.

"We need to go practice concealing ourselves." He smiles at our puzzled looks. "Let's go to the beach."

There are large walls surrounding the private beach behind the palace. They guard us from prying eyes while DeLuca attempts to manipulate the ocean's water. Droplets glisten down his abdominal muscles in a way that makes me want to catch them with my tongue. I have to bite my lip so I don't openly drool. He is trying to learn how to maneuver water as Dover had. Which is proving harder than he originally thought. So far, each time he tries, he fails. He is able to split the water just enough, but when he pulls it back over him, it crashes overhead. Each time he reemerges, the frustration is carved deeper into the lines creasing his face.

Lysette, Audrina, and I watch while sitting in the sand, soaking in the delicious warmth from the sun. After spending days in a glorified book dungeon, the fresh sea breeze is most welcome.

"You're doing great, DeLuca. Let the water become an extension of you. Don't overthink it!" Lysette calls after he almost drowns himself for the fifth time.

"I don't think he has it." Audrina shakes her head.

I grimace as DeLuca curses the water. "He'll get it." I try to sound more sure than I feel.

"It would be really helpful if we hadn't lost valuable members of our team with abilities." Lysette crosses her arms.

"Well, this is what we've got, and I'm thankful for you who stayed."

"Where else would I go? This is *my* home," Audrina says.

"True." I let out a laugh. "Remember when we were at the Astoria Academy and you told me instead of getting married that you and I would govern Sutton together?"

"And by together, I meant you'd do all the boring things and I'd just get to live *my* life in *my* house forever," she adds.

"That sounds reasonable," Lysette says. "Ailie has a head for running a household."

I snort. "Not according to my mother, hence why I was sent to Astoria in the first place."

"You were probably sent because you are a bastard," Audrina reminds me.

I give her a dirty look.

Lysette adds, "At this point, who isn't?"

I think while pretending to count on my fingers. "By my count, only you two." I shrug.

The three of us break into uncontrollable giggles, interrupted by DeLuca shouting more curses. I let out a sigh, and I rise to my feet, dusting the sand off and jumping into the cool water with him.

"You need to calm down."

"How can I when so much hangs in the balance? It's *your* life, Ailie. He wants *you*. This is the smallest thing I can do to protect you from him, and I can't fucking do it. Dover could have at least stayed to teach me...and Cass." He seethes.

"They didn't. But you have me. I may not be able to teach you, but I believe in you." I grab both of his hands in mine. "Lysette said to be one with the water, to clear your mind, clear your emotion as well because it clearly rules over your control. Close your eyes and listen."

He obeys, taking a deep breath and shutting his eyes.

"Now inhale through your nose to the count of five, and exhale out your mouth to the count of seven." I place my hand on his chest, waiting until he breathes out a few times and his heartbeat slows beneath my palm. "Good, now envision the water is a part of you, no different than an arm or leg. Tell it what to do as you would command your foot to take a step."

With his eyes still closed, the sea parts around us. We crouch down. A wall of sea water surrounds us. He then pulls the blanket of ocean over us, creating our own sanctuary below the water.

"You did it!" I clap my hands.

He opens his eyes, wearing a proud smile of accomplishment. We sit for a minute and watch colorful little fish swim through the wall of water all around us. It is truly one of the most incredible experiences, possibly even topping the Tears. DeLuca is digging around a pile of wet sand he picked up. His eyes grow wide, and he rinses something off in the water behind him.

"Here baby, for you." He takes my hand and places an enormous sand ruby in it.

"It's beautiful!" I roll it around on my palm with my finger feeling the smooth edges. When the light catches it just right, it looks like there are tiny flames embedded inside.

"When this is all over, I'll have it put in a ring for you." His thumb rubs along my cheek. "If you want that."

Unexpected emotion consumes me. Lust. Fear. Love. All the emotions. It's hard to keep my head straight. This tiny gem in my hand suddenly feels heavy, and I realize the implications it has. I want them. I want this future with him.

I pounce. He has no time to prepare for my kiss as I press my entire body into his. The skin of my abdomen rubs with his, and a shiver of excitement swims up my spine. His hands wrap around my exposed waist. The moment of intimacy results in the sea water flooding back in from all sides and submerging us completely. It fills my nose and mouth. I spit out the salty water and gasp for air as my head breaks the surface. I can't help but laugh.

"Maybe I should practice some more on my own." DeLuca smiles. "You're far too distracting." He emphasizes his point by pulling me closer and kissing me again, harder and full of intention.

"There are other people present on the beach!" Audrina shouts from the shore.

We both laugh in response. The sun catches his eyes, and they match the hue of the water around us yet, somehow, shine much brighter. Any beauty I found in the ocean is lost in the depths of his eyes.

"You're right, I will be of no help. I am far too selfish right now. But you did it, so now you know you can do it. You're amazing, Rainier DeLuca."

"Yeah, I'd still like to practice more, maybe on my own. No room for mistakes." He pushes his wet hair back.

"I'll just see myself out then." I do a mock curtsy.

"Oh, allow me madam." DeLuca parts the water from us to the shoreline.

"Well, now I think it was all just a ploy to get me to come out here with you."

"At least it worked." He kisses my cheek before I walk down the path he cleared. Wet sand squishes beneath my toes. I keep my fist clenched tightly around my ruby. I'll never let it go.

"Were you kicked out of the ocean?" Audrina fake-pouts.

"I was too distracting." I bat my eyes innocently.

"Should we give DeLuca time alone, or should we taunt him incessantly?" Lysette asks playfully.

"It would definitely be more fun to taunt him, but I fear angering Sir God of Vengeance."

"Ah, yes, DeLuca! Great God of Vengeance. We mustn't turn his wrath upon us." Audrina pretends to be frightened with a hand to her forehead as if she may faint from the very thought.

"We should go anyway. I'm sure your mother will have a fit if we don't bathe before dinner," I say with a sigh.

"Ah yes, Lady Soleil, the true God of Vengeance." Audrina's face falls cold and serious.

We make no attempt to hold back the laughter.

THIRTY-FOUR
ALREADY TOO LATE

This has been the most successful dinner we've had in a while. No outbursts to speak of. No tension. We enjoyed one another's company and pleasantries. My ruby is tucked safely in a small circular gold locket Audrina had lying around. It stays close to my heart and complements the white summer dress I chose to wear. Once everyone else has retired to their rooms for the night, DeLuca asks if I want to go for a walk in the moonlight. Not feeling the least bit sleepy, I happily agree.

We walk past the open area and down to the gardens which are filled with exotic island flowers and trees blooming in the brightest color I have ever seen. The air is thick and humid, but the gentle salt breeze makes it tolerable as it blows through my tangle of hair and sticks my dress against my legs. We find a stone bench that has a view of the ocean that is currently blanketed in dim silverlight from the night sky.

DeLuca holds my face and looks as though he is memorizing it. "You look beautiful in the moonlight, like it shines for you and you alone."

I smile and look down.

"Don't do that. Don't hide from me ever. I think you are the most beautiful creature to exist. In this realm or the next." He plants a gentle kiss on my temple and then pulls me into him so my head naturally rests on his shoulder.

"When we go tomorrow, if things don't go our way...you have to leave me. You have to be able to protect everyone else." I can't look at him when I speak. I know the hurt I'd see upon his face as he visualizes what I am saying, of something happening to me.

"You can't ask that of me."

"I need to know I can rely on you to take care of the people I love."

"Ailie, without you...I don't see myself being able to go on...."

"You can't say things like that, Luc. I am not immortal." I let out a small laugh. "Well, I don't think I am immortal. You *are*. As a true born god, you will live forever. Whether it's tomorrow or in eighty years, you are going to out-live me. You'll have to find a way to live with that."

His voice breaks. "I can't, baby."

"What is it even going to look like? You will look relatively the same forever while I wither away into nothing but a shadow. What kind of future actually lies ahead of us?" My fingers instinctively stroke the locket around my neck as my worries threaten to consume me from the inside out.

DeLuca doesn't waste a beat. Doesn't hesitate. He captures my head with his hands and looks me in the eye. "I have no life without you, Aislinn Theodora. No family. No friends. No home. You are everything. If we can make Erebus mortal, we can make me mortal too. I don't want any of this without you. I'd rather live eighty years with you than an eternity alone with nothing but a beautiful memory to haunt my every waking moment."

Tears slide down my cheeks. The sheer intensity of his love is overwhelming. No one has ever loved me the way he does. I'm not sure anyone has ever loved me truly, except maybe Audrina. But to give all of it up... all that power? Giving up being a god and living eternally. It's too much. "I can't ask you to do that, Luc. Not for me."

"You're not asking. It's what I want. A mortal life with you. Carving out a place of our own in this realm. A home. A family... children."

"Children?"

"Eventually." He wipes my tears away with his thumbs and sighs. "If things don't go our way I can't promise my first instinct will be to help your friends... I'd hunt him down, Erebus. I'd tear the realms open searching. He'd never be safe from me. But, *after* I kill him, I'd watch over your loved ones to honor you."

I give him a small satisfied smile. "I love you, Rainier DeLuca."

"And I love you, Aislinn. More than you could ever know."

A thick raindrop falls on my cheek. For a second, I mistake it for another loose tear. He brushes it with the back of his finger and studies it for a moment before we hear the crack of thunder and the sky lights up in a flash of purple. Before we have time to process, rain pelts down on us as if we've walked directly under a waterfall.

We run back through the courtyard holding hands, and we're laughing at our misfortune. Not cute laughter, the kind that hurts your sides and makes you snort like a hog while gasping for air.

The cracks of thunder and lightning grow closer behind us as if screaming at us to go faster. We run up the courtyard steps and into the palace. We're under the cover of one of the balconies when we stop for a breath. I'm still laughing, but I notice DeLuca staring at me.

"What is it?" I ask.

"I think your laugh is my favorite sound." I bite down on a smile and look up at him with hooded eyes to find his stare has only intensified. "Will you dance with me, baby?" he asks.

"Dance with you? There's no music!"

"Dance with me to the sound of the rain." He holds out his hand, and I accept. DeLuca pulls me in close and begins to slow dance to the sound of rain falling around us. It soon becomes my favorite song. I'm not sure how long we stay like this, but it's definitely not long enough before the wind starts blowing viciously. Pelting us with the water drops so fast it feels as though they are slicing into my skin. With a shared look, we both take off running to get inside.

We're still running as we make our way up the grand stairwell and back to our hallway. Our clothing is thoroughly soaked. His light blue button up clings to each ripple of muscle below. I'm covered in goosebumps, chilled to the bone. My white dress is now translucent and hugging my body so tightly it might as well not be there at all.

Breathing heavily from the run, we finally stop at my doorway. DeLuca's eyes travel the length of me. His eyes darken, and I can see how much he wants me right now. And I am ready for him. He leans down to kiss me. My head tilts expectantly. When his lips find my cheek, I pull back in confusion.

"Goodnight, Ailie. Get some rest." He traces my bottom lip with his thumb.

"Why don't you come in for a while?" I ask, pushing the door open in invitation.

"Aislinn." The way he breathes my name causes a stir in my lower belly. "If I come in right now, I won't have *any* self control. Not with you looking like that. I'm barely holding on as it is." I look down to his hands which are curled into fists and indeed trembling.

I smile mischievously, letting the straps of my shoulders fall down, revealing my breasts, puckered from the cold. "Then *don't* have any self control."

He groans. "Not tonight. Not here, under this pressure. I don't want you to look back and feel I took advantage of the situation. I don't want to give you anything to regret. I want your first time to be perfect. Anything else is far less than you deserve. It's not time."

I open my mouth to argue, but he silences me with a quick kiss and whispers, "I love you," before he turns on his heel and disappears on the other side of his door.

I'm going to die a virgin.

My breath comes out in an annoyed huff as I close the door. I'm still shaking from a mixture of cold and arousal. I light a few of the candles and open the balcony door to listen to the fierce storm outside and pull off the rest of my soaking wet dress— tossing it in a corner. Just as I'm about to pull out a nightgown from my dresser, DeLuca bursts through my door, a deep hunger in his eyes.

"It's already too late. I need you, Ailie, and I need you *now.*" He picks me up and pushes me back against the wall, taking my mouth with a possessiveness that has my eyes rolling back. My body aches for his touch. All of it.

"It took you long enough." I breathe into his ear. The resulting effect has him pushing deeper against me. My legs are wrapped around him tightly. He pushes my lips open with his tongue. His hot sweet breath mingles with my own. I take his bottom lip between my teeth. He lets out a throaty groan, his hands tightening below my thighs, slightly digging into them with his nails. There is no denying how much he wants this as he grows against me.

DeLuca carries me to the bed, laying me down and climbing over me. He throws one hand back, and the flames from the candles I lit jump to every candle in the room—basking our surroundings in a flickering orange glow. The storm still rages outside. Rain is pelting the glass of the windows. I'm thankful for the noise concealing our desperate moans. He kisses his way from the bottom of my jaw down my collar and to the tips of my breasts, his tongue tasting my flesh along the way. His mouth is warm. I want it all over me. His hands explore every soft curve of my body, which arches in response.

"Now, Luc, please." I can no longer stand not being fully connected. I'm desperate for him.

"Not yet."

"DeLuca!"

He laughs against my hip bone and plants a feather-light kiss that causes my body to shudder.

"What are you doing?" I say with shaky breath.

He looks up at me from between my legs. "Don't you trust me, baby?"

"I trust you."

"Good." His mouth lowers, and I'm ready to come undone with the first flick of his tongue on the sensitive center. I moan, and he continues to taste me as if he's starving and I am the only sustenance, deliberately licking and sucking in ways that threaten to drive me to insanity. My fists clench on the blankets. Everything inside me tightens. It's building. He notices how I've tensed, and I can feel his smile as he drags a finger below his mouth and pushes it against my entrance. He uses his other hand to hold my hips in place as I start to lose control over my movements. His finger is now fully inserted into me, and the way it curves mixed with his tongue is the end for me. The built up pressure releases with a vengeance, and I cry out in absolute ecstasy. DeLuca slows his motion but doesn't withdraw completely until I stop quivering.

He reemerges from my legs with a look of triumph, glistening with the evidence of my undoing on his mouth. "I will happily die tomorrow with the taste of you on my lips."

I think I laugh. I'm not sure. My thoughts are still incoherent from what he just did.

"Now that I know what that tongue can do, you're not allowed to die. Ever. In fact, I may just have to find a way to make myself immortal too because that is surely better than *anything* the Afterlands has to offer me."

He smiles and kisses my neck. "We can stop now, if you want. I'll finish in my hand if I have to." And I know, without a doubt, he means it.

"What I want is you, Rainier DeLuca, all of you."

"Are you absolutely sure?" he asks with a shaky breath, as though he might explode from his desires.

He searches for any sign of hesitation. I refuse to give him a morsel of doubt. While wrapping him between my legs, I smile deviously before flipping him onto his back.

I lean down to whisper beside his ear. "I have never been more sure about anything."

The flames on the candles triple in size, burning almost as bright as the fire in his eyes. My mouth takes his in a messy kiss while guiding him into the place I crave him. I go slow, fighting through the slight burn of him stretching me as our bodies become one, and when I fully sink down on him, we both let out a satisfied groan. This is nothing like I had imagined. It's infinitely better. We fit so perfectly together that the Weavers had to have created us specifically for each other. There is absolutely no denying it now.

With his hands holding my hips, we find a perfect rhythm of our hips rocking together. I grind on him, using his chest to brace myself. The pleasure builds again, but it's an entirely different experience than the last time, because this time we're experiencing it together. I didn't know anything could ever feel so good.

I cry out, "Oh gods," when I think I am about to come undone again.

DeLuca stops, stilling my hips before rotating so that he lays on top of me. He takes my chin with his hand and drags my lips to him. The kiss is bruising and has me rocking against him, begging for more. "Baby, there is only one god here tonight. In this bed I want you to only call out *my* name." He grabs my leg from behind the knee to angle himself deeper.

His name falls from my lips like a prayer, over and over again.

His thrusts become more erratic. Our breathing syncs to his movements, and my head tilts back in pure bliss. He uses the movement to his advantage and lowers himself so that he can kiss my exposed neck. "I love you," he whispers.

I can barely get the words out between moans. "I—love—you—Luc."

His movements become more desperate. Our moans grow louder. My climax hits like the rush of the ocean waves below, and he follows immediately as if he was fighting it back, waiting for me. Another loud crack of thunder sounds as DeLuca yells out with his final thrust. He collapses on top of me, and we lay there, our hearts synchronizing as we listen to each other's breath and the storm raging outside.

If I could have any power, it would be to freeze time, and lay here with him forever.

The light bursts through the open balcony door, signaling the morning's greeting. The naked man beside me is still sleeping soundly. His smooth toned chest rises and falls at a steady pace. His hair is wildly tousled from a full night of my hands being in it. There is a hint of a smile in the bow of his lips, beckoning me to kiss them. But I dare not disturb him. I've never seen him so relaxed. My head rests on my pillow, and I trace some of the scars on his arms with a delicate finger.

"Are you going to stare at me all morning, or are you going to kiss me?" he asks, his eyes still closed. I smile and oblige, gently kissing his warm lips.

"Good morning, Aislinn Theodora," he says softly. "Did you sleep well?"

I shake my head. "I didn't sleep at all. I kept worrying I was already dreaming."

"I assure you, it was not a dream. If it were, it would be mine, and I would choose to never wake up."

"You are the best thing that's ever happened to me. I mean that. I didn't know what it was to be loved...or cared for really...until you." I roll my body on top of him. He kisses the top of my head. "When this is over, let's go away. Anywhere. Away from everyone for a while. No rebellions, no Caeliss, no secrets. Let's just be together."

I can tell from the look on his face he's remembering the ticking clock the sun now represents. "I'll follow you anywhere. Until the end of time." He dances his fingers along my spine, carefully so that he doesn't accidentally touch the mark.

A knock on the door startles us.

"Uhm, I'm indisposed," I call to whoever is on the other side.

"I figured when Mr. DeLuca wasn't in his chambers," Aurelia's voice says calmly from the other side. "If you've both finished, we received word from Caeliss."

I roll off DeLuca. "We will be down shortly!" I suppress a giggle. We're both consenting adults, but it feels as though we've been caught in the act. I'm about to throw the covers off and get dressed when the door quickly opens.

Audrina's amber eyes bare a wicked gleam as she takes in the pair of us naked beneath the sheets. "I heard Aurelia. It's about damn time. That is all." She bows and closes the door.

"Someday, she will learn boundaries." DeLuca laughs.

"I've known her for six years, and I can tell you without any use of visions that Audrina will *never* learn boundaries."

"All the more reason for me to sneak away with you." He pulls me back to him and kisses me.

"Come on, I'm sure they're waiting for us."

"A few minutes won't hurt." His arms around me tighten.

"What happened to 'I won't be with you for a fleeting moment of passion. I want hours blah blah blah.'?" I say, mocking him.

"That was for our first time. Now that I've had you, I'll take every spare minute we can get." He smiles hungrily.

I wiggle myself free of his grasp and make my way to take a bath. I stop in the doorway and turn over my shoulder. "Are you coming or not?"

"We grant full pardons to the Children of Astoria by the names of Aislinn, Audrina, Lysette, and DeLuca so long as they return within a week to the safe haven known as Caeliss. In addition, they will bring all known information on the Guardian families mentioned by the Lady of Sutton Isle. Furthermore, Caeliss shall send an emissary to Sutton to collect the pardoned Children and speak with Lady Soleil of Sutton about other safety concerns in person. We are thankful for your services rendered in protecting Caeliss and the families that remain there peacefully. We are sorry for anything that may have made you feel unwelcome or unsafe. No need to reply. We will see you shortly.

Signed,

The Elders of Caeliss."

Lady Soliel finishes reading the letter from Caeliss out loud for all of us to hear together. She then flips the letter over. "Oh, there is more—"

"P.S. Heidon is still in a coma. No change but he's stable. Hadleigh misses you, Aislinn. Leighra is sorry about...everything. The stress really got to us all. Hope to see you all soon. Rett and Iris are doing

good. Well, Rett has been brooding. I'm sure that won't change until you're all back safely.

Xx Cass"

"A nice way to say they're coming to force us back." Audrina rolls her eyes and burns the letter over a candle flame.

"They can't force you back. If you don't want to go, I won't let them take you," Lady Soliel assures her. "You forget, your Mama has an army and strong friends, and you bet I'd go to war for you." She brushes a hair behind Audrina's ear.

"We can deal with them tomorrow," Lysette says, mirroring Audrina's eye roll.

"She's right, if we make it through this day, everything else can be discussed tomorrow. Today we need to keep focused," DeLuca adds.

"Focused on what? You've practiced all you can manipulating the water so you can come undetected. Lady Soliel is providing us with a Siphon Stone so that I can stab a god with it. It's pretty straightforward. There's nothing more to practice or focus on. I will have one shot to catch him by surprise and stab him. I'll be sure to be near the water so that DeLuca can finish him with the Child Blade. I want to spend this day with all of you. If it goes wrong, it may very well be our last day together. Let's make the most of it," I say. I'm tired of making plans, and I'm tired of worrying about what is to come. I want to live this day as though it is my last because it very well could be.

"Aislinn is right. We've prepared all we can. We've been through more the last few weeks than most people have in a lifetime. Let's take the day as our own," Lysette adds.

"I know what Aislinn and DeLuca want to do today," Audrina says, teasing us.

A hot blush rises to my cheeks and DeLuca bites down on a smile.

"It's settled then. We take the day as our own." Lady Soleil claps her hands together.

THIRTY-FIVE
THIS IS A TREASURE

Audrina insisted we spend the morning exploring the village she grew up in. From what I have seen of it, there is a strong sense of community between the people. Everywhere we go, we see neighbor helping neighbor. Like the palace, most of Sutton's colorful structures are on stilts, not as high as the palace, but high enough to withstand flooding that often plagues islands. Audrina takes us to her favorite shops and gives us a full tour of the village surrounding her home. The old buildings are worn and warped from moisture swelling, causing the bright paints to crack and peel. It's beautiful in an unconventional way.

She points to places and shares the memory they stir. I've never seen her so relaxed and in her own element. It's hard to believe she has been away from it for so long. She always talked about Sutton, but it never hit how much she loves this place until seeing her here.

Fully alive.

The Soleil family transport arrives at the edge of a thick jungle at Audrina's request; she said she has one last place she absolutely has to show us. The air is incredibly humid, and my neck is immediately damp with sweat. There is a musk given off by the foliage around us, not entirely unpleasant but exceedingly pungent. We walk barefoot atop the soft wet soil, carefully maneuvering around fallen tree limbs and rocks for nearly an hour. My top is almost soaked through with sweat despite the lightweight material, and DeLuca has lost his shirt entirely by the time we finally hear the sound of a waterfall.

We stop before a wall of vines and tangled tree limbs, Audrina turns back toward us, her signature grin spread wide from cheek to cheek. "Lysette, do you mind?"

"Not at all." Lysette takes the cue and parts the vines like a curtain, revealing water tumbling from atop a golden structure built into a cliff and pounding the rocks below it before joining with a clear lagoon.

Audrina smiles with pride as DeLuca, Lysette, and I still, taking in the splendor. "I told you it was worth it." She strips to her underthings and jumps into the lagoon with full force. When her head pops up, she spits out some water and splashes about. "What are you waiting for? Oonaugh to bless it?"

"You don't have to ask me twice." Lysette peels off her sweat-drenched clothes and joins Audrina in the water.

My movements are slow and deliberate as I remove my clothing, savoring each intense flicker in DeLuca's eyes as he watches.

"Are you just going to stare, or are you going to join?" I ask as I dip a toe in the water. It's the perfect temperature. I submerge completely before DeLuca even has his pants off. "This really is incredible," I say while looking toward the golden ruin.

DeLuca swims to where I am and follows my gaze. "Should we get a better look?"

"Good luck. I've tried to find a way in my whole life. It's sealed off." Audrina gestures to the cliff. "No way in from the top or sides.

"What about through the water?" DeLuca asks smugly.

Audrina's eyes light up. "I've never had someone with me who could manipulate the water."

"What are we waiting for then?" Lysette swims ahead of us toward where the water is tumbling down.

The gold ruin stretches from below the water level to the tip of the cliff. It has words etched down the side in Old Daeil.

"Lut dasi katalvitok." I struggle to say the words.

"My children?" DeLuca guesses, "Katalvia is child, maybe Katalvitok is plural."

"For my Children," Lysette corrects.

"It's for us then," Audrina concludes.

"One way to find out." DeLuca parts the water pouring down, revealing only a solid gold wall.

"Maybe we go under?" I suggest.

"I'm not sure if I can hold all of us under," he admits.

"Why don't you go alone and see if there's anything to see at all?" Lysette suggests.

"Okay, wait here." He kisses my cheek before going below water.

"You two make me sick." Audrina pretends to gag.

"I think they're sweet," Lysette says, coming to our defense.

"Exactly." Audrina rolls her eyes.

"I never thought I'd be with someone who makes me feel the way he does. Imagine, the life our parents had perfectly planned and tailored for us. Imagine never having the freedom to find the love that I've found with DeLuca. That's a life not worth living, and I would've done it blindly and without question."

Lysette smiles. "And Rett too, with Iris. He's been like a love sick puppy ever since returning home from his tour in the army."

"I thought they've been together longer?" I think back to Rett saying she'd been in the house for years prior.

Lysette shakes her head. "Iris kind of always followed Rett around and tried to get his attention, but you know him. His sense of duty has always been high, and he didn't pay attention to other girls. He was waiting for you. Something changed when he got back though. We've never talked about it. I always assumed something in the army changed his way of thinking."

"It feels like a lifetime ago that he and I were supposed to be married."

"It truly does," Lysette agrees.

DeLuca springs up from the water and shakes off his hair. "There's an opening. I'm going to try to create an air pocket. I can't have any distractions though so it doesn't come crashing down. The opening is submerged by water so there's no way to access it except by going under," he explains. "Everyone stay close."

We huddle close, careful not to touch him as he creates a pocket of air big enough for our heads. The pressure of the air within the bubble is enough to push us to the bottom of the lagoon, making it possible for us to walk beneath the water. We follow DeLuca under the cliff. Gold shimmers in distortion through the water above us, and just under it is a square entrance.

"We're going to have to swim. I don't know how to carry all of us up there." DeLuca looks apologetic. "On the count of three, I'm going to release the air bubble. One... two...three...."

I take a deep breath before water floods the air around us and prepare to swim. As I kick my legs, it feels as though the water is fighting back, as if the water is trying to push me back down and keep me as a treasure on its floor. But I fight back, swimming with all my might until I'm able to move through the opening.

The stale air is welcomed in my lungs when I finally pull myself to the ground above, flopping on my stomach and then rolling to my back once clearing the entry point.

My ears are ringing.

"Are you okay?" DeLuca's face hovers above mine.

"I'm fine, just catching my breath," I say.

We are in an almost empty chamber, only filled with three faceless statues. I believe they are supposed to be early depictions of Haile, Millena, and Egon. There is little detail, which makes it hard to be sure, but the medallions around their necks are similar to the sigils I've seen used for each god. A sun for Haile, skull for

Egon, and balanced scales for Millena. The walls are made of gold and have engravings on every inch. The floor is a slick black and white marble.

"Now *this* is truly incredible." Lysette is practically shaking with excitement.

"What is this place?" I ask.

"Probably one of the earliest temples made that is still standing!" Lysette exclaims.

Audrina is examining the statue I believe to be of Egon. "I always imagined it to be full of treasures."

Lysette scoffs. "This *is* a treasure. An almost perfectly preserved temple? It's probably a thousand years old...maybe older. Who knows how early man made something so spectacular with none of the modern tools or technology we now possess!"

"Okay, okay, I forgot you were such a *scholar*." Audrina throws her hands in front of herself defensively.

I'm drawn to the statue of who I believe to be Millena. She's standing between her two brothers as she is often depicted. When learning the myths...or I guess stories...of the gods I'd always wondered how Haile came to be the king. Wouldn't it make more sense for Millena to rule if she was really the balance? I trace the smooth carved edge of what would be her cheek if she had a face. A flash of light blinds me. When I blink it away, I'm in a palace. One I've been to many times in visions. I'm once again in the realm of the gods.

"*How dare you? How dare you not punish her for the death of my wife?*" I hear shouting. It's a dark haired god with broad shoulders and impeccable bone structure.

"*She died by your hand, Egon! How can you expect me to punish another for your own action?!*" The retort comes from a larger god. He has golden hair and clovered-honey eyes.

"*It was as a result of her making us forget our love. Brother, please, allow me this. Allow me to avenge Kaliel.*"

"*Edwissa is under my protection. You wanted there to be a divide between us, brother. You wanted to claim yourself King of Gods in my stead. You kidnapped the muses. All of this has been caused by you. I will not punish another for it.*" *His decree is finite.*

A flurry of gods enter the room to pay witness to the spectacle. I recognize Astoria who is without chains or tears. Her light hair flows in graceful waves down her back. Her blue eyes, DeLuca's eyes, sparkle with life. It appears as though she has a silver glow around her, an indication she has not yet been affected by Erebus.

"*You all see it. You see how the mighty Haile hesitates to enact justice!*" *Egon snarls to the gods huddled around.* "*If you will not act, I will.*" *He points a finger at a goddess with flowers weaved through her hair and wearing a gold pointed crown. Her face turns to fear, and in a flash, there is a blood curdling scream. The goddess who wore the flowers in her hair is kneeling beside the lifeless body of another goddess. One whose hair is both dark and light and whose deep brown eyes now look out into nothingness, void of life.*

"*What have you done?*" *Haile whispers.*

"*No,*" *Egon says under his breath.*

"*What have you done?*" *Haile shouts. The entire palace shakes.*

"*I didn't mean to, Millena. I didn't...I'm...I didn't....*" *Egon is shaking.*

An angry yell sounds from behind. A god comes hurtling past me, spear in hand, aiming for Egon.

"*Enough!*" *Haile's voice vibrates through every bone of my body. The angry god obeys and throws his spear to the ground begrudgingly.* "*Put him in aietal shackles and take him to the holding cells.*" *Haile gives the order, and three men wearing cloaks of gold pick Egon off the ground, shackling his wrists and ankles.*

"*Father, this has gone on long enough. There will be no peace. Especially now.*" *Astoria points at her dead aunt.* "*I need to do it. I have to accept the shadow-bond and take Erebus as husband. We can no longer wait. It restores the balance." A silver tear drops from her eye, but she holds strong, her voice never wavering.*

Haile looks at his daughter with pride and pity. "My dear, I had such great hopes for you. My heart is swollen with pride at the goddess you've become. I wanted more for you. Wanted the realm for you, but I fear you're right. To bring balance you must accept the shadow-bond."

"Go back now." Astoria's attention fixes on me. I look behind me to see if there is another standing there. The hall is empty. She is speaking to me. "Go back. Hurry, Erebus is coming. Go back."

A ball of light flies at me, surrounding me completely. When it dissipates, I am once again in the golden temple. In the arms of another god. One that I know and love.

"Thank the gods." DeLuca hugs me to his chest.

Audrina's voice noticeably cracks with fear. "Was it Erebus again?"

"How did he get to you?" Lysette asks.

I rub my temples, warding off a headache. "No it wasn't him. It was Astoria."

"Astoria?" DeLuca's voice is hopeful.

I nod. "When I touched the statue of Millena, I had a vision of the day she died. Of when Egon killed her and when Astoria agreed to marry Erebus to bring peace. She looked so different, so strong and alive." A knot forms in my throat thinking of the other visions I've had of her. What she must have endured as the wife of Erebus.

I shutter.

DeLuca puts his hand below my jaw and pulls my gaze to his, searching. "You're okay though?"

"I am."

The vision dampens the mood. We head back to the transport through the jungle. We barely speak. Our hearts and heads are heavy as we mentally prepare for the hours to come. The sun signals the sixteenth hour, meaning we only have three more until dusk.

Three more hours until the Isle of Shadows becomes visible.

Three more hours until I face Erebus.

THIRTY-SIX
FICKLE GOD

At dinner, I can hardly eat. I push the food around the plate. If I have already taken a bite, I don't recall the taste. I'm not afraid of Erebus. What I'm afraid of is losing...of never seeing my friends or DeLuca again. It's unbearable to think of this as the last day we will be together.

"Mama, have you ever used a Siphon Stone?" Audrina's question pulls me out of my thoughts.

Lady Soleil's eyes darken at a memory. "Once. A long time ago." She doesn't elaborate.

Audrina doesn't care about her mother's reluctance to answer and presses further. "Tell us, Mama. We need to be prepared. I need to know how it works"

Lady Soleil sighs. "Very well. When the Guardians were still regularly meeting, there was one among us who was too strong...with too dangerous a gift. Sorena could conjure lightning—at will. She didn't need to draw it from anywhere. She became jealous of another amongst us, Bea. Sorena attempted to kill Bea and turned on an entire province. Her storms brought forth furious fires, eating through everything. She had to be stopped. We used the stone. Well, Finnigan did. He was the only one who could get close enough to her. She loved him, but his heart belonged to Bea. He embraced Sorena and stabbed the stone through her back. The Siphon Stone turned purple. You could see the lighting pulse through it, forever caged."

"And what happened to Sorena, Finnigan...and Bea?" Lysette asks.

"Well, Finn and Bea married a few years later. You might have heard of them, Lord and Lady Williston of Azelean, in the west." She smiles.

"And Sorena?" I ask.

She glances at Audrina quickly before finding composure. "She lost her mind without her ability. She lives within her family's walls, still in Rilysse. Her sister, Petra, now governs along with her husband. They keep her hidden away. I do not know the extent other than she never stops talking. That's not so surprising though."

She lost her mind without her ability. I wonder if it would have the same effect on a god wishing to become mortal....

"Poor girl," DeLuca says.

"Excuse me?" Lady Soleil's face turns.

"I said 'poor girl.' She was heartbroken and friendless."

"You wouldn't feel such sympathy if you saw what she did." Lady Soleil grows cold. Her attention turns to me. "Aislinn, dear, I had yours and DeLuca's flight suits cleaned and laundered. I thought given its water resistance, it may be the best attire for your...outing this evening."

I laugh at the polite description. "I appreciate the thought, thank you."

Just as I finish fastening the top of my suit, DeLuca slowly opens my door. His eyes dance wildly over the skintight fabric clinging to my skin. A wicked smile forms with a flicker of flame lit behind his eyes.

"The first time I saw you in this suit, I wanted to tear it off. I might just have to live out that fantasy now." He pulls me tightly against him and gives me a long and wanting kiss.

I breathe heavily against his lips. "We don't have the time." Sadly, my words ring true. The sun is readying itself to fall below the waves.

DeLuca sighs and releases me from his grasp. "I have something for you. I found it in town earlier." He holds up a leather strap engraved with stars that has a small pocket and loops attached.

"What is it?"

"A garter, of sorts. Go sit." His head points toward the bed.

I obey and he takes the garter from my hands, wrapping the leather around my upper thigh. As he notches the buckle tight enough to not let the garter fall, he kisses the inside of my thigh. Heat from his lips lingers and radiates, lighting my nerves ablaze. I bite my lip and grab at the quilt to keep from grabbing his hair and forcing him to where I really want him to kiss.

I curse under my breath, "Damn you, Erebus."

"Speaking of him, open the pocket." DeLuca points to the side of my thigh.

I lift the little flap. Nestled perfectly inside is a clear cylindrical stone with pointed edges. "The Siphon Stone," I say. He nods. It's smaller than I would've thought. Maybe only two or three inches long.

"Thankfully, Lady Soleil had a few, so I have one, and you have one. And here's this," he says rummaging through one of my drawers. He pulls out the Child Blade and very gently slips it through one of the loops of the garter. He kisses my knee and rests his head on my lap. I gently rub my fingers through his hair.

He pulls away, and I realize his fist is clenched around something. When he sees me staring, he unclenches his fist and reveals the bloody shred of veil I kept as a momento. A reminder for why I push forward. DeLuca sticks it in the pocket of the garter with careful fingers. The fact that he knows me so well, that he knows what that tiny piece of fabric means to me, that he takes such care with it, I love this god. "When this is over, let's go back to Astoria. It's where I feel most at home. I want to make a home there with you. We don't need much. Just us. Screw governing families. Screw Caeliss and their rules. You and me." An image swarms my mind of a quiet life with a god as a husband and small children with raven curls running around the meadows. It's something I never let myself picture before, but now I realize it's all I want.

A quiet life with DeLuca.

He pulls me to my feet and kisses me softly. "Anywhere, baby, as long as you're there."

Our goodbyes to Lysette, Lady Soleil, and Audrina are brief. Though we say, 'We will see you when it's done' rather than a formal goodbye. Audrina was shaking. I think she is more afraid than she lets on. DeLuca and I take a small rowboat into the open ocean. As the sun disappears and a shadowy moon shines its first obstructed light, an island appears to apparate from nothing but sea. With its appearance, DeLuca kisses me, hard and fierce before jumping into the water. He disappears from sight, but I know he won't be far. I hold tight to the locket around my neck, the one containing the ruby DeLuca gave me. Taking a deep inhale of salty air, I continue rowing. The waves push the boat forward sending a smile to my face. DeLuca must be under me.

I pull the small boat onto the shore so it won't float away. The island is dark. No structures are visible with lines of thick trees and shrubs surrounding the beach like a crescent moon. I think it's best to stay near the water, near DeLuca. For a long time, I stand and pace. After what feels like an hour, I finally sit.

Where is he?

"Okay. You can come out whenever now."

Silence.

"I'm here, Erebus. Where are you?"

Silence.

"What a fickle god. Demanding I show up, only to back out yourself."

Silence.

My fingers trace the outline of the stone in my pocket. An idea pops into my head. I'm usually careful not to touch the mark Erebus gave me, but when I do, I can feel him.... I wonder if he can feel me? The thought causes me to shudder in disgust. I unclasp the front of my suit and roll a shoulder free. My fingers slightly shake as I place them onto the shadowed place behind my shoulder. The entire mark feels as though it is trying to pull free from my skin. It's so cold that it burns, and I feel a hollowness wrap around me like chains. A tiny scream of pain escapes my lips. The hairs on my arm raise to attention. That's when I feel eyes on me.

"Hello, *pet.*" His voice makes my skin crawl.

"Hello, Erebus." My voice is hard through clenched teeth.

A shadowy figure appears beside me as I jump to my feet. "You came."

"Did I have a choice?"

"You did. There's always a choice, and you chose me. I'm delighted."

"I did not choose you. You told me if I didn't come you'd kill everyone I love and destroy Caeliss."

He lowers his hood, revealing his handsome yet wrong face and wicked eyes. "Ah yes, but you did have *that choice*. You chose to come to me rather than let them die."

"That's no choice. If you knew love, you would know that."

"But I do know love, *pet*. It is at the very core of all of my actions." He looks around. "Where *is* my wayward son?" Erebus asks with amusement.

"You told me to come alone."

"I didn't expect you to listen. You rarely do as you're told." His predatory smile catches a glimmer of moonlight.

"I'm here. What do you want?" My fingers clasp around the Siphon Stone.

"I want you to come with me."

"Come take me then," I say, readying myself.

"Tsk tsk. Not so easy, I'm afraid. The moon has to be fixed just right. We need to be in the correct position, and"—He smiles deviously—"you have to *desire* to go. We must form a connection...that connection being a kiss."

My stomach turns, and bile fills my throat. "I'm not kissing you." The disgust pours through each word.

He shrugs. "You say that. I feel soon you will *beg* to kiss me." *I would never. Could never.*

My thoughts shift. If he thinks I'm going to, he will get close enough for me to plunge the stone into him. I only have to break skin.

"Okay, Erebus. I'm ready to go when you are. Lead me to the spot."

"Come, *pet*, take my arm. Let us away from this dastardly realm." He offers an arm as a gentleman would. I have the stone in my hand. I loop my opposite arm through his. It's hideously cold and sends ice to my core. Before we take another step, I hold him tightly in place with my looped arm and twist my body with all my might to throw the stone into his shoulder.

"DeLuca!" I shout as I plunge the sharp point of the stone into him. Shadows seep from the wound in place of blood.

Erebus laughs as he pulls out the stone and throws it into the sand. A wave of realization washes over me as his form turns entirely to shadow.

"That was very foolish of you." He cackles. "I have a little surprise for you. Call it a gift, repayment for the one you gave me. Come forth now; it's time to be revealed," Erebus calls to the treeline.

Two figures emerge from the darkness. I can't quite make them out. The smaller one appears to be dragging the larger one toward us.

Why didn't it work?

"For it to work, I have to be actively using my abilities. You can only take them while they're at work." Erebus answers my unvoiced question.

The dark figures get closer. I recognize them.

"This is a trick," I say under my breath. I feel my entire world crash. I feel sick, cold, and utterly alone. "This is a trick!" I shout at Erebus.

"While I do enjoy many forms of trick, this, dear pet, is no trick." His shadows wrap around a limp body with wet black curls matted to his forehead. His eyes are closed, but I know them to be electric blue. DeLuca. He has DeLuca. My eyes scan him quickly, looking for signs of life or movement, anything. Launched into his abdomen is a Siphon Stone. I look to the ground where Erebus threw the one I tried to use. It's still there. The other figure comes to light. Her amber eyes glow when the moon strikes them. She looks down, hiding her face with shame.

"Audrina? What the Haile? What are you doing here? You were supposed to stay home. I don't—I don't understand what's happening..."

"Don't you, pet? Can you not see what is clearly before you?"

"Audrina! What is happening?"

"I'm sorry, Aislinn. I told you, you deserved a better friend." Her voice is small.

"For what?" I demand, rage consuming every morsel of my being. "Say it, Audrina. For what?"

"It was me. I stabbed DeLuca with the Siphon Stone...I ...betrayed you."

THIRTY-SEVEN
NOT DEAD, JUST BROKEN

"How could you?" My chest feels as if an invisible force is squeezing all the life from me. Audrina's betrayal. Failure to catch Erebus by surprise. DeLuca suspended in the air, unmoving. It's too much. My knees weaken as my will to live slowly drains.

You're brave. Audrina's whisper echoes through my thoughts. My veins fill with a mixture of anger and steel.

"Why?" I demand.

"To save Sutton." She speaks while looking at her feet.

"To save Sutton? From what? Him?" I nod to Erebus who is watching our interaction with glee.

She nods.

"We were going to *kill him*." I grit my teeth.

"You probably would have failed. I had to have assurances. He also has sworn to the future safety...against the uprisings, wars, all of it. Sutton is a safe haven under the protection of Erebus." She straightens her back.

"So you agreed to whatever he had planned?" I ask.

"Not my plan...no, I was going to simply take you and let my shadows take care of anyone you might have brought. No. She summoned me...days ago, asked if I could help her get home, and in exchange for the favor and the safety of the island, she'd give me you." He practically giggles.

"No." I seeth.

434

"Yes." He smiles, eyes dancing with delight.

Days ago?

"Before or after Pierce?"

"Before. The visions you had may have been tampered with." Audrina moves closer to me. "You have to understand—"

"I understand *nothing*. You've always been a self absorbed manipulative bitch, but I never would have expected you to betray *me* like this. To betray *DeLuca*."

All I see is red. I'm practically vibrating with anger. My best friend. She was my *best fucking friend*. Someone I thought was my family. She sold me out for her own selfish desires and a fucking island. An island that wasn't even in immediate danger.

Audrina tries to reach out to me. The rage takes control of my body. I don't even know what's happening until I pull the blade from the garter and plunge it through her chest. A trickle of crimson flows down from the wound. Her eyes grow wide. I lean in until we are nose to nose. Blood starts dripping from her lips when I push the dagger upwards.

"I hope you rot in the Shadows for this," I say quietly before ripping the blade free of her chest. She falls to her back. Blood stains the sand around her.

When the amber of Audrina's eyes dulls to a muddy brow, Erebus claps his hands wildly. "Be still my heart. There is a fire in you yet." He looks at me with admiration.

"Is he alive?" I say through clenched teeth, pointing at DeLuca.

Erebus suddenly looks bored. "He is in a deep state of sleep."

"Wake him up."

"Oh, so mighty holding that blade. Tell me, *pet*, are you faster than a shadow? You think you could best me?"

I consider his words. Without the element of surprise there is very little chance that I'd be able to beat him.

He smiles and cocks his head. "I thought not."

Looking at Audrina's lifeless body and DeLuca's floating in an orb of shadows, I realize I won't win this. I've already lost.

"I'll go with you," I say quietly. "If you leave him unharmed, I will go with you."

"You have to *desire* it, pet." He reminds me of the terms of entering the god's realm.

"My desire to save him will provide my desire to go with you."

He muses over the thought. "A loophole." He smiles wildly. "I do enjoy a good loophole. Yes, let us go to the portal."

"Portal?" I repeat.

"Yes, this Viisolo is home to my own personal portal between realms. Tricky things, portals. Always so many rules to adhere to. Here, allow me to brisk the three of us away, much quicker. We haven't much time before the Shadow Moon is in position."

I glare at Audrina's body lying beside me, silently cursing her for putting me in this position, then to DeLuca's. His hard features have gone soft in whatever trance Erebus has him in.

"Let's go." The second the words pass my lips, a swarm of shadows surround me completely. They block my view. Everything is dark and cold. When they dissipate, we are standing in the mouth of a cave, surrounded by large trees. I can no longer see the ocean or other islands. My legs buckle, and my head is dizzy from such swift movement. A cold hand firmly grasps beneath my elbow so I don't fall.

"Steady yourself, pet. I'd hate to see you hurt." Something in his eyes softens. Almost like he means what he says.

I pull my elbow away quickly and march forward toward the cave, which is quite unremarkable. It's empty. To anyone else, it wouldn't earn a second glance. It's small but big enough to fit the three of us comfortably. There is a large opening through the top, giving view to thousands of twinkling stars.

"My wife's work." Erebus follows my gaze to the night sky. "She was quite remarkable."

"Was?" I ask.

"Oh, she's not dead, just broken." He sighs.

I glare at him. "I suppose if you smother light with enough darkness, it's bound to suffocate."

A muscle in his jaw twitches. "We are waiting for the Shadow Moon to shine through that hole. Once it does, you must stand with me and place your lips on mine. You must not break away until we've arrived. It will tear you to pieces if you do."

"Comforting," I say, feeling numb. "Why a kiss?"

He smiles wickedly. "We must be bound. Trick the portal into thinking we are one. There are...other ways...but I thought a kiss would be most savory for your taste."

Gross.

"When will you release DeLuca?"

"I will release him when you're securely in my arms and the transaction is done."

"That's smart. I suppose you're afraid of him." I smile at the thought of DeLuca enacting his vengeance against Erebus.

"He is untrained and young. He *currently* poses no threat to me. I am older than your entire realm."

The word he chose, *currently*, means something. I take care to protect the memory.

"How much longer?" I ask, slumping down on a large boulder.

He shrugs. "Not much, though I am immortal. Ten years of your time feels insignificant for me."

I roll my eyes.

"Would you like to be immortal?"

"I don't know. The short life I've lived has already felt like enough."

"Yes. You have known such tragedies in your small life."

"How long have you been watching me?"

"Long enough."

"How? Why is there a connection between us?"

Mischief twinkles in his eye. "Now that, pet, that was the right question. You see, I possess something. Something I took many years ago. Decades. From a shadow I happened to be watching."

"What is it?" I grow tired of the way he dances around my questions.

"I possess the Opari Stone," he exclaims proudly. The Opari Stone was born from the Utikalo. An Isoot of sorts, but not only could it see, it could go. Opari had the gift to see anything happening at that specific moment of time and go to any specific point, if so desired."

"I don't understand the connection." My ears ring and my brow knits as I try to connect the dots.

"Think, pet. What do you have in common with the Utikalo?" He waits.

"We're both Seers?" I ask.

"And what does it mean when a god passes forth their power?"

"They have mated with a mortal."

He smiles. "And so that makes you?"

I take a deep breath. "A descendant of the Utikalo."

"Correct, that also means...you aren't one of mine, therefore, pose no danger to my realm. I also believe you possess something. Something sacred passed down for generations beneath your skin." His eyes burn into my flesh. The mark he left on me awakens, calling to him. His eyes flicker to my flight suit. I shiver from the cold he brings forth.

"We must do something about your hideous clothing," he says.

"My flight suit? You're worried about my flight suit, of all things?"

"You will never be accepted in our realm like that."

"I didn't exactly have time to pack."

"Rise, pet," he orders.

When I refuse, he sighs and uses a shadow to push me to my feet, and I find I am again completely surrounded by shadows. They pull and tug. My feet are off the ground. I'm suspended in the air, completely blind. Spinning in every direction.

The spinning slows, and my feet touch the ground. My boots are gone. In their stead are a pair of strappy sandals with strands of black diamonds wrapping up my leg past my knees, tying behind my thigh in a black ribbon bow. They are hidden beneath a long dark gray skirt that flows out from my hips and is nearly sheer, exposing the black slip underneath. The top of the dress is entirely encrusted with black diamonds, the straps matching that of my sandals. I'm unsure what my hair looks like, but it is no longer loose behind my back. It's swept up, exposing my shoulders which lay mostly bare, my mark on display as the dip in the back of the dress plunges to the top of the skirts. I feel ridiculous.

Erebus runs a finger along the opening of my back, admiring his work. "You look like a queen of shadows. Now all in my realm will know you're *mine*."

"I'll never be *yours*." My eyes fall to the unconscious DeLuca.

"You already are, pet. I've marked you. You're mine."

He sniffs the air. "It's about time, come." His hand gently touches the small of my back and leads me to the center of the cave. "You have to want to go. You can't break our kiss. Wait for me to." He looks into my eyes. I see a flicker of what looks like concern, but I know that can't be right.

"Fine. Wake DeLuca up," I demand.

The Shadow Moon casts its dark silvery light through the hole. The cavern illuminates, and words in Old Daeil appear on its walls that were not visible before. There is a glimmer in the air, and it smells like a crisp winter night.

"Hold on to me." He breathes against my ear. "Don't break contact, no matter what,"

"Wake him up."

"Kiss me," Erebus demands. His hands tighten around my waist, drawing my hips closer to his. I roll my eyes and stand on my toes to reach my lips to his. My eyes never leave DeLuca. Kissing Erebus is like kissing snow, bitterly cold. He deepens the kiss, wiggling his tongue through my tightly pressed lips. I try to bite it, and he laughs against my mouth. One hand flies off my waist, releasing DeLuca from his sleep. Erebus and I are lifted above the ground. His hold on me tightens, afraid I'll leave or afraid I'll fall. It's unclear.

He brings his free hand behind my head and pushes me into him further. I fight the urge to throw up. His frozen kiss feels nothing like the fire in DeLuca's. My eyes shift down below us to see DeLuca rise from the ground. He rubs his head and pulls the stone from his chest. It shimmers blue. Relief washes over me. DeLuca will be okay. He looks around in confusion before looking up and seeing us. Seeing me wrapped in Erebus and being pulled away in a stream of moonlight and shadows.

My heart breaks for him. What he must think.

"Aislinn!" he shouts. Anger and hurt cut through his voice.

I try to pull away, but Erebus holds me firmly in place.

"Aislinn!"

A tear slides down my cheek. We disappear into silver light and shadow. But not before I see an ocean of fire erupt from below us.

DeLuca.

SON
OF
ASTORIA

J.B. WRIGHT

Sneak Peak: Son of Astoria

Open your eyes, DeLuca.

Just open them.

Come on, damn it.

I strain to hear the muffled voices.

Aislinn.

I'd know her hypnotic voice anywhere. The way it sends off little bells in my ears each time I hear it. Like a symphony the Weavers wrote for me.

Who is she talking to?

Open your eyes, DeLuca.

My head threatens to split down the middle, as if another head is trying to grow in its place. I rub it. I'm finally able to open my eyes.

Where am I?

I was just in the water when...*Audrina.*

My hand curls around the Siphon Stone lodged in my abdomen. I grunt as I pull it out. The once clear crystal swirls blue, like waves of water are trapped within. Once my vision returns to normal, I realize I'm in a cave. A glowing cave. Silver is scattered through the air. The walls light up with writings in the language of gods. A beam of dark moonlight shines through a hole above

Wait. Is that...

"Aislinn?" I say out loud.

She is wearing a dress I've never seen. She looks like some kind of beautiful nightmare. Her body and hands wrapped around another man, their lips touching. She noticeably twitches, but the man's hands pull her hard against him.

"Aislinn!" I shout.

That bastard got her.

I begin to shake with rage. All that control, all that I have held in. It's slipping. The blood in my veins boils. My vision burns red. Flames erupt from every inch of me. My fingertips. My eyes. My legs. Even my gods damned toes. My entire body is a flame. Nothing on this island is safe. The fire grows. It surrounds me completely as far as I can see. My clothes burn off, but my body remains unharmed. My blaze burns until I find my breath.

With a final frustrated yell, the flames extinguish, leaving only charred ground in its stead. The forest is gone. I lit the whole damn island on fire. My fire. It came from within me. I didn't have to manipulate it from something else. It's mine.

Clenching my teeth together, I pick up the Siphon Stone. Then I head back for the water. Our boat is still safely floating near the shoreline, thank the gods. It's untouched by my flame. After I climb in, I call upon a wave to push me to Sutton's shore.

Nothing. Not even a ripple.

I curse under my breath while I row as quickly as my arms will allow. The adrenaline helps to push me faster.

"DeLuca?" Lady Soleil looks surprised to see me. "Where's Aislinn?"

A line of fire dances between my shoulders. She looks at it in shock.

"He took her," I say through clenched teeth. "You seem surprised to see me, Lady Soleil. Is it because I'm supposed to be dead? Because you and your treacherous daughter planned to kill me?" The anger feeds the flames, and they dance violently around me. It takes all the control I have to reign them back in.

"I'm surprised because you're standing completely nude and slightly aflame in my entryway." Her hands fall to her hips. "What about my daughter? She snuck out shortly after you left. Where is she? What happened?"

"*Your daughter* stabbed me with a Siphon Stone. I don't know after that. When I came to, Erebus was floating away *with* Aislinn." The memory nearly sends me into a full blaze again until Lysette comes down the stairs. She only needs to look at me to know I failed. Her eyes well up.

"Get your things, Lysette. We're leaving," I order.

"Leaving? Where?" she asks in a voice remnant to a frightened child. As if she is afraid of *me*, as if I am the monster.

"I'm taking you back to Caeliss, to your brother. You're not safe here."

"Not safe?" She looks at Lady Soleil with horror.

"Audrina betrayed us. Lady Soleil is her mother. We can't trust her." My fingers tingle with tiny flames begging to be released.

"You are perfectly safe here. I know nothing of a betrayal," Lady Soleil says.

"Is she perfectly safe even though your daughter is dead?" I ask, looking her in the eye.

She pales in an instant. "Dead? Aud-Audrina?"

"I would assume by Erebus or Aislinn. If not by them, then when I laid waste to all of the Isle of Shadows. There's nothing left of it."

Lady Soleil looks as if she might faint. Aurelia is quickly by her side.

I start toward the stairs "We are leaving, immediately."

"DeLuca, wait," Lysette calls.

The flames along my shoulder blades flicker a little higher as I turn around, digging my nails into the banister.

"We should stay. The transport from Caeliss will be here in a few days. It would be quicker to wait than to go on foot through a hostile country."

"We can't stay here."

"Go without me then. I'll wait for the transport." She crosses her arms.

I groan. "I can't leave you."

"Why?"

"I promised Aislinn. I promised if something happened to her I'd look out for you, all of you."

"Oh." She looks somewhere beyond me, presumably trying to keep her eyes off my still naked body.

"I can't stay here, Lysette. I have to go after Erebus, after Aislinn."

"I know," she says quietly, "but you don't know how to get into the Realm of Gods...and we honestly don't have any way off this island."

Godsdamn it.

Lysette's hand reaches for my arm, but I shake my head in warning, remembering when Aislinn was burned from my explosive anger.

"I can't just do nothing."

"Then don't do nothing. We have a room full of information about the gods. Maybe we can find a lead to getting to the Realm of Gods." Her voice sounds hopeful.

"There wasn't anything in there!" I shout.

"We weren't looking for a way in before!" Her voice raises to match mine, which I would find amusing on a regular day. Not that we have ever had one of those.

"Well, I don't have much of an alternative at the moment." The stairs bow beneath my heavy steps.

Lysette is right. I hate that she's right. But it makes the most sense to wait here for the transport to take us back to Caeliss. If anyone knows where to find a portal it would be Priestess Alis.

After I dress, I begin pulling clothing from the drawers and march across the hall, throwing them in an empty drawer in Aislinn's room. If I'm going to be stuck here, I'm going to damn well be staying where I feel closest to her.

While throwing my things in the closest, I spot the blue dress she wore on our first day on this cursed island. My fingers trace the straps, and I feel the memory of her skin beneath it.

Damn it.

I split the wood of the dresser beneath my fist.

My knees give out, and I sit beside the bed. The wooden frame digs into my back. The quilt falls with me. I can still smell her on it as if she were here with me now. Lunalillies and Freshwater, not like that of the ocean, but like the waterfalls in Caeliss, completely pure.

My gaze turns toward the window.

A single star shoots across the night sky.

I straighten up, remembering who I am.

I am the Son of Astoria.

Born of shadow and light.

A descendant of both Haile and Egon.

Life and Death.

I *am* the God of Vengeance.

And I am coming for you, Erebus.

I'm coming for you, Aislinn.

Acknowledgments

First and foremost I need to thank my husband and kids for their extreme patience with me while I underwent this journey into writing and self publishing. Some nights were very long. There were days where I was so absorbed into the writing that I forgot everything else around me. You guys stood rock solid through it all. I love you and couldn't have made it without your support.

My alpha moms; Alison, Meghan, and Edwina. My first readers and biggest cheerleaders. I wouldn't have finished if it weren't for your immediate interest and excitement.

My Betas; Perci Jay, Chelsea, Haven, Jessica, and Kayla. Y'all were the best group I could ask for! Your notes and comments helped strengthen the story as a whole and I loved working this process with you. It was something I looked forward to daily. Literally. I checked my email a dozen times a day waiting to read your thoughts and got so excited each time you finished reviewing a chapter.

Finally, my editor. My knight in shining armor. Kate. You are incredible. Thank you for the endless hours and read throughs. I'm so glad I don't have to embarrass myself with my lack of knowledge, thanks to you no one will know how illiterate I truly am.

- Ada (*ay-duh*) I am

- Aeikpo (*ike-poe*) Danger

- Aietal (*aye-tal*) Death

- Dasi (*das-ee*) My

- Dailotta (*day-low-tah*) Mother

- Dauuk (*dao-ck*) Moon

- Dauteiol (*dah-tay-all*) Mortal

- Daeiliot (*day-lee-ot*) Maker

- Eika *(ike-ah-)* And

- Eiolol (*aye-oh-low*) all

- Eikvidalis (ike-vid-all-lee) Animals

- Goloeiyu (*gal-loy-ooh*) Please

- Katoeieut *(kat-oh-eet)* Creator

- Kaoket (*kay-oh-ket*) Center

- Katalvia (*kat-all-vee-ah*) Child

- Katalviatok *(kat-all-vee-ah-tok)* Children

- Ku (*coo*) No

- Istaleia (*is-tah-lay-ah*) Shadow

- Isoie *(is-oh-ee)* Sea

- Isoot *(eyes-ut)* Seer

- Isukis *(is-oo-kees)* Sons

- Iseilo Talewok *(is-ay-low— tah-lay-walk)* Save Haven

- Iselota *(ice-low-tah)* Stellera

- L'Vito *(lah-vee-tow)* Fire

- Leietalot *(lay-tah-low)* Father

- Lut *(l-oo-t)* For

- Peiolrikkao *(pay-ol-rik-koh)* Balance

- Putk *(pah-ck)* Born

- Tuiiso *(twee-so)* Rousse

- Utikalo *(oo-tah-kay-low)* Oracle

- Uldaoka *(ool-doh-kah)* Friend

- Ukolsi *(ooh-kol-see)* Only

- Ul *(ool)* Of

- Yeitk *(y-ate-ck)* Warn

- Viisoleika *(vee-sole-ay-kah)* Island

- Viisolo (vee-so-low) Isle

- Yviol (*yiv-ee-ol*) Free

- Yoiso (*y-oi-sow*) West

- Yeitk (*yay-tik*) Warn

- Yutalo *(you-tah-low)* She

Keep in Touch!
If you want to keep updated about book releases
or just hang out you can find me on social media.
Facebook – Author J.B. Wright
Instagram – HeyJ.B.Writes
TikTok – HeyJ.B.Writes

Early Readers can join
the private facebook group — Wrighters

If you're interested in becoming an early reader
reach out to me at: Author.J.B.Wright@gmail.com

Mail can be sent to:
J.B. Wright
PO BOX 6357
Abilene, TX 79608

Milton Keynes UK
Ingram Content Group UK Ltd.
UKHW012114271123
433389UK00002B/25